"Stay," Rio whispered, and Phoebe tipped her head back, challenge lighting her eyes.

He breathed in—breathed *her*—as a shiver of anticipation snaked up his spine. Beneath the towel at his hips, he was hardening.

He cradled the side of her head and let his fingers inch back, finding the pins that held up that thick, silky hair. He pulled them free and let them drop to the floor as she laid both palms, flat, against his bare chest.

"There," she said, almost smiling. "I feel it. A definite heartbeat. You're human, after all."

He bent for a kiss.

She gave him one, a quick, angry one. And then she slipped down a hand, got hold of his towel and whipped it away.

Also by Christine Rimmer

MARRIED IN HASTE
THE RELUCTANT CINDERELLA
†BRAVO UNWRAPPED
*BRAVO BRIDES
LORI'S LITTLE SECRET
STRANDED WITH THE GROOM

†Signature Sagas
*Signature Miniseries

Christine Rimmer

Ralphie's Wives

ISBN-13: 978-0-373-77230-8
ISBN-10: 0-373-77230-0

RALPHIE'S WIVES

This edition published by arrangement with Harlequin Books S.A.

www.HQNBooks.com

Printed in U.S.A.

For Rebecca Reynolds

ACKNOWLEDGMENTS

This book was an adventure for me, from start to finish. And so many people reached out helping hands along the way.

To my sister-in-law Millie Stratton and my niece, Lily Dunning—thank you so much for sharing your stories of the Prairie Lady Music Hall. Those lucky enough to remember the Prairie Lady will see echoes of her in the Prairie Queen. To Susan Mallery, thanks always for the endless support and unflagging encouragement. To my plot group, I so couldn't have done it without you. And to Susan Crosby, who read the first draft and suggested some great fixes—you're the best.

For a variety of information about the OCPD and the workings of law enforcement in Oklahoma City, I am eternally grateful to Captain Jeffrey Becker of the OCPD and to Maggie Price. For last-minute medical counseling, thank you, Darlene Graham. And for help with my somewhat rusty Spanish, thanks to Leslie Crosby. All errors and omissions, medical and procedural, are completely my own.

Ralphie's Wives

PROLOGUE

Remember. If it has tires or testicles, you're going to have trouble with it.
—from The Prairie Queen's Guide to Life, *by Goddess Jacks*

AT A LITTLE AFTER 4:00 a.m. on April fifteenth, Ralphie Styles lay spread-eagled in the middle of an Oklahoma City street, face up, dizzy and bleeding. That was right after the beat-up red van rolled over him and drove off.

He heard a groaning sound and then, a moment later, realized the sound was coming from his own mouth. He stared up at the night sky and tried to move his legs. Nothing.

He tried his arms: no luck. His hand. No. A damn finger…

Wasn't happening. Zero response from the various extremities. The control tower was operating on its own.

The good news was that he felt absolutely no pain.

Or maybe that was the *bad* news….

He listened. Heard water dripping nearby and a siren, far off, fading to nothing—not coming for him.

He smelled asphalt and he tasted his own blood in his mouth.

Darla, he thought, the blood in his mouth mingling with his stunned awareness of her betrayal, making a taste like rusted iron. He remembered. All of it. Every day, every hour, every moment he'd had with her: Darla Jo Snider, who was now Darla Jo Styles.

Ralphie had known a lot of women in his fifty-eight years of life. Known them and loved them. It was his greatest natural talent: to love a woman and love her well. When Ralphie loved a woman, he loved her all the way and over the moon. When Ralphie loved a woman, she was the *only* one—for a while, at least. And when it was over, well, he went on loving her. Just in a different way.

Darla, though. Darla was…special. No. That wasn't it. They were *all* special, every woman he had loved. But Darla? Well, with Darla, Ralphie had been certain that he'd found *her* at last—found the woman he'd always been looking for, the one he'd hold on to for the rest of his life, the one from whom he would never stray.

A tiny smile tipped the torn edges of what was left of his mouth. He'd been right about Darla. Oh, yes, he had. Because in spite of everything, he still loved her. He couldn't help himself. And since the rest of his life was beginning to look a lot shorter than anticipated, it was pretty damn likely he'd be loving Darla Jo when he died.

Ralphie stared up at the faint, faraway stars and managed to whisper her name to the night. "Darla Jo."

And he felt pain then, though that particular pain did not reside in any of the broken parts of his body.

It seemed so wrong, for this to be happening. He hadn't even mailed in his tax return yet. And damn, he could use a smoke. Just one more. For the road…

Ralphie swallowed blood. Everything was kind of slowing down. And he was floating, not exactly able to care much that he was lying in the middle of the street in the darkness before dawn—all alone, bleeding, his arms and legs limp and unresponsive as slabs of raw meat. Yeah. A dead man. No doubt about it. He knew with growing certainty that he wasn't going to be around to put this current problem to rights. And what would the cops have to go on? His killer was clever. His killer just might get away clean.

But then again…

There *was* Rio. Mustn't forget Rio. A good man, Rio. The best—and what about Phoebe?

Phoebe Jacks was Ralphie's first wife and his current business partner. She'd be in the mix, too. Phoebe was something. You didn't mess with Phoebe—or with anyone she called a friend.

Ralphie smiled his torn smile again. Yeah. Rio and Phoebe would take care of it. They wouldn't stop until they got to the bottom of it. And since Ralphie had never gotten around to changing his will as he'd kept promising Darla he would, if this *was* the end for him, Rio would be his only true heir. Rio would be partners with Phoebe.

That was good. That was the one thing that had worked out just right, after all. Ralphie wished he could be there when Rio and Phoebe came face-to-face for the first time. That would be something. Yeah. Something to see. Sparks would fly….

What was that sound?

Music.

Ralphie sighed. Beautiful, the music. Heartbreaking.

It had started far away and it was coming closer. A Bruce Springsteen ballad from the early nineties, "If I Should Fall Behind." A woman was singing it….

Phoebe. Oh, yeah. Phoebe was singing that beautiful song, her husky voice so rich and true.

The music swelled in volume and then a vision burst wide open, bright as day, before him.

He saw the Prairie Queens: Phoebe, Cimarron Rose and Tiffany, onstage in their glory before it all went to hell, before Phoebe divorced him and the band broke up. Cimarron Rose on the keyboards, Tiff on bass guitar. Phoebe, who played lead, stood at the mike, the lights catching bright gleams in her long dark hair, green eyes shining as she strummed and sang so slow and sweet.

Phoebe's face changed and she was Darla, singing just for him. Darla, wearing a long, white dress, her stomach jutting high and proud with the baby she was carrying, a halo of golden light around her angel's face.

"Darla Jo," he whispered to the darkness and the distant stars. "It doesn't matter. All your lies. Or what you did. I love you. I'll always love you. And I'll wait for you where I'm goin'. I swear I will."

The song faded. The vision melted away. Ralphie Styles let his eyelids droop shut.

He never opened them again.

CHAPTER ONE

> If life is a waste of time, and time is a waste of life, then let's all get wasted together and have the time of our lives.
> —*from* The Prairie Queen's Guide to Life, *by Goddess Jacks*

AT THREE IN THE AFTERNOON on her thirtieth birthday, Phoebe Jacks stood behind the bar wearing strappy sandals with four-inch heels and a black sundress printed with roses. She was polishing a beer glass. Phoebe found polishing the glassware calming, and she needed a calming activity right then. Her ex-husband, Ralphie Styles, had screwed her over royally—from the grave, no less.

Oh, yeah, she thought, blowing a coil of dark hair out of her eyes, happy birthday to me.

"And what I want to know is, who the hell is Rio Navarro?" Cimarron Rose Bertucci, one of Phoebe's two best friends since birth—and Ralphie's second wife—pounded the old oak bar with her fist. She did it hard enough that the jumbo margarita in front of her bounced. Luckily, Rose's drink was half-empty, so not a drop was spilled.

Phoebe set down the freshly polished glass. Ralphie had mentioned Navarro's name now and then, in passing, over the years. "Some old friend of Ralphie's," she said. "Not from Oklahoma. Lives in California, I think."

On the stool to the right of Rose, Tiffany Sweeney, Phoebe's other lifelong best friend—and Ralphie's third wife—was shaking her blond head. "Not even from Oklahoma." Tiff did not approve. "Who *is* he? What does he *do?*"

"Well, I guess I'll be findin' out soon enough." Phoebe grabbed another glass and set to work bringing out the shine.

"That's Ralphie for you," muttered Tiffany. "Never met a heart or a promise he couldn't break."

Rose shook a finger and made a tutting sound. "You know how he was. Such a sweetheart, really. He always *meant* well."

Tiff's blue eyes grew suspiciously misty. "Yeah. Yeah, I know..." She blinked away the emotion and turned to Phoebe again. "And Pheeb, who says you'll ever even have to deal with your new partner? Ralphie knew a whole lot of shady types. Most likely Navarro's one of those. I wouldn't be the least surprised if that cheesy lawyer of Ralphie's hasn't got a clue how to find the guy."

Phoebe sighed. "I called the lawyer yesterday when I got my copy of the will in the mail. The lawyer told me he sent Navarro his copy by FedEx a week ago. It *was* delivered and Navarro signed for it."

"Doesn't mean a thing," Tiff insisted. "Take it from me. Mr. Rio Navarro is some grifter or cowhand who never stands still long enough to sign for his mail. His drunk girlfriend probably signed for it and then promptly passed out. It's probably waiting at the bottom of a tall stack of unpaid bills, totally ignored. Don't expect to meet your new partner any time soon."

Rose took another gulp of her drink. "Leave it to Ralphie," she muttered, the words both tender and exasperated.

Ralphie Styles had died broke, but he'd always had a need to leave a legacy behind. As a result, over the years he'd compiled a detailed will in which he doled out every piece of junk he owned. Rose and Tiffany had both received bequests. Rose got a wall clock shaped like a cat. Tiffany was now the proud owner of a gold-plated keychain with the finish wearing off. Both items apparently had special meaning. At lunch a little earlier that day, Rose had got a sad, faraway smile on her face when she'd mentioned that clock. Tiff's eyes had gleamed when she'd spoken of the keychain. Tiff said Ralphie always used to carry it, when she and Ralphie were in love.

To Phoebe, Ralphie had left all the old Prairie Queen publicity stills that decorated the olive-green and brick walls of the bar he and Phoebe had jointly owned since their divorce eight years ago. In those decade-old pictures, Rose, Tiff and Phoebe smiled wide for the camera. They'd been on their way then, with gigs all over town and a record contract in the works. Ralphie had been their manager.

Phoebe herself had collected those photographs, framed them and hung them on the walls. Only Ralphie would will a girl something that already belonged to her.

And oddly enough, that he'd left her own pictures to her had touched her, made her feel all soft and dewy-eyed, like Tiff with her keychain, like Rose with her clock. As if by willing her what she already owned, Ralphie was somehow reminding her of all that had been—of the passionate, wonderful, long-ago love the two of them had shared, of what a great time they'd had.

As to Ralphie's half of the bar itself, which now belonged to the mysterious Rio Navarro, well, Phoebe knew she should have got it in writing one of those dozen or so times that Ralphie had told her how it would all be hers when he was gone. Those times were mostly when Ralphie needed money. He'd hit her up for a loan and remind her of how it would all shake out in the end, that one day Ralphie's Place would be hers and hers alone. He'd died owing her over twenty thousand dollars.

Phoebe polished another glass.

Yeah, she of all people should have known better than to take Ralphie Styles at his word.

Phoebe had been nineteen when she eloped with him. He'd been forty-seven: the legendary Ralphie Styles. In love with *her.* At last. That he was finally seeing her as a woman had meant everything to Phoebe. She'd known him all her life, been in love with him since she was old enough to speak the word and mean it. He'd never married anyone until he'd married her. She'd thought that made her different than the rest.

It hadn't. He'd broken her heart they way he did all

the others—broken her heart and then, over time, become her true friend.

And no. Phoebe couldn't say she was all that surprised to learn that she had a new partner. It was her new partner being some stranger from out of state that made her want to break a few glasses instead of polishing them. Since three weeks ago, when Ralphie had got himself nailed in a hit-and-run, Phoebe had been more or less expecting to end up in business with his fourth wife, Darla Jo.

And speaking of Darla Jo…

Back at the table in the corner that Ralphie had always called his "office," Darla Jo was nursing a plain tonic, hunched over her very pregnant stomach, sobbing her little heart out. She'd received her copy of the will yesterday, too, same as Phoebe, Rose and Tiff. Devastated to learn that some stranger was getting Ralphie's half of the bar when she was his wife and it ought to have gone to *her,* Darla had called Phoebe and sobbed in her ear. Phoebe hadn't been able to stop herself from inviting Darla along for her birthday lunch with the Queens.

After lunch, they'd all come on over to the bar. It was Tuesday, which was usually slow, so they'd figured they would have the place pretty much to themselves. Darla's brother, Boone, who'd been working the day shift for almost five months now, had already been there when they arrived.

Now Boone sat with Darla, his chair scooted close to her. He had his arm wrapped around her and his sandy-colored head bent close to hers.

"It's okay, sweetheart." Boone tried to soothe her by rubbing her back a little. "Darla, come on, it'll be all right." But Darla Jo only wailed all the louder. She was inconsolable.

The two women at the bar glanced toward the back table and shook their heads some more.

"Sad," said Tiff. "No. Worse than sad. Downright depressing."

Softly, so the two in back wouldn't hear, Rose stated the obvious. "It's tough to lose a husband when you're twenty-one and pregnant with no job skills to speak of."

"Yeah," said Tiff. "But that girl has been cryin' every day for three weeks now. It can't be good for the baby. She needs to lighten up a little."

Phoebe spoke then, quietly, bending close to her lifelong friends. "She loved him and now she just can't deal with the fact that he's gone. It's tearing her up inside."

The other two looked at her, looks that displayed the endless wisdom acquired once a girl approaches thirty and has had plenty of opportunity to witness—and participate in—what goes on between women and men.

At last Rose said low, "Pheeb, darlin'. She may be brokenhearted. But she's also flat broke. Ralphie left her nothing. No money, no life insurance, no bar. I'd say at least half of all this endless bawlin' is about a total lack of *c-a-s-h.*"

Tiffany burped—but delicately. "Oh. 'Scuse me." She hunched to the bar and whispered so Ralphie's sobbing child bride wouldn't hear, "Well, she did get the double-wide, didn't she? Not that it's paid for, or anything."

"Pardon me." Rose kept her voice low and faked a snooty accent. "That is no double-wide. It is a manufactured home." She slapped a hand on the bar. "Music. Now." Sliding off her stool, Rose straightened her jean jacket—causing the rhinestone appliqués on it to glitter wildly in the dim light—and sauntered to the jukebox. Draping her lush self over the side of it, she punched out a few tunes. First off was Creed: "My Sacrifice."

"Oh, God." Tiff whined. "Did you have to?"

But Rose only grinned and strutted back to her stool, black salsa skirt swaying. Just as she was settling in, the unmistakable roaring rumble of a Harley-Davidson motorcycle rattled the wide window across from the bar.

Phoebe glanced up from polishing yet another glass as a big guy with shoulder-length crow-black hair rolled a gleaming two-wheeled hunk of chrome and steel off the street and into one of the spaces out front. The afternoon sun glinted off his black sunglasses. Phoebe had to squint against the glare.

The girls at the bar had also turned to look.

"Oh, my, my," said Cimarron Rose. She pretended to fan herself.

"Nice Harley," added Tiff out of the side of her mouth.

Rose loudly cleared her throat. "But back to the task at hand…" They both faced the bar again and lifted their glasses. Rose proposed the toast. "Ralphie. He was one of a kind and that is no lie."

"Ralphie," Tiff echoed after her, eyes glittering with moisture again. They drank in unison as Darla sobbed all the harder and, beyond the window, the black-haired hunk, in faded denim, a black T-shirt and a black leather vest, got off the Harley. He kicked down the stand with his big black boot. And then, for a moment, he just stood there, muscular arms hanging loose at his sides, staring at the front window as if he could see Phoebe in there behind the bar, staring right back at him. He couldn't, of course. It was darker inside than out and the window was tinted. But still, a shiver like a dribble of ice water slid down her spine and a sizzle of heat flared low in her belly.

"Darlin' Phoebe, another round," said Tiffany.

Phoebe set to work on two more margaritas, glancing up as the big guy came strolling in.

Rose had got it right. *My, my, my…*

The stranger in question claimed a stool at the end of the bar and took off those black sunglasses. Tossing them down by the ashtray, he sent a glance Phoebe's way.

"Be right with you." She gave him a nod and he nodded back. Phoebe served the Queens and then moved on over to stand opposite him.

"Shot of Cuervo." He had a deep, kind of velvety voice. With a little sandpaper roughness around the edges. "Beer back." He laid down a twenty and as he did that she looked at his hands. Big hands.

She glanced up and their gazes caught. *My, my, my.* Eyes as black as his hair. And a mouth that made her think of deep, wet kisses….

Inside Phoebe's head, alarm bells started ringing.

Don't you even think about it, girl.

Phoebe had made plenty of mistakes in her thirty years, but she liked to think she'd learned from them. There had been other men in her life since Ralphie, every one of them big and wild and dangerous.

No way. Not again.

She broke the eye contact and concentrated on setting the guy up, free-pouring the tequila with a flourish, plunking the salt in front of him along with the fresh wedge of lime, tipping a beer glass under the tap, topping it off with a perfect inch of head.

"Enjoy," she said, flashing him one dead-on glance, not letting the look linger.

"Thanks."

Down the bar, Tiff complained, "Enough of this Creed shit."

"Baby, your wish is my command," said Rose.

Right on cue, the song ended and Rose stuck a fist in the air as though she'd been personally responsible. Phoebe moved back to her post near her friends and the Queens laughed together as the jukebox whirred and a much mellower Dave Matthews tune came on.

At Ralphie's table, Boone was helping the still-sobbing Darla Jo to her feet. She sagged against him and he tightened his hold on her. Swaying together like a pair of bomb victims staggering away from a deadly explosion, they started for the door at the end of the bar that led through the storeroom to the employee parking area in back.

"Mind if I see she gets home all right?" Boone asked, steadying Darla as she stumbled.

"Go ahead," Phoebe said. "Take the day. I can handle things here till Bernard shows up."

"Happy birthday, Pheeb," Darla Jo said in a tiny, broken voice, leaning heavily on Boone. Her honey-brown hair hung lank around her pale baby-doll face.

It caused an ache in Phoebe's heart to see her hurting so much. "Thanks, sweetie. Take it easy, okay?"

"Take care, Darla Jo," said Rose.

And Tiffany added, "Later, hon."

They all watched, wearing solemn expressions, as Boone guided Ralphie's pregnant widow to the swinging door and on through.

"Ralphie, Ralphie," Rose pondered aloud, casting her gaze heavenward, once the door swung shut behind Darla Jo and Boone. "Ralphie, what were you *thinkin'?*"

Tiffany was nodding, looking severe, her famous dimples nowhere in sight. "You are so right, Rose. He never should have gotten the poor little thing pregnant. Almost sixty years old, and he didn't have the sense to put a raincoat on that big thing of his."

"Sense? Ralphie?" Rose made a scoffing sound low in her throat. "Now, *there* are two words never meant to be spoken in the same sentence." They all nodded at that, even Phoebe. Then Rose's face softened. "Think about it, though. That baby will be the only child that wild man ever had."

Tiffany corrected her. "Well, that we know of."

Tiff did have a point. Chances were Ralphie had other children somewhere. Ralphie had loved women. And women had loved him. It didn't matter that he was too skinny and too old and his nose was too big for his face. When he turned those lazy-lidded eyes on a girl, she would fall hard and fast and not give a good damn that the landing was bound to be rough.

Back when Phoebe and Ralphie were married, both Tiff and Rose had been in love with him, too. Though she knew her friends would never betray her, Phoebe had resented them for not being able to keep themselves from wanting *her* husband. Secretly, she'd feared that the day would come when Ralphie started falling out of love with her, the way he had with all the others before her. She'd dreaded that the unthinkable just might happen: she'd find him doing the wild thing with Rose or Tiff.

As it turned out, Ralphie *did* fall out of love with her. And into bed with someone else. Not Rose or Tiff, though. Thank God. In her pain and rage at his doing her that way, she'd divorced him and taken her half of the bar in the settlement. She'd dropped out of the band, and Rose and Tiff hadn't had the heart to carry on without her.

For a while, Phoebe had hated Ralphie Styles with a passion as powerful as her love had been. But her hatred didn't last. She just couldn't stay mad at him forever. He'd give you the shirt off his back if you needed it. Only later would you find out it was a shirt he'd borrowed from someone else.

You just had to love him, even when you weren't *in* love with him anymore. Besides, once a couple of years had gone by, Phoebe really was over him in the romantic sense and truly immune to the passionate insanity he could inspire.

Rose and Tiff weren't immune to him, though. They'd each married him—Rose first, Tiff later; short marriages that ended the same way his marriage to Phoebe had: in heartbreak and divorce. Eventually, both Rose and Tiff had forgiven him. And in time, each found herself calling him a friend.

Down the bar, the big biker caught Phoebe's eye and raised his empty shot glass. She went on over there and served him up another round, her throat kind of tight suddenly with all the memories swirling around in her brain. That time, when she set the beer in front of him, she gave the guy a longer look. He looked back. Another shiver went through her—one that crackled with heat all the way down to where it went liquid and spread out into a warm pool low in her belly.

No, she thought.

But deep inside someone was sighing out an endless string of yesses—yesses, she reminded herself, she would do nothing about.

It was a bad day, that was all. A day that had her polishing every glass in the place and imagining what it might be like to celebrate turning thirty by doing something dangerous with a guy she'd just met—a guy who'd spoken exactly six words to her so far: *Shot of Cuervo. Beer back. Thanks.*

No doubt about it. Soulful eyes. Lots of muscles. Coal-black hair and a couple of shots. These were the beginnings of a truly deep and meaningful relationship.

When she returned to the Queens, they'd moved on to the subject of Ralphie's suspicious demise.

"I'm sorry," said Rose. "But I do believe we are dealing with foul play here." Whoever had run Ralphie over and then fled the scene had yet to be apprehended.

"Well, duh," said Tiff. "A hit-and-run *is* foul play by definition." She sipped her margarita, frowning. "Isn't it?"

"A hit-and-run is foul play by *accident,*" Rose clarified. "And I don't believe Ralphie's death was any accident. I am talking about someone finally getting fed up with Ralphie in a murderous way. I am talking premeditation. You hear what I'm saying? And it's not like it's never been done before. Remember that woman up in Tulsa last year? Got into her SUV, drove to where her husband was doing the nasty with his girlfriend, and ran the bastard down when he and the other woman came out of their favorite motel. Ran him down and then backed up over him, slammed it into drive and ran over him again."

"I don't think that was in Tulsa," said Tiff. "It was on *Law and Order,* wasn't it?"

Rose gave her a look. "Not the point—and think about it. As long as nobody sees you and you don't blow it and leave the guy alive to identify you, a hit-and-run would be better than a bullet or rat poison or a stabbing to the heart." She paused to gaze deeply into her jumbo margarita glass. Glancing up again, she added, "Yeah, you'd need a way to get rid of the car...."

"Well," said Tiff. "*Somebody* did find a way to get rid of the car. Or to hide it. Or somethin'. They got rid of it *after the fact.* They don't want to face the consequences of their actions. That doesn't mean it was pre-planned or anything."

"Oh, yeah," said Rose. "I think it was."

Phoebe, who'd heard all this before, just wished they would stop. But they didn't.

Tiffany insisted, "Some drunk, that's all. Or some soccer mom on her cell phone."

"Ha," said Rose. "That's a stretch. A soccer mom driving around in the Paseo in the middle of the night, calling…who?"

"I'm only trying to get you to see," said Tiff in her most patient and reasonable tone, "that we basically know nothing beyond the fact that someone hit him and then drove away."

"Huh. Pardon me. We know he was in the Paseo, on foot, after midnight." The Paseo, the old Spanish district, with its stucco buildings and clay-tile roofs, was best known for its thriving artists' community. Ralphie was no artist. He didn't live in the Paseo, have friends there or do business there that the Queens knew of. "I ask you," said Rose. "What was he *doing* there?"

Tiffany blew out a hard breath. "I'm only saying, why assume it had to be murder?"

Rose had her margarita glass in her hand again. She took a big gulp and set it down hard. "Because it was Ralphie who got killed, that's why. We all know how he was. Everybody loved him—except for when they hated him."

Phoebe had heard enough. More than enough. She grabbed the cast-aluminum ice scooper from the top of the ice machine, pulled open the slanted steel ice machine door, braced her free arm on the rim and stuck the scooper in there. Taking a wide stance for balance on her pointy little heels, she used the scooper to beat at the ice. It had been clumping for a few days now, which meant the machine was leaking. She'd need to call a repairman.

Haven't done that *in a while,* she thought as she pounded away. Not since Ralphie came back to the city—to stay, this time, he'd told her—and started in with Darla Jo.

"Tiff, you are in denial," she heard Rose insist.

"*I'm* in denial….?"

Phoebe pounded harder, glaring into the globs and clumps of ice as she attacked them with the scooper, every blow beating back the voices behind her.

She pulverized that ice and in her mind's eye, he took form.

Ralphie…

She could just see him, see that road map of a face with the laugh lines etched deep as craters on either side of his fleshy mouth, see the wild hair he dyed a reddish-black not found in nature, which in the past few years was thinning so high at the temples, the bare spots threatened to meet at the top of his head.

He'd always been handy with machines. "Step aside," he would say when the equipment started acting up. "Let Ralphie work his magic—and hand me that wrench over there, will you, babe?"

Phoebe beat the ice harder. She wanted to smash every clump to a sliver, crush it all into powder.

"Phoebe, hon." It was Rose. Phoebe slammed the

scoop into the ice one more time. Rose shouted, "Hey!"

Squinting hard to hold back the gathering tears, Phoebe pulled her head out of the ice machine and sent a glare over her shoulder at the Queens.

Rose told her tenderly, "Honey, put that scoop down."

Phoebe tossed the scoop into the machine, slammed the door and whirled to face her friends. "I am sick of hearin' about it."

"Sorry," said Rose.

"Not another word," vowed Tiffany.

Phoebe wrapped her arms around herself and looked down at her high-heeled sandals. They were red as the roses on her dress. Red was a power color—she'd heard that somewhere. Lately, since Ralphie's death, Phoebe felt like she needed all the power she could get.

Tiff said weakly, "Aw, Pheeb. Come on."

Phoebe squeezed her arms tighter around her middle, lifted her head and jerked her sagging shoulders back. "I miss that sorry sleazeball, I truly do." Her throat locked up. She had to whisper the rest. "I just can't believe he went and got himself killed."

There was a silence, except for Gwen Stefani bopping on the jukebox, singing that "Hollaback Girl" song.

Rose got that soft-eyed, mother-hen look. "Oh, honey…"

Phoebe pressed her lips together and tightly shook her head. "Uh-uh." She put out a hand. "I am not going to lose it. I am going to be fine." There'd been enough crying. Darla Jo had done plenty of that for all of them.

"It's okay," Tiffany said in a careful voice. "Sometimes a girl can't help herself. She just needs a good cry."

But Phoebe wasn't going to cry. Not now. Not today. She gulped to clear the tightness from her throat, pressed her fingers under her eyes to ease the burning ache of tears unshed and drew herself up tall again. "So. 'Nother round?"

But the fun was over and they all knew it. Phoebe looked from Tiff to Rose and back to Tiff. They both wore that shiny-eyed, tears-on-the-way look. One more drink and things would get seriously weepy.

Tiff, who'd driven Rose, pushed her half-full glass Rose's way. "Finish that if you want it. I need a quick minute and then we're outta here." She got up and went to the ladies' room, past the stage and down the hall.

Rose looked into the depths of Tiffany's unfinished drink and then up at Phoebe. "I took the whole day off. Come on over to my place for a while. Give yourself a damn break for a change. It *is* your birthday."

Phoebe considered, but decided against it. "Thanks. No." She swept out an arm, indicating the mostly empty room and the lone biker down at the end of the bar. He wasn't looking their way. Instead, he stared straight ahead at the rows of bottles on the mirrored back wall, as if pondering the mysteries of the universe. "Who'll handle all these customers if I take off?"

Rose forced a chuckle, then asked doubtfully, "You sure?"

"Positive. And Bernard'll be in at six." Bernard, one of Phoebe's two full-time bartenders besides herself, had the closing shift that day. "If things stay slow, I'll go home when he gets here. Put my feet up. Call my mother. Floss my teeth..."

Rose groaned. "Pheeb, you need to watch yourself."

"Oh? And why's that?"

"Lately, your life is becoming downright boring."

"And you know what? I like it that way."

"But a girl needs a thrill now and then."

"I've had enough thrills to last me a lifetime—and then some."

Peruvian earrings dancing against her white neck under the soft waves of her blond hair, Tiffany emerged from the back hallway. "Y'all ready to go?"

Rose took a long pull off Tiff's abandoned drink and set the glass down with finality. "Ready."

Phoebe followed them to the door, answered their duet of goodbyes and happy birthdays, and moved to the wide window to watch them as they got into Tiff's ancient, perfectly maintained Volvo sedan, which Ralphie had presented to her two years ago when her rattletrap compact car finally gave up the ghost. They hooked their seat belts and Tiff backed onto the street.

The gorgeous old car slid out—and slammed to a stop as a Mustang came roaring down Western and almost plowed into it. Honking ensued, from both vehicles. The guy in the Mustang swung around the Volvo, yelling something rude as he went by. Rose stuck her arm out the passenger window, middle finger raised high.

Phoebe shook her head. Rose had the attitude, always had.

The Volvo rolled forward, made the light onto Thirty-Sixth Street and disappeared the same way the Mustang had gone. Phoebe leaned her forehead against the cool glass of the window and shut her burning eyes.

She missed the Queens already, though five minutes ago she couldn't wait to see them gone. The song on the jukebox ended. It whirred for a moment and then it was quiet.

Quiet enough to hear the rubber hit the road out on Western and the faint cries of four starlings on a wire above the furniture store across the street. She could even hear the damn ice machine dripping, back there behind the bar. And the balls of her feet were sore. She lifted her left foot and slid off her sandal. Heaven. She took off the other one. The cool, scuffed boards of the floor felt so good against her bare feet. Sandals in hand, she turned for the bar.

The biker had turned, too. He sat facing her, watching her through those black, black eyes.

Phoebe let a naughty little thrill shimmer through her—and then shrugged and swung the sandals over her shoulder to dangle by a finger. "Don't tell me. You're the new health inspector." It was a bad joke and it fell flat.

He shrugged. "Not me."

"Ready for another shot?"

"Two's my limit."

"Smart man."

They shared a look. It lasted a second or two longer than it should have. Then he tipped his dark head at the empty stool beside him.

Better not, she thought. But what do you know? Her bare feet ambled on over there anyway, carrying her with them. She hopped up on the stool, facing out as he was, tugging lightly on her skirt so it didn't slide too far up her thighs.

Dropping the sandals to the floor, she eased around his way and stuck out her hand. "I'm Phoebe Jacks."

After a slight hesitation, he took it. His big, warm, rough hand swallowed hers and she felt that thrill again, that heated excitement searing upward along her arm, spreading all through her.

Lust at first sight, she thought, trying to be philosophical, reminding herself, again, that it was just a bad day for her and she would not follow through on her urge to rip off her sundress and jump into his lap. Maybe once upon a time she would have. But not anymore. She was older and wiser now. She'd lived through a marriage to Ralphie and after that, through a definite weakness for bad boys in black leather. She was done with all that now.

They shook.

She prompted, "And you are?"

"Rio," he said. "Rio Navarro."

Phoebe's heart stopped dead, and then started racing. Carefully, she pulled her hand away. "My new partner." Her tone was level. Absolutely calm. Just as if she were polishing the glassware.

"That's right."

"Ralphie's dead," she said, as if he didn't already know.

"So I heard."

She looked at Rio Navarro and she wondered how this—how any of it—could possibly have happened. Ralphie gone forever. Darla crying all the time. This black-eyed, sexy stranger showing up out of nowhere on her birthday and turning out to be the man who owned half of her livelihood.

It was too much, all of it, just too damn much.

"Excuse me," she said, and had to pause to gulp hard. "I'll be back in a minute." Phoebe jumped from the stool, scooped up her sandals and raced around the end of bar, headed for the swinging door that led to the prep and storage areas in back.

Though it took every ounce of pride and self-respect she possessed, she didn't burst into tears until after the door swung shut behind her.

CHAPTER TWO

A Prairie Queen has a sparkling comeback for every bad pick-up line.
Example: Man: Haven't I seen you someplace before?
Prairie Queen: Yes, that's why I don't go there anymore."
—*from* The Prairie Queen's Guide to Life, *by Goddess Jacks*

RIO WAITED FOUR AND A half minutes for Ralphie's former wife to reappear through the swinging door with the round window in the top of it.

When she did, her eyes and nose were red. She'd also put on some flat-heeled black shoes. She pushed through that door with her dark head high and marched right over to him—keeping to her side of the bar so that the long oak surface stood between them.

She met Rio's eyes dead on, no sniffling, and he thought of what Ralphie had always said of her: *Phoebe's a stand-up gal. A rock.* "Sorry about that."

"No problem." He knew she wouldn't want his concern, but he found himself leaning closer and asking anyway, "You okay?"

"I am just fine." Each word was strong and final, even with the Oklahoma lilt adding a twang to the vowels. Her gaze shifted away, and then back. "So. You come all the way from California on that big bike out there?"

"That's right."

"You travel light."

"I've got a pack and a helmet. I left them at the motel."

She kind of squinted at him, leaning in. He got a whiff of her perfume. Tempting. Like the rest of her. Then she backed off again and braced a hand on the bar. "Not meanin' to insult you or anything, but I wonder if you wouldn't mind showing me some ID."

Her request didn't surprise him. When you met someone through Ralphie Styles, it was always a good idea to ask for ID. "Right here." He eased his wallet from an inside pocket of his leather vest and flipped it open, holding it across the bar to her so she could get a look at his driver's license.

She craned her dark head close to examine it. He stared at the vulnerable crown of her head and breathed in more of the seductive smell of her. When she straightened, he still saw doubt in those red-rimmed green eyes. "I'll bet a good forger could make one of those look just like the real thing."

Rio turned it around so his private investigator's ID in the opposite window was right-side up. She peered at that one for even longer than she had his driver's license. Finally, with a weary little sigh, she waved it away. He tucked the wallet back inside his vest.

"So. You're a private detective?"

He nodded. "I also work for a bail bondsman now and then, bringing home the bad guys."

She looked at him sideways. "Like a bounty hunter?"

"You got it."

"Well," she said, "and now you're half owner of my bar." She put a slight extra emphasis on the word *my*. Her mouth had a pursed look. "We missed you at the funeral." A definite dig.

"When was it?"

She blinked and her mouth loosened, even trembled a little. "You didn't know."

"Not till last week, when I got the will and the letter telling me that Ralphie was dead."

"I'm sorry." He saw real regret in her eyes then. "Ralphie didn't talk a lot about his friends from out of town. But he did mention you, now and then. I guess I should have thought to try and get a hold of you."

Rio had never cared much for funerals anyway. "Not a big deal."

"Well, the times he talked about you, he said good things."

Okay, he was curious. "Like what?"

She waved a hand. "General things. How he could always count on you. Once, when he took off for California, he said something about staying with you. How you were like family. How someday he was going to talk you into coming to Oklahoma, at least for a visit. And then, when he and Darla decided to get married, he said something about inviting you to the wedding."

Ralphie *had* invited him. "He gave me a call. Would have made it if I could." There had been that job in Mexico. He hadn't wanted to pass that one up. Rio found himself wishing what men always wished when it was too late: that he'd chosen his friend over paying the rent.

She said, "You knew Ralphie a long time, huh?"

Sadness scraped at the back of his throat. He swallowed it down. "Yeah. We went way back."

Her eyes got a little wetter. She cleared her throat. "He died on tax day, do you believe that?"

He shook his head. "Ralphie. Always filed his taxes…"

She was smiling, a misty kind of smile. "He hated to do it, but he'd say—"

"'I've seen a lot of highflyers brought low,'" He faked Ralphie's whisky-and-nicotine drawl. "'And all because they didn't bother to do their time with a 1099.'"

She turned slightly away, swiped at her eyes, and then faced him again. "I keep expecting to look up and see him comin' through that door, heading straight for the jukebox."

"Let me guess. 'Home Sweet Oklahoma.'"

"That would be the one." It came out tight. Emotion under strict rein. She swallowed. "Ralphie did love his Leon Russell. No matter where his big dreams took him, he always came home to Oklahoma."

"Which is why Woody Guthrie would do in a pinch."

"So true." Her eyes shone at him, full of memories and the growing awareness that Rio had a few memories of his own.

There was a silence. In it were all the things Rio might

have said, but didn't. Bad idea, he thought, to let himself go tripping too far down memory lane. He'd just met this woman. No need to make a business meeting into a wake.

Ralphie's ex let her gaze drop to the bar. "So what are your plans?" She was getting down to it.

Stalling, he asked for clarification he didn't need. "You mean about this place?"

She nodded, drawing herself up, suggesting grimly, "Thinking you want to get into the bar business?"

He should have answered simply, no. But things were starting to seem a long way from simple. "You're leading up to offering to buy me out, right?"

She raised her slim hands and pressed her fingertips gently to the tear-puffy skin under her eyes. Her bare shoulders gleamed, pearly, in the dim light from above. "Yeah." She let her hands drop. "Yeah, I am."

It was exactly what he'd hoped she might say—or it had been. Until he'd heard those friends of hers discussing the way Ralphie had checked out.

And then there was the little problem of Ralphie's very pregnant bride.

Things weren't adding up. If the dead man had been anyone else, Rio probably would have just let it go. But Ralphie Styles, with all his faults, had been the best friend Rio Navarro ever had. Rio was ten when they'd met, Ralphie in his midthirties. Rio still remembered the first advice Ralphie Styles had ever given him.

"Keep your head up, kid. And never let any sumbitch see you sweat."

The woman across the bar prompted, "So what do you think?"

Rio ordered his mind back to the present—and stalled some more. "You got the cash to buy me out?"

"Not right now. But I can get it eventually. In the meantime, you'd get Ralphie's share, half of what we make here—after operating expenses."

"I'll need some time to think it over."

"Think what over? What do you want with a half-interest in an Oklahoma City bar? Let me buy you out."

He let a few beats elapse before replying, "I think I'll just keep my options open for a while. If that's all right with you."

She was getting that strung-tight look again, the one she'd been wearing just before she fled to the back room. "It's not all right with me. None of it. Not a thing. And excuse me, but did you *know?*"

He sat back a fraction. "About?"

"About this bar. That you were getting his half of it when—" she had to swallow before she could finish "—Ralphie was gone?"

Her eyes pleaded with him. She didn't really want the truth. He gave it to her anyway. "I knew."

She had to clear her throat again. "Ralphie *told* you he was leaving his half to you?"

"Yeah."

"How long ago was that?"

"Three years."

She shut those misty eyes and sucked in a deep breath through her nose. He watched the roses on her dress rise high and recede.

Same old Ralphie, Rio thought. Ralphie had a bad

habit of promising people things that didn't belong to him. And if something *did* belong to him, he'd promise it to *everyone.*

When Ralphie's ex looked at him again, her pretty mouth was set in an angry line and she seemed to have run out of questions—for the moment, anyway.

Rio decided to try getting a few answers of his own. "That was the widow, right? The little pregnant one who left with…" He didn't know the guy's name, so he gave her a chance to provide it.

She did. "Boone is Darla Jo's brother. He works here, for me."

"And Darla is exactly *how* pregnant?"

The woman across the bar made a small, angry sound and her green eyes flashed warnings. "Darla Jo was pregnant *before* she and Ralphie got married, if that's what you're getting at. Does that shock you or something?"

"Not a lot shocks me."

"Is that a fact?"

"Yeah. It's a fact."

"So why even ask?"

"Just curious. Just…putting a few things together."

"Well, you know what? I'm a little curious myself. I can't help wonderin' why you didn't have the courtesy to introduce yourself when you first walked in here." She tipped her head at the twenty he'd laid on the bar. "Why'd you have to fake me out with the paying customer routine?"

"Sorry," he said, though he wasn't. "I wanted to wait. Talk to you alone."

"How *thoughtful.*" She gave the word a whole new meaning. Not a good one.

He couldn't resist turning the knife a little. "And then there were all the interesting things your friends had to say about the way Ralphie died."

She made another of those tight, disgusted noises. "Listening to other people's conversations. Didn't your mama ever tell you that eavesdroppin' is rude?"

"Gets ingrained, in my line of work."

She waved her hand as if batting away a pesky fly. "Well, it's all just talk, anyway, what Rose said."

He gave her the lifted eyebrow. "You have to admit she made some valid points."

For that he got a long, tired sigh. "Listen. It's been three weeks since it happened and the police don't have a thing—and don't give me that look. They did their job. They interviewed everyone in sight. And whenever I called them and asked what was going on, they were great about it, real considerate and helpful. But they've got nothing, not without the car that ran him down or a single witness or anything left where it happened that might give them a clue. A hit-and-run. That's all we know. And like Tiff said, that's probably all it was. An accident."

"Phoebe." He called her by her name for the first time and found he liked the feel of it in his mouth. "Do *you* think there's more to it?"

She simmered where she stood. "It doesn't matter what I think. It's pretty damn clear by now that we're never going to know for sure."

"You mean you don't *want* to know? Or maybe you just don't care…"

She gave him a long beat of frozen silence. Then, with slow purpose, she leaned in close. He smelled that faint perfume again. And liked it. Too much. She spoke low, her voice gone to velvet—velvet over tempered steel. "You can be a real asshole. You know that, Mr. Private Detective?"

"Do you want to know the truth or not?"

"You also ask too many questions."

"Questions tend to bring answers. I like answers."

A stare-down ensued. He won. *Más o menos.*

She broke the eye contact. Shoving off the bar, she stomped on down to where her friends had sat and started cleaning up after them.

Every movement deft and quick, she cleared off the soggy cocktail napkins and the squeezed-out sections of lime. She dumped the half-empty drinks, tossing them into the steel sink behind the bar. Once the debris was swept away, she grabbed a wet towel to swab it all down, the sleek muscles in her bare arms flexing as she scrubbed.

As he watched her, Rio considered her various reactions since he'd walked through the door. What did they add up to? Grief? Guilt? Fury at Ralphie's final betrayal of leaving half of her business to a guy she'd never met? Frustration at not even knowing who had run Ralphie down?

When she'd said goodbye to the childlike, big-bellied widow, he'd heard a definite softness in her voice. Motherly almost. Protective. What was that about?

Rio consulted his instincts. They told him that Phoebe Jacks was okay, that if Ralphie *had* been murdered, she wouldn't have—*couldn't* have—had anything to do with it. But instincts could lie. And his were probably a little skewed in her case.

Scratch that.

More than probably.

He liked her—as Ralphie had always been so damn sure he would. He liked her coffee-brown hair, piled loosely on her head, getting free in little wispy strands that curled around her cheeks. He liked her pearly skin, her slanted green eyes and straight, no-nonsense black eyebrows. And then there was the way she'd refused to cry in front of him. And that sexy little black dress splashed with red roses that tied behind her neck and left her upper back and shoulders bare.

He'd like to see the parts of her the roses covered. He'd like that a lot.

Even if she did have a scrotum-shrinking way about her when she was ticked off.

Once she got the bar cleared, she trotted out to the table in the back where the loudly grieving widow had sat with her brother. She scooped up the glass the widow had left and wiped away the water ring beneath it. She straightened the chairs, holding the ladderbacks with one hand, kicking them under the table so the chair legs screeched against the floor.

She flew back behind the bar and dumped the glass,

folded the wet towel into a neat little square. Rio waited for her to look at him again.

Before she did, the door to the street swung open and three guys in short-sleeved dress shirts, red ties and cheap slacks came in. Obviously regulars. Phoebe greeted them by name, pushed an ashtray toward the balding one in the center, and served them without having to ask what they'd have.

The balding one lit a cigarette and told her she was looking good. She flashed him a smile of acknowledgment—with zero invitation in it.

Then she marched down to stand opposite Rio again. "Anything else?"

He was being dismissed. Leaning toward her, he pitched his voice low so the locals wouldn't hear. "Happy birthday."

"Thanks," she replied good and loud in a tone that said, *Get lost.*

"And one more thing. For now." His bike was too attention-getting. He needed something a little quieter and less eye-catching to get around in while he tried to find out what the police hadn't. "I'll need to rent a car."

"Call Hertz."

"I'll do that. And when I do, I want to put my bike someplace safe. Is there a garage or a loading area in back, something with a lock on the door?"

The guys in cheap slacks were watching. Rio caught the eye of the smoker and held it. After a count of five or so, all three looked away. A few seconds later the skinny one on the far end started in with some story about buying surround-sound for his digital TV.

Phoebe fumed at him a little, and then she gave in. "Just a minute." She headed off through the door with the porthole in it and banged back through seconds later.

"There's a garage around back." She slapped a key down on the bar a few inches from his shades. "Take the alley on the side of the building."

"Thanks."

"Why thank me? That garage is half yours. And pick up your money." She nodded at his twenty. "Didn't Ralphie tell you? An owner never pays."

He left the twenty where it lay. "Got a pencil?"

She huffed about it, but she did step over to the cash register, where she yanked a Bic from a happy face mug full of pens. She came back and handed it over.

He took a business card from another pocket of his vest and wrote the name of his motel and the number to his cell on the back. "In case you need to get in touch with me." He slid the card her way.

"Great," she said, meaning it wasn't. And then, huffing some more, she returned to the register and got a card from the little plastic stand next to the mug full of pens. "Here's my cell." She scribbled on the back. "And my home number, too. Also, there's an alarm inside the roll-up door in back. You'll need the combination." She scribbled some more, then passed the card to him. The front had a line drawing of the exterior of the bar with the bar's address, phone number and *Phoebe Jacks, proprietor* in the lower right hand corner.

"Thanks."

She gave an elaborate shrug of those smooth shoulders. "If I didn't give it to you, you'd find it all out anyway, right?"

"See you later, Phoebe." He stood from the stool and put on his shades. "It's been educational."

Phoebe watched him go. He had an excellent butt on him. But then, she could have guessed that by looking at the front of him. She wanted to despise the guy, though she knew she really didn't. It was Ralphie she was mad at.

But not really even Ralphie. Uh-uh. When she thought of Ralphie, she only wanted to flee to the back again and indulge in a Darla Jo–sized crying jag.

That wasn't an option. She had a bar to run. Tonight, just maybe, she could get away early. She could go home, throw herself across her bed and sob to her heart's content.

Outside, Rio straddled his bike and started it up. The powerful engine rumbled and then roared.

Pointedly ignoring the twenty that still waited on the bar, Phoebe turned to her customers. "Everybody doing okay?"

"You like a man on a big bike?" asked Dewey, puffing on his cancer stick. "I can get myself one of those."

Andy, to Dewey's left, piped up. "Phoebe darlin', for you, I will join the Hells Angels."

"Now, I don't know," said Purvis, to Dewey's right. "I'm not sure we approve of you goin' out with a Hells Angel."

Phoebe reached for the rack over her head and pulled down a wineglass. She grabbed a dry towel.

"Purvis, that is no Hells Angel. And I'm *not* going out with him." She put a strong emphasis on the *not,* partly because she personally needed to hear herself say it.

"But you said he could park that Harley-Davidson around back. And you gave him your phone number." Dewey looked deeply wounded. "You never would give it to me."

She said it again. "I'm *not* going out with him."

"Well, then why'd you give him your number?" Andy demanded.

Phoebe polished that wineglass for all she was worth. "That's my new partner."

There was a moment of awestruck, disbelieving silence.

Andy broke it. "You're shittin' us."

"No," Phoebe said. "Unfortunately, I'm not."

CHAPTER THREE

A Prairie Queen knows that most of a woman's problems start with men. Think about it: MENtal illness, MENstrual cramps, MENtal breakdown, MENopause…
—from The Prairie Queen's Guide to Life *by Goddess Jacks*

IF RIO HAD KNOWN HE WOULD have a job to do when he got to Oklahoma City, he would have come better prepared.

After he left the bar, he went to work. He made some calls. He got a haircut and bought a few clothes. Then he tracked down the accident report through the usual channels, paying a visit to police headquarters downtown, digging up the case number first, then trotting over to records to pick up the report.

After a quick study of the report, he talked to an OCPD public information officer. He left police headquarters and made a few more calls. Then he shopped some more. Got himself quality binoculars, a high mega-pixel digital camera and a video camera, also digital. He also needed a decent computer with high-speed Internet—and his motel had no Internet access, so he'd have to find one that did.

All in good time.

That night, he stretched out on the hard bed in his current motel room with the accident report and a map of Oklahoma City, and zeroed in on his target area, a ten-block radius from the spot where Ralphie had been hit. Most likely, the police would have covered that ground already, cruising the neighborhood, possibly even going door-to-door, looking for witnesses. But Rio would do it again. A lot of people didn't like talking to the police, for any number of reasons. They would talk to a friend, though. And when he put his mind to it, Rio Navarro was very good at making friends.

And speaking of friends…

He needed one. Or at least, an ally. Not for doing the scene and the neighborhood around it. For that, he could dig up some recommendations and hire an assistant, a pro. But for getting information out of Ralphie's friends and associates, he could use the help of an insider.

He already had his insider picked out. Phoebe Jacks.

The dead man himself recommended her. Ralphie had always said that Phoebe was a smart woman, a woman a man could count on. Plus, Rio had his own sense of her from that afternoon. She had pride. And *cojones;* she sure hadn't taken any crap off him. Also, he kind of liked the way she'd attacked that ice machine.

And then there was what she'd said a moment later, the anger and the pain in it: *I miss that sorry sleaze-ball, I truly do....*

Yeah, Ralphie's death had really gotten to her.

Rio wasn't kidding himself. His sense of his new business partner had a little more to do with his dick than it should have.

Too bad. His dick aside, she struck him as the perfect choice.

Next step on the Phoebe front would be to make her see that she wanted answers, too.

DUE TO ALL THE UPHEAVAL in her mind and heart, Phoebe had managed to forget that the second Tuesday of every month was open-mike night. Open-mike night brought in the wannabe musicians and singers with their Sears keyboards and cheap acoustic guitars. The wannabes brought all their friends. It wasn't a call-brand crowd. No pricey flavored martinis. They drank well liquor and a lot of beer. But cheap drinks added up if you sold enough of them. And on open-mike night, Ralphie's Place was packed.

At seven, when the two extra cocktail waitresses and the second bartender came strolling in, Phoebe remembered what the night held in store. No way would she be going home early. Her crying jag would have to wait.

She worked without a break straight through till closing time and didn't pull into the driveway of her little house in Mesta Park until almost 3:00 a.m.

By then, she was too tired to cry. She dropped her

dress on the floor and crawled into bed without even bothering to brush her teeth.

The phone woke her at eight: her mother, Goddess Jacks.

"Listen to this. 'Five tips for a woman. Number one. Find a man who helps you around the house and has a job. Number two. Get yourself a guy who makes you laugh. Number three. Don't forget that a man you choose should be one you can count on, who doesn't lie to you. Number four. You need a man who loves you and spoils you. Number five. It is important that these four men do not know each other.'" Goddess let out a musical laugh full of wicked delight. "So. You think?"

Phoebe thought her mother ought to try and remember not to call her before ten. She said, bleakly, "I love it."

"Oh, hon. It's going to be *so* good."

Goddess Jacks was writing a self-help book: *The Prairie Queen's Guide to Life.* Originally, she'd titled it *The Prairie Goddess's Guide to Life,* after herself, since she was the one giving the advice. But then she'd decided that *goddess,* with an apostrophe and an *s* at the end, didn't sound right. She'd settled on *queen,* in honor of Phoebe, Rose and Tiff—and the Prairie Queen Music Hall, long defunct and torn down.

"I've got more." Goddess was on a roll. Phoebe tried to remind herself that at least the call wasn't about one of her mother's visions. Goddess had visions all the time. She swore she had second sight. Goddess said, "A good friend will come and bail you out of jail, but a *true* friend will be sitting next to you in that cell saying, 'Damn. That was fun!'"

"Mom."

Goddess accused, "You are not laughing."

"I got in at three."

"Don't whine, hon. Whinin' makes those ugly little lines between your eyebrows—though I do know what's got you down. It's that will, isn't it?" Goddess had received her copy the same day as Phoebe, Darla and the other Queens—and probably everyone else in central Oklahoma. "I still can't believe he left me that foosball table. How could he have known I always wanted one of those? He was a genius that way, now wasn't he?" Goddess paused to indulge in a long, sentimental sigh. "Ralphie. More faults than Swiss cheese has holes. But didn't he always just *know* what a woman might want? Now, if I can only find somewhere to *put* the dang thing—and I know, I know. Figuring out where to put a foosball table doesn't exactly stack up against discovering you've got a partner you've never even met. Any news on this Rio Navarro character?"

It was not a question Phoebe wanted to be asked.

Her mother, using her psychic powers no doubt, read Phoebe's silence correctly. "He showed up. Oh, my. What's he like?"

Black hair, black eyes, lots of muscles and a great ass. "He's okay. I guess. He got in from California yesterday. On a Harley."

"Ooooo. Black leather jacket? Tight jeans? Interestin' tattoos? Chains hangin' off him?"

"Get a grip, Mama."

"Your new partner got a job out there in California?"

"He's a private investigator."

"Hmm. Not exactly your average nine-to-five. But still refreshing. A friend of Ralphie's who *works*. What's he going to *do*—about the bar?"

"He hasn't decided yet."

"I do hate a man who can't make up his mind."

"Yeah. Me, too."

"Hon, you do sound down."

"I'm fine," she lied.

"You're lyin'. You have a nice birthday lunch with Tiff and Rose?" Not giving Phoebe any chance to answer, Goddess kept right on, "Thirty years old. I can hardly believe it. My baby is thirty years old..."

"Happens to everyone eventually."

"That it does. And you're still all broke up, aren't you? You haven't made peace with the fact that Ralphie is gone." Phoebe decided not to reply to that. After a pause long enough to drive a fifth wheel and a horse trailer through, her mother said, "I am picking up nothing about that hit-and-run. But you wait. The spirits always come through. In fact, I've been thinking that we all need to make ourselves more open to communications from—" her mother's voice cut out and Phoebe heard a beep on the line "—the grave. After all, the spirits can't be heard if nobody's listening and—"

"Mom, I have to go. I've got another call."

Goddess harrumphed. "And if you think I believe

that, I've got some swampland to sell you. You can build you some condos on it."

"'Bye." Phoebe punched the call-waiting button. "Hello."

"Just checking to see if you gave me your real number."

Already, she recognized his voice. Probably a bad sign. "Rio."

"Too early for you?"

"Yeah. But don't let that stop you. It never stopped my mother."

"Goddess. Now, there's a name for you."

She tightened her grip on the handset. "How did you know my mother's name?"

"Ralphie told me. It's not the kind of name a man forgets. Ralphie also said he knew your mother from back in the seventies. And that he knew you and his other ex-wives back then, too, when you three were only kids."

"Ralphie talked too much."

"True. Rose and Tiffany. Your friends from the bar yesterday. Right?"

"What about them?"

"You know what. They're the ex-wives I just mentioned. And I've been nosing around a little…."

"Nosing around, where?"

"Various places."

"Oh, I'll just bet—and *why* have you been nosing around?" she asked, as if she didn't already know.

"Information is power."

"Hold the phone. Let me write that down."

"Don't be crabby, *Reina.*" His voice changed when he said the unfamiliar word, became softer, more musical.

"What's that, Spanish?"

He made a sound in the affirmative. "*Reina.* Queen."

She started to tell him not to call her that, but couldn't quite do it. Why not? It was a question she refused to analyze. She said, "I'd be a lot less crabby if you'd agree to sell me your half of my bar."

"Help me get what *I* want. Then we'll see about the bar."

"And you want?"

"Take a wild guess."

She didn't have to guess. She knew. She muttered, "Answers."

"Got it on the first try. And my take is that you really cared for the old SOB. I can't figure out why you don't want answers, too—unless you already have them."

She tried to whip up a little outrage, but it just wasn't happening. Wearily, she accused, "Meaning that you think I had something to do with what happened to him."

"My instincts tell me you're not involved."

She ladled on the sarcasm. "I am so relieved to hear that."

"But I do wonder…" He let the sentence wander off. She waited, refusing to prompt him. He went on at last. "Maybe there's someone you feel you have to protect."

"Why would I be protecting some drunk driver I never met?"

"You wouldn't. If it *was* some drunk who hit him. But what if it wasn't?" Before she could respond to that one, he said, "He was killed by a flat-fronted, high vehicle—an SUV, a full-sized van or a big pickup."

"And you know this...how?"

"Accident description. Force applied above the body's center of gravity. Forward projection—the body is flattened against the high front of the vehicle, accelerated to the speed of the vehicle, then thrown to the roadway *ahead* of the vehicle. In Ralphie's case, the vehicle went right over him after hitting him."

Phoebe's stomach was suddenly queasy. She shut her eyes—and saw Ralphie's lined, leathery face; his too-charming scam artist's smile. Her eyes popped open—wide—and she argued, "They never *found* the vehicle, so there's no way to know for sure what it was."

"But they *do* know what I just explained to you. And they got paint transfer. Off the body. Red paint. I had a little talk with someone down at the OCPD. Paint analysis here takes four to six months. The FBI does it. Did you know that from one tiny flake of paint, it's possible to get the make and model of just about any vehicle?"

"So in six months, they'll know what to look for."

"I don't want to wait that long. Do you?"

Phoebe had a powerful urge to disconnect the call, throw the phone across the room and pull the sheet over her head.

And then what? Cry until she couldn't cry anymore? Sleep?

Wake up, go to work, wait six months to find out whether it was a van or a pickup that had killed Ralphie Styles?

Rio said, "Come on, Phoebe. You're not the little widow, wailing away at a back table as if turning on the waterworks is going to get you somewhere. You're a strong woman who knows that if something's not getting done, it's time to roll up your sleeves and do it yourself."

"The little widow has a name. Darla Jo. And you don't know a thing about who I am."

There was a silence on the line. For a moment, Phoebe thought he had hung up on her.

No such luck. "I could use a cup of coffee."

Phoebe speared her fingers through her sleep-scrambled hair and growled at the phone.

"I heard that."

"I'm not meeting you for coffee."

"Fine. I'll come there."

"Forget it. I'm not givin' you my address."

"I've already got it." Now, why didn't that surprise her? "Ten minutes."

That time he *did* hang up—before she could tell him to go to hell and stay there. She yanked the phone away from her ear and glared at it, then slammed it down on the nightstand.

And then she got up, pulled on some old jeans and a wrinkled Oklahoma State University T-shirt, and went to put the coffee on.

PHOEBE OPENED THE DOOR scowling. Rio saw the unwilling smile tug at her mouth as she took in his freshly cut hair, his cheap suit and square-framed glasses. "You look like Clark Kent." *She* looked like the unmade bed she'd probably just crawled out of. It was a good look for her. Rumpled and sexy. Made him want to reach for her and rumple her up some more.

He kept his hands at his sides. "You'd be surprised the way people open up to a harmless-looking guy in a bad suit."

"I'll bet." She craned her head toward her driveway where his Softail gleamed in the morning sun. "Maybe you ought to rethink that Harley, though. Puts a real dent in the mild-mannered image."

"I'm on it. I'll pick up a car this morning. A beige sedan. When I'm working, I like a full-sized car. A nice, dependable model. With a big engine. A guy never knows when he'll need to get away fast."

"In your case, I completely understand." She moved back.

He took that to mean she was letting him in and stepped over the threshold directly into her living room, which was painted a buttery-yellow with white trim. The furniture was simple, Pottery Barn meets fifties retro. One of those square fifties couches, lamps that looked like spaceships, a blond wood coffee table in a kidney shape. A plain sisal rug on the hardwood floor. It was nice. Very little clutter.

"Come on back to the kitchen. I'll see about that coffee you just *had* to have." She turned to lead the way.

He didn't follow. A framed black-and-white photograph over the television had caught his eye. He stepped a little closer.

It was an old building, two stories, stone below, clapboard above, the upper story jutting on round pillars above the lower, leaving a natural porch beneath. A sign in old-time script crowned the upper story. He read, "The Prairie Queen."

She turned back to him. Her mouth, pinched at first, softened. "It was a music hall. An Oklahoma legend in its day. I was born there." He waited as she decided whether to say any more, though he already knew the basic facts. Finally, she went on, "My mother and father and a bunch of their friends pooled what money they had and bought the building in the early seventies. They renovated it, doing all the work themselves, using salvaged materials. For a while, the Queen was a going concern. She drew bands from all over—some big names, too. That was where Ralphie came in. He showed up, calling himself a promoter, after the Queen had been in operation for a few months. He helped my parents and their friends book the bands. He was pretty good at it, too."

"You said you were born *in* the building?" That part was news.

She hitched her chin up. "Yes, I was. There were rooms in back where everyone lived. No money for hospitals. Later, after the Queen closed down, my dad did pretty well for himself, buying old houses, fixing them up and reselling them. But in the days of the Prairie Queen, he and my mother were as broke as the rest of them. Tiff and Rose were born in the Queen, too."

"And you three are like sisters."

"That's right." Defiant. Proud. Then she shrugged. "They called themselves a commune, my parents and their friends. But the commune didn't last. The doors closed in seventy-eight. They tore the building down about fifteen years ago. There's a strip mall there now."

"And you named your band after the music hall."

She fell back a step. "Ralphie told you about the band." Rio nodded. Her dark brows drew together. "Did he also tell you he was our manager?"

"Yeah."

She gave him a long look and then huffed out a breath. "Well, the band had a shorter lifespan than the music hall."

"Ralphie's fault."

She glared. "You want that coffee or not?" She turned away again, started walking.

"Wait," Rio said. She stopped, but didn't face him. He spoke to her back. "Ralphie told me. How he screwed around on you. He always said when he lost you, he lost one of the best."

She did turn then. Slowly. "He didn't lose me. I'm still right here."

Rio held to his point. "You know what I'm saying. He lost you…as a woman. And he always regretted that."

She folded her arms across her middle. Classic body language: listening, maybe. Receptive? Not in the least. "It doesn't matter. That was a long time ago—and Ralphie was who he was."

"So true. Just when you'd think he couldn't make things any worse, leave it to Ralphie. He'd find a way.

Take your friends. First he betrays you. And then he marries your friends, one right after the other."

"I was long over him by then. And he loved them both."

"Like I said. One right after the other."

If looks could kill, he'd have been fried to a cinder. She demanded, "What are you getting at?"

"That Ralphie trusted me. Maybe you should, too."

"I haven't even figured out who you are yet. Yesterday you came in on a Harley. Today you're Clark Kent. Which one's the real you?"

"Both. Neither."

"Thank you for clarifyin'."

Before she could whirl away again, he said, "I was a kid when I met Ralphie. He…loved my mother and she loved him. He was the father I never had, took an interest when no one else gave a damn. Yeah, he screwed up a lot. I know what he was. I've always known. Where I grew up, you face the truth or you don't last too long. But he had heart. He taught me to respect myself and how to get along. I loved him. I owe him. In spite of all the crap he put you through, I think you loved him, too. Work with me."

She pressed those soft lips together—and let her arms drop to her sides. He was making progress. She wasn't ready to throw in with him yet—but she wasn't saying no anymore, either. She turned.

He didn't try to stop her that time. Instead, he followed her to a sunny sea-blue kitchen at the back of the house, where she flung out a hand in the direction of the red chrome and Formica dinette. "Have a seat."

He pulled out one of the red vinyl chairs and dropped into it. She served him in silence, pouring his coffee into a big yellow-green mug, setting out the sugar and a little red pitcher of milk. Then she got herself a mug, too, and sat down opposite him.

More silence. Outside, he heard a lawn mower start up. They both sipped, eyes meeting, then shifting away.

Eventually, he tried a compliment. "Nice place."

She doled out a grudging, "Thanks." There was more sipping. She set down her mug. "You really think you could find out what happened?"

"No promises. I could work my ass off on this and still come up blank. But it's possible—and that it *is* possible is enough for me. I need to know I did everything I could."

"Yeah," she said, resting her forearms on the table, wrapping her hands around her mug, her expression both grim and determined. She stared down into the mug for a moment, as if looking for the answer to a question she didn't know how to ask. Then she glanced up. "What would I have to do, if I helped you?"

"You could start with a list—everyone you know who knew Ralphie. And *how* they knew him. Special focus on anyone who had issues with him, anyone he cheated or messed over, anyone he owed money to."

She tapped the mug on the table and a low sound escaped her. "That's a long list. My own name would be on it."

He allowed a soft chuckle. "Hell. Mine, too."

"So I'd give you this list…"

"And we'd take it from there. You'd answer my questions. *All* of them, to the best of your knowledge. Provide addresses and phone numbers if you have them, so I don't have to waste time tracking people down. Back me up, say you know me and I can be trusted, if someone wants to know why I showed up on their doorstep and started asking about things they didn't want to go into."

The silence stretched long again. At last, she said, "All right. I can do that." She got up, topped off her mug and held out the pot to him.

He shoved his cup her way. "Thanks." She gave him more and then carried the pot to the counter. When she slipped back into her seat, he said, "Tell me about Darla Jo."

She stiffened right up on him. "I thought I was supposed to start with a list."

"That's right. You also agreed to answer my questions."

She slumped in her chair, looked down at her lap, then slanted a suspicious glance up at him. "Why the big interest in Darla?"

"You're protective of her. Why?"

There was some huffing, but in the end, she answered him. "I just know she would never do anything to hurt Ralphie. She loved him. Truly."

"You sound pretty sure about that."

"I *am* sure. You should have seen them together. They were crazy about each other. She made him quit smoking. A woman who would run a man down wouldn't make him stop smoking first. And there were times, especially lately, in the past two or three months, when I would see her looking at him—when he *wasn't* looking at her. Pure adoration. No woman could fake that kind of a look. And why would she bother to try, if the guy wasn't even looking her way?"

Rio was thinking that what she'd just told him was probably more about Phoebe than it was about Ralphie and Darla Jo. Against his own better judgment, he found himself taking a stab at helping her see that. "It's important to you, is that it? To believe that Ralphie Styles was finally in love for real and forever? That Darla Jo loved him back? That they were having a baby, making themselves a happy little family?"

She sat up straighter. "You go ahead. Put it down, what they had. Tell yourself it wasn't real. But it *was* real. He loved her and she loved him. I know it." She speared her fingers through her tangled brown hair, raking it back off her flushed face. Then she grabbed her mug again—and plunked it down without drinking from it. "No. I'm never going to believe that Darla had anything to do with Ralphie getting run over in the middle of the night. Never. Not in a hundred million years."

Rio saw there was a point he hadn't quite made clear to her. He said, keeping it low and even, "You don't have to believe it. You don't have to do anything. You can run your bar and wait. Get together with Ralphie's other ex-wives and argue about what might have happened. Maybe someone will talk who hasn't yet. Maybe the OCPD will come up with something. Maybe *I* will. And maybe we'll just never know."

Taking care not to let the chair scrape the floor, he pushed it back and stood. "Thanks for the coffee."

He knew he had her when she stopped him before he could take a single step. "Sit back down."

He allowed a solid five seconds to elapse before obeying. Then he dropped to his seat again and laid out the ground rules. "You'll have to talk to me. Nothing held back. About anyone." The demand was a little over the top. He'd take less, if that was all he could get. A lot less. But there was no reason Phoebe Jacks had to know that—at least, not at the moment.

"Fine. Okay."

"About Darla…"

"Okay."

"How did Ralphie meet her?"

"She came in the bar looking for work last September."

"Ralphie met her at the bar?"

Phoebe nodded. "Darla was just twenty-one, fresh out of some tiny town in Arkansas. She met Ralphie the night she started working. He was gone on her at first sight. It took her longer. But not *that* long. Within a few weeks, she'd moved in with him. They got married last December, though I guess you know that, since he invited you to the wedding."

Rio took a small spiral notebook and a pen out of his breast pocket. He flipped the notebook open and jotted down the major points. "The brother?"

"Boone's twenty-six. He's Darla's half brother. Same mom, different dads."

"Last name?"

"Gallagher." She spelled it out for him. "Darla's name was Snider—with an *i*."

Rio nodded. "Go ahead. About the brother."

"He'd been living down in Texas. Came up for the wedding and decided to stay in town. I hired him. He's a good worker, dependable."

"Did they fill out applications before they went to work for you?"

"Yeah."

"They give you social security numbers?"

"Of course."

"That'll help. A lot. I'll want to have a look at those."

"An employment application is strictly confidential."

"Think of it this way...."

Her sweet mouth turned down at the corners. "I don't like the sound of this."

He almost smiled. But not quite. "You use the information on an application to check your people out, right?"

She qualified, "I *can* check them out, if I think checking them out is necessary."

"Because you're their employer."

She put it together. "Oh. And now, so are you."

"Which means I have every right to run a few checks on Darla Jo and her half brother Boone."

She leaned in, craning that smooth white neck across the table, her sleep-wild hair swinging forward, brushing the tabletop. "I just want to know. Why are you after them?"

He set down the notebook. "I'm not after them."

"You know what I mean. Why are you suspicious of them?"

Rio considered evading some more. But to get information, you had to be prepared sometimes to give a little back. "I'm not suspicious of either of them. I *am* a little curious about Darla."

"Why?"

He went ahead and laid it on her. "That baby she's having? It's not Ralphie's."

Outrage sparked in her eyes. "How do you know that?"

"Ralphie told me."

She blinked. "Ralphie told you that Darla was havin' some other man's baby?"

"No. He told me I was the son he could never have. Ralphie Styles was sterile."

CHAPTER FOUR

More on the subject of sparkling comebacks.
Man: I want to wake up with you beside me. How do you like your eggs in the morning?
Prairie Queen: Unfertilized.
—from The Prairie Queen's Guide to Life *by Goddess Jacks*

"STERILE." PHOEBE repeated the word. It tasted dry in her mouth. And also impossible. A word without meaning in relationship to Ralphie Styles. "No..."

The man across the table from her didn't speak. He didn't have to. Those black eyes said it all. She saw sympathy in them at that moment—sympathy that went well with the ugly suit and the glasses. With the rest of him? Not so much.

Then again, why shouldn't a big, dangerous macho-type guy be capable of showing a little sympathy? It could happen. Maybe not in Phoebe's own personal experience up till now.

But there was always a first time.

And the sympathy in Rio Navarro's eyes wasn't the question, anyway. The question was: Could Ralphie have been sterile?

And more to the point, if he was, shouldn't Phoebe have been the first to know?

Phoebe had been Ralphie's wife for three years. Once, for all the wrong reasons—because she knew she was losing him, because she needed a way to bind him to her—she'd begged him for a baby.

"Now, babe..." A rueful, tender smile had curved those big, soft lips of his when he'd answered her. "It's not the time and you know it."

"No. I *don't* know it."

"Come on. Ease off. Maybe later, huh?"

"When?"

"Can't say. But don't you worry. We'll both know when it's right...."

She'd known him well enough, even then, at a still-starry-eyed twenty-two, to get the message: The time would never be right; Ralphie would never have a baby with her.

Not for one second had it occurred to her that maybe he *couldn't.*

But there had been a whole lot of women in his life. And, until Darla Jo, he'd failed to father a single baby or even get a woman pregnant that Phoebe had ever heard of—and she was staring into her coffee cup again, feeling a definite reluctance to meet Rio's waiting eyes.

"Phoebe." He said it softly, coaxingly.

So she looked at him, making her lips a flat line, narrowing her eyes a little, sending the clear message that just because he said something didn't make it true. "How, exactly, do you know he was sterile?"

Beneath that cheap suit, one hard shoulder lifted a fraction in a hint of a shrug. He took off those absurd square-framed glasses and hung them from the breast pocket of his jacket. "I told you. He said so."

She canted forward, sharply. "Why would he tell you if he never told me?"

He eyed her with wariness. "You about to go off on me here?"

"Just answer the question."

Carefully, he suggested, "Come on, Phoebe. What does it matter, who he told—or why?"

She tightened her fingers around her coffee mug. It mattered. Probably more than it should have. "Ralphie lied all the time. He was a master at it. He made lyin' the next thing to an art form."

Rio shook his head. "All right. It's no secret that Ralphie never put a lot of emphasis on honesty. But a man doesn't lie about something like that, not without a damn good reason."

What he said made sense. Too much sense. She swore under her breath. And then she slumped back in her chair, lifted her arms and scraped her hair back hard off her forehead with both hands.

The movement had her braless breasts poking hard at the thin fabric of her old T-shirt. Rio looked. She caught him at it. One black eyebrow canted up, but he didn't say anything. Neither did she. She was too busy feeling hurt and defiant. Too wrapped up in ignoring the sudden sluicing of heat, down low, where it had no damn business being, and remembering…

Ralphie. That evening in early December. Sitting

across from her in the same chair where Rio sat now….

Her stove had gone on the blink again and Ralphie had come over to fix it. As always, within ten minutes, he had it working like new. She'd offered him a beer and he sat down and got out his Marlboros. Squinting through the curling smoke, he'd announced, "This is it. My last pack of smokes."

Phoebe had to laugh at that one. "Ralphie, you've quit more times than any man I know."

"This time's for real, babe. Darla asked me to." He sucked that coffin nail hard, tipped his head back and tapped his cheek. Five perfect rings rose toward the ceiling, quivering a little on the still air before they slowly faded to nothing. He gave Phoebe that charming, naughty-boy smile. "I'm marryin' her, babe. She's the one."

Phoebe felt so happy for him that night. She saw in his face that this one would be different. She *knew* it, deep down, no matter what anyone else said. She reached across and laid her hand over his long, skinny one, all ropy with veins. "Go for it."

"Oh, I most definitely am."

Later, when Ralphie was leaving, he told her he was inviting Rio Navarro to the wedding. "Damn, I hope he comes. I been trying for half my life and most of his to get his ass to Oklahoma. I want him to meet you."

She'd seen the matchmaking light in those watery blue eyes and she'd *almost* warned him not to even go there. But no. Let Ralphie imagine his two longtime friends falling hard and fast for each other, the way he had for Darla. What could it hurt for him to scheme on that? It wouldn't cost her any money, the way most of Ralphie's big plans did….

Phoebe blinked and shook her head, and ordered her mind back to today, to the large man in the bad suit sitting across from her—and to Darla, about to have a baby that might not be Ralphie's, after all.

She let her arms drop to her sides. "So what now?"

He rose and circled the table to set his mug on the counter. "You make that list. And I'll go have a talk with Darla Jo. See if I can find out who the real father of that baby is—and if maybe he had a problem with Ralphie claiming his child."

She was on her feet before he finished that sentence. "No." He stuck his hands in the pockets of his ugly slacks—and waited for her to explain herself. "Just let me do it, okay? Let me talk to Darla."

He studied her for a few seconds more. "That's not how I operate," he finally said.

"Maybe not. But we're working together on this, remember? And she knows me. She *trusts* me. She's a lot more likely to tell me her secrets than a stranger."

His look took her measure. "You have to decide, *Reina*. Which you want more. The truth, or holding on to your romantic fantasy about Ralphie and his little widow."

She realized she was biting her lower lip—and made herself stop. "I don't think it's a fantasy. But if it turns out that's all it is, fine. I do want the truth. I want it more. I want it most of all."

OUTSIDE, THE MUGGY morning had turned cloudy. When Rio left Phoebe, he rode his bike to Ralphie's Place and took the alley around to the back as per Phoebe's instructions of the day before. Behind the bar, he found a small loading area. A big green Dumpster stood against the building next to a wide roll-up aluminum door with a bolt-type lock. When he stuck the key Phoebe had given him into the lock, an alarm began beeping a warning from inside. The door slid upward with one easy shove and the alarm box was right there, on the wall inside, next to the door. He whipped out the card Phoebe had given him and punched in the code.

Silence. A low-wattage overhead light had come on. It cast a dim glow over a combination garage and storage area. Boxes and crates lined the bare brick walls and a red Chevy van, dinged and dented and probably about twenty years old, was parked nose-in on the left.

A red van.

A steel door a few feet from the front of the van would take him into the back rooms of the bar—if the key to the garage fit the lock, which Rio had a pretty good feeling it would.

First things first. Rio wheeled his bike in and parked it next to the van.

Then he gave the area a cursory check, reading the labels on the boxes, peering into an old microwave that had been left on top of a crate. He checked out the van, which was full-size with a flat front—the kind of vehicle—and the color—that had put an end to Ralphie Styles.

Inside, the van smelled of dust, with a faint hint of dampness. The rear seats had been removed and lint-spotted gray shag carpeting covered the floor.

In front, a dreamcatcher hung from the rearview mirror and a half-empty Aquafina bottle waited in the cup holder between the seats. Rio sat in the captain-style driver's seat, leaned across to the passenger side and popped open the glove compartment: insurance up to date; registered to Phoebe Isabel Jacks.

He got out and went around and looked at the grill. It was original, he'd lay heavy odds on that. Original and intact. Around the edges of it you could make out the van's original colors: silver and maroon. But the red paint job wasn't new, just badly done, the shine faded out, dinged and rusting in spots. Rio got down on the concrete floor and looked under the front end. No surprises there. The undercarriage, like the grill, was worn but undamaged.

Whatever had smashed Ralphie flat, it wasn't Phoebe's old red van.

Rio got to his feet, brushed off his slacks, and moved on to the steel door that would take him into the bar. He was just sticking the key in the lock when he heard the soft whir of an engine and the crunching of tires on bits of gravel in the loading area behind him.

Pocketing the key, he put on his Clark Kent glasses, turned and strode between the van and his Softail. He stopped in plain view, just beyond the garage door.

The car was a yellow Camaro. Boone Gallagher

unfolded his long frame from the low front seat. He had his left hand on the window of his open door, in plain sight. His right arm was down at his side, the hand not visible, tucked around behind him.

"Who the hell are you?" Gallagher demanded.

Rio raised both hands high and wide and put on his most harmless, ineffectual expression. "Rio Navarro. Phoebe gave me a key, said I could store my bike here." He tipped his head back, in the direction of the Softail behind him.

Gallagher's frown deepened, but his lean body relaxed a little. "Navarro. You the one Ralphie Styles left half this bar to?"

"That's me."

Gallagher bent slightly toward his car. When he straightened, he brought his right hand up: empty. He'd either decided he didn't need his weapon, after all—or there was no gun. Rio figured the former, but in his line of work a man learned to suspect the worst. "No offense, man," said Boone. "Things have been kind of tense around here lately, if you know what I mean."

"I understand."

"So I need to see a little ID."

Rio almost smiled. Yesterday, Phoebe. Today, Darla Jo's brother. They all had to see a little ID. "No offense taken. I'll just ease it out. Slowly."

"Yeah. Slowly." Gallagher remained covered by the door of his car. "Good idea."

Rio produced his wallet, flipped it to his driver's license, and passed it over the driver's door window to Boone, who grunted at the proof, and then flipped it down and studied Rio's P.I. card.

Finally, with another grunt, he stepped free of the car door, shoving it shut, and gave Rio back his wallet. "Didn't mean to be unsociable. I saw the garage wide open and you standin' there and—"

"No need to explain."

Boone tipped his red-brown head to the side and smiled in a cautiously friendly way. "Hey. I seen that bike before…."

Rio gave him an easy shrug. "I stopped in for a shot of tequila. Yesterday, around three or so. I met Phoebe then."

Boone was frowning again. "I was here. I don't remember you."

"I got a haircut since, and I cleaned up a little."

Boone nodded. Slowly. "Yeah. Okay." He grinned. "My sister hates your damn guts even though she's never met you, in case you didn't know." Rio decided he'd be wiser to say nothing to that. Boone held out his hand. "I'm Boone, Darla's brother. Darla was Ralphie's—"

"Wife. Yeah, I know."

Boone's grip was firm and dry. "You're a P.I., huh? From Los Angel-eez."

"That's right."

"Well, come on inside. I'll brew us a pot of coffee and you can tell me about all the movie stars you know."

RALPHIE AND DARLA'S marital bliss had begun and ended in a trailer park south of Northwest Tenth, a few blocks east of Meridian. Phoebe pulled into the park an hour after she showed Rio the door. The whole drive over there, she had a nervous feeling in her stomach and a heaviness in her heart. The sign at the entrance did bring a grin, though: Rose Rock Suburban Estates.

"Come on out to my estate," Ralphie used to say with a wink.

Through the gray day, a misty rain was falling. It dripped from the sign, dribbled like slow tears from her windshield. Phoebe cruised past single- and double-wides in a rainbow of colors, each with its own little carport jutting off the side, shading small squares of patio with plastic lawn chairs and cast-iron smoker barbecues.

Ralphie's trailer, down at the end and around the corner, was one of the nicer ones. White, with blue shutters, striped awnings and a small redwood deck, it boasted a cheerful row of dwarf nandinas behind a low brick border in front.

Things were looking a little ragged, though, since Ralphie's death. A couple of potted daisies on the deck steps, thriving the last time Phoebe had come by, had dried up and died. The grass, once pristine, was scraggly and uncut, dotted with dandelion flowers. Phoebe shook her head at that. She'd talk to Boone, see if he could make a little time to mow the yard for his sister.

Darla's three-year-old red Sebring convertible, bought a few months ago in one of Ralphie's deals, sat alone beneath the two-car carport. They'd repoed

Ralphie's V-series Cadillac, hauled it away from that street in the Paseo where he'd left it the night he died. After the police had gotten through with it, the dealership had claimed it. As usual, Ralphie was behind on his payments.

Ralphie had always driven Cadillacs. He'd cruised through life in style behind the wheels of an endless series of Fleetwoods, Eldorados, Sevilles and sedan DeVilles.

Beyond the carport, at the end of the driveway, stood a cute shed shaped like a miniature barn. It was blue and white to match the trailer.

Phoebe pulled in under the carport, sliding out of the sluggish rain and into Ralphie's empty space. She got out and shut the door quietly, and then stood for a moment, breathing in the warm, wet May air and wishing that being there didn't make her feel as depressed as the dead daisies on the deck steps.

DARLA PULLED OPEN THE door as Phoebe raised her hand to knock. Ralphie's widow wore a red lace flyaway baby-doll top with matching bikini panties. Her tangled hair hung limp around her tear-puffy face and her giant stomach, the navel distended, poked out between the open sides of the lacy pajama top. "Hey," she said in a tiny, lost voice.

"Oh, honey," whispered Phoebe on a heavy sigh.

Darla pushed open the glass storm door, grabbed Phoebe's wrist and hauled her over the threshold. The storm door shut by itself. Darla shoved the inner door closed. "Pheeb..." With a sound midway between a moan and cry, Darla threw herself at Phoebe, who gathered her in and held her, rocking her, stroking her dirty hair, breathing in the slightly sour smell of her skin, amazed that her distended belly felt every bit as hard as it looked.

Phoebe whispered sweet lies meant to soothe. "It's okay. It'll be okay…." Darla held on tight and sobbed against her shoulder until the baby kicked Phoebe a good one and she pulled back. "Wow." She laid her palm right over the spot where she'd felt the kick as Darla continued to sniffle and moan. "She's a strong one…."

Darla hiccupped, a sound of pure misery. "It's a he. I just know it. And he does that all time."

Phoebe dropped her purse on the floor and reached for her hand. "Come on."

Darla's lip quivered. "What? Where?"

"A bath. And then breakfast."

THE TUB HAD A RING OF greasy dirt in it and the small square of bathroom floor was littered with used tissues and wrinkled clothes. Phoebe quickly swept the clutter away and found a can of cleanser under the sink. She dropped to her knees, gave the tub a quick scrub and a cursory rinse and then put in the plug and ran the water, sprinkling in some bath beads to make it more inviting.

Darla sank into the froth of bubbles with a tiny sob and a surrendering sigh. Phoebe bathed her, washing her back and shampooing her hair. Darla cried softly through it all, murmuring now and then, "Oh, I don't know. I just don't know how I'm gonna go on…."

Once Phoebe had her washed up, she left her long enough to find a pair of reasonably clean maternity cargoes, a top and some underwear. She got Darla out of the tub, dried her off.

Darla stood before the steamy bathroom mirror, naked. "Oh, I just don't know…." She traced a heart on the mirror, wrote her name and Ralphie's, dotting the *i* with another tiny heart, the way she always did.

Phoebe looked at that sad, tiny heart and heard Ralphie's voice in her mind. "Now, there's a woman made for love. Even dots her *i*'s with little hearts…"

Darla turned from the mirror, big eyes stark with loss and pain. "Oh, Pheeb…"

"I'll be in the kitchen," Phoebe said firmly. "Get dressed and get in there."

The kitchen was worse than the bathroom. A tower of dirty dishes filled the sink. More dishes littered the counter and the table. Every burner on the stove had a pot on it and each pot contained something old and dried and unrecognizable. Phoebe cleared herself enough space to cook in. She found a box of oatmeal and a can of Eagle Brand milk in the nearly empty cupboard.

Twenty minutes later, she set a steaming bowl of oats in front of Darla, picked up the can of milk and poured some over the oats, then shoved the sugar bowl in closer. "Eat."

Darla sniffed and scowled at the bowl. "I hate oatmeal. And that weird canned milk is gross. Ralphie used to eat that. Yuck…" Her face crumpled. "Ralphie. Oh, Ralphie…" The waterworks started in again.

Phoebe grabbed a Kleenex from the box on the table and shoved it Darla's way. Grudgingly, Darla accepted it. She dabbed at her eyes and blew her nose.

"Eat," Phoebe repeated, more firmly than before. She dropped into the chair across from Darla and waited, keeping her expression stern. Eventually, Darla ladled on some sugar, picked up the spoon Phoebe had washed for her, and dug in.

As she ate, Phoebe lectured. "It's enough, Darla Jo. And you know it, too. I know how much you loved Ralphie. But there's grieving and there's grieving and you have let this get way out of hand. I'll send someone over this afternoon to help you clean up this place." She figured she could get Bernard or Tiff to help out. If not, she'd come back herself. "Whoever I send will take you to the store so you can buy groceries."

"I'm broke. You know I am. The man I love died on me—and he left me nothin'."

So Phoebe got up, got her purse and laid two fifties on the table. "You're buying food. Today."

Darla slid a glance at the money, then muttered sulkily, "Thanks."

"No thanks are needed. You clean up this place and get yourself some food and show up at the bar tomorrow afternoon."

"Why?"

"I'll put you back on the payroll. We'll find something you can do."

Darla shot her a calculating look. "Give me Ralphie's share." Her voice went wheedling. "Pheeb.

Please. He woulda wanted me to have it. He *promised* it to me…."

"I can't. You know that. Ralphie's share belongs to Rio Navarro."

Darla's spoon clattered into the half-empty oatmeal bowl. She threw up both hands. "Rio Navarro was not supposed to get my half of that bar. It was all a big mistake that he got it, and you know it was—and you know what else? That Rio Navarro, he couldn't even be bothered to come to our wedding, you know that? We invited him, and he didn't show. Ralphie said he could never talk that guy into coming to Oklahoma. He'll probably never come. The time will go by and he'll never show up and it won't even matter, if you give Ralphie's half to me. Nobody's gonna care. And I'll have something to get by on, me and the baby. I'll—"

"Darla—"

"Uh-uh. Don't say different. You know I'm right. That Navarro guy is never even coming around." She picked up her spoon again, flicked a hank of hair back over her shoulder and wheedled some more. "So come on. You can just split the till with me, at least until you hear from that Navarro guy and he—" Phoebe put up a hand. Darla stuck out her lower lip. "What?"

"Have I got your attention?"

"Stop ragging on me, okay? Just say it. What?"

"I've heard from Rio."

Darla paused—but not for long. "Well, until he gets into town, you could—"

"He *is* here in town."

"That bastard. No."

"Yeah. You're going to have to give up your plans for the bar, Darla. You're going to have to accept the fact that Ralphie's half went to Rio and move on."

"Real easy for you to say. You got *your* half...."

Phoebe refused to reply to that. She sat very still and she looked at Darla in a steady, unblinking way.

Darla gave it up. "Okay. I'm sorry. That was a mean thing to say to you and you didn't deserve it. I love you, Pheeb. You're the best friend I ever had next to Ralphie and I'm grateful you're lookin' after me."

Phoebe said softly, "Finish your breakfast." Obediently, Darla scooped up another spoonful of oatmeal and poked it into her mouth. Phoebe waited until she'd eaten it all. Then Phoebe picked up the bowl and carried it to the sink. She ran water in it and put the can of milk in the fridge while Darla sat at the table, slumped over her big tummy, staring out the window beside the back door. Phoebe went to her and put her hands on those sad, sagging shoulders. "Come on. Let's go sit on the sofa."

Darla dragged herself upright and plodded along behind Phoebe into the other room, where she plopped down on the ugly brown corduroy sofa. Phoebe sat beside her and wrapped an arm around her. Drawing the younger woman close, Phoebe guided Darla's still-damp head to rest on her shoulder. She stroked Darla's arm.

Darla snuggled in. "Thanks for comin' over. And you're right, what you said. It looks like crap around here and I need to pull myself together."

Phoebe made a low noise of agreement and then spoke gently, "Darla?"

"Umm?"

"The baby…"

"Umm?"

"It's not Ralphie's, is it?"

With a soft little sigh, Darla snuggled in closer still. "Oh, Pheeb…"

"Is it?"

Darla answered at last in a dreamy voice. "Strictly speakin'? No, it ain't."

CHAPTER FIVE

The gene pool could use a little chlorine.
—from The Prairie Queen's Guide to Life *by Goddess Jacks*

DARLA KEPT HER HEAD on Phoebe's shoulder and continued, in that same dreamy voice. "It was…a one-night thing, you know? I met this guy in a bar before I even came to the city. I never got his number and I ain't seen him since and I never would've had sex with him if I'd'a known that in a few days I would be meeting the man I would love until death." She rested her hand with its chewed-down nails on her bulging stomach. "Ralphie knew the baby wasn't his. I told him. I always told him *everything.* He didn't care. He said the baby would be *our* baby and that was that. He said we'd tell everyone he was the daddy—because he was going to *be* our baby's daddy in all the ways that really count. And Pheeb?"

Phoebe rubbed Darla's shoulder and stared blankly at their shadowed reflections in Ralphie's big-screen TV across from the sofa. The last thing she'd expected was a straightforward confession.

The baby was not Ralphie's. Impossible—and apparently, true.

"Pheeb?" Darla asked again.

Phoebe smoothed Darla's hair. "What, honey?"

"As far as I'm concerned, this *is* Ralphie's baby." A thread of steel had found its way into Darla's voice. The sudden determination surprised Phoebe as much as the confession had. Darla might beg you or con you. She had a certain frail, needy charm about her, a charm that was sexy and innocent and too wise all at once, a charm that could knock certain types of men right off their feet. But determined? Uh-uh. No way, not ever. Darla lifted her head. Phoebe met those red-rimmed brown eyes. "I told you because I love you," Darla said. "And Ralphie loved you. I know I can trust you to understand, and not to tell another soul."

Phoebe nodded, keeping her expression fittingly solemn, knowing that she would betray Darla's confidence to Rio the first chance she got.

"AND YOU BELIEVE HER about the real father being a one-night stand," Rio said.

They were sitting in Phoebe's kitchen. It was eleven-fifteen at night. "I do," said Phoebe, thinking that those were the words a woman says on her wedding day, the words of a witness swearing an oath….

"*¿Por qué?*"

She blinked. "What?"

He gave her one of his patient looks, eyes soft, mouth firm. "Why do you believe her?"

"I just do."

"Blind faith. It's hardly an argument."

"No. It's more than blind faith."

Rio eyed her sideways, clearly doubtful. "How?"

"It…makes sense, that's all."

"Why?"

"If there was some other guy in the picture, he would have come around by now."

"Not necessarily. And maybe he *has* come around, but nobody told *you* about it. He's come around—and killed Ralphie while he was at it." Before she got a chance to argue, he asked, "Did Ralphie seem happy to you, about the baby?"

"Oh, yeah. Ecstatic. He built a crib, helped Darla fix up the baby's bedroom. He was into it. And I wasn't surprised. When he came home last August, he told me he was through with the footloose life. He only wanted to stay home and be happy. Then he met Darla, married her, settled down with her. And if he *was* shootin' blanks, well, being the father of Darla's kid would have been a way for him to have a baby he could call his own, to have it all—Darla and a kid and the settled-down life he'd finally realized he wanted."

Rio leaned both big arms on the table. Sleek, hard muscles bulged beneath the sleeves of his black T-shirt. Gone were the cheap suit and geeky glasses of that morning. Tonight, he was all in black. Ready to creep around in the dark, snooping into other people's secrets. "Okay," he said. "For now."

She eyed him sideways. "And by that you're telling me…?"

"At this point I'll buy Darla's story." Phoebe felt

relieved for Darla's sake. And yeah, she knew she was too protective of Darla. But so what? Ralphie would have wanted her to be. Rio added, "I ran into Boone this morning at the bar when I dropped off my bike."

"So he told me. He said he thought you were ripping us off."

"We got past that, Boone and me."

"He said he took you in the bar and gave you some coffee and a microwaved cinnamon roll."

"That's right. I tried to get the guy talking about himself."

"Learn anything?"

"Nothing you didn't already tell me. He and Darla are from Arkansas. Boone moved to Texas a couple of years ago—and then came here for Darla's wedding. He liked Oklahoma so much, he stayed on."

"He knew you were pumping him for information."

"The ones who are hiding things always do."

In the center of the table stood a red napkin holder and red Fiestaware salt and pepper shakers. With great care, Phoebe straightened the napkin holder and lined up the salt and pepper beside it. "Boone also told me that he thought your glasses were fake and he had a sneaking suspicion you might be up to no good, nosing around into stuff that's none of your business. He said you asked way too many questions."

"Busted." Rio chuckled low, an intimate sound, one that shivered down through Phoebe like a physical caress. "And what did *you* say to Boone when he told you all that?"

"I reminded him that, as of Ralphie's death, you're

my business partner. I said I gave you a key and he should keep in mind that you're now his boss as much Ralphie ever was."

"How much is that?"

"Seriously? Not a lot. Over the years, Ralphie pretty much left the running of the bar to me. He was gone so much anyway and he always had some deal going that demanded all his attention. Whenever it was time to count up the cash, though, he'd get his hand out fast."

"Nice work if you can get it."

"So I told him, more than once."

Those dark eyes held a teasing light. "Before Boone showed up, I was about to go inside and have a long, in-depth look around."

"Why shouldn't you? It's half yours."

"I'm glad you see it that way."

"And what else did you do today, besides parking your bike and having coffee with Boone?"

"I got a car. I changed hotels." He shoved one of his cards across the table, face down. On the back was the name of a residence hotel over on Northwest Expressway, including a room and phone number. "I hooked up with an associate who'll help me go door to door, interviewing people around the area where Ralphie got hit." He pushed another card her way, one for a local detective agency: Red Wolf Investigations. He pointed at the name in the lower right-hand corner. "Mac Tenkiller. In case he comes looking for me, you can trust him."

"Thanks." She glanced up from the card and into

his eyes. They stared at each other, unspeaking. It was no hardship for Phoebe, staring at Rio. He looked good and she felt…what? The word came to her: *safe*. She felt safe around him. Safe and all shook up, both at the same time. Already she was getting used to seeing him at her kitchen table. Before you knew it, if she didn't watch herself, she'd be offering to tie on an apron and whip him up a little something special.

He asked, "Did you have time to make that list of people who knew Ralphie?"

"I made a list. I can't say it's complete. Ralphie knew a lot of folks."

"Give me what you've got."

"Hold on." She rose. "I'll get it."

Phoebe's house had three bedrooms and a bath all in a row on the east side of the house. The living areas—front room, dining room and kitchen—were lined up on the west side. She used the middle bedroom, accessed through a bath and through the central dining area, as a home office. In the office, she scooped up the manila envelope she'd left on her desk and whirled to return to the kitchen.

Rio was right there, in the door to the dining room. She gasped at the sight of him.

"Didn't mean to scare you." He lounged against the door frame, hard arms crossed over his deep chest.

"I had a cat like you once," she grumbled, whacking his chest with the envelope. "His name was Shadow. Big and black, with a real attitude. I never knew when he'd come creeping up on me. I'd turn around and there he'd be. Watching me with a smirk on his face."

Rio took the envelope. "So I remind you of your *gatito....*"

Phoebe realized she liked it when he spoke Spanish. It was a beautiful language, soft and musical, and it sounded real nice coming out of that sexy mouth of his—not that she was telling him that. "My what?"

"Your kitten."

"Shadow was no kitten."

"*Gato,* then. That's good, right? A woman loves her cat."

"You wish. I finally had to tie a bell around that cat's neck so I'd know when he was nearby. He died a little over a year ago. Now and then, I think I see him, in the corner of my eye. But he is gone, gone, gone." Just like you'll be, soon enough.

"Hey," Rio said again, too gently. He touched her chin. The contact was electric, sending little bolts of excitement zipping all through her.

She met his eyes and tried to pretend he didn't thrill her in the least. "I put copies of Darla's and Boone's employment applications in there. Bernard's, too."

"Great."

She wanted him to understand...what? She wasn't quite sure. She said quietly, "I do want to know, Rio. I want to know how Ralphie died. Since we talked this morning, I'm only more certain about my priorities here."

"That's good."

Her heart was doing the old lub-dub, beating heavy and hard and much too hungrily. She could so easily take one step closer, reach up, hook her fingers around his big neck and haul that tempting mouth down on top of hers. She could do him right here, standing up in the doorway between the dining room and her office, just hike up her skirt, shove down her panties, unzip those worn black jeans of his and…

Uh-uh. And maybe it would be better to get this issue right out in the open. "Rio?"

"¿Sí, mi reina?"

"I'm not ending up in bed with you."

"Liar." He said it with such easy tenderness.

She wanted to slap him—or kiss him. Or both. "I'm not. I've had guys like you—more than one. More than two. Big guys who like it rough, guys who were never going to be around for the long haul. I'm not complaining. I had a real good time, in a strictly temporary way, with those guys. But more than two is enough, you know? I want something a little more dependable now."

"Reina." The dark eyes reproached her. His scent came to her: green and earthy at once, like geraniums in morning sun. And with a hint of something spicy and exotic. Cinnamon, maybe. Or cloves. He asked, "Who told you I like it rough?"

She almost laughed. "Notice how you skipped right past my main point?"

"Just because I didn't mention it, doesn't mean I didn't hear you—and who told you I like it rough?"

"No one. I guessed."

"Maybe you guessed wrong."

"It doesn't matter. What I'm telling you is, I'm not going to find out."

"But *Reina.* There's no need to tell me. Either you are or you aren't."

"I'm not."

"And that's the fourth time you've said so in under a minute." He touched her hair, catching a lock of it between his fingers. "Why say it so many times if you really believe it?"

Carefully, she reached up and eased the strands from his grip. "Just never you mind. I'm sorry I said anything." The way he looked at her turned the heat on high and set the candy to melting in all her sweet spots. "You should go."

He peeled his big self away from her door frame. "See you. *Mañana.*" He turned and left her.

She stayed where she was until she heard the front door click quietly shut behind him.

CURVING UP OUT OF WALKER Avenue at Northwest Twenty-Eighth, Paseo Drive began barely a mile from Phoebe's house. The Paseo, Rio had learned by using the free Internet connection provided by his hotel, was a tiny district of five square blocks. Paseo Drive cut through the heart of the district, going north and south.

Some said Paseo Drive *was* the Paseo. In any case, the street defined the district as the heart of the Oklahoma City artists' community. The Paseo was lined with studios and galleries, many of them housed in buildings of bright-painted stucco with red tile roofs. If any of the galleries had surveillance cameras, Rio didn't spot them. And the police hadn't mentioned any. Apparently, Ralphie's killer had managed not to have his or her picture taken as the deed was done.

Ralphie had died at the upper end of the street, a block or so before Paseo petered out into Dewey. He'd died a few feet from the sidewalk, next to a cinder-block-and-clapboard building with a yellow For Lease sign draped across the front. Two young sycamore trees, growing out of planters cut into the sidewalk, partially masked the phone numbers on the yellow sign. On the opposite side of the street stood the Galileo Bar and Grill.

At midnight, loud music spilled from Galileo's. After the rain that morning, the sky had cleared. Customers sat outside beneath a pair of ornate matching Victorian streetlights, under the wide Oklahoma sky.

Rio managed to corral both a chair and a small black iron table in a corner of the front patio. He nursed a couple of Coronas, listened to the music, which was alternative something-or-other, and watched the people. He scribbled notes to himself, including the two phone numbers on the yellow sign across the street. Whenever the band would give it a rest, he would strike up conversations with anyone willing to talk.

Most of what he learned in conversation that night, he already knew.

Yeah, the Galileo's crowd had heard about the guy who got run down. No, they didn't know squat about the accident itself except what they'd read in the *Daily Oklahoman.* The police hadn't found the one who did it, had they? He learned that the building across the street had once been a club, but had been vacant for years.

One fine-looking little blonde in a see-through shirt told him she'd known Ralphie. "Sweet guy. Kind of…hot, for an old guy." She said she went to Ralphie's Place often. "They get some good bands there. Sometimes Phoebe, the other owner, will get up and sing. She's got a voice on her. She used to be in the Prairie Queens, back in the nineties. You ever hear of them?"

"'Fraid not," Rio lied.

"Back then, everyone thought the Queens would break out big-time." She scribbled on the inside of a matchbook. "My number. Give me a call sometime." She smiled at him from under her lashes.

Rio slipped the matchbook in a pocket, knowing he would never call her. If he ended up in any woman's bed during his visit to Oklahoma, it was going to be Phoebe's.

And scratch the *if.*

Phoebe would have him. The more she swore she wouldn't, the more certain he became that she would.

He felt minimally guilty about knowing that he wouldn't do the right and noble thing; he wouldn't say no when she finally gave it up to him.

Minimally guilty…

Yeah. He was that. But not guilty enough to make him pass up a chance for something sweet and hot with a woman like Phoebe. A strong woman, a woman of power and dignity and loyalty until death…

Galileo's closed at two. By three the street was as

quiet as the day after the end of the world. Rio sat at the corner in the Buick he'd rented, watching. Traffic was light. As dawn approached, he saw a couple of dog-walkers: a thin, sparse-haired woman of about seventy walking a perky ball of white fur, and later, a paunchy middle-aged guy with a limping shepherd mix.

Since the guy with the shepherd showed up around the time the police would have already arrived at the scene, Rio gave up the site surveillance and followed him home. He noted the address.

Investigative work, Rio thought with a yawn, as he headed for his hotel at six in the morning. Sometimes it took boredom to a whole new level. He stole a few hours sleep, and he and Mac Tenkiller started working the neighborhood.

Rio checked out the scene in daylight. Bloodstains can last a month on pavement. As a rule, though, on a city street, some enterprising shop owner would make sure to clean up a stain like that.

And someone had. In the general area where Ralphie would have breathed his last, Rio found not even the shadow of a bloodstain. There would also have been clothing transfer: a drag mark from whatever Ralphie had been wearing. That was no longer visible, either. Rio took his time, walking the area, looking for any debris from the accident that the police might have missed: a button, a bumper decal. It was a long shot, especially after all that time. And it gave him nothing. He went on to the interviews, visiting the lone witness listed on the accident report first.

Fayreen Mavis Montgomery had found Ralphie's body and called the police. As it turned out, Fayreen was also the elderly lady Rio had observed earlier walking her little white dog.

She answered all his questions. Rio nodded and thanked her accepting the fact that she had no more to tell him than she'd told the police.

The guy with the shepherd knew even less. By the time he'd walked his dog that morning, he said, "The sirens were screamin' on the Paseo. Danged if I was gonna go over there and get myself in some kind of trouble. A man has enough of that in his lifetime without chasin' after it. I tugged on Rex's leash and we went the other way."

The rest of the day turned up a big, fat zero. No one they talked to knew, saw or had heard anything—except sirens wailing about 5:30 a.m., which would have been when the police and the paramedics had shown up.

At five in the afternoon, Rio dropped by Ralphie's Place to tell Phoebe his news, which was nada. He could have called her. It would take maybe thirty seconds to pass on all he *hadn't* found out.

But he wanted to see her, to look in those green eyes and admire the shine on that coffee-colored hair, maybe get up close enough to breathe in the tempting womanly scent of her. Was his dick leading him around now?

Kind of looked that way.

He went in the front. The jukebox was playing Dwight Yoakam and there were six guys and two women at the bar. Customers at the tables, too. More than one turned to look when Rio entered, including Phoebe's friend, one of Ralphie's exes, the slender blonde—the one they called Tiff. She wore a snug white shirt and black pants and carried one of those round cocktail trays, complete with a trio of full margarita glasses. Rio nodded a hello. She nodded in return, and then gave him her back as she served the margaritas to three young secretarial types at one of the tables.

Rio moved on to the bar and introduced himself to the handsome, burly black bartender.

"Rio Navarro."

"Yeah." The bartender stuck a beer glass under the tap and drew a tall, cold one. "Phoebe's new partner. I'm Bernard." He set the beer in front of one of the guys at the bar, then reached across. Rio took his hand and they shook. "She's in the back." He tipped his big, smooth-shaved head toward the door with the round window in it.

"Thanks."

Rio found her sitting in her dark little office, staring at a computer screen. He waited there in the doorway until she looked over and saw him.

She blinked in mild surprise, then gave him a slow grin. "There you go again. Sneakin' up on me."

"Didn't want to break your concentration."

"Just counting our money." She gestured at the chair in front of her desk.

He shook his head. "Sad to say, this won't take long." He told her where he'd been and what he'd done.

She leaned back in her chair. "Nothin', huh?" she said when he'd finished.

"A pretty little blonde I met at Galileo's said she's been here. Heard you sing. She says you're good."

She turned her face slightly away and slid him a glance. "Should I be jealous?"

"No."

She looked down, dark lashes like fans of silk against her skin, creamy cheeks coloring. "I don't know why I said that...."

He did, but he let it go. "You gave me the names of eight guys that Ralphie did business with."

"There were a lot more than eight. Those are just the ones whose names he mentioned over the years, or ones who came into the bar now and then, that I got to know a little."

"What kind of business did he do with these guys?"

"You knew Ralphie. Always making a deal." She smoothed her hair back with a slow hand. "One's his bookie. But mostly he liked to get things cheap and resell them. Or trade up and then sell what he'd traded for. He did that a lot with cars and antique furniture."

"He got my Sebring on a trade," said a soft, slightly sullen feminine voice behind him.

Rio turned. Ralphie's widow stood behind him. She clutched a clipboard and wore jeans with a loose white ruffled top that ballooned out over her big belly and fluttered in wispy handkerchief-style points around her thighs. Now that she wasn't red-eyed and sobbing, he could see how pretty she was: a sexy, ripe little *muñeca,* more child than woman.

"You're Rio," Darla said. It was as much an accusation as a statement of fact.

"And you're Darla." He delivered his condolences. It wasn't hard. He meant them. "Rotten deal, Ralphie going. He was good to me, over the years. A true friend. He'll be missed."

The pouty lips hinted at a sneer. "If you're so regretful, you can give me his half of this—"

"Darla." Phoebe cut in, sounding way too much like an adoring mama warning a naughty child to behave.

Darla stuck out her lower lip and muttered, "Sorry," in a tone that said she wasn't, not in the least. She lowered the clipboard to her side and stroked her big stomach. "Phoebe says you're gonna find out what happened…" That plump lower lip quivered. She pressed both lips together to make the quivering stop and whispered the rest. "…when he died."

"I'll do what I can."

Darla's big eyes brimmed. "That's somethin', anyway."

Rio could see how this one had gotten to Phoebe. He could almost buy her act, himself. The weak, he thought, have always known how to work the strong; they have to know, in order to survive—and he had a few questions for Darla. But not while mother-hen Phoebe hovered nearby.

Phoebe asked Darla gently, "Finished?"

"Yeah. We need Chex Mix, club soda and straws." Darla held up her clipboard. "I marked it on the chart like you told me."

Rio saw his cue and took it. "Nice to meet you, Darla."

Darla stuck out her lower lip again. "Yeah."

"Later," he said to Phoebe. "I'll let you know if there's news."

Did she want him to stay? She didn't say so, just "Thanks," and a nod as she held out her hand for the clipboard.

He left through the back way.

RIO GOT HIMSELF A chicken wrap at Galileo's, and lurked there for several hours—moving from the front patio, inside and then later on out to the patio in back, pumping the locals for information, of which he got little. Once the place closed, he spent a second night watching the scene.

It was a repeat of the first night: endless unproductive hours of mind-numbing boredom. Both dog walkers appeared like clockwork, at five-seventeen and five-thirty-two respectively. The old lady spotted him. She gave him a jaunty wave and that tight, proper smile of hers. Her little dog looked right at him, pink tongue lolling, as it lifted its leg on one of the sycamore trees.

That second morning was a Friday, the same day of the week that Ralphie had died. If anything different happened on the Paseo Fridays before dawn, Rio didn't see it.

PHOEBE HAD GIVEN BOONE Friday off.

She took his shift, arriving at eleven to set up for opening at noon. The morning routine was long-established. First, the bank drop. A lot of places did the drop at night, after closing, so the safe would be empty in case of a robbery. But a night drop could be dangerous. Since Phoebe had yet to suffer a break-in, she stuck with doing her banking in the bright light of day.

Back at the bar, she put the chairs down from the tables where Bernard had left them after mopping up at night. She set up the cash drawer.

She was moving by rote, her mind where it shouldn't be: on Rio. She wondered if she'd see him soon, hoped she would—and called herself a fool because after swearing she wouldn't, she was…

Falling.

No. Scratch that. She wasn't falling. Not at all.

It was nothing but animal attraction. And the good thing about attraction was that if you just left it alone long enough, it would fade away all by itself.

She hoped.

She was grinning, shaking her head at her own foolishness, when she shoved open the ladies' room door to make sure that the stalls were stocked with toilet paper and the towel dispensers full.

Phoebe glimpsed the lurid lipstick scrawl on the mirror, registered the word *Bitch,* just as her feet flew out from under her.

With a sharp cry, she went down, grabbing for the edge of the sink, missing it, crying out again as she landed on her tailbone and her head hit the outside wall of the first stall.

The head blow jolted her. But the hot knives of pain

that shot up from her tailbone and sang through her spine left her momentarily paralyzed.

After a moment, as the waves of pain receded, she lifted her hand from the floor and looked at it.

Gooey stuff, pink and thick and shiny, dripped down her arm. Liquid soap. She sniffed at it, smelled that distinctly soapy perfume. "What the…?" Someone had refilled the soap dispenser and gotten sloppy, spilling a *lot* of it on the floor? And then just left it there…?

Who would do such a stupid thing?

Bernard and Tiff had closed up. Neither of them would make a hazardous mess and walk away.

Phoebe let out another low moan. Her butt ached in a big way. It was also covered in gooey wet soap. So were the backs of her thighs. By some miracle, her cute ribbon-tied wedge sandals had been spared—probably because her feet had whipped out from under her so fast, only the soles had gotten soapy. She might have broken her tailbone, but at least she hadn't wrecked a favorite pair of shoes.

Things could be worse, right?

She had no change of clothes in her office locker. So she'd have to go home. But if she hurried, she could make it back to open on time.

Since her skirt was already covered in soap, she wiped her hands on it. Then she untied the ribbons and took off the sandals, tossing them free of the mess. Finally, she planted her bare feet in the soapy goo and reached for the sink rim again, groaning at the fresh, sharp pain in her backside as she braced to pull herself to her feet.

That was when she got a good look at the scrawled lipstick message on the mirror.

Bitch. It's not your business. Leave it alone.

Each of the three small *i*'s was dotted with a cute little heart.

CHAPTER SIX

> To be happy with a man, a woman needs to understand him a lot and love him a little. To be happy with a woman, a man should love her a lot and not try to understand her at all.
> *—from* The Prairie Queen's Guide to Life *by Goddess Jacks*

AFTER A MORNING NAP, Rio spent a second afternoon on the neighborhood—a day as fruitless as the first had been. He interviewed more residents. Zip. He posed as a prospective club owner and got a Realtor to take him through the vacant building at the scene. Nothing in there but tables and chairs, some restaurant equipment, an empty stage and a dusty bar.

At five, he traded his ugly suit for jeans and a T-shirt and headed for Ralphie's Place, thinking that most of his day had been a total bust. But soon he would see Phoebe. He was getting used to that, to seeing Phoebe. Getting to like it.

Maybe too much.

He went in the back way. Gave him a chance to check on his bike, for which he'd picked up a cover.

The chrome and the pricey black paint job gave off a real nice gleam, even in the dim light of the big garage. He dropped the new cover over it and went on inside.

Phoebe wasn't in her office. He moved on through to the front, where he found the curvaceous strawberry-blonde, Cimarron Rose, working the floor along with another cocktail waitress Rio hadn't seen before.

Rose lifted an eyebrow at the sight of him. "Didn't you have long hair the last time I saw you?"

"It's a whole new me." He asked after Phoebe.

"She went home early," Rose told him as she set up drinks on her tray. "We sent her." Rose and the bartender shared a look. "We got more help coming in and we can handle this place without her now and then—*and* she needs a break."

Bernard chimed in. "Someone spilled soap in the women's room. Phoebe slipped in it. She went down pretty hard, I guess."

Rio's pulse ratcheted up a notch. *Chill,* he thought. She fell in the restroom. How bad can it be? "She okay?"

Rose nodded as she dirtied a martini with extra olives. "Just shook her up. But she's been stressed lately, anyway, with Ralphie dead on the street—not to mention a new partner ridin' in from Cali, movin' in on her, parking his bike in the back and opening his own little private investigation into our ex-husband's suspicious demise." Rose paused to give him a look that could only be called disapproving, then added, "She told me I should answer any questions you got. Fine with me. You just give me a call."

"I'll do that."

"Let me guess. You've already got my number."

He nodded. "*Gracias,* Rose."

"She really got on me, about the soap," said Bernard. "Jumped hard and fast to the conclusion it had to be me. I told it her it wasn't and she eased off, but she's usually not the type to go freako, especially before she's got all the facts."

"I'm tellin' y'all," Rose said, sliding her tray smoothly off the bar. "*S-t-r-e-s-s.*"

FIFTEEN MINUTES LATER, RIO WAS knocking on Phoebe's door.

She answered in seconds, barefoot in white pants and a plain white T-shirt, her hair pulled back loosely into a thick ponytail. "How did I know it would be you?"

"Can't stay away."

She ushered him in. The TV was on. She switched it off. "Coffee?"

"Got a beer?"

"I can do beer." She turned for the kitchen. He took up the rear and admired the view. The white pants cradled the back of her, snug and tight. She had an ass that matched the rest of her. Firm and very fine, enough sweet flesh to fill his hands. Her walk swayed easy. If she'd been hurt, it didn't show—at least not with her clothes on.

He allowed himself to imagine what it might be like to peel those white pants down and check for bruises….

That got him going. Beneath his jeans, his dick swelled to attention. Down, *vato,* he thought with a grin.

In the kitchen, she veered toward the counter. While her back was still turned, he slipped a hand down his pants to straighten his bad self, and then slid into his usual place at the table as she uncapped him a Corona. She came around beside him to set the beer in front of him, her ponytail swinging forward, brushing her shoulder, a whiff of her sweet scent drifting to him.

Before she could step back, he caught her wrist. She made a small, sexy sound of womanly surprise and those green eyes went wide—open to him, even though she didn't want to be. Her skin was so soft, and velvety, too, like the petals of a rose. He didn't want to let go, but he did. Long enough to push his chair back. Then he took her by the hips and guided her, sideways, onto his lap.

She surprised him, coming down to him without resistance, even leaning close with a surrendering sigh. He brushed a kiss on her neck. At her nape, a row of silky curls had escaped her ponytail. He caught a few dark strands between his lips, tugged at them lightly, let them slide free. A shudder went through her.

"You okay?" He kissed that soft neck again. "Bernard and Rose told me you fell."

She nodded, still snuggled against him. "It hurt. Bad. But I'm fine now…." He stifled a groan as she shifted in his arms, stroking him at the same time as she drew away from him. "I went in the ladies' room to check the paper goods. There was liquid soap. On the floor, in front of the sink. I slid in it, that's all…."

Something about the way she said *that's all* didn't sound right. Her head was down, her gaze on her hands, folded now, in her lap. He needed to see those green eyes, so he took her chin and made her look at him. "What else?"

"Oh, Rio…"

"*Dígame,*" he coaxed. When she let out a confused, throaty sound, he translated, "Tell me."

She jerked her chin free of his hold and looked down at her hands again. He waited. At last, she confessed, "There were words on the mirror. In lipstick…"

"What words?"

She swallowed, hard. "Um. 'Bitch. It's not your business. Leave it alone.'"

"That's it? Exactly?"

She slid off his lap and turned to look down at him. "Yeah. It's real vivid in my mind. Believe me."

He caught her hand before she could escape to the far side of the table. "Why didn't you call me?"

She let out a small, strangled sound. "Oh, I don't know. Not thinking, I guess…"

"I suppose you already cleaned that mirror."

Her fist tightened in his grip. "Rio, please. I'm constantly fighting the graffiti in the bathrooms. At least, when it's lipstick on the mirror, I can wash it off when I find it."

"And so you did. You cleaned the mirror." She nodded, three quick bobs of her head, that silky ponytail bouncing. "Did anyone else see the mirror before you cleaned it?" Her head went back and forth, sharply. He gave her hand a tug, to make sure she was listening. "I don't think that was just graffiti, *Reina.* I don't think *you* think so, either. I wish you'd called me, let me see for myself."

"I just…it didn't occur to me. And there's no way to know for sure *what* those words really meant. Come on. Spilled soap and words in lipstick on a restroom mirror. That kind of thing happens all the time."

He instructed patiently, "If it happens again, don't touch anything nearby. Do not erase the words. Call me, right then, right that minute, on my cell. I'll get there as fast as I can. Are we clear?" He released her.

She wrapped her arms around herself. "We are. I will. I'll call."

"Tiff was there last night, when I stopped in to see you…."

"Yeah. She and Bernard closed up."

"And Rose was there today. They work for you, then, Tiff and Rose?"

"They help me out, and they like the extra money. But they both have other jobs. Rose owns a vintage clothing store, a few blocks up the street from the bar. Tiff works for her boyfriend, Dave Tolby, in the office at his body shop."

"Dave Tolby. He's on the list you gave me, right?"

"Yeah."

"I talked to Bernard. He said *he* didn't spill any soap. He didn't mention the message on the mirror."

"I didn't bring it up to him, or to anyone, until now. I just…I don't know. I landed on him so hard about the soap. And I'd already cleaned off the mirror…."

"What about Tiffany?"

"I haven't talked to her yet—and you're right. I blew it, didn't I? I should have called you. I messed up...."

He rose and pulled her to him. She didn't object. In fact, she let out a breath that had relief in it and rested her head on his shoulder, sliding her arms around his waist, linking them at the small of his back. He breathed in her scent again, thought about how he didn't want to let her go.

But he still had questions. He took her arms and held her away so he could capture her gaze again. "The words on the mirror. The soap on the floor. Is that all? Was there anything else out of the ordinary? Anything on the floor, in the sink, whatever? Anything noticeable about the handwriting on the mirror, anything not quite right?"

Again, she was looking everywhere but at him.

He shook her, gently. "Come on, *Reina.* You said you want the truth, about Ralphie, and I said I'd do all I could to find the truth. How can I keep our bargain if you hide things from me?"

"Let me go."

So. There *was* more. He released her.

She went back around the table and dropped into the chair across from his. Rio sat back down, too. She started fiddling with the salt and pepper shakers. Rio kept silent. He let her work through her reluctance in her own time.

Finally, she met his gaze. "Okay. The *i*'s were dotted with hearts. Darla does that, dots her *i*'s with little hearts...." She let out a pained cry and tapped the salt shaker, sharply, against the table. "Oh, don't look at me like that. I know she didn't write that message."

"*How* do you know?"

"I just do. Come on. 'Bitch. It's not your business. Leave it alone.' That doesn't sound a thing like Darla. Darla doesn't give orders, she whines and pouts to get her way. And she wasn't in the bar last night. I sent her home before six, not long after you came by. Plus, she *wants* to know what happened to Ralphie. She told me herself—she told *you,* yesterday, remember? She—"

"Could she have come back later? After closing, when everyone else was gone? Or in the morning, before you got there?"

"What? I don't—"

"I'm assuming Ralphie had a key to the bar?"

"Well, yeah. But—"

"And if Darla doesn't have Ralphie's key, her brother has one, right?" He waited until she gave him a tight nod. "So. One way or the other, Darla could get access when no one else was there."

"But she wouldn't. There's just no point in her doing something like that."

"Oh, come on, Phoebe. There's a point. If she had something to do with Ralphie's death, there's a real good point and that is to scare you, to get you thinking that maybe it's not such a great idea to look any deeper into this, to put it in your mind that it could be bad for your health if you keep digging into what really went down in the Paseo the night that Ralphie died in the street."

Her slim shoulders drooped. She pushed the salt

and pepper to the left, then moved them back to the right again. "Okay. All right. I'll talk to her."

"No, you won't. I will."

"But I'm the one who saw the message. I'm the one who knows..." He was shaking his head. "What?" she demanded.

"The question hasn't changed, *Reina.* Which do you want? The truth, or to protect Darla?"

She shut her eyes, breathed out through her nose and then drew her shoulders up tall. "Fine. *You* talk to her."

He kept up the pressure. He wanted this clear. "And I'll talk to Tiffany, too. To everyone on that list you gave me. That was our deal."

"All right. Everyone. Okay."

"Reina..." He reached out, to touch her, to ease her fears.

She jerked her fingers away before he made contact. "You'd better go now."

SATURDAY, WHILE MAC finished up the neighborhood interviews, Rio moved on to the names on Phoebe's list. He tried the long shots first. Before noon, he caught a couple of Ralphie's "business associates" at home. Both men were still in bed when he knocked on their doors. Neither was especially happy to see him. He gave them his best nice-guy routine, kept up a pleasant, relentless pressure until each said they'd been out of town the morning Ralphie had died and had friends to vouch it was true.

When he left the second guy, Rio took serious stock of the situation.

He'd staked out the scene and gotten nothing. He'd talked to the lone witness and scoured the neighborhood. He'd interviewed a couple of suspicious-looking characters with airtight alibis, neither of whom appeared to know a damn thing about why or how Ralphie had ended up dead.

All the above had gotten him nowhere, fast.

Time to go with his instinct on this for a change, time to take the search a little closer to home.

As he made that decision, he realized that even today, after he'd told Phoebe he would talk to Darla, he'd avoided going through with it. He'd been covering all the bases first, so that Phoebe wouldn't accuse him of jumping too fast on the people she cared about.

So, fair enough, he decided, as he treated himself to a couple of slices of pizza and a big Pepsi in a cafeteria downtown. It had all been ground that needed covering. Now for the stuff with some real potential in it.

Time to pay the little widow a visit.

DARLA WASN'T HOME—OR AT least, when he knocked on the door of her trailer, she didn't answer. No car in the driveway, either. Rio figured she was probably over at the bar, walking around with her little clipboard, counting the straws and the toothpicks.

Rio tried both doors: locked. He checked all the windows: latched. Even the barn-shaped shed near the back fence, which was minus any windows, was locked up tight. To get in, he'd have to break in. He wasn't up for that. Not yet, anyway.

Next subject: Tiffany Sweeney.

He had a hunch she might be at her boyfriend's body shop not far from Will Rogers Airport in what Mac had told him was called Southside. And even if Tiff wasn't there, he was kind of curious about the boyfriend, anyway. And about the body shop, which could be a very convenient business to have if for some reason a man decided to run down his girlfriend's ex.

Dave's Dent and Ding was a long metal-sided building—two work bays on one end, the office area at the other—surrounded by vehicles, most of which had suffered some kind of collision. A chain-link fence corralled it all. The front gate was wide open.

Rio drove through the gate and parked around back, which gave him a reason to circle the building, checking out the damaged vehicles—especially the ones that could have run over Ralphie. He counted three big pickups, four vans and six SUVs. None of them looked as if they'd hit a human body head-on recently—not that he'd expected he'd get that kind of lucky. If Dave or Tiff was involved, the vehicle that had hit Ralphie wouldn't be waiting on Dave's lot for someone to stumble over. It would have been stripped and parted out long before now.

When he reached the office door, he went in.

The room beyond the door was small, with a high counter and a cash register in front, a desk crammed in behind that. Corkboard lined the walls, dirty invoices and wrinkled sticky notes pinned to it, along with two out-of-date pinup calendars and an autographed glossy headshot of Toby Keith. In the corner stood a couple of dented file cabinets. A smudged window on the inside wall opened onto the first service bay.

Tiffany sat at the surprisingly immaculate desk, stapling a stack of papers together. She looked up at the sound of the door buzzer, her friendly smile of greeting turning cool when she saw who it was.

"Rio Navarro." She slid the stapled papers into a plastic sleeve, hung the sleeve on the wall next to her desk and got up. "Phoebe warned me you'd probably be coming by sometime."

"How are you, Tiffany?"

"Just fine." She got right to business. "Phoebe said you'd have questions and I should answer them."

"I'd appreciate that."

Tiff huffed out a breath. "Phoebe's all obsessed with what happened to Ralphie."

"And you're not?"

She pressed her lips together. "You make it sound like I don't care."

You never catch a fly with vinegar and Rio knew it. He softened his tone. "I'm sorry. I know that Ralphie meant a lot to you."

Tiff sniffed, delicately. "I married him, too, you know. Even if that marriage only lasted six months, I loved him. I did. And by the time he died, he was my friend as much as he was Phoebe's or Rose's. He looked after me, when things were bad for me. He got me my car for me, traded it for some pickup he had and gave it to me without charging me a cent. He was good to me. He was. And I do care."

Rio watched as she paused to brush at her filmy-looking skirt and smooth her hair, which was loose and softly curling around her triangular face. Her makeup was light, her nails well cared for, filed straight across, coated with clear polish. As she stepped out from behind the desk, he saw that she wore delicate high-heeled sandals with straps that wrapped around her trim ankles.

Out of place, he thought. Tiffany Sweeney looked out of place there, in that cramped, messy office with the smell of motor oil tainting the air.

She moved up to the counter and folded her arms on it, leaning slightly toward him, lifting her cute pointed chin. "So, okay," she said briskly. "What do you want to know?"

"Did Phoebe call you about what happened to her yesterday?"

"You mean the soap on the bathroom floor, the weird message on the mirror? Yeah. She called me last night. She told me about how she fell, asked me if I maybe spilled the soap…."

"Did you?"

Tiff straightened. "No way. I make a mess, I clean it up. And Bernard checked the bathrooms at closing, anyway. If there was soap, he spilled it. And if there was some weird lipstick message on the mirror, well, I didn't put it there and I don't know who did."

"Did Phoebe tell you what the writing on the mirror said?"

"'Bitch. Mind your own business,' something like that—and I agree, that's creepy. But I don't know how it got there. Well, unless Darla did it."

"Why Darla?" he asked, just to see if her answer might surprise him.

It didn't. "Phoebe said the *i*'s were dotted with hearts the way Darla does hers, but she also said she'd called Darla just before she called me. Darla swore she didn't do it."

So Phoebe had been busy after he'd left her last night, checking in with her homegirls, hungry for reassurance that no one she loved could be messing with her mind. "Do you think Darla's lying?"

"How would I know? Darla could have done it, I guess. She's been acting pretty damn desperate and strange lately." Tiff tossed her blond head. Small silver earrings shaped like crescent moons swayed against her neck. Then she grew more thoughtful. "You know what? On second thought, no. Darla may not be the sharpest pencil in the drawer. But everybody knows about how she dots her *i*'s with hearts. Even she would have sense enough not to give herself away like that. It's a lot more logical that someone wants it to *look* like Darla did it. And, the more I think about it, if the message really was meant for Phoebe, no way. Darla just wouldn't do that to her."

"Why not?"

"Darla can be a total pain in the ass. But she loves Phoebe. Phoebe has done a lot for her and Darla knows it. Darla trails after her like a little lost lamb. And besides. Maybe the message wasn't even meant for Phoebe. Did either of you think of that? She didn't say it had her name on it. A message like that could be for anybody, could mean a lot of things…."

Right then, the service window into the shop area slid open. A guy in greasy overalls leaned a pair of weight lifter's arms on the sill and stuck his head through the open hole: shaggy brown hair, gray eyes, faded acne scars, good-looking in a rough-trade kind of way. He flicked a wary glance at Rio, then asked Tiff, "What's goin' on?"

Tiff smiled at her boyfriend, a nervous smile—and a hopeful one, too. "Dave, honey. This is Rio, Phoebe's new partner…."

The gray eyes turned on Rio again. He muttered flatly, "Hey."

"Hey." Rio's cell vibrated. He slid it from the carrier at his waist and glanced at the display. Phoebe. He put the phone to his ear. "Yeah?"

"You said to call if I got another message…" Her voice was wound a little too tight.

He kept his own voice easy. "That's right, I did."

"I got one. More or less…" Dave and Tiff were watching him, looking way too interested.

He told Phoebe, "Hold on a minute, will you? I'll be right back." He muted the phone. "It's Phoebe. She needs to meet with me."

Tiff was frowning. "Is something wrong?"

"Not a thing," Rio baldly lied. He put on his most harmless smile. "A pleasure talking to you, Tiff." He nodded at Dave. "Later…"

Dave gave him a grunt and a scowl.

Rio turned and got out the door before Tiff or her boyfriend could say anything more. Moving fast toward his car, Rio spoke to Phoebe again. "Still there?"

"Right here."

"The message. Drawn in lipstick?"

"Yeah."

"When did you find it?"

"Just before I called you. Here at the bar. On the mirror inside the door of the locker in my office."

"Are you there, in your office, now?"

"Yeah."

"Stay there. Don't clean it up. Don't even let anyone near it till I get there—who's tending bar this afternoon?"

"Just Boone. He was here to open up."

"Make sure he stays until I can talk to him."

"Okay."

"I'm on my way."

CHAPTER SEVEN

A Prairie Queen knows everybody's first name:
Honey
Darlin'
Sugar.
—from The Prairie Queen's Guide to Life *by Goddess Jacks*

RIO PARKED AROUND BACK, grabbed his digital camera and went in through the side door. Phoebe was there, in the office, waiting for him. She rose from behind her desk as he entered.

There was another woman with her. Slim, with a short cap of snow-white hair, she sat with her back to the door, rising when Phoebe did and turning to Rio with a big smile. Even with the white hair, the woman seemed youthful. She had green eyes very much like Phoebe's, and wore a loose black velvet shirt and snug jeans, turquoise earrings and a silver-and-turquoise bracelet. There was also a wedding ring.

"Rio," said Phoebe. "My mother, Goddess Jacks."

"Rio Navarro." The older woman's drawl was more pronounced than Phoebe's, as warm and slow as poured honey. "At last." She took his hand in both of hers. Her touch was cool. "Oh, my yes. Nothin' like a big, strong man to the rescue, now is there?" She shut her eyes and crooned, "Oh, yes. Yes, yes, yes..."

"Mama," said Phoebe in a warning tone. "Dial it back a notch, will you?"

Goddess released him and turned on her daughter. "Don't you get snippy on me, baby. I only came to help." She whirled to Rio again. He got another thousand-watt smile. "No formalities, now. You call me Goddess."

Phoebe explained, "My mother suddenly got worried about me, so she raced right over here to check on me."

Goddess's blinding smile dimmed. "What else could I do? Not forty-five minutes ago, while looking for a synonym for the word *foreboding,* I had a chilling sense that something wasn't right, an overwhelmin' awareness that Phoebe needed me with her. What would any mother do? I rushed to her side."

"A phone call would have covered it," Phoebe suggested hopefully.

"And have you say there was nothin' wrong? Oh, no, thank you."

Phoebe told Rio, "My mother has visions." She sounded resigned.

"I do," Goddess confirmed with pride. "But this, today...it was no vision. Just a heavy, draggin' sensation, a premonition of possible doom. I thought, *Phoebe,* and I felt a chill of cold and darkness brushing dank, bony fingers across my heart."

"She's also a writer," Phoebe said drily. "In case you didn't already guess."

"Self-help, with humor." Goddess was beaming again. "Very hot right now."

Rio wondered what dog Phoebe's mother might have in this hunt. He asked her, "You knew then, about Phoebe's fall in the restroom yesterday?"

"No, I didn't know." Goddess sent a hurt frown Phoebe's way. "Not until five minutes ago, when she finally saw fit to tell me."

"Mama, please. I didn't want to worry you, that's all."

The look on Goddess's face said she wasn't buying that one. But she didn't argue. "Well. At least I'm here now. And I've finally been told something about what is going on."

Rio cut to the chase. "Let's see what you found."

"There." Phoebe gestured at the open door to the tall metal cabinet on the side wall. A big, sloppy red lipstick heart—a heart split jaggedly in two, with a ragged space between the halves—covered the eight-by-ten mirror mounted at head height inside the door.

"Did you touch anything in here after you opened the door?"

"No. I pulled it open and I saw that someone had drawn that thing on the mirror and I called you, like you told me to."

"Good." Rio switched on the camera and snapped several pictures—of the door and the mirror, of the blue sweater drooping from the hook inside, of the two pairs of flat-heeled women's shoes lined up neatly on the cabinet floor. Then, with his elbow on the edge of the door, he carefully guided it shut, not letting it latch. He took more pictures of the front of the cabinet and then from either side. "When was the last time you looked in here?"

"I don't know," Phoebe said after a moment's thought. "It's been a few days. I use it more in the winter, for my coat and boots and stuff…."

He lowered the camera and turned to her.

Dark smudges of fatigue showed under her eyes. He had to resist the sudden, insistent urge to close the distance between them, to haul her into the protective circle of his arms. And beyond the urge to protect her, he felt the heat—as he'd felt it from that first moment he'd seen her—the arc of attraction between them.

"Well…" Goddess spoke low, in that slow-honey voice of hers. "I am getting a sense of…great energy. Oh, my yes. This is really very excitin'…."

Phoebe ignored her mother. She stared at Rio and her straight brows drew together in a frown. "The last time I opened that cabinet was Tuesday, my birthday, the day you came to town. Remember?"

He did remember. "You came back here and changed your shoes."

"And later, at the end of the night, I opened the cabinet again to get my red sandals and take them home. There was no lipstick on the mirror then—and that was it. I haven't been in there again. Until today."

"Why today?"

She pointed at the blue sweater sagging on its hook. "I kept forgetting to take that sweater to the cleaners.

I was going to set it out where I could see it, so I wouldn't leave it behind again."

Almost four days. A lot longer than he would have liked. It was possible this "message" came first, before the one in the bathroom. He might make a guess at how long it had been there, by the feel of the lipstick, its relative dryness. But he didn't want to touch anything until he'd dusted for prints.

He asked, "Got a flashlight?"

Phoebe took one from a lower desk drawer and passed it to him. He used the end of it to guide the door open again and then shone the light on the mirror. "Come over here. Both of you." The two women stepped up. He moved the light across the lipstick heart. "What do you think? How fresh?"

Goddess said, "Got me, darlin'."

Phoebe shook her head. "Couldn't say."

Rio leaned close and sniffed. Nothing. If there had been a smell, it was gone now. How long did it take the scent of lipstick to fade? Did it have a scent in the first place? The police might be able to answer those questions, with the tools at their disposal.

"The police?" asked Goddess, as if she'd plucked the word right out of his head. "Shouldn't we call them?"

Phoebe made an impatient noise in her throat. "And tell them what, Mama? I washed off the other message, the one with actual *words* in it. So they'd have to just believe us when we said what this one means—and what *does* this one mean? What exactly have we got here? A lipstick drawing of a broken heart. That'll really get them going down at headquarters, I'll bet."

"But it's *threatening,*" Goddess insisted.

"Is it? Most people would probably think it's just a silly prank. And a prank is a big 'so what?' You don't call the cops because some bratty kid T.P.'s the house or chalks the driveway."

Phoebe had it right. But if and when the police had to come in on this, Rio would have the pictures he'd just taken and any prints he could get, plus scrapings of the lipstick, all ready for them, cataloged and under lock and key.

Rio asked, "Who has access to this room?"

"The safe's in here," Phoebe said. "After closing at night, the take from that day and evening goes in the safe. Bernard and Boone each have a key, beyond the one that I have."

"They have keys to the safe, too?"

"It's a combination lock—and yes, they both have the combination. I trust them and they haven't disappointed me. But I'm not stupid. I make bank runs five days a week. There's never *that* much cash in there at one time."

"And if you're not here?"

"The room stays locked. I leave it open when I'm in the building."

"Did Ralphie have a key?" If Ralphie did, Darla might have it now.

"Not to my office, not in the past three years or so. You know how he was. Always short of cash. He 'borrowed' from the safe without telling me. We had a long talk. He agreed that he wasn't real good at resisting temptation. So I changed the combination to the safe and the lock on the door, too. He didn't get a new key."

Ralphie, Rio thought, hiding a grin. A man you could trust with your life—but not with the combination to the safe.

Phoebe dropped into her chair. Goddess made a clucking sound and hurried over to stand behind her. She put a reassuring hand on Phoebe's shoulder. Phoebe reached up to clasp her mother's fingers. "Anyone could have done it, anytime the door was open. Anyone could have snuck in here and drawn that heart and snuck right out again, with nobody the wiser."

Goddess gave him a sharp-eyed look as she brushed a motherly hand down her daughter's shining hair. "Where were *you* today, Rio?"

"Asking around. Trying to get closer to what happened to Ralphie."

"How you doin' with that?"

"Not great, so far."

"You want to get closer," Phoebe's mother said in a scolding tone, "I'm thinkin' you'd be smarter to stick around here."

RIO SCRAPED A LIPSTICK sample off the mirror, dusted for prints and talked to Boone, who had arrived before Phoebe to open the place up. Boone said he'd been in the office once that day, to get the cash to set up the drawer. No, he hadn't gone near the locker. He'd opened the safe, taken out the bills and change he needed, locked up the safe, left the room and locked the door behind him.

"Where's Darla?" Rio asked Phoebe, once he was through with Boone and she had rejoined him in the office.

"Well, I don't know. I have her coming in at three today, working until six. She's almost eight months along, so she can't work a lot."

"I'll talk to her first thing, as soon as she gets here."

"Why not?" She didn't sound thrilled at the idea, but she didn't argue against it, either. That was progress, Rio supposed.

Goddess, who'd made herself scarce so he could talk to Boone, appeared in the doorway with a can of Fresca in her hand. "Rio, I would like a few words with you." She sent Phoebe a look. "Alone."

"Mama. Stay out of this. Please."

Goddess continued as if her daughter hadn't spoken, "So Rio. How about a nice walk? There's a cute little park not far from here and it's not all that hot out."

"Damn it, Mama..."

"It's okay," Rio said. "A walk sounds good to me."

"Oh, I'll just bet it does," Phoebe grumbled.

Rio spoke to Goddess. "Let me lock the evidence and the camera in the car and I'll be ready to go."

IT WAS A QUICK WALK ALONG Thirty-Sixth and over to Shartel and Edgemere Park. Goddess led him to a bench beneath a sweet gum tree. "Now isn't this nice?" She sat and he sat beside her. She drained the last of her soft drink and set the can on the grass at her feet. Then she straightened the wide neck of her velvet shirt and granted him another of those brilliant smiles. "All right. I'm sure you have plans to question me. You go on ahead." The smile turned sweet and saintly. "I believe in layin' it all right out there. A life is so much fuller, so much freer and bursting with light, when it's lived out in the open, don't you find?"

"Absolutely. Where were you the morning Ralphie died?"

"Home safe in my bed."

"Alone?"

"Yes."

"From a few things Ralphie told me, I got the feeling he was in love with you, years ago, when he came to the Prairie Queen and started booking acts for you."

She shrugged. "I'm a one-man woman and that man was Hank Jacks. If Ralphie Styles ever got some crazy idea he was in love with me, well, he must have known it would go nowhere, because he displayed the surprising good sense never to say a word about it to me."

"Ralphie told me you were angry when Phoebe eloped with him."

Goddess let out a musical chuckle. "Angry, huh? The word *angry* does not begin to describe my emotional state when I learned that Phoebe and Ralphie Styles had run off to Vegas together. I was furious. I was livid. Yes. Livid, furious, outraged and beside myself when Ralphie Styles ran off with my only child."

"Why?"

She laughed again. "Oh, Rio. You knew Ralphie. That man was not, and never would be, husband material. And besides, Phoebe's daddy had passed on not six months before they eloped. Phoebe was in no emotional condition to go makin' any life-changing decisions. She was the one who found Hank, did you know that? She found him slumped over his desk in his office at home. A heart attack, out of nowhere. It was blessedly fast, the doctors assured me. I took comfort in that, that his suffering was brief. I tried to be grateful for all the years of love we had together. But Phoebe could not be consoled. She loved her dad, more than she has loved anyone before or since. He...understood her, and she could tell him anything. With Phoebe and me, well, the love is there and always will be, but we don't often see eye to eye on things...."

Rio listened to Goddess chatter away, giving him a boatload of information, most of which had nothing to do with what had happened to Ralphie on April fifteenth. It did, however, have everything to do with Phoebe. And that interested him. A lot. More than it should have. "You're saying Phoebe married Ralphie as a...reaction to her father's death?"

"That is exactly what I'm saying. Phoebe had always adored Ralphie, but I doubt she would have married him, would have made such a foolish move as to put her tender heart in his untrustworthy hands, if that poor heart wasn't already broken from losin' her dad." Goddess sat very straight, staring off toward the sidewalk and the cars rushing past on Thirty-Sixth Street. The breeze ruffled her silvery hair. "I hated

Ralphie Styles when he took my baby away with him. I was fit to be tied. If you'd put a pistol in my hand and locked me in a room with him then, I can't guarantee I'd have let him out alive. But I got over it. Life goes on and the rent comes due, if you catch my drift. He did what I knew he would do to my baby. And in time, she got over him and I found it in my mother's heart to forgive him for what he'd taken from her—her innocence, her sweet and trusting hopeful youth…." Goddess paused. She looked down at her folded hands and then back out toward the street again.

When she spoke, her voice was very soft. "In spite of how furious I was with him once, when Ralphie died last month, I did grieve for him. While he wasn't a man that a woman could pin her hopes on, he had a kind heart and a tender way about him. He was generous to a fault." Goddess looked at Rio then. Her eyes were as deep as oceans. "I sense a hard time coming for my baby. I sense a storm and great, grave danger. I sense you're the one to help her through it. I want to know she can count on you, to stand beside her, until the storm is past and the sun comes out again. Will you be here, to take care of my baby, until this is over?"

The buildup had been way too dramatic for Rio's taste. Still, the question itself was easily answered. "Yeah. Until it's over, I'll be here."

"Swear it."

Why not? It was only what he intended to do, anyway. "I swear it."

Instantly, Goddess was all sweetness and light again, her handsome face wreathed in smiles. "I am so pleased. And grateful. And the moment I receive any messages, I will let you know."

Apprehension tightened Rio's gut. Had he missed something important here? "Messages?"

"Yes. From the other side."

"What side, specifically, is that?"

"Why, from beyond the grave, of course. Messages from the spirit world. If Ralphie, or any other restless soul, should decide to communicate with me on the subject of Ralphie's death, I'll let you know immediately."

"Uh. Thanks," he replied with a straight face, wondering if Phoebe's mother might be just a little *loca.* "I'd appreciate that."

"Anything I can do. *Anything*—and shouldn't you give me a number where I can reach you?"

"Just tell Phoebe. She'll let me know."

"Well, all right, then." Goddess dipped to the side to pick up her empty soft drink can. "Everything is settled, for now. Let's go back to Ralphie's Place, why don't we? I have got to get on home. All this excitement has decimated my flow."

"Your flow."

"That's right. My creative flow. My writing goal today is five pages. I've barely got a paragraph."

When they reached the parking spaces lined up in front of the bar, Goddess headed straight for a big Ford F-150 pickup, which was painted a glittering metal-flake midnight-blue.

"Some paint job," said Rio, as he held the door and Phoebe's mother jumped lightly up behind the wheel.

"Yes, I just love it," said Goddess. "It looks like a night full of stars, don't you think? Tiffany's boyfriend Dave did it for me." She patted the dash the way a horsewoman would stroke a pony's neck. "Dave does beautiful work."

"When did you have it done?"

"A few weeks ago." She handed Rio the Fresca can. "Take this in for me, will you, sugar? Thank you so much—for everything. I will be in touch."

Rio pushed the door closed. Goddess started up the pickup, checked her mirrors and backed carefully out onto Western. Rio stood there, holding the empty Fresca can, watching as she drove away.

Once she disappeared around the corner, he tucked the empty can beneath his arm long enough to slide his spiral notebook from a back pocket and write down her plate number. He'd ask Phoebe later what she knew about that new paint job.

CHAPTER EIGHT

Face it, darlin'. In life and love, there are no guarantees. If you want a guarantee, buy yourself one of those nice washer-dryer combinations from Sears.

—from The Prairie Queen's Guide to Life *by Goddess Jacks*

HOURS LATER, LONG AFTER Goddess had climbed in her pickup and headed for home, Rio was still at Ralphie's Place. Phoebe wasn't sure how she felt about his hanging around.

On the one hand, his presence did soothe her. Something about him just made her feel safe. With Rio around, those creepy lipstick messages on the mirrors seemed…not so scary, somehow. With Rio nearby, whatever happened, she knew the two of them could deal with it just fine.

That was on the one hand. And anybody who'd ever loved a good country song knew that "on the one hand" always led straight to "on the other hand."

On the other hand, even letting herself think of the two of them in one sentence was a bad idea. Phoebe was way too attracted to him and she knew it. She didn't need him around to remind her constantly of what a big ol' hunk of manliness he was, of how, if she had a "type," Rio was it, only better. He was big and dark and dangerous-looking, like the leather-wearing bad boys she'd been drawn to after she and Ralphie had split up. But he also had a sweet side, a side that meant he could wear a cheap suit and geeky glasses and people would buy it, let him coax them into telling him all of their secrets.

He kept himself busy.

First, he interviewed Darla, led her right into the office when she arrived—late, as usual—and kept her in there with the door closed for half an hour. But Darla seemed okay when Rio finally let her out, so Phoebe figured whatever he'd said to her couldn't have been all that bad.

After he finished with Darla, he spent an hour and a half fixing the ice machine—including a quick trip to the hardware store to buy some rubber seals that he said had worn out and needed replacing.

Phoebe thanked him.

He shrugged. "I'm here. Might as well make myself useful."

It seemed a good opportunity to ask, "And how long are you stayin'?"

"Why? There some reason you don't want me around?"

Yeah, you make me want to climb you like a tree. "No. None. Really. You've got every right to be here." After all, he owned the place as much as she did. "I just thought, you know, that you would want to get back out on the street, collect more clues, talk to witnesses, do whatever it is you do when you're, uh, on a case…."

"Reina." He said his secret name for her softly, so no one else would hear. "I've been out there. Nothing's happening. I'm taking your mother's advice and sticking around here for a while."

"Oh."

She saw that smile—the one that kind of played at the edges of his fine, sexy mouth. He said, "I think I'll have a talk with Bernard next. If that's okay with you…."

"Well, sure. Whatever you need to do."

"Gracias."

Rio led the night bartender into the office and shut the door.

That night, Phoebe had booked a popular fusion band, Aberrant Behavior, for four sets between nine and 1:00 a.m. Since it was Saturday and Saturdays were killer busy as a rule, both Rose and Tiff came in to help out. Rio took them to the office one at a time.

After Rose came out and Tiff went in, Rose joked, "I got no secrets left. He wanted to know about how it was with me and Ralphie. I said, 'How did it always go with Ralphie? True love, a weddin' ring, a broken heart and a *d-i-v-o-r-c-e.*'"

Bernard mixed a pitcher of margaritas. "He asked me where I was the night Ralphie died. I gave him the lady's name and number." His smooth dark forehead crinkled as he frowned. "I hope the lady doesn't mind…."

Rose laughed as she salted the glasses. "He asked me the same question. I was with Dexter DuFrayne. Remember him?"

"Yeah," said Bernard. "Never washed his hair. Carried around that old Fender Stratocaster. Claimed it once belonged to Jimi Hendrix."

"Ex-actly." Rose made a scoffing sound. "Dexter and me. So not meant to be." She shook her wild, red-blond head. "I have to tell y'all. So much can happen in a month. Four short weeks and nothin's the same."

Phoebe opened the ice machine and looked inside. It was filling up nicely, not dripping at all anymore. Who would have thought it? Rio. Good with machines, just like Ralphie…

AFTER RIO FINISHED WITH Tiff, Phoebe waited for him to leave.

But no.

He stayed, washing glasses and carrying in supplies from the back when Bernard or the other bartender asked for them. When he wasn't giving the bartenders a hand, he sat at the bar and drank club soda and listened to the band.

A tall guy—brown-skinned with a broad face and unreadable dark eyes—came in at eight-thirty or so.

Rio introduced him to Phoebe. "This is Mac Tenkiller, with Red Wolf Investigations. He's been helping me out with some of the legwork." Phoebe nodded in greeting and Mac Tenkiller nodded back. Rio asked, "Mind if we use the office for a minute or two?"

"No. That's fine."

So Rio led Mac to the back. A while later, they both came out and the other P.I. left.

Between sets, when the jukebox wasn't blaring, Rio struck up conversations with anyone and everyone. Since Phoebe was all over the place on a busy night like that one, pitching in wherever she was needed—tending bar, working the floor, bussing tables—she found it pretty easy to keep an eye on her new partner as she worked.

Women really went for him. He was friendly and low-key—and then there was the way he looked in a pair of jeans, not to mention how his dark blue T-shirt showed off those fine arms of his. Every time she glanced his way, a new female was chatting him up, tossing her hair and laughing too loudly, laying a hand on his big, strong, brown forearm.

Yeah, the women liked him. Phoebe was pretty sure he didn't hook up with any of them, though. After a while, each one seemed to give up and go away—not that Phoebe was paying all that much attention or anything.

At two, Phoebe sent Tiff and Rose, the other waitress and the extra bartender home. She and Bernard could handle cleaning up, especially since Rio had been restocking the bar and helping them keep on top of the glassware as they went along.

Rio was still sitting there, at the end of the bar, all by his lonesome, when Phoebe let the last three customers out and locked up behind them.

When she turned from the door, she saw that Rio had spun on his seat so he faced her. She got that warm, hollowed-out feeling down below, felt the shimmer of heat sliding slow and sweet all through her.

Here they were again. Alone in the bar, just like that first day…

Well, except for Bernard, who'd gone off into the back somewhere.

"¿Qué ahora?"

"Pardon me?"

"What now?"

"I'll bet you talk Spanish to all the girls."

"Only the special ones."

She slanted a glance at the floor and then back up at him, knowing exactly what she was doing, giving him the come-and-get-it look. "Are there a lot of special ones?"

He shook his head, slowly.

She thought of last night, of his lips on her throat and his powerful arms around her. She'd let him pull her to his lap….

But she hadn't kissed him.

She looked at his mouth, imagined what it would feel like, to kiss him: the warmth and the wetness, that green, manly scent of his, the taste of him.

That would be something. Just a kiss. Maybe.

A kiss didn't have to go anywhere, did it? A kiss could just be a kiss and nothing more….

Taking her sweet time about it, enjoying the way that he watched her, she reached back, took the pins from her hair and finger-combed it when it fell to her shoulders. "Well. That's it. Another Saturday night has come and gone. Nothin' else happening here at Ralphie's Place."

He stood from the stool. "Come on. Let's finish whatever needs doing around here. I'll follow you home."

A hot gladness spread through her. She thought, I am a fool and you know what? At this particular moment, I don't care in the least.

Still, she did ask, "Why?"

"We have a few things to talk about."

"Just…talk?"

"Más o menos."

She knew what that meant. "Oh, right. More or less…"

He raised a midnight eyebrow. "*Reina.* You speak Spanish."

"Only when I'm talkin' to you."

RIO INSISTED ON WAITING until Bernard had left and then going through the whole place, opening every cupboard, closet and cabinet, making certain no more messages had appeared.

"See?" Phoebe said when he was finally done. "Nothing."

"Never hurts to check."

He followed her to her place. She found she kind of liked that, his headlights in her rearview mirror, the feeling that someone big and strong and dangerous was covering her back.

At her house, she got a pair of Coronas from the fridge and they took their usual seats at the table.

"So?" she asked, and sipped.

His beer sat untouched on the table in front of him,

the little beads of condensation sliding down the sides, pooling at the base of the bottle. He looked at it and then across at her. "Your mother asked me to stick by you. Until this thing is over."

Five or six really down-and-dirty swear words scrolled through Phoebe's mind. She didn't say them. "My mother is...my mother. If she didn't butt her head in, she'd worry I might think she doesn't love me."

"I said I would. Stick by you."

She felt another warm jolt of gladness—and then got the bigger picture. "Until this is over..."

He nodded, then picked up the beer and drank. She watched the smooth sliding of his Adam's apple along that strong, tanned throat of his. He set the bottle down in the exact same spot, so the little ring of wetness curved perfectly around the base again. He studied her for a long moment, dark eyes so deep.

Then he said, "My mother loved Ralphie...."

She took another sip. "You told me."

He ran a thumb down the side of the bottle in a thoughtful sort of way. "You know how it was with Ralphie. He loved her, too. She was the only woman for him."

Phoebe did know. "For six months, or a year, or even two, if she was extra lucky, she was the only woman in the world...."

Rio nodded. "And then he broke her heart. She hated him."

"For a while..."

"Eventually, they became friends."

Almost, she reached across and put her hand on his.

Almost. But not quite—and her throat was suddenly dry. She drank again, tossing her head a little before putting the bottle to her lips, so her hair fell back away from her throat. She knew he watched her. She wanted him to. With care, she set the bottle down. "I know this story. I know every chapter. After all, I lived it myself."

Rio kept talking, his voice tender, his eyes far away. "She never fell in love with anyone else. My father had died in Mexico, in their tiny village in Jalisco, about a month after I was conceived. She made three trips across the border, with me in her belly, trying to get me there before I was born, so I would be an American citizen. *La migra,* the border patrol, kept catching her, sending her back. She was just another of *los mojados,* a wetback, to them. The fourth time, she succeeded. I was born the next day. She named me after the river she crossed four times to make me an American."

"Her name?" Phoebe heard herself ask in a near-whisper.

"Maria. She was *muy fuerte,* very strong, my mother. She worked hard, to give me more than she'd ever had. She was murdered, in our house in East L.A. when I was seventeen years old. Some assholes were after me to join up with them. I'd promised *mi madre* I'd never run with gangs. They drove by our little house, shooting. They didn't get me, they got her. Right through her heart."

Phoebe did reach out then.

But Rio pulled his hand away. "Ralphie came when I called him. He stayed with me, through the funeral, until I finished high school. He kept me from going after those worthless pieces of shit. He told me to wait, not to ruin my life, that guys like that will do the job for you if you just give them a little time. He was so right. I went in the army. Two years. When I got out, those three *pinchis cabróns* were dead."

"What did you do next?"

"Went to college for a couple of years. Considered joining the LAPD, decided I'd rather run my own business. I met Soledad Licea five years ago. She was a nurse in the clinic where I would go when I needed patching up. She had thick red-brown hair and soft brown eyes. She was brave and good and sweet as sugar."

"And strong…"

He looked at her, narrow-eyed. "How did you know that?"

"Just a guess."

"She was. Strong. I asked her to marry me. She said yes. We were so happy…." He paused, shrugged, raised the beer to his lips again. Phoebe waited, saying nothing. She had a pretty good idea what was coming.

He set his beer on the table again. "Soledad was raped and murdered in our bed, by a lowlife bastard I'd brought in to face trial three years before. The son of a bitch got early parole for good behavior and he got my woman to get back at me. That time, I took out the garbage myself. When I went to bring him in, I made sure he tried to kill me, so I had no choice but to kill him. It wasn't all that satisfying, watching him die. And it didn't bring my Soledad back."

She said what she felt, as inadequate as she knew it to be. "I'm sorry, Rio."

He grunted, low. "Say it in Spanish. It sounds so much sweeter."

"I don't…have the words."

He gave them to her. *"Lo siento."*

She gave them back. "*Lo siento*—and it wasn't your fault. Not your mother. Or your fiancée. I hope you know that."

"Yeah. I know it. I got no guilt about either of them. Regret? A mountain of it. No guilt, though. But given what goes on in my line of work, I've learned that everyone is better off if I don't get too involved. That way, when the assholes come after me, the people who matter to me don't get caught in the middle."

She sank back in her chair. "Meaning?"

"When this is over, I go back to L.A. I'll do what you wanted me to do at the first—be your silent partner until you can get it together to buy me out. And I'll fix it so if some dirtbag finishes me off before that happens, my half of Ralphie's Place goes to you."

"You'll put it in your will, Rio?" She ladled on the sarcasm. At that moment, she couldn't seem to stop herself. "Put it in your will, just like Ralphie always promised to do?"

For that, she got a long, steady stare. "I'm not Ralphie."

Shame moved through her, sluggish and sad. She sat a little straighter and spoke more gently. "I know that. I'm sorry. How do you say it? *Lo siento…*" He gave one regal dip of his dark head in acceptance of her apology. She held up her empty bottle. "You?"

"Yeah. One more."

She opened two fresh ones, slipping back into her chair and then sliding his beer across to him.

He picked it up, then set it down without drinking from it. "You mad at me now?" His mouth hiked up on one side and he was Clark Kent again, shy and sweet, the kind of guy people open up to.

Damned if that act didn't work just fine—even on Phoebe, who should have known better. "No. I'm not mad."

"I'm sticking close to the bar, for a while. I'll be in and out, but mostly in."

"Yeah. I got that. It's okay. You can even use my office when you need it."

"You are so generous."

"Oh, yeah. That's right." She wrapped her fingers around the cold beer bottle—but she didn't raise it to drink.

They sat there for a while, just looking at each other. Phoebe thought how some things were like a flood. Or a tornado. Some things just happened. There was no stopping them, no bargaining with them. If you were smart and lucky, you got out of the way in time—before they mowed you down and left you, bloody and broken, to try and pick up the pieces and get on with your life.

Finally, he said, "What color was your mother's pickup, before she got Dave to paint it?"

She almost had her beer to her lips that time. She plunked it back on the table. "You are kidding me, right? Not my mother. No."

He didn't say anything. Just waited, watching her through eyes that saw too damn much.

Finally, she told him. "Silvery gray. *Factory* gray. She bought it a year ago and she never liked the color, so last month, she got Dave to change it." She saw in his eyes that he'd be checking on that. Fine with her. He could waste his time looking for another answer if he wanted to. He wouldn't find one because there wasn't one. Her mother's pickup had never been red, like the paint chip the police had found on Ralphie, and that was a plain fact. "You get anything interesting from all those little talks you had in my office today?"

He drank. "Darla told me Ralphie left without telling her, the night that he died. She said that wasn't like him, to leave after midnight without a word to her about where he was going. She said he would always at least tell her he had business to take care of, give her kiss and a general idea of when he'd be back. But that night, the baby was kicking a lot and she was tired. She went to bed at ten. He said he'd be in soon. She woke up at three, she said…."

"And no Ralphie."

He softly accused, "She already told you that."

Phoebe nodded. "Several times, usually while sobbing and wailing."

"You never told me."

"You never asked, and besides, if I had, you'd still have had to go and ask her yourself, to make sure I gave it to you straight."

"*Muy lista,*" he said. "You're a smart woman, *Reina.*"

"That's right."

He sat forward in his chair. And then he reached across.

She thought again of floods and tornadoes. *Be smart. Stay out of the way.* But she didn't—somehow, she couldn't. She gave him her hand.

"Come on," he said.

She let him guide her, up out of her chair. He wove his fingers with hers and led her into the front room. They sat down on the sofa. He wrapped his big arm around her and she let him, resting her head on his hard shoulder with a contented sigh.

It was all so…natural. Like two follows one, like night comes after day. She lifted her mouth and his was right there, waiting.

He whispered the name he'd given her. "*Reina…*"

And then his lips closed over hers.

CHAPTER NINE

Lead us not into temptation. It's simply not necessary. We know how to get there on our own.
—from The Prairie Queen's Guide to Life *by Goddess Jacks*

RIO'S KISS WAS SLOW. Exploratory. Tender.

Phoebe felt they had forever, sitting there in the hour when the morning was so new it couldn't be distinguished from nighttime. She opened for him when his tongue touched her lips and he deepened the kiss with a low, pleasured sound. She smiled against his mouth and thought that he tasted exactly as she'd expected.

Exactly the same—and completely different. There was more kindness, more sweetness, in his kiss than she had imagined.

And for her?

The heat and the hunger that drove her when she looked at him, the anger she felt, the frustration, the fear…all that was changed, somehow, tonight, at this moment. Changed not only by the tenderness he showed her, but also by what he had told her, about his mother, Maria.

About Soledad Licea.

About his birth and his name.

He stroked her hair—gentle, brushing strokes, starting at her temple, combing back and down so tenderly through the strands. And then he caught her head. His fingers, warm and sure, cupped her skull, cradling her as he drank the kiss from her willing lips.

She gave him her tongue and he sucked it, running his own tongue beneath it in a slow, wet, delicious glide, then circling it, so his tongue was on top. She moaned in excitement, a low moan that promised him everything she had sworn she would never give.

He smoothed her hair out of the way and ran the back of his hand along the side of her throat, following the stroke outward, to the curve of her shoulder—and inward. His hand closed on her breast.

She sighed in delight, opening her eyes to look at him, at his crow-black brows, at the thin, vulnerable skin of his eyelids and the silky spikes of his lashes against his tan cheeks. He seemed to know she was watching. His lashes flickered up. His eyes were so dark. A girl could get lost in them—get lost and never want to be found.

She let her head fall back, her throat stretched for him. He nipped her chin with careful teeth and he stuck out his tongue. He licked her throat. And then he nipped where he'd licked.

Phoebe moaned again. She couldn't stop herself. She moaned and he made another low sound—an answer and a promise, both at once.

And what had happened to her shirt? He had the

row of little white buttons all undone. She looked down her body, at his big, brown hand cupping her white breast in its nest of black lace.

How had this happened?

Silly question. How could it be any other way?

Oh, and it did feel so good, his touch on her breast, the warmth of his breath across her cheek, the sounds of arousal rising from her own throat. She let her head drop back once more and rolled it lazily, from side to side, feeling her hair catch and cling to the sofa, crackling with static electricity.

There was an ache now, inside her, an ache with a definite glow to it. She felt the wetness, the humid heat between her thighs and she moved, restlessly, against the sofa cushion, as Rio lowered his mouth to her breast.

She cried out at the thrill of it—his warm mouth over the barrier of lace, encompassing her nipple and the sensitive flesh surrounding it. He blew out a breath and her nipple, already hard, drew up even tighter. Between her breast and her womb, she felt that sweet thread of yearning, felt it tug and release in that magical, hot rhythm, like a secret, perfect internal dance.

His teeth found her nipple through the lace. He toyed with it and she lifted her hips, moaning out a wordless invitation. He nudged the lace aside.

His mouth closed over her bare breast.

At last…

He suckled her, slowly, as his hand stroked her belly, his thumb dipping in her navel, his fingers moving on, across the fabric of her slacks and lower. Her moan deepened as he cupped her mound, fingers sliding between her open thighs, claiming her, even through the layers of clothing she still wore.

She lifted higher, raising her hips, offering…

Everything.

All he wanted. All he could take.

All she could give.

And more…

Yes. More…

"More. Yes. More…" She said it out loud, whispered again, "More…" as he teased her breast with his teeth, as he stroked her through her clothes, cupping, then pressing, his middle finger exploring the hidden shape of her: the secret lips, the tender cleft. She raised her hips higher still, straining to be closer. He helped her, holding her, lifting her as he stroked.

She came in an instant, just shattered out of nowhere. With a hard cry, she bucked up into his cupping hand, straining as the pleasure broke and skittered outward. She tossed her head from side to side, seeing fireflies, little points of golden light, glowing in the darkness behind her shut eyes.

WHEN SHE DRIFTED BACK TO herself again, she felt him tenderly pulling the lace of her bra up over the curve of her breast. She blinked and looked down and he was buttoning her white shirt, smoothly, with one big hand, pulling the sides together, guiding the buttons through the holes with a deft movement of his third finger.

Phoebe let him finish, let him button her all up.

When he was done he looked at her and smiled his sweetest Clark Kent smile.

"You look so pretty, *Reina.* Soft and relaxed…"

She cut her eyes down again. No missing that lovely, hard bulge along his zipper. "Are we stopping? Why?"

He laughed, a low, sexy laugh. And then he tipped up her chin and brushed a light kiss on her lips. He pressed his forehead to hers. "You sure? Tonight?"

Now, why did he have to go and ask her that?

"Your hesitation says it all," he whispered. "I don't want you hesitating. I want you…" He seemed to seek the word. And found it. "Ready."

She wondered how much more ready she could get. But she didn't say it. Now he'd stopped making his own special brand of magic on her too-willing body, she was thinking all over again that this—the two of them doing the wild thing together—was a long way from a good idea.

They were partners. In Ralphie's Place. In the hunt for whoever had run Ralphie down. Did they need to be partners between the sheets, too?

For months she'd been telling herself that hot nights with temporary lovers just weren't for her anymore. And yet, here she was, rolling around on the couch with Rio, coming before he'd even gotten her pants down—not a half an hour after he'd patiently explained to her why he wasn't sticking around after his job here was done.

She put her hands on those big shoulders of his—but only to push him back so she could get her feet firmly planted on her own hardwood floor. She stood and looked down at him. "You're right. I'm not sure. I'm not ready. Maybe I'll never be."

It was a flat-out lie and they both knew it. But he didn't argue the point. He only grinned up at her, giving her one of those looks that a man gives a woman when they both know exactly what they want from each other. His dark eyes made a slow pass, from her static-wild hair, over her flushed face, down the shirt that hung loose from her pants and had a moist spot at the nipple, marking the place where his wet mouth had been. His gaze swept lower, over the swell of her hips and the line of her legs to the flats she wore on busy nights.

"We'll see," he said finally.

She could have said a hundred really sour, mean things. But she didn't. She knew she was just feeling cranky because it was late and things weren't right in her world. Because she wanted him and she didn't *want* to want him. Because *he'd* been the one to be sensible and call a halt and a man doing that can hurt a woman's pride just a tad.

Until a month ago, when Ralphie had visited the Paseo in the middle of the night and hadn't come back, she'd thought things were going so well, too....

After her dad had died, after the disaster that was her marriage to Ralphie and the end of the dream that had been the Prairie Queens—after the balls-up she'd made of her young adult life—Phoebe had pulled it together. She'd taken Ralphie's run-down bar and she'd made it into something profitable. Something kind of special. A place where there was good music and good times, a place she could be with her friends and make a living at the same time. Her own little corner of the world.

A safe place…

She looked down at Rio and she told him the truth. "What I really hate, what rags me the most, is I don't feel safe anymore in my own place, you know?"

He rose then to stand with her and he gathered her close. She let him hold her. It felt good—safe. She rested her head against his hard chest and she heard his heart beating, steady. And sure. He stroked her hair and after a minute or two, she tipped her head back.

"Stay," she said. "I have a spare room and it would make me feel better—safer, you know? To have you here, in the house."

He touched her cheek, a breath of a touch. "It's a bad time, eh, *Reina?*"

By way of answer, she shrugged. And then she whispered once more, "Stay."

CHAPTER TEN

It is a known fact that whatever hits the fan will not be evenly distributed.
—from The Prairie Queen's Guide to Life *by Goddess Jacks*

PHOEBE SLEPT TILL NOON. She woke to the smell of coffee brewing.

She pulled on some clothes and went to the kitchen, where she found Rio, barefoot and shirtless, bent at the waist, staring into the wide-open refrigerator, one big arm braced on the door. His black hair was wet and the steam from a recent shower lingered in the air—and my goodness, he did have a gorgeous back, smooth and brown and thick with muscle.

Oh, yeah. So nice to have a man around the house—even if you're not sleeping with him…

"See anything you like in there?" She went to the coffeemaker and poured herself a cup, then braced a hip against the counter and sipped. By then, he'd pulled out the eggs and a green pepper from her nearly empty crisper drawer. He'd already found the picante sauce. It was waiting on the counter.

He shut the fridge door and piled the food next to the jar of picante sauce, adding a white onion from the shallow basket on top of the microwave. "You need chorizo," he said, adding, "hot Mexican sausage," in case she didn't know.

She resisted the tasteless urge to make a really bad sausage joke. "Speak for yourself." She sipped some more. "What are we having?"

"Scrambled eggs, a little sweet pepper and onion."

"Thanks. I'd love some." She sat at the table and watched him cook, getting up when the food was ready to take down the plates and grab a pair of forks from a drawer. He dished up from the frying pan. "Good," she said, after a bite or two. He nodded and they ate in silence.

She cleared off the plates when they were finished, poured them both more coffee and sat across from him again. "So what's up for today?"

"The bar's closed, right?"

She nodded. "Sundays and Mondays."

"Then I'll finish up with a few long shots on that list you gave me, maybe spend some time on the Internet, see what I can dig up…."

"You can get your stuff from that hotel, too." She kept her voice strictly offhand. "Get settled in here."

She saw the flare of surprise in his eyes; he wasn't expecting that. When she'd asked him to stay, he hadn't realized she meant for more than just last night.

Then again, neither had she.

After a second or two, he asked the same question he'd asked the night before. "You sure?"

"No. But I got eight hours' sleep with you in my spare room. That's a first, since Ralphie died. So you can check out of your hotel, bring everything here."

He didn't answer for a moment or two. She tried not to stare at his smooth chest and amazing abs. Finally, he said, "I need a fast Internet connection."

"I've got cable on my home computer. Stop in at Best Buy and pick up one of those wireless router things." She pushed her chair back, went into the laundry room and snagged the spare key from the hook near the door, returning to set it on the table in front of him. "There's a basic alarm system. The box is inside the front door." She repeated the four-digit code.

He reached for her hand, slowly, giving her plenty of time to pull back.

Which she did. "Uh-uh," she said, shaking her head.

He only grinned. "You want to torture me a little, *Reina?*"

She grinned right back. "Oh, now. Of course not. I just want you…ready."

RIO LEFT TO GET HIS STUFF a half an hour later. Phoebe cleaned up the kitchen, made the bed, started a load of laundry and watered the ficus tree by the high window in the dining room. Then she went out and puttered around the yard for a while. She was setting the sprinkler on her patch of front lawn when her new roommate pulled back into the driveway.

He took his things in, waving her off when she asked if he needed help. A few minutes later, he reappeared, got in the car and left again.

Phoebe wandered inside—and kept going until she reached the added-on back bathroom off the laundry room. She stood in the doorway and stared at his leather shaving kit, which he'd left by the sink. That shaving kit somehow made it official: he was actually staying in her house.

Bad idea? Beyond a doubt. But he was staying and she was glad, in spite of the fact that she knew she shouldn't be.

She'd given him the back bedroom, the one off the kitchen. And what do you know? He'd left the door open.

A duffel and a backpack sat side by side on the trunk at the foot of the neatly made bed and a laptop lay flat on the desk in the corner. She didn't peek into the closet to see if he'd hung that ugly suit of his there. She wasn't that far gone. Yet.

And really, she did need to pick up a few groceries….

AT KAMP'S, IN THE DELI section, she just happened to notice that they had chorizo. So she bought some. Because he was staying at her house and her mother had brought her up to be a person who made her guests feel at home.

Yeah. Right.

Back at home, his car was in the driveway. She started to smile at the sight of it, felt like a hopeless fool, and scowled instead.

He came out of his room when she got to the kitchen, saw she was bringing in groceries and went out to get the rest. She thanked him and told him to put the bags on the table.

"Need help putting all this away?"

When she said she could handle it, he disappeared into her office room to install the router he'd bought. A half hour later, he was back in his own room, at his laptop, probably finding out all kinds of awful things about her mother and all of her friends.

Phoebe took the *Sunday Oklahoman* into the front room. Her butt had barely hit the sofa when the phone rang. It was Rose. Phoebe went into her bedroom, shut the door and told Rose that Rio was staying at her house.

"Well," said Rose with a definite snort. "That was fast."

Irritation prickled through Phoebe. Suddenly Rose had an attitude about Rio? "I didn't say I was sleepin' with him. I gave him the spare room."

Rose made a humphing sound. "Oh, well, I guess that makes everything all right, then."

Phoebe didn't get it. "Hey, what's the deal? Last week you were griping because my life is so boring, telling me all about how I need a thrill."

"So you *are* sleepin' with him."

"No. I am not."

"But you will be."

"And this is some big problem for you?"

"I'll take that as a yes, you are doin' him, or you will be soon—and no. It's not a problem for me at all. I like Rio…."

Phoebe blew out a hard breath—one she meant for

Rose to hear. "The way your voice kind of wandered off there, I'm taking that to mean there's a big ol' *but* at the end of that last sentence?"

"Oh, come on, Pheeb. He's stirring up shit. Tiff bitched about him all the way home last night, how he's always asking questions, sticking his nose into people's private lives…."

"He's trying to find out what happened to Ralphie. So am I. And until this moment, I thought you wanted to know, too."

"I *do* want to know. But the sad truth is, I don't believe we ever *will* know. Face it. The police have got nothing."

But the police did have something: that bit of red paint. Eventually, the OCPD would hear back from the FBI on that. They'd have something to go on then. She considered telling Rose and decided not to—and *that* made her heart ache. She'd always told Rose and Tiff *everything….*

Rose was still talking. "…And if the police can't figure it out, how does Rio think he can do it?"

Phoebe bit her lower lip, saw herself doing it in her dresser mirror and made herself stop. "Listen. If anyone's got a chance at finding out what happened, Rio does. And a chance is damn well good enough for me."

There was a silence on the line. Finally, Rose said, oh-so-wearily, "Phoebe."

"What?"

"You're just getting so invested in this whole thing, that's all. Throwing in with a stranger to—"

Phoebe couldn't let that pass. "Rio's not a stranger. Ralphie loved him and trusted him."

"What makes you so sure about that?"

"Ralphie left him his share in the bar, didn't he? There's no reason Ralphie would do that, not unless Rio was the son that Ralphie never had."

Another silence from Rose, then she said, "The son that Ralphie never had? Oh, puh-leese—let me guess. Rio told you that, right?"

"Yeah. So?"

"Well, and that's what you've got, isn't it? That's why you trust him. Because of what *he* told you."

"What he told me adds up."

"I'm sure you think it does. You need to think it does."

"No. That's not how it is."

"Yeah, it is."

"No, it's not—and do you know what? This conversation is goin' nowhere. I'm thinking that maybe, about now, you and me should just agree to disagree."

"Sure. Fine with me—but then there's that weird situation with the lipstick messages on the mirrors."

"What, Rose? You think Rio's the one leaving them?"

"He's not from around here. You don't know what he might do."

"Oh, well, now. That makes a whole lot of sense. He shows up in the city, opens an investigation into what happened to Ralphie—and then tries to scare *himself* off the case?"

"Okay. You're right. That makes no sense."

"Thank you."

"I told you. I *like* Rio. But I'm kind of getting that feeling, you know? The feeling that says this is a giant can of ugly worms and we don't want to go openin' it."

"And that's just what whoever wrote those messages *wants* us to feel, now isn't it? Rose. Think about it. Whoever wrote those messages is someone close, someone who's been in my office at the bar. And that could mean it's someone we know well, someone from right here in the city—someone we trust. And *that* could mean we're getting close to whoever's responsible for Ralphie's death. You want to just turn your back on that?"

"I'm only saying it's not a job for us. It's a job for the police."

"Who have gotten nowhere so far, as you so clearly pointed out a minute ago."

"Look. You loved Ralphie. I loved Ralphie. But now and then he would get himself into some weird shit. You got to watch out for weird shit, Pheeb, or you'll end up with it all over you."

RIO CAME OUT OF THE GUEST room maybe an hour later. By then, Phoebe was back on the sofa, checking the sale inserts for Dillard's and Target and trying not to get too depressed over her argument with Rose.

Rio dropped into the easy chair. "Silver, with dark shadow-gray interior." She gave him a what-are-you-talking-about look and he explained himself. "Your mother's pickup. It was silver before she had it painted."

"Didn't I tell you that?"

"Yeah, but now I've checked it for myself."

As if she hadn't known that he would. "You found that out on the Internet?"

"That's right. Using special techniques developed over years of snooping around in other people's business. Not to mention a certain Web site where I pay good money to have access to otherwise-unavailable DMV information."

The way he'd said "snooping around in other people's business" was just a little too close to Rose's recent remarks. Phoebe sent him a sharp look. "You been listening in on my phone conversations?"

His teasing expression vanished. "I wouldn't do that. Not to you."

"Seems to me you take your information wherever you can find it."

He actually looked wounded—in a noble, oh so manly, very Latin kind of way. "There are limits, *Reina.* This is your house. I'm a guest here. *And* we're partners. I don't take partners, as a rule. I'd never take one I didn't trust—and respect."

Now, see? There she was. Doing exactly what Rose had accused her of doing: believing him just because he said it was so. "Right. Like the way you trusted me when I told you the original color of my mother's pickup."

His midnight eyes turned softer—and so did his tone. "You might lie for the sake of *tu madre,* might do it for love, because you believe she's innocent and you don't want me finding out otherwise. I couldn't blame you for that. So I checked. But if I was going to invade your privacy, I'd have the good manners not to stay in your house."

Phoebe, believing him though maybe she shouldn't, made a low, grumbling sound and picked up the Target inserts.

Rio asked, "Who's telling you bad stuff about me?" She flipped through the insert. They had Tide on sale. And Biz, too… "Hey…"

She looked up from the Biz ad to meet his eyes. "That was Rose on the phone a while ago. I told her you're staying here. She wasn't thrilled over the idea. She says she likes you, but I wouldn't say she trusts you, exactly. She said Tiff was complaining that you keep sticking your nose in everybody's business."

He seemed to consider all that for a moment. Then he nodded. "*Es verdad.* What can I say?"

That you'll find out who killed Ralphie. That everything will be all right….

She tossed the insert on the coffee table. "Suddenly you're so damn philosophical."

He grew serious again. "I will never spy on you, *Reina.*"

Okay, she did believe him. Did that mean she was one of those women who couldn't tell a skunk from a house cat? Probably. "Well," she muttered. "All right. Good to know."

"I might watch you sometimes." Now his voice was rough velvet. "A man will do that. Watch a woman he wants…"

There was one of those moments. The kind with shivers in it. The kind heavy with promise.

The kind she wasn't letting spin out into dangerous territory—at least, not right now. "What else did you find while you were looking around on those special Web sites of yours?"

He shrugged. "I searched the Social Security Death Master File. Neither Darla nor Boone is dead—or at least, if they are, they didn't die since 1980. Before 1980, the list is inconclusive." He frowned. "Okay, the list is inconclusive, period. But before 1980, it's a lot more so."

"Oh, come on. They're both still breathing. We didn't need any fancy Web site to tell us that."

"My point is, people up to no good sometimes steal the social security numbers of the deceased."

"You mean, you were checking to see if they're not who they say they are?"

He nodded. "And I got no new information from the Death Master File. I checked their credit reports. Boone's got a lot of debts he hasn't paid up on. He's a bad credit risk."

"I'll keep that in mind if he ever asks me for a loan."

"Good thinking. Darla's credit report is virtually nonexistent. Boone incurred debts in both Arkansas and Texas, so that fits with the story he gave you."

"Maybe it wasn't a story. Maybe it was just the truth."

"Maybe. Darla was arrested once for shoplifting in a Little Rock department store. First offense. She didn't do any time. As far as I could find out, neither of them has ever been in prison."

"All this to say, you got nothing on either of them that you didn't already know—well, except for the shoplifting, which I'm not all that shocked about, frankly. From what Darla's told me, she hasn't had an easy life. Her daddy beat her. Often. And she had an uncle and a cousin who paid *too* much attention to her, if you know what I mean. It's not a big surprise she made a mistake or two."

Rio put up both hands. "Don't shoot me, okay? I'm only the messenger."

She cut her eyes away. "Sorry." *And don't you dare ask me to say it in Spanish....*

He rose to his feet. "I've still got a few names on that list you gave me, guys I haven't talked to yet...." Meaning he was leaving.

She forced a smile. "See you later." She picked up the Target insert again. Maybe she'd head over there. Stock up on laundry supplies...

"*Reina.*" He was still standing there, waiting for her to look up at him.

Okay, fine. "What?"

"Maybe you want to think again, eh? About me staying here. Maybe that's not such a good thing for you."

Funny. She *didn't* have to think again. Not about that. She wanted him there. "No," she said softly. "Please. Stay."

RIO DIDN'T GET BACK UNTIL after midnight. Phoebe knew when he came in. Her room was off the living room, at the front of the house, so she heard the front door open, and him working the alarm—plus, she was wide-awake, unable to sleep, as usual lately.

She considered getting up, asking him if everything was all right, if he'd learned anything new….

But why? Just because she wanted to see him, maybe touch him, maybe tease him into stealing another kiss? Or more…?

Better not. If he needed to talk to her, he'd have knocked on her door.

She turned her pillow over to the cool side and pulled the sheet a little higher with a sigh. Now he was here, nearby, she could relax a little, maybe even get some sleep….

HE MADE BREAKFAST AGAIN in the morning—chorizo and eggs.

Once they'd eaten and cleared off, as they lingered over second cups of coffee, he told her he'd managed to talk to everyone on her list. None of Ralphie's past business connections looked especially promising. For now, he was crossing them off as of "interest" in the case.

He added, sounding much too casual, "Last night around eleven, I drove by Boone's place." Boone rented a duplex over on Northeast Seventeenth. Phoebe had that sinking feeling. The one you got when the other shoe was about to drop. Rio said, "That fine old blue Volvo of your friend Tiffany's was there in front, cozied up to the curb. Around eleven-thirty, she came out, got in the car and left."

Whatever he thought he might be on to here—he wasn't. Tiff would never cheat on Dave.

He asked, "She good buddies with Boone, or something?"

She told him coolly, "Not so much Tiff and Boone, but Boone and Dave are pretty tight." She gave him a look. "So. Did you creep around in the photinia bushes, peeking in the windows?"

His gorgeous mouth hitched up in that sexy half grin of his. "Photinias? Is that what they're called? They're prickly as hell, I can tell you that much."

"See anything you shouldn't have?"

He shrugged. "All the blinds were drawn—so what are you up to today?"

"Nice save," she muttered and tried not to get all dewy-eyed over the way the morning sun slanted in the window and caught blue lights in his thick black hair. "Work."

"But you're closed, right?"

"I've still got deliveries to take, a bank drop to make, bills to pay and supply orders to approve."

"Give me a ride over there?"

A shiver went through her—and not a sexy one. "You think you need to protect me, that there will be more messages on the mirrors when I get there, or even something worse?"

He reached across the table then. She let him cover her hand with his big, warm one. "Did I say that?"

"You didn't have to."

He squeezed her hand. "I just want to pick up my bike and move it into your garage, if that's okay."

That's all? Honestly? she thought. But she didn't ask. "Sure."

"Give me a ride, then?"

She eased her fingers out from under his. "Of course."

AT THE BAR, PHOEBE PULLED around back as always and parked to the side, out of the way. Rio got out and unlocked the roll-up door. He gave it a shove. Phoebe ran in and dealt with the alarm.

When she turned and went around the old red van to the center of the shadowed garage, she found him pulling his bike up off the concrete floor.

"What happened?"

He had the bike upright by then. "Someone knocked it over." He whipped off the cover. The left mirror dangled loose from the handlebars.

Their gazes met and held. She had zero doubt they shared the same thoughts. The place had been closed yesterday and the bike had been upright when they'd left in the very early hours of Sunday morning. Nobody had called her to borrow the van or to tell her they needed to pick up something they'd left behind. That meant no one should have been in here between 3:00 a.m. or so Sunday morning and now. "Could it have just…fallen over?"

He shrugged. "Anything's possible—and it's only a broken mirror. Not a big deal."

Phoebe knew about men and their bikes. When you knocked a man's bike over, he didn't shrug and say it was no big deal. Rio was only putting a light face on this because he didn't want to spook her.

Which was great. Really. She didn't *want* to be spooked. In fact, she chose not to be. She said brightly, "Well, that's why you're moving it to my house, right? Cut down the chances for accidents."

"Right. And I'm thinking you need motion-activated cameras, at least one at each entrance—the back, the front and the side door. It takes time to review the tapes—but there'll be no need to, unless there's a problem. We can put a hidden one in your office, too. See what goes on in there when you're not around."

Cameras? She'd never seen the need for them at Ralphie's Place. Until now. "Whatever you think."

"I can get on that today."

"Great," she said, and tried to mean it. She reminded herself that she was way behind the times. Most businesses used some kind of video surveillance now.

Rio followed her inside. She was just nervous enough about what they might find there that she didn't remind him he'd only come with her to pick up his bike.

They went through the storeroom, the prep room, the two pantry-type closets and the break room. Rio did the honors. He pulled a latex glove from his back pocket, put it on and systematically opened every cabinet and door. Phoebe stood out of the way while he checked things out, her heart knocking hard against her ribs, her mind locking on the fact that he'd actually brought that glove with him, which meant he'd suspected they might be in for more trouble—the kind where you didn't want to disturb the evidence.

Wasn't this overkill? Oh, yeah. Overkill. She would think of it that way.

He found nothing. The sick, heart-pounding, adrenaline-induced dread she felt faded a little.

"The office," he said.

She led him to her office door, unlocked it, flipped on the light in there, and gestured Rio in ahead of her. She waited in the doorway as he checked the locker, the file boxes, all the drawers in her desk.

Nothing.

"The safe," he said, glancing up to catch her eye. "We should see if everything in there is the way you left it."

So she went to the hidden wall panel in the shadow of the file cabinets, eased it back and opened the safe. It looked undisturbed. Swiftly, she checked the stacks of bills and rolls of change. "It's fine. No one's been in here." She locked it back up and slid the panel into place on the wall.

"Okay," said Rio. "Let's check the front."

She was feeling almost cocky now. There was nothing suspicious here. So Rio's bike had fallen over. It just wasn't a big deal. "Rio, I have to ask. Don't you think you're going a little overboard on this?"

His smile was rueful. "Humor me."

So she let him lead the way, back up the short hall, into the prep room, through the swinging door and out into the bar area, feeling absolutely certain by then that they wouldn't find a thing. The main room looked fine, shadowed and waiting in a golden slant of morning light, chairs upended on the tables, the floor swept clean and mopped.

Nothing to be the least concerned about.

Or so she thought until she turned and got a look at the mirror behind the bar.

The words were big and bold and bloodred, each *i* dotted with a perfectly shaped heart.

Back off, bitch. Final warning.

CHAPTER ELEVEN

An itch you don't scratch just itches all the worse.
—from The Prairie Queen's Guide to Life *by Goddess Jacks*

RIO CALLED THE POLICE and somehow managed to convince the dispatcher to send someone over. It took a while for the guy—a regular beat cop in uniform—to show up, and he only said what Rio had warned Phoebe he would say: that he would file a report. The officer asked questions and wrote down the answers and made all the right noises, but Phoebe could see in his eyes that a veiled threat written in lipstick on a mirror wasn't reason enough to call in the police, who had real crimes to deal with, things like murders and robberies, rapes and assaults.

"At least there's an official report on file now," Rio said after the cop left.

Phoebe slumped in the chair she'd taken down off one of the tables. "Yeah," she said sourly. "When someone gets hurt, we'll be able to tell the cops we told them so."

For a moment, he only looked at her. His look didn't judge her, but still Phoebe felt shame. Rose had said it: when you dig around in shit, you're going to get some on you. Whining to Rio wouldn't make the shit go away.

Finally, he said, "I've been giving these threats some thought…."

Somehow, she didn't like the sound of that. "And?"

He lifted a chair down, flipped it onto its legs and sat in it backward, hard thighs spread. "We could play this differently."

She eyed him warily. "How?"

"You could pull back, disassociate yourself from me. Tell everyone you're fed up with me, you don't think I'm getting anywhere, you don't think any of this is worth it, whatever. I'll move back to the hotel and you're out of it. Let me take whatever heat comes down. Let whoever left those messages believe that they worked. They scared you off."

She folded her hands in her lap and looked down at them. "No."

He said his name for her, so softly, *"Reina…"*

After a moment, she made herself lift her head and face him. "Nobody's scaring me off. This is my place and Ralphie was my friend. I'm in. And I'm staying in." He started to speak. She put up a hand. "Don't, okay?"

"Don't what?"

"Ask me if I'm sure. I am sure. And whatever happens, no matter how much I grumble and moan about how I hate what's going on around here, I'm not changing my mind."

RIO TOOK HIS BIKE TO THE house and got his car and his equipment. He was back in twenty minutes, snapping pictures and dusting up the mirror the way he had the time before.

Then he went out and bought the surveillance cameras and the recording equipment. He took the afternoon to install them. Once they were in, he showed Phoebe how to work everything.

That night, Rio took her out to dinner in Bricktown, the old warehouse district, renewed and revived in the past couple of decades so it was now a thriving tourist attraction and the hub of OKC night life. They went to Chelino's, always a favorite of Phoebe's, and sat out on the balcony over the canal and watched the colors of twilight turn the wide prairie sky a thousand shades of orange and purple. They drank margaritas, shared a basket of chips, and ordered chili verde burritos.

It was...nice, everything so peaceful and normal, as if they were just a guy and a girl getting out for an evening, enjoying each others' company, as if simple mutual attraction had brought them together, rather than the sudden, brutal death of a man they'd both loved.

By tacit agreement, they kept the conversation light, discussing harmless things, like the mild weather and the Oklahoma Redhawks, who played at Bricktown Ballpark nearby.

They got back to the house around ten.

Inside the door, she turned to him. She looked into those tempting dark eyes and she wanted...his arms around her, his lips on hers, to sink into his touch, let the pleasure close over her, blocking out everything.

And then, the next morning…what?

"Maybe not," she said in a whisper.

He understood. "Good night, *Reina. Sueños dulces.* Sweet dreams."

So instead of wild, hot, forget-everything sex, Phoebe treated herself to a long, lazy soak in the tub in the main bathroom. When she'd finished with her bath, she climbed into bed, grabbed the novel she'd been trying to get into since Ralphie's death and read herself to sleep.

RIO WENT WITH HER TO THE bar again the next day. Phoebe had that sick, heart-pounding feeling all the way over there. But when they let themselves in, they found everything as it should be: nothing knocked over or broken, no bloodred messages scrawled on the mirrors.

Boone arrived shortly after they did.

"I notice we're all under surveillance," he joked, tipping his head back toward the loading area where Rio had installed one of his motion-activated video cameras.

Rio told him about what they'd found the day before.

"Damn," said Boone. "This is getting beyond it. When we catch the dickhead who's doing this, I want fifteen minutes alone with him before you get your turn."

Rio added with a noncommittal shrug, "*I*'s dotted with hearts again."

Boone swore some more. "That's the worst. Whoever this jerkwad is that's messin' with our minds, he's got to try and make it look like he's my little sister? On second thought, fifteen minutes alone with him is no way long enough."

Rio said, "You sound pretty sure it's a guy."

Boone's grin was not a cheerful one. "Okay, if it's a woman, fifteen minutes'll do it."

THE REST OF THE DAY AND evening, Rio was in and out. He was around when Darla came in for a four-hour shift at two. He helped her check stock, getting up on the step stool to reach the highest shelves for her, moving boxes around so she could get to stuff in back.

Phoebe knew that Ralphie's widow still topped Rio's list of suspects, yet he treated her with a careful, patient sort of kindness. Phoebe wondered about that at first, but then she remembered the things he'd said about his mother. Maria Navarro would have been the kind of mama who made sure her son learned to show a pregnant woman respect.

Every time Phoebe just happened to pass through the storage areas, she heard Darla giving Rio orders.

It was "Get that out of my way." And "Move that over there." And "I can't get up there. You do it." Darla wasn't smiling, either. She never once said *please.* She made it very clear that she had no problem letting Rio do the heavy lifting—but she didn't like him and she wouldn't trust him as far as she could throw a full-size party keg.

When Darla left, Rio wandered out to the bar area and over to where Phoebe was clearing off a table.

She piled the dirty glasses on a bar tray before pausing to look up at him.

He said, "Darla just left."

Phoebe straightened and glanced at her watch: 6:05. Right on time. Darla's short shift ended at six. "Okay. So?"

"She's driving that red convertible of hers."

Phoebe picked up the tray of dirty glasses. "What are you getting at, Rio?"

He raked a hank of silky black hair back from his forehead. "She's so…big, that's all. She could have that baby any minute now. A woman in that condition shouldn't be driving." Dark brows drew together. "Should she?"

He looked so very male at that moment. So perplexed and concerned—and so completely out of his depth.

Phoebe hid her woman's smile as she turned for the bar. "It's okay. Really. She's only driving short distances." She glanced back and paused when she saw that he was still standing there by the table where she'd left him, his frown deeper than before.

He said, "I think someone should drive her."

Phoebe set the tray on the bar. Bernard, who'd relieved Boone not long before, set to work emptying it as she returned to Rio's side. "Listen." She kept her voice down. They had several customers, including Purvis, Andy and Dewey, hardcore afternoon regulars who'd been there the day Rio had come to town and who always showed way too much interest in what went on at Ralphie's Place—and in Phoebe herself. "Darla's had a normal pregnancy," she told Rio. "It's perfectly safe for her to drive herself around town. Plus, it's good for her to know she can get herself around, not to have to count on other people for every little thing."

He hadn't stopped frowning. "You think so?"

"Absolutely." A woman at a table a few feet from where they stood signaled that she wanted another round for her and her girlfriends. Phoebe gave her a smile. "Right away."

Rio, still looking doubtful, turned and wandered off through the door to the back again. Phoebe returned to the bar and ordered the drinks. Purvis, Andy and Dewey, holding down stools along the far end, were looking her way.

She garnished the drinks as Bernard set them up. "Okay, whatever it is, you guys just go right ahead and get it off your chest."

"That there's the Hells Angel from a week ago, inn't it?" Andy's giant Adam's apple worked as he sipped his beer.

Phoebe sighed and shook her head. "He's my partner, remember?"

Purvis had his mouth pinched up. "I do believe someone said he was livin' with you."

"He's staying at my place, yeah," she corrected him sweetly. "Temporarily."

Dewey sucked on his cigarette. "Well. At least he got himself a haircut…"

FOR THE REST OF THE WEEK, Rio went with Phoebe to the bar every day. No more sinister messages appeared.

Final warning, that last one had read. Well. Maybe so. Or maybe the cameras Rio had installed were doing the job, keeping the culprit at bay for fear of discovery.

Rio continued to dig for clues. He was shameless about pumping any and everyone for information. Rose complained some more and so did Tiff.

Darla griped that she'd rather lift the heavy boxes herself, "than have that big Mexican there beside me every dang moment, making my skin crawl with knowin' he's just waiting for me to see the light and admit that I drove out to the Paseo on April fifteenth and ran the man I love down in the street—which I did not."

Phoebe asked her friends to please just cooperate. That didn't go down with any of them too well. They were getting pretty tired of being constantly on the hot seat.

At the house, Rio and Phoebe were careful with each other. They came home from the bar at night and they went to their separate rooms. There were no stolen kisses, no dangerous moments when the heat between them threatened to catch fire. No such moments…

And there weren't going to be.

After a lot more serious thought than was strictly necessary, Phoebe had decided she wasn't going there, after all. No way. The more she considered their situation, the more certain she became that it would be a seriously bad idea for her and Rio to hook up.

Did Rio think so, too? No way for her to know. She certainly had no intention of asking him.

But yeah. It did kind of get to her, having him close by all the time and constantly reminding herself not to touch.

Goddess called on Friday morning while Phoebe and Rio were at the breakfast table. "Did you notice? It's been six days since you talked to your mama. You *could* pick up the phone."

"Sorry," Phoebe said, feeling guilty. She should have called and she knew it. "It's just been *so* crazy...." It hadn't, not really. Not since Tuesday morning and the last message on the mirror. But too bad. When a daughter fails to call her mother, she has to say *something.*

"Rose tells me you got Rio livin' with you."

See, now? There. Why call? Why volunteer to try responding to remarks like that? She carefully avoided looking at the man across the table. "We're roommates, Mama."

"You are thirty years old, baby."

"Did you think I'd forgotten?"

"I *mean* that you are long past the age when it's your mama's business who you've got in your bed."

"Well, how nice of you to realize that."

"I'm glad he's there, glad he's lookin' out for you."

"Great."

"I *told* him to look out for you."

"Gee, Mama. Have I got a choice here? I think I'd

rather have you deciding who I sleep with." Rio arched an eyebrow at her. She pretended not to see. "I can look after myself just fine."

"Don't be sarcastic, now, darlin'. It's just not all that feminine. Put him on, will you? I need a few words with him…."

So Phoebe passed the phone to Rio. She watched him talk to her mother, watched that little half smile come and go on his fine mouth, admired the breadth of his shoulders and the dark male beauty of his face….

What was it her mother always said? An itch you don't scratch just itches all the worse….

Rio said goodbye, set the phone down and picked up his fork. "*Tu madre* had a dream."

"Yeah. Her and Martin Luther King."

He looked at her reproachfully and speared up a bite of scrambled eggs. "You feeling kind of edgy, *Reina?*"

She ignored the question. "Okay. My mother had a dream about…?"

"In the dream, she and Ralphie were playing table soccer."

"Foosball, you mean?"

"Yeah. Table soccer. Ralphie won. He looked up from the table and winked at your mother and said, 'Tell Rio it's a problem of storage.'" Rio forked up more eggs.

Phoebe watched him take two more bites before prompting, "And?"

"That's all." He gulped some coffee.

"Wow. That was…really helpful."

"Hey. I'll take a tip wherever I can get it."

IT WAS A RED-LETTER morning.

For the first time that week, Rio let Phoebe go to Ralphie's Place alone. He told her he would spend the day coming at the situation from a different angle, that she should call him right away if there were any problems.

"What angle?"

"I'll let you know if anything pans out. Just remember—"

"I know, I know. If there's a problem, call."

But there weren't any problems. The day went along like any other Friday, kind of slow in the early afternoon, but picking up by happy hour. And by eight at night, when the band, a great retro-rock group, GreenWave, launched into their first set, there wasn't an empty seat in the place.

Phoebe had Rose and Tiff and two other waitresses to help her, with both Boone and Bernard behind the bar. Even with a full crew, it was a lot to handle. Customers stood at the tables, clapping, dancing in place, shouting out lyrics whenever the lead singer threw them a cue: a good night. And a profitable one, too. The bank drop tomorrow would be a fat one.

Rio arrived at midnight. Phoebe spotted him through the crowd. Their eyes met. The usual naughty thrill went cascading through her, just from catching sight of him. She sent him a smile and a hopeful look. He shook his head.

So much for that different angle, apparently. She forged on through the press of customers with a tray full of drinks to serve.

A little later, she noticed he was down at the end of the bar, in the corner near the door to the back room, talking to Dave, who'd come in with Tiff and hung around to hear the band. Rio must have said something Dave didn't like, because Dave leaned in on him, got right up in Rio's face. Scowling, Dave gestured with both hands. The band was so loud, Phoebe couldn't hear what Dave said, but she had a very strong feeling there was about to be trouble. Dave went on gesturing, talking fast, looking furious, but Rio just stood there. He seemed so calm, completely unaffected. Finally, Dave spun on his heel and stalked away, shoving people aside as he went.

"Hey. Waitress!" a guy right beside her yelled to be heard over the pounding, high-decibel throb of the band.

Phoebe went back to work. Whatever had happened between Dave and Rio, at least it hadn't turned into a brawl. And right then, she had no time to look into the problem.

The band finished their final set at five to one. The place was still full of customers partying down. They played the jukebox, loud, all the hardest-rocking old-time artists: the Stones and Bob Seger, ZZ Top and Led Zeppelin. They all stomped and danced and sang along to great classic hard-driving numbers: "Sharp Dressed Man" and "You Can't Always Get What You Want," "Night Moves" and "Whole Lotta Love."

At one-forty-five Phoebe took her old acoustic Martin from the back, turned the spotlight on the stage again, got up there and announced, "This is it, folks. It's been great. Thanks for comin' and… last call."

It happened like it always did on nights like that one, when it all came together so fine and everyone was rockin' and no one wanted to go home yet.

Someone yelled out, "Hey, Phoebe. Sing us a song."

And the others picked up the call. "Come on, Phoebe…."

"Sing for us."

"Yeah. We see that guitar."

"Yeah. Come on…"

"Sing us a song."

"Rock it!" yelled some guy from back in the corner.

Phoebe laughed. "Uh-uh," she said to the guy in the back. "This'll be a slow one. Slow. And sweet…"

The guy whistled and stomped and a few other yahoos joined in. Phoebe waited. She'd always known how to work a crowd.

In no time, the whistling faded off and there was silence in Ralphie's Place—except for the whisper of swift feet across the floor as Tiff and Rose and the other two waitresses took the orders for last call.

Phoebe slid the strap over her head and cradled the old guitar. It felt good there, the way it always had. Her only baby, coming home. She didn't play enough anymore. As a rule, she didn't have the heart for it.

But sometimes, on a night like this one…

It was right.

It was okay.

She spoke into the mike again, using the husky voice

audiences always loved. "This one's for Ralphie." A smattering of applause. Someone said, "Oh, yeah…"

When the silence found the room again, Phoebe repeated, "For Ralphie—and his wife, Darla Jo."

She strummed the first chord and the song took over.

It was one of Ralphie's favorites, from all those years ago. That old Springsteen song about a wedding, about lovers matching step to stay together, about one dying and the other, left behind.

She sang it slow and she sang it sweet, just like she used to, back in the day, sang about the beautiful river and the valley below, about a vow to keep till death and beyond.

When it was over, as the last chord faded away, Phoebe smiled, dashed a couple of stray tears from her eyes and told them all, "That's it."

They clapped and they stomped their feet, they whistled and yelled. She stood there and waited, until they settled down. Then Bernard, who knew the routine, did a slow fade with the spotlight.

Phoebe came down off the stage.

Within fifteen minutes, the place was empty, except for the waitresses and bartenders cleaning up. Phoebe was just sliding a tray full of empties onto the bar when Tiff slammed in through the swinging door from the back. She marched right over to Phoebe, grabbed her arm and hissed in her face.

"Rio's beating the crap out of Dave. You get out back this instant and drag that big beaner of yours off my boyfriend!"

CHAPTER TWELVE

Some guys are just begging for it—and by "it"
I don't mean a long night of good lovin'.
—from The Prairie Queen's Guide to Life *by Goddess Jacks*

PHOEBE RACED OUT BACK, Tiff and the others at her heels, to find Dave crouched in a boxer's stance in the clear space next to the old red van. Blood trickled from his nose and over his mouth and chin as he circled Rio. Rio, so far uninjured, wasn't doing much of anything that Phoebe could see, except turning in the center of the clear space as Dave circled him.

"Stop him," shouted Tiff. "Phoebe, make him stop."

Phoebe took a crack at it. "Okay, you guys. Knock it off."

"Be glad to," said Rio, still turning as Dave, making jabbing boxer moves with every step he took, continued to circle. "Dave," Rio said patiently. "What do you say, man? Let's give it up."

Dave punched the air and tossed his head. Blood flew. "No way, you spic motherfu—"

"Uh-uh," Rio warned, shaking a finger. "Don't go saying bad things about my mother."

That did it for Dave. He came out of his crouch with a shout of pure outrage, ejecting himself straight at Rio—who danced lightly aside. Dave, flying forward, failed to put on the brakes. He collided with the passenger door of the van. Metal crunched.

Dave staggered back, cradling his now-bloody fist, swearing a blue streak as Bernard whistled and remarked, "Now, *that's* gotta hurt…."

Tiff grabbed Phoebe's arm again, whipping her around so her back was to Rio and Dave. "Damn it, do something!" she screeched. "Make Rio stop. Do something *now*…."

Phoebe yanked her arm free. "Tiff, what the hell? Rio's not the one who—"

"Yeah, he is! This is all his damn fault, showin' up here out of nowhere, getting everyone stirred up, digging around in stuff that's got nothing to do with him…."

Phoebe felt a scary tightness in her chest. "What are you saying, Tiff?"

Tiff gaped at her blankly, then shouted again, "Stop him!"

"Tiff, have you got something to do with what happened to Ralphie?"

"Ralphie." Tiff blinked, her eyes unfocused, her face blotchy with rage. "It's always about Ralphie with you, lately. Hello, hello. Ralphie is *dead* and it was a simple hit-and-run and you are never going to find out who the damn fool was that killed him—and no, of course not. I had nothin' to do with it. How can you ever think that I…" Tiff didn't finish. She let out a cry instead and threw out a hand. "Look! Just look at them."

Behind her, Phoebe heard a heavy male grunt. She jerked around to face the action as Dave tackled Rio and they actually connected.

They went down, clasped together, and rolled on the concrete. The punching started. Phoebe winced at the heavy thuds as fists hit flesh.

Tiff was still hollering, "Stop them! Make them stop!"

"Stop it, you guys," Phoebe shouted. "Stop it now…."

The two on the floor ignored her. They rolled, paused, delivered a few punches, rolled some more, ran into the big door, which clanged and rattled, rolled again, traded more blows. As they struggled, they made all the wordless, painful noises men always make when they're fighting.

It was "Oof, agh, ungh, arrr…"

Phoebe turned to her two bartenders. "You guys get in there and stop them."

Bernard backed up a step. "No way…"

Boone shook his head. "Uh-uh. No, thanks…"

"You damn useless…dickwads!" Tiff shrieked.

"Tiff," scolded Boone, shaking his head. "Be nice…."

Tiff let out a cry of frustrated fury and grabbed an old pool cue with the rubber tip missing that someone had propped against the garage wall.

"Tiff. Don't!" cried Rose, who stood back near the inside door with the two other waitresses. Tiff ignored her.

Phoebe pleaded, "Tiff. No..."

Tiff sent her a killing look and waded in.

Rio was on top right then. Tiff raised the pool cue and set to beating him about the shoulders and head.

"Hey!" Rio ducked away from the blows, taking his attention off his opponent—and giving Dave the upper hand.

Dave claimed the top position and started punching at Rio. By then, Tiff was so far gone in her fury that she didn't care who she hit. She started beating on Dave, shrieking, "You stop it, I told you. Stop it, stop it, stop it, I said...."

The pool cue snapped as Tiff delivered a blow to Dave's shoulder. The broken part went flying toward the knot of cocktail waitresses over by the door. They ducked in unison and the foot or so of cue end hit the door, bounced off and rolled under the van.

About then, Rio and Dave stopped fighting and scooted apart to escape the endless battering from Tiff's broken cue. Tiff hit Dave a few more times, paused, shook her head, blinked, and finally seemed to realize she was whupping her own boyfriend.

She was a sight. Her hair hung in her eyes, and all the buttons on her shirt had popped open, revealing her cute little flowered push-up bra and the round swells of her breasts, shiny with sweat now, and heaving with each agitated breath she took.

Dave put up an arm to protect his face just in case

she took it into her head to hit him again. "Tiff? Damn. You crazy?"

Tiff threw her head back and shrieked at the ceiling. Then she lowered her gaze and homed in on Rio. A low, growling sound came from her throat.

"Tiff," said Phoebe, sharply.

But Tiff didn't seem to hear her. She stepped over Dave, pool cue raised and kept walking until she stood above Rio. She raised the broken cue again. Rio caught it as it whistled down.

For a moment, Tiff gripped the end of that cue in a white-knuckled fist, her arm shaking with the hopeless effort to break Rio's stronger hold. Her lips drew back from her teeth and she growled some more.

And then, in an instant, the fight went out of her. She let go of the cue and stepped back, raking her hair off her forehead, making a lost kind of whimpering sound, her shoulders drooping, head hung low. With a tiny cry of pure dismay, she stared down at her open shirt. Tiff had always been the modest type. Standing around in a garage full of people with her shirt wide open just wasn't her style.

"Oh, Tiff…" Phoebe moved in to help.

But Tiff threw out both hands. "No. Uh-uh. You stay away from me, Pheeb. I don't need you. I don't need anything from you…."

Rose stepped forward then. "I'll talk to her."

Phoebe, aching inside, moved back. And Rose approached the wild-eyed Tiff. "It's okay," Rose chanted softly. "Okay, hon, all right…" Tiff whimpered and moaned as Rose buttoned her up and smoothed her hair.

Finally, Tiff turned to Dave, who was sitting up on the floor by then, head hanging between his spread knees. "Oh, Dave…" She struggled free of Rose's comforting arms and staggered over to him. "Dave?" Dropping to a crouch beside him, she reached out her arms. With a groan, Dave sagged against her and she gathered him in, cooing, "Aw, honey, oh, baby…" as Dave's sweat and blood smeared the front of her white shirt. She clutched him close, rocking him like a child, stroking his sweaty hair—and lifting her furious gaze to look daggers at Phoebe. "This is what you get, Pheeb. This is what happens, when you turn on your *real* friends for a little hot action with some slick, nosy operator, some stranger you just met."

Phoebe knew if she answered Tiff right then, she'd say something she'd always regret. So she sucked in a long breath, let it out slowly, and turned to Rio, who had already pulled himself to his feet. "Okay. What's going on?"

"It's about *him,*" Tiff screeched. "It's about—"

Phoebe whirled on her—and shut her up with a look. She waited. Tiff, mouth quivering, glared, but said no more. Phoebe turned back to Rio. "Well?"

Rio used his arm to wipe blood from a cut on his forehead. "When I first came in tonight, I tried to talk to Dave."

Dave swore and muttered from the circle of Tiff's cradling arms, "There's no law says I have to talk to you, asshole."

Rio spoke wryly. "Dave told me no. After that, every

time I'd turn around, there was Dave. So I'd move away. Then, a few minutes ago, he followed me into the back."

Phoebe asked, "So you hit him?"

"No. I told him that if he didn't want to talk to me, I'd appreciate it if he'd quit following me around. He threw a punch, back there, in the storeroom. He missed. That was when I suggested we ought to take it out here."

Dave jerked free of Tiff's tight embrace. "He's got no right to question me. Who the hell is he? Movin' in here, actin' like he owns the place."

"I do own the place," Rio said.

Phoebe qualified, "Half of it, anyway."

"Yeah," sneered Tiff. "And, Pheeb, you act like that's okay with you. Some guy you never met in your life until two weeks ago, some guy who got half of the place that you built up from nothin'. He's got you wrapped around his finger, Pheeb. You gotta face that he does. You're not thinking straight about the way things are, not lately, not since *he* moved in on you. You're so hot for him, you don't care what—"

"Enough." Phoebe looked at Tiff. A long look. Finally, she asked, "You through?" Tiff turned her eyes away. And Phoebe tried again. "I just want to know what happened. Now, tonight. That's all."

Dave mumbled, "It was like *he* said."

"How?"

"Well, he pisses me off, always after everybody, always nosing around, always dragging people into that office of yours for a little private interrogation. I told him I wasn't going to tell him shit. And then I had a couple more drinks and…it all just kind of got to me, the way that guy won't leave it alone. I followed him into the storeroom, just like he said. I threw a punch at him there. Then we came out here. You know the rest."

"And you know the rules, Dave," Phoebe said regretfully. "You start a fight in Ralphie's Place, you don't come back."

"What?" Tiff jumped to her feet, her face flushed a hot pink, her slender body shaking with fury. "You're kickin' Dave out…for good?"

Phoebe looked in her lifelong friend's eyes and… she just couldn't do it. Couldn't hold the line that tight. "Okay." She forced a smile for Dave. "At least you waited until after hours—and you took it out here." Thanks to Rio, not to Dave. But there was no need to put too fine a point on it. "So let's say a couple of weeks, all right? And when you come back, check your attitude at the door."

Tiff was not mollified. "That cuts it," she announced, more furious than ever. "That cuts it clean. If Dave doesn't come in here, neither do I."

Phoebe turned to her friend again. "Well, Tiff. Okay." Her heart ached to do it, but she felt she'd backed down as far as she could go. "I guess you'll be taking a couple weekends off, then."

Tiff's mouth was trembling again. Phoebe could see the tears pooling in those blue eyes. "Fine. You know what? Maybe I'll never come back."

"Tiff—"

"Uh-uh. Don't talk. Listen. You don't want us here? Fine. Me and Dave, we're gone. For good."

CHAPTER THIRTEEN

Look at it this way, darlin'. Wild, uninhibited sex won't solve your problems. But it *will* improve your complexion, step up your circulation and do wonders for your attitude. Having great sex not only feels good while you're doing it. It's also a way to ensure you'll be at your best, wearing a winning smile, lookin' on the sunny side when your life is going all to hell.
—*from* The Prairie Queen's Guide to Life *by Goddess Jacks*

RIO GOT BACK TO THE house before Phoebe did. He took a quick shower in the small back bathroom she'd assigned to him, wrapped a towel around his waist and opened the bathroom door to let the steam out.

He heard her come in, tracked the sounds of her footsteps moving lightly across the hardwood floors, going through the living room, the dining room, the kitchen. He could so easily have reached out an arm and swung the door to the laundry room closed.

But he didn't.

She appeared in the doorway behind him. He met

her angry eyes in the bathroom mirror as she folded her arms beneath those fine breasts of hers, leaned in the doorway and watched him put a butterfly bandage on the small cut at his jaw.

"Hey, *Reina*." He winced as he pressed the cut a little too hard. Then he waited, for her to speak, say *hey* in return, or even to call him a bad name. She didn't. She said nothing. So he shrugged. "That Tiff." He squeezed a little antibiotic cream on a finger and dabbed at the split-open spot on his forehead where the pool cue had come down. "She's a mean one when she gets mad."

Phoebe's pretty mouth tightened. He knew she was swallowing harsh words. She broke eye contact, her gaze moving to his back, lingering there for a moment too long, before she caught herself—and met his eyes again. "Believe it or not," she said, her voice trying hard to be offhand and not quite managing it, "Tiff's a true romantic."

He flicked on the water. "Yeah?"

"Yeah." She looked down at her shoes and then back up at him. He watched her watching him as he wet a washcloth and dabbed at the cut on his chin where blood still oozed on either side of the bandage. She added, "She married Ralphie. You know how that went. And she married again. Big disaster. In between and since, there were other guys. Each one was supposed to be *the* one. She really wants that. One special guy to spend her life with…"

"Like all women."

She gave him a cool look. "Believe it or not, some

women are perfectly happy all on their own. Or with just their kids. Or with other women…"

He couldn't resist asking, "What about you, *Reina?*"

"I told you about me. I'm looking for a nice, steady guy. But in the meantime, I like my life just fine the way it is."

"And Tiff doesn't." He rinsed the blood-smeared washcloth, wrung it out and turned to hang it over the shower door, adding, "Tiffany Sweeney needs that special guy…."

"That's right."

He turned and faced her fully. "And since she hasn't got that guy, she beats men with pool cues?"

She stiffened. "I didn't say that." He resisted the need to take a step toward her. She wasn't ready for him coming at her in only a towel. He watched as she forced a shrug. "Tiff's…a little bit desperate, that's all. It can happen when a true romantic gets close to thirty and her own private Prince Charming is nowhere in sight. Maybe she…settles."

"For a guy like Dave?"

"Yeah. And up till now, things have gone pretty well with her and Dave. She doesn't want to lose him."

Rio recalled that day at the body shop, how out of place Tiff had looked there. "Maybe she should think about whether Dave is a guy worth keeping. Maybe she's better than Dave."

Phoebe made a rough noise in her throat. "You want to try and tell her that?"

"Not my job."

"Oh. Well. All right, then. I get it. You're full of suggestions—but the dirty work is up to me."

He spoke gently. *"Lo siento, mi reina."*

She blew out a breath. "Sorry for what?"

"To make trouble between you and your friends."

"My friends…" She shook her head. "If you'd told me a few weeks ago that the day was comin' when Tiff wouldn't be speaking to me, I would have called you a stone liar—or an ignorant fool."

"She'll get over it."

"Easy for you to say." Her eyes were so sad, suddenly. "Rio?"

"Yeah?"

"It's…someone I've trusted, isn't it? No matter how much Tiff keeps insisting it was only an accident, something that just *happened* because some drunk wasn't paying attention, it wasn't any garden-variety hit-and-run. It was…someone who hangs out at Ralphie's Place, someone who works for me. Or someone I call a friend. Maybe Tiff herself. Or Darla or even Rose. Or Dave or Boone or Bernard…" A shudder went through her. "I hate that. I hate that so much…."

He sought the words to soothe her. All he came up with was "We've got no proof of anything, *Reina.* It's still wide open."

She wasn't soothed. "No, it's not. If it was wide open, you wouldn't be hanging around the bar every day, watching for Ralphie's killer to mess up and betray himself. Uh-uh. You see what I see. They're all way too stirred up about it, about you. If they didn't have secrets, stuff they have to hide, they'd be helping you, not on me all the time to get you to back off, not picking fights with you…" Her voice faded away and she waited. For him to agree with her.

He did agree, but saw no need to rub it in.

She prodded, "Go ahead. Say it. Tell me I'm right. You know that I am."

But he only shrugged and let the silence happen, let it soften the distance between them. Finally, he said, "Your song was beautiful tonight. *Muy dulce.* So sweet…"

She tightened her arms around her middle and glared at him. "Yeah, right. So sweet. So sweet that you immediately went out back and beat the crap out of Dave."

He turned to the mirror again, granting her the continued illusion that they were just talking, that there was nothing else going on here. Bracing his hands on the sink rim, he worked his jaw back and forth. It was tender, yeah. But nothing serious. In a few days, he'd be good as new.

He reminded her, "Dave wanted to fight me. I tried to back out of it. You were there. You saw. Sometimes, there's no stopping a man…." He was talking about more than a fight. But he didn't think she realized that.

Not yet.

She hadn't put it together that he'd left the bathroom door open on purpose, that he'd wanted her to come to him. Talk to him.

Maybe yell at him a little.

Maybe something more…

He'd been keeping his distance from her, as a man.

Because he knew that it would be better, for both of them, if this hot thing between them went no further than it already had. He'd respected her wariness after that night last week, he'd taken her cues and kept his hungry hands off.

But tonight…

Well, tonight things had gotten pretty out of control. Though the fight was over, Rio's senses still hummed: a low, insistent adrenaline buzz. It was nice. Like a bad drug that felt so good, a drug that whispered through his veins, urging him to do the things he really wanted to do: to touch, to taste, to take…

He thought of Soledad, her beautiful face, her fragrant auburn hair. Phoebe and Soledad, so different. And yet so much the same.

Strong and good and loyal to the core.

After Soledad, he'd thought he'd learned his lesson. The good women he wanted deserved more than he could ever give them—a safe life, a life free of the danger loving him could bring them.

And then…

There was Phoebe. And inside him, hope and desire were stirring again.

The hope? He could deny that. He could remind himself that whatever happened between them, it wouldn't be permanent. In the end, he'd go back to L.A. And she'd stay here, in the world she had known for all of her life.

The desire, though? Uh-uh. Against his desire for the woman in the doorway, denial was a weak dam destined to break.

She said, "I know that Dave came after you. Strictly speaking, it wasn't your fault." Her green eyes snapped with accusation. "Still, you could have kept that fight from happening."

"No. I couldn't. Not after he tried to hit me and I got him a good one right in the nose. After that, Dave was bound to mix it up with me. His pride wouldn't let him have it any other way."

"Well. Before that, then…"

"No."

"Yeah."

"*Reina.* Some things are destiny." He held her eyes in the mirror. "Some things are bound to happen. You can put them off, maybe, for another hour, another day. But you can't deny them forever."

Again, her gaze skittered away. "Tiff got you a good one," she muttered, staring hard at the stack of towels on the shelf above the toilet, "from your right shoulder blade down at a diagonal, to the middle of your back…"

He laughed, low. "Oh, yeah. I can feel it."

Her glance strayed his way, but she carefully avoided looking right at him. She frowned at his back. "Like a whip mark, angry. Red…"

He picked up the tube of antibiotic cream and gave her a questioning look.

Her body swayed toward him—but she caught herself and settled against the door frame again. "What happened today, that other 'angle' you said you were trying?"

He turned, slowly, and dared to face her a second

time. "I went back for another visit with some of those business associates of Ralphie's. I was hoping to dig up a reason why he was in the Paseo that night…."

"And?"

"Nada."

She swore, low. "Great." Her arms dropped to her sides as she pushed away from the door frame. "Give me that." He held out the tube. She moved in closer and took it from him, her fingertips whispering across his palm. "Turn around."

He obeyed and watched her reflection, her dark head tipped down, her hair, which she'd pinned back before going to work, coming loose in little curls at her temples and along her smooth cheeks. She squeezed the cream onto a finger, looked up, saw he was watching, broke the glance quickly and focused on his back. Her finger, light and so gentle, traced the diagonal mark from his shoulder, and down.

It felt so good, her touch. So right.

And much too brief.

Too soon, she was reaching around him, setting the uncapped tube on the sink rim. "Better put the lid on that."

He caught her arm before she could back away. "Don't go…."

She froze. He was sure she'd jerk free—but no. She stepped in that fraction closer, so her slim body brushed his.

"Stay," he whispered and she tipped her head back, challenge lighting her eyes. He breathed in—breathed *her*.

She asked in a harsh whisper, "What? You ready now?"

His throat had locked up tight and a shiver of anticipation snaked up his spine. Beneath the towel at his hips, his dick leaped to attention. Somehow, he managed a nod.

"Let go," she commanded low.

He opened his fingers wide, but kept his open palm pressing the smooth flesh of her arm as he waited for her to step back.

She didn't. She held her ground, her eyes daring him. So he slid his palm up the soft, firm flesh of her arm, stroking his way over the curve of her shoulder, and up along that fine, white neck. With a finger, he guided a stray curl to curve behind her ear.

And then he waited. It was her move.

She made it, reaching up a hesitant hand to touch the cut on his jaw, and after that, to trace the red line at his forehead where Tiff had hit him. "What a mess…" He knew she referred to more than his scrapes and bruises.

His turn…

He cradled the side of her head and let his fingers inch back, finding the pins that held up that thick, silky hair. He pulled them free and let them drop to the floor.

The dark waves fell to her shoulders. He combed them, fingers sliding through the strands, as she laid both palms flat against his bare chest.

"There," she said, almost smiling. "I feel it. A definite heartbeat. You're human, after all."

He bent for a kiss.

She gave him one—a quick, angry one. And then she craned her head back, warm palms pressing against his chest.

He asked, *"¿Qué, Reina?"* just as she slipped down a hand, got hold of his towel and whipped it away.

CHAPTER FOURTEEN

All women look the same in the dark. What idiot said that? Some fool with bad night vision, I'll bet.
—from The Prairie Queen's Guide to Life *by Goddess Jacks*

PHOEBE GLANCED DOWN between them—and then back up at him. She smiled then, a real smile. "You're right. You *are* ready. And may I just say…wow."

He took her by the shoulders. So fine—her soft skin, the slender bones beneath… "You think you're pretty damn smart."

"Oh, yeah."

He stared at her mouth. There was not a more tempting mouth *en todo el mundo:* in the whole of the world. It hurt him, to look at that mouth of hers, hurt in the way that all great pleasure brings pain. Since his first sight of her, in that dress with the roses and those sexy sandals with the mile-high heels, he'd wanted her. It was a need that had only got stronger while they'd both played the yo-yo game: knowing they would; pretending they wouldn't.

And now, tonight…

To hell with the games. Fuck denial. Life was too short and tonight was *their* night.

His dick gave a jump—for joy, more or less. She blinked at the feel of it tapping her belly and grinned all the wider.

He suggested a lot more calmly than he felt, "Since you took my towel, I think you better kiss me. Again. But slower, this time."

She let out a low laugh. "Excuse me. But what does your towel have to do with a kiss?"

"Nothing." He pulled her closer, so her breasts brushed his chest. Heat sluiced through him, a heat with a pulse to it, slow and deep and sweet beyond belief.

"Nada?" She said his word for it, her breath hitching, betraying her own need.

Keeping her close with one hand, he ran the other down the curve of her back and over the firm swell of her pretty bottom, tucking her into him, sharply, so she could feel what he wanted from her. "On second thought…everything." He watched her eyes change. They went hazy and soft. *"Sí,"* he added, *"todo."* He lowered his mouth until it was almost on hers. She smelled so good…a little like a rose, a lot like something he couldn't define. Something musky and female and perfect for him. He told her once more, "Everything. I want it all."

Before she could pull back, he dipped his head that extra inch and caught her lower lip between his teeth. He played with it—just for an instant—and then let it go.

She stuck out her tongue and licked the place where his teeth had been. Her eyes were softer than ever now, her body pliant against his. "Oh, Rio. I wasn't going to do this. I honestly wasn't..."

"Liar," he said tenderly.

"No. I wasn't—and then I was. And then I wasn't..."

He understood what she meant, then. "But here you are."

She gave a slow nod. "It was bound to happen and deep down, I knew it. Since that first moment, when you got off your bike in front of Ralphie's Place. I saw you through the window. I think I knew since then...."

"*¿Reina?*"

"Um?"

"Are you telling me yes?"

She swallowed. Her face was flushed now. "I am, I... Yes."

"Say that again."

"Yes... *Sí.*"

"Good." He lowered his head and took her mouth—hard—pulling her tight against him, wrapping his arms around her. She gave no resistance, only a sigh of surrender as she opened to him, letting him have her tongue to suck.

Was there ever a woman who tasted so fine?

Nunca. No way.

She had too many clothes on. He wanted—needed—her naked. Naked as he was. *Ahora mismo.* Right now and not one second later.

He turned her slightly, bracing an arm at her back

to hold her as her body swayed beneath his kiss. With his free hand, he undid the buttons on her shirt and peeled it wide.

She cried out into his mouth. He drank in the sound, letting his fingers stray along the silken flesh of her rib cage, under her shirt to where her bra hooked in back.

With a flick of thumb and forefinger, he released the clasp. The bra fell open.

Keeping his mouth locked tight to hers, he fisted the shirt and bra in either hand and stripped them down her arms. She did the rest, tossing them away.

The feel of her was magic, the flesh of her shoulders so soft and so smooth. He let his fingers trail inward and down until he cradled a fine bare breast in either hand. First he tested the tempting weight of them, then he flattened his palms to rub the nipples, to feel them draw up, tight and hard. She moaned at that.

Below the waist, she was still fully dressed. He tried to remember his goal: to get everything off and to do it now.

But there was also the stunning pleasure of each brushing touch, and the swift heat that pulsed through his veins, setting his body on fire, tempting him to track the shape of her naked back, to clasp the impossible, beautiful curve of her waist.

Her hands weren't still, either. They stroked his chest and wandered downward. He should have caught her before she went too far. But he was too busy touching her, kissing her, too busy drowning in the feel and the taste of her.

When those soft fingers closed around him, he knew he would lose it. He had to break the never-ending kiss to warn her, "No. Not yet, or I'll die...."

She grinned a woman's grin against his mouth, a low, purring sound rising in her throat—she grinned that grin and she failed to obey him.

But then, she never had obeyed him.

Her hand opened—he dared to think he was saved—until she took him, warm and snug, in her grip again. She milked him, stroked him slowly, from root to rim.

He caught her wrist. "*Por favor...*" and he groaned again.

And at last, with a small moan of regret, she let go.

He kissed her some more, devouring her mouth, as he unbuttoned and unzipped the black pants she wore, took them by either side at her hips and shoved them down, hooking her panties, taking them, too.

He got everything halfway down her thighs, but he couldn't reach lower without losing her mouth. With an impatient growl, he broke the kiss.

She sighed, letting her head fall back, giving him the long, velvety line of her throat. He scraped his teeth over her chin and lower, licking his way down, kissing her neck, and pausing there to suck the skin against his teeth, marking her as his.

The scent of her filled him, the taste of her...all the heaven a man is ever allowed. He swept downward, going to his knees before her. She braced a hand on the sink rim and lifted one foot and then the other, helping him to get rid of her pants and her panties, as well as the soft, flat-soled shoes she wore when she worked.

He stopped to look at the wonder he'd uncovered and saw the tiny tattoo at the silky hollow where her hip joined her body: a sunflower. He kissed it.

She whispered his name on a rising inflection, "Rio?" The fingers of her free hand tangled in his hair.

He dipped his tongue in her navel, catching her hips in both hands, sliding his fingers inward from behind, parting her. For that, she gave him a long, hot moan.

She was wet for him. Slick and ready. He parted those secret lips, fingers gliding along the slippery folds.

Bending his head close to her again, he nuzzled the dark curls that covered her mound. With a moan, she lifted toward him, bracing her straining legs wider, offering him better access.

He took what she offered, hands cupping her bottom, pressing her closer, his mouth locking on, tongue delving in. He found her: that little nub, all swollen and needful. He flicked it, sucked, flicked it some more.

In seconds, with a hot cry, she went over. He held on, sucking gently, as her body quivered and more low, growling moans rose from her throat. He drank her in, tasted that liquid spill of greater sweetness, felt the faint pulsing that came with her release.

Then, quickly, before she could sink down to the floor with him, he got his feet under himself and stood.

"Rio?" she asked again, her head falling back,

clutching his shoulders, her eyes unfocused, voice sighing and tender, lost in sensation, drowned in the aftermath of her pleasure.

She was *his* in that moment, and that was the best part. He looked down into her glowing, soft eyes and he saw there what he knew he shouldn't, what, since Soledad, he'd sworn to himself never again to know: A full life with a good woman—this woman—beside him. Hope.

Rio saw hope. Hope and the sweetest promise of all, the one about forever.

Always. *Siempre…*

A lie, yes. But a beautiful one. A lie that, right then, at that magical moment, almost seemed true.

He scooped her up against his chest and carried her to his bedroom, lowering her carefully to the bed and coming down beside her. He laid his head on her belly and felt her hand, slow and lazy, stroking his hair.

It was good. The best. Just to lie there with her, his cock hard and hungry, causing him the sweetest kind of pain, his mind and heart satisfied already—to have her naked, here with him, at last.

He lifted up on an elbow and touched her again, laid his hand on the damp curls that covered her womanhood. She rolled her hips with an eager moan and for a few minutes, he played with her, spreading her, his fingers gliding so easily into her wetness.

He watched her as he touched her, his index and middle finger sliding, in and out. She tossed her head on the pillow and her hips worked, moving in rhythm to each stroke, until she broke wide open a second time, catching his wrist, holding it to her, then, with a low groan, pushing his hand away.

"Rio," she grabbed for his shoulders, urging him up along the length of her body. "Now, okay? Can it be now?"

"*Sí*," he whispered, "There. In the drawer by the bed…"

She took his meaning. Her eyes glowed as green as a deep, still pool in a secret place. "Wait…" Sliding away enough to open the drawer, she found the condoms he'd put there so he'd be ready when this moment finally came.

She took one out, peeled off the wrapper.

Gently, he edged her sleek thighs apart and rose up on his knees between them.

She crooked a finger. "Come closer. Come here. Let me do it…."

So he lowered himself over her, bracing up on his fists so she could reach down between them to clasp him. He shut his eyes and held his breath as she rolled the condom over the length of him.

And then, with a sure hand, she guided him into her, lifting her legs so he slid in so easy, all the way into the heat and the wet of her.

She clutched his back and wrapped those legs around him—and he knew he would lose it, right then, right away.

He commanded, "*Reina*. Wait. Don't move. Don't you…" He broke off on a groan as she surged up against him, taking him deeper. Impossible, to go deeper, but somehow, he did. She sheathed him so tightly, down to the root, and he was a drowning man, going down for the third time, happy to die.

Once she had him deep and sure, she gave him what he'd asked for. She stilled. Her eyes opened. He stared into those shining green depths.

And then he *had* to move, hard and fast…then slow and long, withdrawing to the tip—pushing in all the way.

She held on. She answered him, picking up his rhythms, and giving them back to him. He rolled and she rose up over him, her hair falling forward, tickling his chest, breasts swaying above him; he grabbed her close and rolled to take the top once more.

And then, there it was, like a wave closing over him, a roaring in his ears and his body turning inside-out. In the middle of it, he felt her coming, too, her slick inner muscles milking him, contracting, pumping around him. He heard her soft, triumphant female cry.

It was too much. The world spun away. There was only hot, pulsing pleasure as he thrust in deep and his climax rolled out along every nerve, ripping him open, laying him bare.

CHAPTER FIFTEEN

Friendly spirits are reaching out, calling you, ready to share great wisdom from the world beyond. Believe it. And pick up the dang phone.
—*from* The Prairie Queen's Guide to Life *by Goddess Jacks*

THE PHONE WOKE PHOEBE at seven in the morning. Shocked from sleep by the sound, she lay there not moving through three rings, getting her bearings, remembering last night and everything that had happened, frowning when she thought about the fight and the riff with Tiffany, and then grinning like a long-gone fool when she recalled what Rio had done to her in the bathroom—and later, right here, in this very bed.

Before she pulled it together to reach across the naked man beside her and answer the guest-room extension, he did it for her, sticking out a big, hard arm, picking it up, passing it over.

Her mother's voice gritched in her ear. "I was beginning to think you weren't going to answer."

"Well, here I am."

"I feel I really *have* to say something."

"Fine. Say it."

"Tiffany called me a few minutes ago, in tears. She's just brokenhearted about what happened last night. Just completely devastated. I've never heard her that miserable and upset, not in all her life—now it's true, she's always had that morose side, that just slightly whiny side. But this is more than whinin'. This is a deep and terrible emotional wound. You and she and Rose are *bonded.* You know that. Bonded from birth in the truest, strongest way. Why, you were *babies* together, all three of you, born in the back of the Prairie Qu…" Phoebe knew the rest. She tuned it out.

Blinking sleep from her eyes, she pulled herself to a sitting position. Rio, the covers down to his waist, rolled his big head on the pillow and lifted an eyebrow at her. The phone cord stretched across his gorgeous chest. She made a mental note to pick up a cordless extension for the guest room.

She mouthed, "My mother," at him as Goddess continued to chatter away, repeating ancient history, and then launching into what Tiff had told her, which was basically a recap of the fight between Rio and Dave.

Rio gestured for her to climb over him to the phone side. She did, shoving back the covers, scrambling up and over him. It was awkward, to put it mildly. She tried not to let the cord get hung up in the process, feeling way naked, which she was, holding back a snort of pretend outrage when Rio made a show of looking up her crotch—not that there was anything there he hadn't already seen. At last, she ended up next to the night table. She grabbed the blankets and covered herself, which was pretty absurd, really. Talk about shutting the barn door after the mare wandered out….

Goddess stopped in midrant and asked sharply, "Hon, what is all that gruntin' and heavy breathing I'm hearing?"

"Nothing, Mama." Rio was watching her. She flashed him a big, fake smile and turned so she was facing away from him. Carefully, she tucked the covers up over her breasts, preserving a modesty she so didn't have.

"Phoebe," said her mother. "I think you need to get with Tiff and work this out between you."

Okay, it wasn't bad advice, not really. And if Tiff had actually called Goddess to talk about it, then maybe she'd changed her mind about the whole *Dave goes, I go* routine. "I'll call her, okay?"

"When?"

"Today."

"Oh, hon. Good. Real good. Now I've got to get back to my book. I'm upping my page goals as of this morning. Ten pages. I know I can do it."

"That's the spirit, Mama."

"But first, put Rio on."

So Phoebe turned back over to face the man who now had intimate knowledge of every inch of her body. She shoved the phone at him.

He took it. "*Hola,* Goddess… Yeah?" He was silent, except for an occasional encouraging grunt. Phoebe lay on her side, the phone cord nestled in the curve of her waist, feeling all syrupy and sentimental, watching him as he listened to one of her mother's stories, not quite able to resist reaching across and smoothing his hair back where it fell over his forehead. He smiled when she did that and a giddy wave of pleasure cascaded through her. He had that raw red line on his forehead where Tiff had hit him, a big bruise under that little bandage on his jaw and several more bruises on that amazing torso of his. But other than that, he looked pretty good.

Well, more than good. Terrific, actually. Just supermanly and extremely fine.

He said goodbye to her mother and passed her the phone.

She put it in the cradle and turned on her side facing him, tugging at the sheet some more, settling it over her just so. "And my mother said…?"

He touched her shoulder with the side of his finger and then traced a line down her exposed arm. Little tingles of excitement followed in the wake of that caress. When he reached the back of her hand, he eased his big fingers between hers. "Your mother had another dream."

"About Ralphie?"

He nodded. "They played table soccer again. Ralphie won. Then he took her out for a spin in Darla's red Sebring. They had dinner…."

"In the dream? My mother and Ralphie?"

"That's right. At Pearl's. The original one, your mother said. Great margaritas there, she told me."

"Is there any point to this dream?"

"Wait. We're getting there—after the meal, your mom and Ralphie went out and got in Darla's car again. He took her back to her house. When he let her off, he leaned across the console and said, *Goddess. Remember. Sometimes I'd get two.*"

"Two?" Phoebe echoed. They stared at each other, and then they both burst out laughing. As the laughter faded, he brought her hand to his mouth and pressed a kiss on her knuckles.

Inside, she sighed and melted and thought, *Hey. I'm up for this. As long as it lasts, I'm gonna have me one fine, sexy time….*

But back to her mother's dream. She asked Rio, "Two of what?"

"Goddess didn't say."

"Wonderful. Let's see. 'Sometimes he'd get two' and foosball games and margaritas at Pearl's, a ride in Darla's convertible and 'A problem of storage.' How vague and disconnected can you get?"

"*Reina.* They're only dreams."

"My mother. One of a kind and that is no lie."

"No argument there."

"And you won't believe this, but sometimes her weird dreams and visions actually do turn out to amount to something."

"For instance?"

"Things like, once, her next-door neighbor's dog got lost. No one could find it—until my mom had a vision and told them where to look. And then there was the day Tiff's mom, Brenda, died. That was awful.

Brenda was in the hospital for a hip replacement—serious surgery, but routine. People have hip replacements all the time and get through it just fine."

"But Tiff's mom didn't?"

"She had some weird reaction to the anesthetic. They lost her on the operating table. My mother called me in tears, at what turned out to be about five minutes after Brenda's heart stopped beating. She'd just seen Brenda, standing in her hallway, waving, a golden light all around her, wearing nothing but one of those shower cap things they make you wear before they wheel you in for surgery…." Phoebe shivered. "Very scary. And Brenda was all the real family Tiff had. Her dad was long gone, some druggie from the commune days at the Prairie Queen. My poor mama. She and Brenda were like sisters, you know? And then to have to see her, standing naked in the hallway, waving goodbye…"

"Hey," Rio said, his voice tender and low. He reached out and gathered her close, turning her so he could curl his big, hard body around hers. He smoothed her hair back from her ear and whispered, "You love *tu madre* very much, don't you?"

"She makes me crazy." He nipped her earlobe. She swatted at him—not hard, purely for effect. "Hey. Knock it off."

He caught her earlobe in his teeth again. That time, he licked it with his clever tongue.

She snuggled in closer and sighed. "On second thought…"

"¿Qué?"

"Do that again…"

AN HOUR OR SO LATER, THEY got up. They showered and Rio made them breakfast. Phoebe cleaned up the dishes. He poured himself more coffee and disappeared into his room where his laptop waited. Phoebe straightened up the house a little, putting off calling Tiff and having to face the possibility of more harsh words between them.

Finally, at a little after ten, she picked up the phone.

Tiff answered immediately, as if she'd been sitting right there, waiting for Phoebe's call. "Okay, Pheeb. What?"

Phoebe didn't much care for her dismissive tone—but then Tiff sniffled, a sound that spoke of held-back tears. Phoebe spoke gently. "We should talk, okay?"

"Go ahead." More sniffling. Bad-attitude sniffling. "Say what you have to say."

This was not looking promising. "Face-to-face, all right?"

"Sure. Fine. Whatever. Come on over. Dave's already gone to work. We'll be alone."

TIFF AND DAVE SHARED A small brick house on Northwest Eleventh, not all that far from the trailer park where Darla now lived alone. The house had a steep-pitched roof and a semienclosed front porch with arches opening onto the front walk and the steps to the driveway. The storm door and all the windows were barred in black iron. It wasn't a rough neighborhood, exactly. But it was borderline, a place where you might as well go ahead and bar the windows and not have to deal with some drugged-out burglar paying you a visit in the middle of the night.

Tiff had the door open and the storm door pushed wide before Phoebe had finished mounting the steps to the porch. As soon as Phoebe got close, Tiff let the door go.

"Cute," Phoebe muttered as she lunged and caught the handle before it swung shut in her face.

Tiff only shrugged. "Come on in," she said, her tone low and sulky, her eyes and nose red from her recent crying jag. Her hair had that mashed, slept-in look. She was still in her bathrobe: a red silk kimono. Her slender feet were bare.

Phoebe followed her in.

It was a nice place. Tiff had made it so. She'd refinished the old hardwood floors, painted the walls in vivid, deep colors, carefully trimmed out all the woodwork in glossy white. A graceful arch separated the living room from the dining room. Tiff padded under that arch and led Phoebe to the narrow kitchen bright with morning sun.

Tiff threw out a hand at the two-person breakfast table and Phoebe slid into one of the chairs. "Coffee?"

"Sure. Thanks."

So Tiff poured them each a cup and took the other chair. They sipped in unison and set their mugs down at the same time.

Tiff was hunched over hers, both hands wrapped around it. She looked up at Phoebe and muttered, "Okay. What?"

Phoebe took a stab at making peace. "Look. Let's

stop this, okay? Come to work tonight. It'll be busy, you know it. Good tips. And you know you always have a good time. I've booked Paula Teal and the Mudruckers." The Mudruckers played country-rock. A terrific band. "You know you love them."

Tiff's graceful bow of a mouth tightened. "What about Dave?"

"Two weeks." Tiff let out a small sound of disbelief and Phoebe hurried to add, "Come on. It's not the end of the world. He can wait that long. It's not like he's hanging out there day in and day out or anything. He doesn't come in all that often as it is."

Tiff shifted her shoulders and smoothed her kimono where it was gaping a little in front. "No. That won't work. I can't do that. It wouldn't be fair to Dave."

Phoebe, who'd just raised her mug to her lips again, carefully set it down without taking a sip. "Not fair to Dave…"

"Yeah. Did you ever give even a single thought to Dave? He's very upset. Very hurt. That you would choose that…" Tiff must have seen the look of warning on Phoebe's face. She stopped before calling Rio an ugly name and corrected herself bitterly, "That you would choose Rio over him."

So much for trying to make nice. "Tiff. Get with reality. Ralphie's Place is half Rio's. I couldn't kick Rio out if I wanted to. And I don't. *Dave* came after *him.* Dave needs a little time to cool off."

"How do you know what Dave needs?"

It was all just so much crap and Phoebe was sick of it. "Tiff. Look. Technically, I shouldn't let *you* back in for two weeks, either, after that stunt with the pool cue. But since you didn't start the fight, I'm letting what you did pass."

"Oh, how *kind* of you, your royal majesty."

"Damn it. What the hell is going on with you?"

Tiff huffed out a big breath. "Oh, right. What's going on with *me?*"

"Yeah. With you. You're actin' real strange lately. All pissed off because Rio is trying to find out what happened to Ralphie. Why should you be mad because Rio cares what happened to Ralphie and is actually trying to do something about it?"

"Dave says—"

"Dave. Right. It's all about Dave."

"Well, he's a very private person and he doesn't like anyone getting in his face."

"Why not? What does he have to hide?"

"Nothing. Not a thing. He just has a right to his privacy, that's all."

"Fine. He's got a right to his privacy. But why can't Dave be a good sport and maybe help out a little, answer a few questions?"

"Well." There was more huffing. "I don't know what to say to you. I just don't."

"How about the truth? You could tell me that."

Tiff scowled. "What are you getting at?"

"I'm getting at how you—and Dave—are acting strangely."

"We are not."

"Well, then, good. Tell me why Dave won't talk to Rio—why he came after Rio. And while you're at it, you can explain what got into *you* last night, why you attacked Rio *and* your boyfriend with that pool cue. You can tell me what's got you so freaked out, why you're callin' up my mom, cryin' your eyes out, playing the wounded party in all this when you know that nobody did a damn thing to you—or at least, nobody *I* know about."

"I…" Tiff looked away.

"You what?" Tiff only shook her head. So Phoebe laid it out for her. "Tiff, you're my friend. No matter what you do, you'll always be my friend. But there *is* something strange going on with you." Phoebe leaned forward, wishing that getting closer would allow her to see what weird stuff was going on in Tiff's mind. "What's happening? Tell me. Tell me the truth and you know I'll be there for you. I always have been and I always will…."

Tiff sat back. Her lower lip quivered. She bit it hard to make it stop. And when it did, she said, "I'm with Dave. I have to…stick by him. That's how it is. And you know what? This is no good."

"Tiff—"

She waved a hand. "There's no point in us talking. You've got your…loyalties. And I've got mine. I'm sorry I called Goddess. I shouldn't have done that. But don't you expect me to be servin' drinks to your customers, don't expect to see me around. Not until Rio Navarro wraps up that little private investigation of his. Not until he gets his ass on that big Harley of his and heads back to Cali where he belongs."

CHAPTER SIXTEEN

Contrary to popular belief, hon, there are some wounds time *doesn't* heal.
—from The Prairie Queen's Guide to Life *by Goddess Jacks*

"TIFF CAME BY THE shop a couple of hours ago."

Phoebe looked up from her computer to find Rose standing in the doorway to her office. "Come on in. Shut the door."

Rose peeled herself off the door frame, nudged the door shut and sauntered over to Phoebe's extra chair, which she dropped into with a big, fat sigh.

"Tough day at the store?" Phoebe asked, hoping against hope to avoid hearing yet again how Tiff was so devastated and it was all Phoebe's fault.

"Busy, yeah." Rose's vintage clothing store, Special Effects, was across the street and five blocks up from Ralphie's Place. Saturdays, she was open eleven to four. Rose wasn't getting rich on the shop, but she made enough to get by, and working for Phoebe a few nights a week helped her pick up the slack. The shop also served as Rose's personal closet. Today, she wore a cropped electric-blue velvet blazer over a sort of Grecian-looking purple silk dress that flowed to mid-thigh, with nicely tattered stovepipe jeans under the dress. She sat forward and braced her elbows on her knees, folding her hands together. "You know. Tiff is just—"

"Let me guess. Devastated."

Rose shrugged and sat back in the chair. "That would be the word."

Phoebe clicked the mouse to shut down her spreadsheet. "I did go to see her. This morning. It didn't do any good."

"You shouldn't let this happen between you."

"I did what I could, Rose."

"Men come and go," said Rose in a lecturing tone. "You, me and Tiff. We're for life."

"Well, when she gets over whatever's really bothering her, I'll still be here."

"You mean, when she gets over Dave."

"I guess."

"Funny. You're waiting for her to dump Dave. And all she wants is for you to get rid of Rio."

Phoebe picked up a stray pen, opened her pencil drawer and dropped it into the pen tray. She shoved the drawer shut. "And what about you, Rose? Is that what you're waiting for? For me to get rid of Rio?"

Rose shifted in the chair, crossing her legs. "I'm not waiting for anything. I'm old enough to know better than that. But I do want my two best friends to work things out with each other. Is that too much to ask?"

"That's all?"

"That's all."

Phoebe thought of the glory of the night before and wished she could be back there now, in bed, wrapped tight in Rio's arms. In bed with Rio, everything seemed right.

But then again, Tiff probably felt the same way about Dave.

"Give it a little time," Phoebe said, trying for diplomacy.

"I'm not sure time will do it."

"Well, for now, I can't do any more."

"Oh, come on. You know the old saying." Just in case she didn't, Rose repeated it for her. "*Can't* lives on *won't* street."

"Okay, Rose. I've done what I'm *willing* to do. How's that?"

"Not so good—and I can see by that look on your face that I am dismissed." Rose pushed herself from the chair, smoothed her purple skirt and paused before turning for the door. "By the way, in case you didn't notice, you've got a hickey on your neck."

Phoebe refused to rise to the bait. "I'll put some more makeup on it."

"I hope you know what you're doing."

Phoebe gave it a mental count of ten before suggesting, "Look. It's bad enough that Tiff and I are on the outs. I don't want to fight with you, too."

Rose put up both hands. "Looky here. No weapons. It seems I have checked my six-guns at the door."

Phoebe grunted. "Right. But you still got that tongue that cuts like a knife."

Rose gave it up. "All right, all right. I don't want to fight, either. Sorry."

"Apology accepted."

"One more question…"

Phoebe shut her eyes, sucked in a breath and let it out slowly. "What?"

"How long is this little investigation of Rio's going to last?"

"Until we get some answers."

"And what if you never do?"

"We will."

"Well. Great. And the sooner the better, is all I have to say."

IT WAS ANOTHER BUSY, LOUD, profitable night. Standing room only, from eight o'clock on. Both Boone and Bernard were behind the bar. Without Tiff, Phoebe, Rose and the other two waitresses had to work all the harder. It was crazy, but somehow they managed to stay on top of things.

At ten past midnight, as Phoebe was serving another round to a table of eight, Rose sidled up and whispered in her ear. "Darla's on the phone. She's having contractions. She wants to know if someone can go over there and drive her to the hospital."

Phoebe passed the tray of drinks to Rose and trotted back to the bar. "Let me talk to her."

Boone gave her the phone.

"Darla?"

"Hey, Pheeb."

"Darla, I want you to relax now. I want you to take deep breaths and—"

Darla actually laughed. "I'm not dyin'. Just havin' a baby, is all. I feel pretty good, except for…" The words trailed off. She let out a sharp, surprised, "Oh!"

"Darla? Darla, are you okay?"

Boone loomed across the bar. "What the—?"

Phoebe put up a hand and shook her head, mouthing, "It's okay. Okay…" She waved him off.

Boone didn't look especially convinced, but he did move on down the bar to serve a couple of yahoos who were calling for more beer.

The place was a zoo. She couldn't hear herself think. Phoebe stuck a finger in the ear not covered by the phone. "Darla?"

"I'm here. That was another one."

Another contraction. Oh, sweet Lord. "Did you call your doctor?"

"I tried. I got a message service. And he didn't call me back yet. I'm getting kind of worried. It *is* a little early. I need to get to the hospital, I think. I'm afraid to drive myself right now."

"You're right. You shouldn't drive. Not for this."

"So I need a ride." She asked in a tiny, hopeful voice, "I guess you're pretty busy, huh? So should I call a cab?"

Phoebe sent a frantic glance around the crowded, noisy room. Packed, to say the least. She couldn't afford to leave the floor. And she couldn't spare Boone to drive his sister—she couldn't spare anyone. She needed everybody she had working, or they wouldn't be able to keep up….

And what was she thinking? There was no question here. Darla and the baby came first. "Forget calling a cab. I'll…" Right then, her gaze collided with Rio's down the bar. In his questioning dark eyes she saw the solution to her problem. "Rio will be there in twenty minutes, tops."

Darla let out a cry—one that didn't have a thing to do with labor pains. "Oh, no. Not *him…*"

"Darla. He's coming. I know you're not crazy about him. But I also know that *you* know you can count on him. He'll take care of you until I can get there."

Darla muttered a very bad word. "Fine, then. Whatever. Tell him to hurry. I need a ride *now.*"

WHEN PHOEBE TOLD RIO WHAT she needed from him, he got right off his stool at the end of the bar and turned for the door to the back. She followed him out to his rental car and shut the door for him once he was settled behind the wheel. He started the engine and rolled the window down.

She leaned in. "Drive carefully—but get there fast." She named the hospital. "They have twenty-four hour emergency. It's at—"

"Don't worry. I can find it."

"And call me as soon as you know anything. I'll be there the minute I can get away."

"I'm on it. Relax."

"Oh, yeah. Easy for you to say…"

He grinned the grin that made her heart do the happy dance. "Hell. I might even get the chance to look around inside that trailer of hers…."

"Rio." She scowled to let him know this was beyond serious. "Hello? Darla and the baby. Top priority."

He grinned even wider and gunned the Buick's engine. "Just kidding—I know. Darla first. Got it."

"And you'd better hurry, or you could end up delivering that baby yourself."

He faked a look of terror. "Never say those words to a man. Men are brave. But not *that* brave."

She leaned in far enough that they could share a quick kiss, then stepped back from the car. Gravel crunched. Rio waved at her as he disappeared into the alley.

INSIDE, THE BAND HAD started their final set. Phoebe grabbed a cocktail tray and hit the floor running.

It was a little before one when the band wrapped it up. Everybody stayed on as they had the night before. Phoebe kept moving, taking orders, clearing off, bringing on the next round. Somehow, she and her crew kept one step ahead of the bar full of thirsty customers.

Rio didn't call. She worried a little about that, about how Darla might be doing. But it had hardly been an hour since he'd left—and no news was good news.

When closing time drew near, Phoebe got up and sang another ballad. In the dark, with the spotlight hard and white in her eyes, she couldn't see much of anything beyond the stage.

Which was fine. In her mind, she pictured Rio's face. She imagined him there, on his favorite stool at the end of the bar, watching her. Listening to her song. She sang for him, letting the music fill her and spill out, letting it carry her away.

She sang and it was all about the feel of Rio's mouth on hers, about the things they'd done together the night before—and what they would do this night. And in the precious nights to come.

Woven into the song was her sadness, the flipside of her joy. The sadness whispered in her secret heart, *It won't last, you know that. He told you up front that it wouldn't. It's not forever, it's just for right now.*

Forever. A lovely word that did not apply.

Forever...

And she thought of Ralphie, could almost hear that whiskey-and-cigarettes drawl of his, whispering to her as she sang. *"Babe, it ain't forever and it sure as hell ain't fair. So you might as well have yourself one damn fine time while you're here."*

Forever...

Her dad used to say that. *Love you forever and ever, Phoebe, my girl...*

But then he was gone, his lifeless body slumped at his desk in his office at home.

Yeah. Ralphie had it right. Not forever. And a girl should have herself a damn fine time while she was here.

Phoebe let the last note linger and slowly fade. And then, before the applause roared in her ears, there was that moment, that hush, that beautiful silence that told her she'd done her job well. That was good, too.

WHEN SHE CAME DOWN OFF the stage, Boone was waiting with the phone in his hand.

"False alarm," he said as he passed the phone across the bar.

She took it. "Rio?"

"Hey, Pheeb." Darla's voice. She sounded sheepish. "It's me."

"You okay?"

"Yeah. I saw the doctor here in emergency…."

"And?"

"He says I'm a little dilated, but not, um, effaced."

"Which means?"

"The baby's coming soon."

"But not tonight?"

"Yeah. He said those cramps I had were Braxel… huh?" Phoebe heard Rio correcting her, then Darla spoke into the phone again. "Braxton-Hicks. It's a kind of contraction, but it's not the kind you have when things get serious."

"But you're okay? The baby's—"

"Fine. Honest—hold on." She didn't bother to cover the phone as she spoke to Rio again. "Could you just stand over there, please? Could you give a girl a little space?" A second later, she was talking into the mouthpiece again. "Rio did fine." She said the words softly, as if she didn't want anyone—namely, Rio—to hear. "He, um, took care of me, like you told him to."

Phoebe grinned to herself. "He's there with you now, right?"

"Well, yeah. But I just sent him over by the vending machines so I could talk to you in private. I don't need him hanging over me every second, now, do I?"

"No, of course you don't."

"He's going to take me home now."

"Good."

"But he said we could stop at Braum's on the way." Braum's was fast food the Oklahoma way. Great burgers. The best ice cream around. "I need me a banana split, Pheeb. I need it bad."

"I understand. Enjoy every bite."

"I will—and I guess you want to talk to *him* now."

"Just for a minute."

"Love you, Pheeb."

"Love you, too."

Rio's deep voice rumbled in her ear. "She's okay. She'll be having that baby soon, but not tonight."

"So I heard."

"I promised I'd take her to—"

"Braum's. She told me. Tell you what? Just go on home after you drop her off. There's no point in coming here."

He teased, "I don't know. You think you can handle closing that place up without me?"

"It'll be rough. But we'll manage somehow."

"Be safe," he warned. "Don't hang around there alone."

She started to argue that she'd stayed on alone after closing a thousand times and never once been mugged. But then she thought twice—and saw bloodred letters scrawled on a mirror: *Back off, bitch. Final warning...*

She promised, "I'll keep someone right here with me till the bitter end."

"Good." He said something soft in Spanish. She didn't catch his meaning—not exactly. But close enough. A slow warmth spread through her. She cradled the phone and imagined his arms around her, his mouth covering hers.... He spoke in English then. "See you at your house."

"Yeah—and Rio?"

"¿Sí?"

"Thank you."

"De nada. Para te, algo..."

She understood most of it. *You're welcome* and, "For me...?"

He translated softly, "For you, anything."

IT WAS TWO-TEN IN THE morning when Phoebe finally ushered the last few customers out the door. Everyone worked fast to clean up. Bernard had a date waiting for him and Boone was eager to go check on Darla. They locked up at 2:35 and the men left, along with the two extra waitresses.

Phoebe still had the count to do, adding the totals for both the afternoon and evening shifts, getting everything ready for the bank drop on Monday. She wanted to get home *now* to Rio's waiting arms, but...

Keeping the books current was part of the job. The nights that Bernard closed up alone, he did the honors. As the boss, though, when she stayed till the end, the job fell to her. And really, it didn't take all that long.

Rose, who'd agreed to hang around and walk out with her, had already changed out of her white shirt and dark slacks into the purple dress and the blue velvet jacket of the afternoon. She sat sprawled in Phoebe's guest chair, chewing gum and checking out the summer fashion bulletins in *Lucky* magazine. Phoebe worked fast, counting the money, entering everything into her computer and zipping a copy off to one of the extra private e-mail addresses supplied by her Internet provider.

Once the count was done, Phoebe put most of the money in the safe, locked it up and carried the cash drawer back out to the register, empty except for six fifties in the twenties slot. In the unlikely event of a robbery, the thief would get three hundred dollars and maybe not bother to look around for the safe.

Phoebe returned to the office, where Rose still sat, flipping through the pages of her magazine. She went to the desk and grabbed her purse. "Ready?"

Rose cracked her gum. "At last."

"Hey. It barely took twenty minutes."

"At three in the morning, twenty minutes is a lifetime."

Phoebe thought of Rio and smiled. "Oh, yeah…"

Rose slid her magazine into the tote on the floor at her side as Phoebe turned for the open hallway door. Just as she reached it, the lights went out, plunging the room and the hallway beyond into darkness.

From over by the desk somewhere, Rose's disembodied voice said, "Terrific." Not a glimmer of light bled in from the big storage room at the end of the hall.

"The main breaker must have tripped."

Phoebe heard Rose crack her gum again. "What now?"

"No biggie." The breaker box was inside the door to the garage. Phoebe turned toward the room again—and Rose's voice. "There's a flashlight in my…"

It was as far as she got. She heard something behind

her—the tiniest sound, a shifting, a movement in the air. Enough to register that she and Rose were not alone.

Before she could whirl and face the intruder, something came down, impossibly hard, on the back of her head.

Rose screamed and called her name as Phoebe's world exploded into a thousand bright stars.

And then, trailing streams of light, the darkness descended again. Phoebe felt her knees give way. With a sigh, she crumpled slowly down.

She was out before she hit the floor.

CHAPTER SEVENTEEN

You know how it goes. Just when you think you understand everything…you regain consciousness.

—from The Prairie Queen's Guide to Life *by Goddess Jacks*

"PHEEB." ROSE WAS CALLING her. "Phoebe. Oh, God. Pheeb… Can you hear me?"

Phoebe opened her eyes. Rose's white face swam above her. "I…where…what?" Her head pounded. She could *hear* the blood beating through her brain.

"Oh, thank God," said Rose. "Pheeb. Do you know who I am?"

Beyond the wild strawberry halo that was Rose's hair, she could make out the ceiling tiles….

In her office. She was lying on the floor in her office.

She seemed to remember…. "The lights. They went out…."

Rose, on her hands and knees bending over her, bobbed her head, eagerly. "Yeah. After the bastards left, I got your flashlight, found the breaker—"

"When? Who? How long?" Phoebe reached up to touch the place on her head where the hideous pounding seemed to be centered.

Rose caught her arm. "Better not."

"Wha…?"

"There's a little blood."

For a moment, *blood* seemed a word in an unknown language. Phoebe repeated it numbly, "Blood?"

Rose held up the cell in her free hand. "Lie still, okay? I just called 911. The paramedics'll be here in no time, along with the cops."

"What about Rio? Did you call Rio?"

Rose blinked. "Uh, no."

Phoebe dug around in her throbbing brain and somehow came up with his cell number. She repeated it, commanding, "Call him. Now."

Rose sighed and punched up the number. "Rio," she said a moment later. "We've got a prob—"

Phoebe stuck out a hand. "Here. Give me that." Rose let her have the phone. "Rio. Oh, God. It's Phoebe…."

"What's wrong?"

She told him, in a disjointed tumble of words, ending with, "Rose called 911, so help is coming, but—"

"Sit tight. I'll be right there."

She heard the click as he disconnected the call and she handed the phone back to Rose. "He's on his way…." She started to raise her arm again. Rose caught it and guided it back down. "What's that under my head?"

"My jacket."

"Oh, no. Not that gorgeous blue velvet one."

"That would be the one."

"But you said there was blood…."

"There is. A little." Rose forced a brave smile. "Don't worry about that jacket. I've got a store full of great clothes where it came from." Phoebe tried a laugh. Not smart. It only made her head pound harder. Rose saw her wince and her smile vanished. "Oh, baby. Is it…?"

"It's okay. It's fine."

"Just hold on. Not too long. They should be here real soon."

"I know they will. And I'm okay. I really am—now, tell me. What happened?"

Rose patted her shoulder. "Maybe you should just rest." She was cooing, sounding downright motherly. "Don't think, don't move, don't do *anything* until the ambulance gets here…."

"Rose. I need to know what happened while I was knocked out."

"But—"

"No buts. I'll lie right here, flat on the floor, bleeding calmly on your pretty velvet jacket. I won't so much as move until the paramedics say I'm going to live. But I have to know what happened." She groped for her friend's hand. Rose gave it. "Please."

Rose sat back on her heels and wrapped her other hand around their joined fists. "Oh, honey."

"Tell me. Come on…"

"I—"

"Tell me. The lights went out and you…"

"I heard that thud when they hit you."

"Yeah?"

"And then I heard you fall to the floor. Freaked me the hell out. For a few seconds, I lurched around in the dark, calling your name. Then someone threw a big bag over me…."

"A bag?"

Rose pointed toward the corner. Phoebe carefully rolled her head to look. "That bag," Rose said. Phoebe recognized one of the oversize white drawstring bags her laundry service provided. A length of rope, as limp as a dead snake, lay a few feet from the bag. "I didn't see either of them. But I know there were two, at least. One of them tied me up in the bag. They both wore those gloves, you know, those surgical gloves…." Rose shuddered. "I felt them, the gloves, on my ankles when the guy at my feet tied them together. And the other guy, the one who put the bag over my head, he brushed the back of my hand with one…."

"So they were men. Both of them?"

"The one with the bag, no doubt about it. Big arms, chest like a slab of rock. Hard thighs. Definitely a guy. The other? I'd say yes, but I can't be one hundred percent sure." She paused to draw a shaky breath. "They shoved me down in the corner and went to work on the safe. See?" She pointed.

Phoebe had to crane her head to see around the barrier of her own desk. It hurt. She groaned as she saw that the file cabinet had been shoved to the side. The safe was wide open, the area where the lock would have been, charred and melted. A busy night's earnings, gone, gone, gone.

Rose said, "They used some kind of torch on it. I heard a hissing sound, smelled smoke…."

Phoebe sniffed. A burning smell still hung in the hair. "How long…?"

"It was quick. I swear, though. It *felt* like forever. Three, maybe four minutes, I guess. Five tops. By the time I was able to get the rope around my body—the drawstring, I mean—loose, they were gone. You were groaning by then, starting to come to. I fumbled around until I found the flashlight in your desk, and I checked on you. Or I tried, anyway. It was so dark, I couldn't tell much with just the flashlight. So I left you to run out and flip the breaker. The lights came on. When I got back to you, you were still groaning, not really conscious yet. I called 911."

Phoebe tried to think. What would Rio ask? "Did you…notice anything familiar about either of the guys who tied you up? Was there anything else about them that stuck with you?"

"It was pitch-black. But there was a split second there…"

"Yeah?"

"I thought I smelled booze, on the guy who grabbed me first."

"You think he was drunk?"

"Don't know. It was only just for that second. After that, I had my head in a bag. And neither of them said a damn word the whole time."

THE PARAMEDICS ARRIVED about ten minutes later. Rio came in right after them.

Phoebe wanted to run to him. But it wasn't in the cards at that moment, considering she was lying flat on the floor with a couple of burly EMTs bending over her. He eased through the door and stepped back out of the way, near the pulled-out file cabinet and the torched-open safe, not far from where Rose sat in Phoebe's desk chair.

They made Phoebe lie there while they poked and prodded her injury and checked her vital signs. They shone a light in her eyes. Finally, they said it was okay for her to sit up. They cleaned up the clotted blood in her hair a little, had her track a pen moving back and forth at eye level, and asked her several simple questions, apparently to find out if they were dealing with brain damage.

"You've had a concussion," one of them said. No kidding.

They seemed to think she was okay now, but urged her to climb in the ambulance for a ride to the hospital. She could spend the night there, they said, let them run a few tests and keep her under observation, just to be on the safe side.

By then, Phoebe was sitting in the extra chair. "No, thanks." She spotted her purse, against the wall by the door where she must have dropped it when they hit her. "My purse…"

Rose got it and brought it to her.

"Phoebe," Rio said darkly, opening his sexy mouth

for the first time since he'd entered the room. "You're going with them."

She clutched her purse to her chest and shook her head. "No."

Rose piped up. "Yeah. He's right. You need to go. You don't want to fool around with something like this. You don't want to be one of those people who gets a bump on the head, wanders around in a fog for a while, and then drops dead." She paused as she noticed that both paramedics were frowning at her. "Well," she told them. "Sorry to get graphic, but it happens and y'all know it, too."

"She's right," said Rio.

Great. For once, Rose and Rio were in complete agreement—over a choice they just plain didn't get to make. She told them so. "It's my decision and I say I'm fine." She forced a wide, perky smile and stuck out both hands, palms to the ceiling. "And see? I'm alert. I'm not in anything remotely resembling a fog." Her head still pounded. But that didn't count as far as she was concerned.

There was more argument. Phoebe held her ground. The med techs gave her more advice. For the next twenty-four hours, she shouldn't be alone. No driving or operating heavy machinery. There should be someone with her at all times to see that she got immediate medical attention if she felt dizzy, vomited or passed out.

"She won't be alone and she won't get behind the wheel of a car," Rio muttered in a threatening tone. "I'll make sure of it."

The police arrived as the paramedics were leaving: two uniformed officers.

The older one, Officer Pulaski, took charge. "I'll need you two—" he nodded at Rose and Rio "—to go out into the bar and get comfortable. Ms. Jacks, I'll take your statement first. We'll need to clear the scene. Do you have another room we can use?"

She suggested the break room, off the main storeroom. "It's pretty small, though, hardly more than a big closet…."

"Someplace to sit down?"

"A table. A few chairs…"

"That'll work."

Phoebe stood up a little too fast. With a groan, she put a hand to the matted goose egg on the back of her head.

Rio was watching. "She's got a head injury," he told Pulaski. "Let me take her home. She can talk to you when she's feeling better, answer all your questions then."

"No," Phoebe said before the cop could respond. "I'm staying."

Rio looked at her, a stark look. "*Reina.*" It shocked her, to hear him use his private name for her in front of two cops and Rose. It wasn't like him to do that.

He was *that* worried about her.

Still, she made herself face him squarely. Those dark eyes pleaded with her to do what he thought was best. But she just couldn't. She knew she was going to be okay. And this was *her* place that had been invaded, her safe that gaped open, her head that pounded where some bastard had hit her hard enough to kill her stone dead. She wanted them caught. And she wasn't leaving until she'd told the cops everything she knew.

"No," she said.

He swore low, in Spanish.

Officer Pulaski said, "Ms. Jacks, a head injury's nothing to fool with. We can call another ambulance for you."

"Please don't. I'm fine and I'm not leaving."

That seemed to settle it. "All right, then," said Pulaski. Rose was bending down to grab her tote. Pulaski stopped her. "Leave that, for now. Don't disturb anything."

So Rose left her tote behind and she, Rio and the younger officer went out to the main bar area. Phoebe, her own purse clutched safely in her hands, led Pulaski to the break room. They sat in the plastic chairs at the round table and Phoebe told him what she knew, up until the big moment when her own personal lights went out.

"And when you regained consciousness?"

She told him the rest, about what Rose had said while they waited for the paramedics.

He talked to Rio next. That was brief. And then he called Rose in. Her statement took longer. Rose had just finished up and rejoined Phoebe and Rio in the bar when a weary-looking plainclothes detective arrived.

He introduced himself as Sergeant Ankerson and then he and Officer Pulaski went off for a powwow in back. The younger uniform stayed in the bar with them. He was the strong, silent type—serious and intense. His presence kind of put a lid on conversation. Phoebe was itching to find out how Pulaski's interviews with Rose and Rio had gone. But she supposed she could wait until the wheels of justice finished turning for the night.

Ankerson came back without Pulaski. He said he'd called in a lab guy who would be there shortly to gather evidence.

And then he went through the interview process all over again, starting that time with Rio. He spent a lot longer with Rio than Officer Pulaski had.

He talked to Phoebe second, leading her into the break room and shutting the door.

He sat across from her at the break table and asked her to repeat the story she'd told Officer Pulaski, up to when she lost consciousness. And then he asked for the rest, from the point when she came to again.

Ankerson told her that her three hundred dollars was still in the cash drawer. "Not surprising," he added.

"Because?"

"They probably figured it wasn't worth the extra time stumbling around in the dark to go out front and check the drawer." He told her that the lock on the side door had been broken. "Were all the doors locked?"

"Yes. We were in here alone, just me and Rose."

"But your alarm wasn't armed."

"I do that when I leave."

"All right. What we have so far, from what you and your girlfriend told Officer Pulaski, is that someone—your girlfriend says there were two of them and one was definitely male—broke in, flipped the breaker, and then robbed the safe using some kind of torch. They worked quickly, they didn't speak, and they were gone within five minutes of their arrival."

"Yes. That's what Rose told me, too…."

The detective paused to check his notes. "The safe is empty." Well, duh. "What was in it?"

"The money from the register."

"How much money?"

"A little over ten thousand dollars." *Thank God she had insurance.*

"That's all?"

She almost laughed, though there was nothing the least bit funny about it. "What? It should have been more?"

He didn't answer, only asked another question. "How much money do you usually keep in the safe?" She named a figure. He said, "That's considerably less than was stolen."

"Fridays and Saturdays are the busiest. So nights like tonight, we really clean up. I make a bank run every day we're open. We're closed Sunday and Monday, but I take what we make on Saturday to the bank Monday mornings. I don't like to leave a lot of money lying around."

"How many people know where the safe is?"

She admitted, "Several. Most of my employees are also my friends, people I trust."

"I'll need a list from you—names, addresses and phone numbers of the people who would know where to go in this building to get to the safe."

She thought of that list. Everyone she cared

about—including her mother, for cryin' out loud—would be on it. "I…sure. Okay. Then, um, you think it was someone I know?"

"Ms. Jacks. The whole thing happened way too fast. And in the dark. I'd guess it was someone who knew this place blindfolded."

Phoebe had been thinking pretty much the same thing. Still, it shocked her to hear him say it. "My two main bartenders have the combination. I think we can eliminate them. They didn't need to use a blowtorch to get the money."

Ankerson only shrugged. "Yeah, and by doing it this way, they'd allay suspicion. I'll need their names and contact information, too."

"Okay…"

He scribbled on his notepad. "Your friend the P.I. says he's been looking into an unsolved vehicular homicide that happened on April fifteenth…."

"Yeah. My business partner, Ralph Styles, was run down and killed on Paseo Drive. Rio and I want to know who did it."

"Ralph Styles, I understand, was your business partner *and* ex-husband…."

How had he found that out so quickly?

The question answered itself: Rio. He would have told the detective everything. He wanted the police interested. And at last, they were. She hiked up her chin a notch. "That's right. Ralphie was my ex. And my friend."

"You got any enemies, Ms. Jacks? Anyone been threatening you lately?"

She frowned. "Didn't Rio tell you?"

"I'd like to hear about it from you."

So she told him about the messages on the mirrors. "Both the second and the third and final time that happened, Rio took pictures and tested for fingerprints."

"So I understand. He'll be handing that evidence over."

"Well. That's good. Right?"

Ankerson glanced up from his notepad. His lips twitched in what was probably supposed to pass for a smile. "How many surveillance cameras you got here?"

"Didn't Rio…?" She looked at his tired face and remembered. He wanted to hear it from her, too. "Three outside and a hidden one in my office. The VCRs are locked in a closet in the main storage—"

"Got that." He cut her off. "Mr. Navarro is giving the tapes to Officer Pulaski."

"Okay. But since the power was out…"

He gave her a look. Patient. Weary. And more than a little condescending. "We need the tapes anyway. With luck, we'll get a look at whoever broke in that side door—at this point, we're assuming they had to get in to throw the breaker. The camera at the side entrance would have been working when they busted the lock."

Phoebe blinked. "Yes. Of course. That makes sense…."

"Mr. Navarro is also your *new* business partner, right?"

The way he said that had defensiveness knotting her stomach and the throb in her head spiking. She took care to answer in a calm tone. "That's right. Ralphie left his half of this place to Rio."

Ankerson wrote on his notepad and a skinny middle-aged guy with thinning hair stuck his head in the door. "Got a minute?"

The detective glanced up. "You bet. Ms. Jacks, Sergeant Tilda. He's with our lab—excuse me a minute."

"Sure."

The detective got up and went out with the lab guy. When he reappeared, he muttered, "Sorry," dropped heavily into his chair again and flipped through his notes. "About those lipstick messages you found on the mirrors…"

Phoebe had to clear her throat. "Um. Yeah?"

"Anything special about them?"

Darla's sweet baby face swam through her aching head. She *knew* Darla hadn't left those messages. But Rio didn't share her certainty. And he would have laid it all out for the detective, anyway. Plus, they'd see the hearts when they got a look at the pictures Rio had taken. They'd be asking about them—and damn it, if she wanted the cops to figure this mess out, she knew she had to tell them everything….

"Ms. Jacks?" Ankerson looked at her probingly. She'd taken way too long to answer.

She rubbed the back of her head where the goose egg throbbed. "The *i*'s were dotted with hearts. Ralph Styles's widow, Darla Styles, who also works for me, dots her *i*'s that way."

He scribbled something else. "This Darla Styles… she knows where the safe is?"

"Yes." Might as well tell it all. He'd find out soon enough—if Rio hadn't already filled him in. "I guess you should know that Darla's half brother Boone is one of my two main bartenders."

He wrote some more on his pad, and asked without looking up, "Darla Styles got a grudge against you?"

"No. Absolutely not."

He did look up then. Those tired eyes seemed to see right through her. "She's the widow of your ex—who left his half of this establishment to your P.I. friend instead of her. And she's not even a *little* bit angry about that?"

"Yes. Darla was angry. But she wouldn't take it out on me. She and I are…very close."

"Close?"

"Yes. Close. That's what I said."

Ankerson jotted something else on the pad. Then he took a moment to flip back through it. When he spoke at last, he didn't look up. "Thank you, Ms. Jacks. I'd like that list of names as soon as possible."

Phoebe's head pounded. She just wanted to go home and to go bed. Wearily, she told him, "If I can use my computer in the office, I can print it up for you."

"Sergeant Tilda ought to be done in there soon. I'll have him tell you when he releases the room. Send Ms. Bertucci in next."

BY FIVE-FIFTEEN, ANKERSON had completed his interviews. The lab guy had taken his pictures and collected the evidence to take back to headquarters. They'd decided against dusting for prints, since Ankerson had learned that virtually all of Phoebe's employees—who also were looking like the main suspects—had access to the office in the normal course of a day. Plus, there was Rose's statement that the men who'd attacked her wore surgical gloves.

Back in the front, at the bar, Sergeant Ankerson passed out business cards to Rio, Rose and Phoebe and said he'd probably be getting back to them with a few more questions. A report would be filed and he'd make it a point to interview everyone on Phoebe's list. "I've written the incident report number on the back of my card. You'll be able to have a look at it in a few days, once it hits records and the girls have a chance to get it typed up. And please," he added, "if you have any questions, or, more importantly, if you think of anything else relevant to this incident, give me a call."

The uniforms, the lab guy and Ankerson left. At last.

About then, the open-all-night locksmith that Rio had contacted arrived. Rio led him to the side door and the broken lock.

Phoebe only wanted to put her aching head down on the bar and not move until Rio took her home. But she couldn't let Rose take off without thanking her for being there. So she dragged herself to the office and hovered in the doorway while Rose grabbed her tote from the floor by the desk. When she straightened and turned toward Phoebe again, she pasted on a game grin.

"Hey." Rose held up the tote. "What do you want to bet that skinny old guy from the OCPD lab knows I carry a condom in my wallet?"

Phoebe looked at her friend's wild hair, wilder than ever right now, and the dark smudges of stress and fatigue beneath her brown eyes, and almost forgot her own pain and exhaustion. Darlin' Rose. Always trying to be so tough. "I know it was awful. I'm sorry. But I can't tell you how glad I am you were here…."

"Oh, come on. What the hell are friends for? One thing, though. That lab guy better not have run off with my license and credit cards." She gestured with the tote again. She looked so…lost, suddenly, standing there, swinging the tote, eyes swimming with tears she refused to let fall.

Phoebe went to her. She set her own purse on the desk and held out her arms. Rose moved eagerly into them. They held each other tight. For a long time.

When Rose pulled away, she sniffled and swiped at her eyes. "They did take my velvet jacket, can you believe that?"

Phoebe squeezed her bare shoulder. "Must've been the blood all over it. What hardcore forensics guy could resist booking something like that into evidence?"

"Yeah. Must be it…" Rose sniffed again. She shut her eyes, turned her head away. "Well. Better get home…" She tried to pull free of Phoebe's hold.

But Phoebe didn't let go. "Rose? You all right?"

Just like that, Rose's brave front shattered. She let out a loud sob and the tears overflowed. "Oh, Pheeb…"

Phoebe grabbed her close again and held on tight. "Hey. What is it? Honey, what's wrong?"

Rose dropped her tote. It plopped on the floor at Phoebe's heels as she whispered in Phoebe's ear between sobs, "That detective…that Ankerson character, he thinks I was in on it…."

"What? No…"

"Yeah. Yeah, he does. Damn it, he does…."

Phoebe hugged her some more and patted her back till the sobbing faded down to a sniffle or two. Then she pushed her gently down into the spare chair, grabbed the box of Kleenex from her desk and held it out. Rose yanked out a handful and blew her nose.

While she waited for her friend to pull it together, Phoebe shut the office door against the possibility that Rio might wander in. Then she went behind the desk and sank gratefully into her chair.

When Rose had it down to a stray sniffle or two, Phoebe said, "Look. It was the same for me. When Ankerson questioned me, I wondered once or twice if he thought I'd set up my own bar to be robbed."

Rose was shaking her head. "Uh-uh. This was different. This was more than him just bein' generally suspicious."

"Different, how?"

Rose shook her head again and sniffled some more.

Phoebe kept after her. "Come on. How?"

"Well. He, um, pointed out twice how you were knocked out cold and they didn't do anything to me except tie me up. He said how *odd* it was that I got away without a scratch, that I managed to wiggle out of that bag they tied me in so *quickly,* that I got the flashlight and got the lights back on so fast, that I must have been dialing 911 within three or four minutes after those assholes took the money and ran."

"And did you tell him that I'd *told* you where the flashlight was just a second before they hit me? That you know where the breaker box is as well as I do, being as how you're my best friend and you've been working here for years?"

"Yeah. Yeah, I told him. I don't think it helped. He was also real interested in the fact that I was married to Ralphie once. Now, how did he know that? Why would Ralphie even come up?" Phoebe knew. Rio. But she decided it would be wiser not to bring Rio into it right now. Rose went on in a bad imitation of the detective's deep drawl, "'Ms. Bertucci. How many wives did this Ralph Styles *have?*' He seemed to think it was pretty bizarre. All of us, Ralphie's wives, being best friends like we are. He wanted to know if my divorce from Ralphie was bitter, if Ralphie had left me anything when he died—and by the way, where *was* I the night that Ralphie was killed…"

"So you told him, right?"

"That I was with my then-boyfriend, Dexter. Yeah. Then he asked for Dexter's number, and I had to tell him that I didn't know where the hell Dexter DuFrayne and his Fender Stratocaster had gone off to, that I *thought* I'd heard he'd left town and moved on down to Austin to try his luck as the next Willie-frickin'-Nelson, but no. I didn't know exactly *where* in Austin…." Rose braced an elbow on the arm of the chair and cradled her forehead in her hand. "You know what? I've got a splitting headache—and I'm not even the one who got whacked on the head."

"Rose…" Phoebe sought the right words.

Before they came to her, Rose added two and two and came up with four. She raised her head and looked straight at Phoebe. "It's that damn Rio, right? I can smell him in this. He talked to Ankerson before I did, filled him in on all the, uh, interesting relationships around here. He probably thinks I helped those sons of bitches break in here tonight."

"Rose. No."

Rose threw up both hands. "No? No, what? No, he didn't get Ankerson suspicious of me? Or no, he doesn't think I'm an accomplice to assault and robbery—of my own best friend?"

"Rose. Listen. Please. Rio is trying to find out who killed Ralphie. He needs all the help he can get. The police have the resources and the manpower to make a difference. They're who we need on our side in this."

"Oh. *We* need the cops. Well, of course."

"Rose. Think about it. Think about the weird stuff that's been happening around here. You have to see that it's possible—likely, even—that Ralphie's death and what happened tonight are connected."

Rose gaped. "Connected."

"Yeah."

Rose leaped to her feet. "I've about had it with Rio and what Rio thinks."

"Rose, come on…"

"Uh-uh. No. Get this. Get it good. And pass the

news on to your boyfriend for me. I had nothin' to do with Ralphie's death. I don't know diddly-squat about it. I didn't write any lipstick notes on the mirrors around here. And all I did tonight was get manhandled and tied up in a laundry bag and kicked to the wall. Got that?"

"Oh, Rose. Please…"

"Uh-uh. Don't. Just don't. I am so outta here."

"Rose…"

But Rose wasn't listening. She bent and grabbed her tote. Then she stomped to the door, threw it open and flew off down the hall.

CHAPTER EIGHTEEN

Occasionally even a prairie queen will have a minor run-in with the law. I'm speaking of those little irritations like traffic tickets. Bear them with dignity, darlin'. Don't lose your head and start giving the officer grief. And *do not* bat your big eyes at him and say somethin' stupid like, "I didn't think you gave pretty women tickets." You will only force him to say, "You're right, ma'am. We don't. Sign here, please...."
—*from* The Prairie Queen's Guide to Life *by Goddess Jacks*

ONCE THE LOCKSMITH HAD replaced the busted lock, Rio paid the man and sent him on to his next job. An older guy, a cowboy type, in faded Wrangler jeans and a straw cowboy hat, he had a hitch to his walk.

Rio watched him limp down the narrow space on the nondriveway side of the building. Beyond him, above the furniture store across the street, the sky bled orange as the sun began its rise. The old guy disappeared around front. Not long after, Rio heard an engine start up, rev and soon fade away.

It was time—past time—to take Phoebe home.

Rio found her in the office, head down on her desk. Beat. He should have made her go home hours ago.

"Reina?"

She dragged her head up and looked up at him through lost eyes. "What a mess…."

"Come on. You need rest. Let me take you home."

She didn't budge, except to reach for her purse at the edge of the desk and haul it over in front of her on the desk pad. She looked beyond the purse—and through him—to some floating spot in the middle distance. "Rose left. Mad." Rio had seen Rose leave. She'd stomped past him and the cowboy locksmith, out through the side door without saying a word. It hadn't taken a lot of brain power to see there was a problem. Phoebe went on, "She says the cops think she was involved in what went down here this morning, and she figured out that you must have told the detective about Ralphie, including that Rose had been married to him." Phoebe paused, met his eyes and waited for him to say something. He knew better than that. The silence stretched. With a weary shrug, she continued. "Rose thinks Ankerson has singled her out as a suspect. She blames you for bringing her to his attention. And since you and I are partners, she blames me, too…."

It wasn't anything he hadn't expected—and nothing they needed to go into right then. "*Reina.* Let it go for now. Come home. Rest. You can call Rose and work things out later."

She blew out a breath and hung her head. "Tiff. And

now Rose. Both pretty much not speakin' to me. Never thought that would happen."

He repeated, "Home. Rest…"

Her head came up, finally. Wincing, she reached back and touched the spot where some lowlife had popped her. "Yeah. You're right. I know it." She put both hands flat on the desk, pushed herself to her feet and then slipped the strap of her bag over a shoulder. "Let's go home."

SINCE SHE WAS UNDER orders not to operate machinery right then, Phoebe left her car in back to pick up later. Rio drove.

When they got to the house, he herded her inside, worked the alarm, locked the door and took her hand.

She let him lead her into her bathroom, where he flipped the taps and got the shower going. As the water ran, heating up, he undressed her. He did it swiftly and efficiently, unbuttoning and unzipping, peeling everything away until she stood there before him, naked as the day she was born.

"Come on," he said with a soft smile. "Get in…"

So she climbed into the tub under the lovely, warm spray of the shower. She looked over at him and almost smiled. He'd moved back a step, but he was still there. Watching her, eyes soft and worried.

"I think I can handle it from here…" She pulled the shower curtain shut on him.

The steam rose up around her and the water flowed down her tired body. It was good. Just what she needed. A hot, soothing shower.

And then sleep.

First, she washed her hair, working up a good lather, flinching every time she bumped the swollen spot at the back of her head. Then she soaped her whole body and let the water run over her until all traces of blood, soap and shampoo were sluiced away.

When she pushed the curtain back, he was waiting with a towel. She let him dry her. He was gentle and so careful, big strong hands rubbing and patting.

Once her body was dry, she took the towel from him and wrapped it, turban-style, over her hair. He grabbed her terrycloth robe from the hook on the back of the door and settled it over her shoulders.

"¿Tienes hambre?" he asked. "Hungry?"

She shook her head. "I should dry my hair. But I don't have the energy…."

He caught her face between those two rough, warm hands of his and frowned into her eyes. "Are you dizzy? Do you feel sick?"

She almost laughed. "Rio. I'm fine. It's been a hell of a night and I'm tired." She caught his wrists, touched her forehead to his. "That's all. I promise you."

He pulled back enough to peer at her suspiciously. "Sure?"

"Positive."

"Okay, then. Come on…."

He led her to her bedroom, shut the blinds against the morning light and folded the blankets down. Then he eased the robe from her shoulders and unwrapped the towel from her head.

Her damp hair fell around her face. She smoothed

a hand down the coiling strands. "Dry enough, I think..."

"Good. Time for bed."

So she crawled onto the clean, cool white sheets. He settled the covers over her. *"Gracias,"* she told him.

"De nada."

She heard the rustle of his clothing and a moment later, he slid in beside her. He gathered her close, his naked body curling around hers. She sighed and snuggled against him. He did make her feel safe.

Safe...

Was there such a thing, really?

Not in her world, not lately. Not anymore...

TWO HOURS LATER, CAREFUL not to wake the woman beside him, Rio eased from the bed. She stirred and sighed, but didn't wake.

He bent close, dared to smooth a coil of silky hair back from her cheek. She shifted, sighed again, made a muffled, sleepy sound.

Her sleep seemed normal....

Didn't it?

She was turned on her side, away from him. He could see the ugly swollen spot beneath her hair where that *pinchi cabrón* had hit her.

The urge was a powerful one, to grab her shoulder and shake her, to watch her open her eyes, to listen to her grumble at him for waking her up.

He'd make her say that she was all right. And then he'd let her sleep again....

But he knew the urge to wake her was only his fear

for her talking. She was going to be okay. A little rest, she'd be fine.

This time.

Slowly, with reluctance, he pulled his hand away without disturbing her. She had a small, padded chair in the corner. He backed up to it, sank slowly onto it, braced his elbows on his naked knees and let his head drop.

He stared at the hardwood floor between his bare feet and thought all the self-accusing stuff he'd been refusing to face until now.

It was happening all over again.

What was his problem? Was he blind? He damn well should have seen this coming. He'd known that first day, in the bar, the kind of woman she was.

His kind.

Looking back, it was all so clear. He never should have chosen her, never should have made her his partner in the search for the secrets behind Ralphie's death. But she was the best choice, the most effective choice. So he'd lied to himself, pretended he couldn't see….

That he was leading her into danger, that what he felt for her was, from that first moment, about more than his dick.

Yeah. From their first meeting, he'd known what she was.

From even before that…

From when Ralphie used to speak of her: her strength, her loyalty, her intelligence…her long dark hair *y piernas bonitas;* beautiful legs. And clear green eyes.

She had intrigued him, even way back then, just listening to Ralphie talk about her. He'd known Ralphie had thought they'd make a match.

Rio hadn't bought that crap. But until Ralphie had turned up dead, he'd also made sure he never had a chance to find out if the man was right.

Yeah. The signs were there....

And he'd ignored them.

And now, here they were, the two of them.

Right where he should have known it would go. Deep into something that could get her killed, something that had almost done the job already.

It was Soledad all over again.

What the fuck had he been thinking? Steps had to be taken. He had to do what he could, get it through to her how things would go from here. And make sure she played her part and played it well.

Even if it was already too late, he had to do what he could to be sure she was protected.

THE PHONE WAS RINGING.

Another ring. Phoebe reached over and snatched it off the nightstand. "What?"

"Pheeb?" Darla sobbed in her ear. "Pheeb?"

Phoebe lurched fully awake. "Darla? You okay? Is the baby—?"

"No. Not the baby. Not right now...right now, it's..." Darla burst into a soggy fit of weeping.

Phoebe groaned and squinted at the bedside clock. Four...p.m.? Amazing. She'd slept the whole day away. And what *was* it lately with most of the women she cared about?

There was altogether too much damn crying going on. Yesterday, Tiff. This morning, Rose. And now Darla, who'd stopped the endless waterworks the last several days, had started in again.

Since you can't hand a Kleenex through the phone, Phoebe dragged herself up against the headboard, reached back to check the still-tender bump on her head, and waited until Darla wound down a little.

Eventually, Darla sniffed loudly and announced, "That detective Rio sent over here just left. He asked me all kinds of questions…about me and Ralphie, about those weird messages some creep left at the bar. I told him I didn't write those messages and I know nothin' about 'em. And I know nothin' about what that cop said happened at the bar at three this mornin'." Darla paused for a sob or two and an extra sniffle. Then she asked, "Pheeb, you still there?"

"Right here."

"That detective said you were hurt. Are you hurt? Are you okay….?"

"I got hit on the head. Knocked me out and gave me a headache. But I'll live."

"Well. At least you're okay." A sniffle. A stray sob. "Pheeb. He acted real suspicious, you know?"

"The detective?"

"That's right. He acted like he not only thought I hit you on the head last night and broke into the safe—*and* wrote those rotten notes on the mirrors. Not only that. He also acted like he was thinkin' that maybe I also killed my own husband." More sniffles. "I just… well, you know. It's not right. It's not fair…."

"Darla, it's what detectives do. When there's a crime, they go around and talk to people who might have been involved. Sure, they act suspicious. They *are* suspicious. Because someone did something they shouldn't have and it's a cop's job to find out who did it and why."

Darla made a low, sulky sound in her throat and then sniffed one more time. "Well. Okay. I guess you're right."

"I *am* right," Phoebe made her voice brisk. "Now. Tell me. How're you feelin' this…" She glanced at the clock. Yep—4:02 p.m. "…afternoon?"

"Okay. I guess."

"No more contractions?"

"A few. But not serious. Those *Braxel*-Hicks kind. But it's not too bad."

"Boone said when he left the bar last night that he was going over to check on you…."

"Yeah. He was here for a few minutes. You know how he is. He had to make sure I was okay. I told him not to worry. I was fine. So he left and I finally got to bed."

"What time was that?"

"What?"

"When he got there—when he left?"

Darla was silent for a moment. Then, carefully, she asked, "Why?"

Because I'm getting to be as suspicious as Sergeant Ankerson.

The thought brought sadness. Phoebe was slowly coming to accept the fact that someone she knew and trusted had killed Ralphie. That same someone looked pretty likely to have been behind what happened last night. And if Boone wasn't with Darla at about 3:00 a.m., he could have been anywhere. He could have been hitting Phoebe on the head, terrorizing Rose and robbing Phoebe's safe.

She said none of that. She only said, so casually, "I just wondered, that's all." Which was the truth, though not all of it.

Darla took a moment to answer. Phoebe steeled herself for another storm of weeping and a little outrage for Boone's sake: *You don't* trust *my brother. Boone would* never *rob you or hurt you and you know he wouldn't….*

But when Darla spoke, her voice was level. Off-hand. "Oh, I'm not sure. It's not like I was watching the clock or anything. I guess he got here a little before three and left at maybe ten after…."

Pretty much the time frame of the incident at the bar. So that ruled him out as one of the SOBs from last night, now, didn't it?

Unless he had someone else do the dirty work.

Or Darla was lying for him…

Sheesh. That was the thing about asking questions. Half the time the answers only created *more* questions. Phoebe rubbed the bump on the back of her head again. It was tender to the touch and it still throbbed in a dull kind of way.

Darla said softly, "Pheeb?"

"Um?"

"You sure you're okay?"

"Yeah. I'm all right."

"I'm sorry."

Phoebe pushed a few strands of hair out of her eyes. "For what?"

"Well, I guess you don't need me sobbin' on your shoulder every time some little problem comes up, now do you?"

"It's okay."

"Well, no. It's not. I gotta stop that. I know I do. I'm, um, workin' on it, Pheeb. I really, truly am—and now I think about, well, it's just what you said. That detective will be talking to everyone who works for you, and to your friends. It's not like he singled me out or anything…."

"Exactly. So. You okay now?"

"I am just fine."

"Those contractions get serious, you call me. Hear?"

"I will, Pheeb. You know I will."

Phoebe no sooner said goodbye and set down the phone than it rang again. She put it back to her ear. "Hello."

"How're you feeling?"

"Mama. Hi. I'm fine."

"I talked to Rio this morning. He told me *everything*. I am worried sick—but at the same time, I know that this terrible challenge is one you were *born* to face. As your mother, I want to grab you and hold you and protect you and never, ever let you go. But I can't hold you. You are your own woman, brave and strong and possessing the power to triumph over any and all adversity. Just know that I am here. Ready. Willing. Able. To help you in your time of trial."

"Good to know, Mama. Thanks."

"Baby, can I get you anything? *Do* anything?"

"No. Right at the moment, I've pretty much got it covered."

"About Tiff. And Rose…"

"Mama. Not right now, okay?"

"This is not pressure. This is just a word or two of wisdom."

With Goddess, it was never just a word or two. Still, Phoebe asked reluctantly, "What?"

"Baby, this, too, shall pass. I have seen you, the three of you. Darla Jo was there, too. I have seen you all, laughing, together. Tiff, Rose and Darla wore emerald green. But you were all in bridal white. It was your wedding day. Hon, I have seen it. I have seen what shall be…."

The bit about the wedding day was maybe a little much. But the rest? "At a time like this, Mama, that's real nice to hear."

ONCE SHE GOT RID OF HER mother, Phoebe grabbed her robe from where Rio had laid it at the foot of the bed and raced for the toilet. Relief and a half. She rinsed her face and washed her hands and spent a bleak moment gaping at her own reflection.

Face haggard. Hair like a bunch of snakes. She'd have to do something about the disaster that was her appearance—as soon as she got a little food in her growling stomach.

Maybe Rio would make her one of those big Mexican breakfasts, with the eggs and the chorizo, the salsa and warm tortillas. Her mouth watered just thinking about it and her stomach growled even louder.

She left the bathroom and went looking for him. It was a small house. She didn't have to look far. She found him sitting on the bed in his room, his duffel, backback and various P.I. paraphernalia surrounding him.

"How you feeling?" he asked.

"I been better."

"But you're okay?"

"Yeah."

He rose. "I didn't want to leave until you woke up."

He grabbed the pack and put it on. "I need to get set up with a place. I'll be back in an hour, okay? We'll talk."

"A...place?"

He hefted his duffel. "Give me an hour. We'll hash it out."

"But—" The chiming of the doorbell cut her off.

He said, "That'll be Mac."

"That other P.I.?"

He nodded. "He'll watch out for you until I get back."

"I don't need—"

"You're not supposed to be alone, remember? Not yet."

"But I don't—"

"An hour," he repeated. And then he brushed past her, headed for the front door.

CHAPTER NINETEEN

More good news about sex: it relieves headaches. A lovemaking session can release the tension that restricts blood vessels in the brain…
—from The Prairie Queen's Guide to Life *by Goddess Jacks*

BY THE TIME RIO'S RENTAL car pulled back into her front driveway an hour later, Phoebe had fixed her own late lunch. She'd spent a little quality time with a bottle of conditioner, a blow-dryer, blusher and a mascara wand—and she was sitting calmly in the living room, fed and made up, watching a *Fear Factor* rerun.

Rio unfolded that big body of his from the car. He adjusted his sunglasses against the afternoon glare and shoved the door shut. She had the sound on the TV up kind of loud. It fit with her mood: watching people eat worms and get covered in bees at high volume, anticipating the big moment when the host, Joe Rogan, announced, "And fear is not a factor for you!" She watched Rio through the window, to the accompaniment of angry bees buzzing and Rogan shouting and the contestants making grossed-out noises.

Mac Tenkiller, who'd gone out to the porch to wait for Rio about the time she turned on the TV to full volume, stood from the steps as Rio approached. The men shook hands and Mac went down the front walk and got into the SUV waiting at the curb. Rio mounted the steps. Once he reached her door, he did exactly what she knew he would do: *He rang her damn doorbell.*

She saw him raise his muscled arm and give the bell a punch. The bell was loud enough that she heard it—another kind of buzzing altogether—over that of the swarming bees.

He rang her doorbell....

Even though he had a key. He rang it because he was moving out on her and ringing the doorbell was more proof of that fact—proof that matched up with his empty room and empty closet.

So considerate of him, to give her all these *subtle* signals, to give her time to prepare herself before they had the *big talk.*

Well, guess what? She was prepared, all right. Just not in the way he meant for her to be.

The sound of the bell faded beneath the buzzing of the bees and Phoebe stayed right where she was. When she didn't answer, he rang it again.

When she *still* didn't answer, he took off his sunglasses and cupped his hand on the window and looked in at her, sitting there. She looked right back at him and she gave him a big smile.

And only then did she point the remote at the TV. It went dark—and blessedly silent. She rose and smoothed her skirt and straightened her cute summer T-shirt and went to let him in.

Yanking the door wide, she blasted him with another blinding smile. "Rio. Hey. Great to see you again."

She stepped back and gestured him inside. He hesitated, his eyes wary.

"Well?" she asked, too pleasantly. With clear reluctance, he moved forward. Once he was in, she shut the door. She gestured at the sofa. "Have a seat."

He stayed where he was. *"Reina—"*

She put up a hand. "Don't." The single word was a sentence and she meant it to be. "...call me that. Not right now, okay? At this moment, I'm not your damn queen."

He gulped. She saw him do it. And then he launched into the spiel he'd probably been rehearsing all day. "It's too dangerous for you to stay involved in this. I want you out of it. Now. I'm back at the hotel and I'm staying there. You're going to tell everyone how I moved out and you don't know anything about what I'm up to. You don't know and you don't care. You're out of it. You're done. I've messed up your life and hurt the people you love. So you want nothing to do with me *or* with trying to find out what happened to Ralphie. You're letting the police take over, letting them handle it, from here on out. *¿Entiende?*"

She said the only word that really mattered right then. "No." He swore. Something very bad. Even though it was in Spanish, she could tell that much. "No," she said again, just to drill the main point home. "I don't understand. We've been through this. More than once. I've told you I'm not pulling out. And you know what? You really should have asked me before you decided that I'd changed my mind."

"There's nothing to ask. You *have* changed your mind. As of now."

"I haven't. And I won't. Not ever."

He frowned and she saw pain in his eyes—for her. "Don't say that." His voice was softer as he tried to make her understand what she would never understand—let alone accept. "It's the only way. After last night—"

"Stop." She raised both hands, palms out, and waited. When he kept his peace, she suggested levelly, "Okay. Good idea. Let's talk about last night."

He swore again. "Phoebe. They could have killed you…." The pain in his eyes intensified—for *her*—for what could happen to her.

She saw that pain and the anger she'd been flogging drain away to nothing. She longed to reach out to him. But she didn't. She knew that *he* had to reach first.

She exerted all the will she possessed not to move toward him as he added, in a low, desolate rumble, "They almost did kill you…."

"Well, not quite." She tried a wry smile. It didn't work. He only stared bleakly back at her, his fine mouth a thin line. So she said, "I know you think you're doing the right thing walking out on me in the middle of this. I know you think it's the best you can do for me. But you're wrong. Oh, Rio, whatever *you* do, I'm not giving up. I just can't."

"You can. You will."

"Uh-uh. I couldn't live with myself if I did. Whatever

you do, I'm not done and I won't *be* done until I know how and why Ralphie died, until the slimeballs who held up my place get what's coming to them, until I find the scum-sucking coward who left those threatening messages in lipstick on *my* mirrors. Maybe I can't do much without you. But I *can* tell everyone that you only moved out to protect me, that I'm still looking for the bastards who've been terrorizing me, that I'm not giving up."

He muttered something under his breath and dropped his sunglasses on the TV. "*Escúcheme.* Listen—"

"Rio, I *have* listened. I've heard every word you've said. I understand you completely. But I'm just not going to do this the way that you want me to."

"Damn it, it's pointless, don't you see, for you to make some *stand* over this?"

"I'm not making a stand. I'm just telling you. I won't give up, whatever you do."

He said nothing for a moment. Then he tried bargaining. "Look. We can stay…in touch on it, all right? I'll keep you informed. Just between us. But I want you to tell everyone you're through, that you're out of it. If you're convincing enough and no one sees us together, it will work. If whoever's doing this really believes that you're done with asking questions, that you and I are finished…"

She looked at him steadily. "But we're not finished. Not yet. And you know it. And besides, it's too late. Whoever's behind all this, I'm a target now. No matter what I do, that's not going to change until we catch the bastard."

"You don't know that. *I* think they want you out of it and if you *are* out of—"

"Rio," she said, tenderly now. "You're repeating yourself."

"Because you're not hearing me."

"It's too late."

"No…"

"Yeah. It's too late, and you know it's too late. And—listen very carefully—*it's not your fault* that it's too late."

"*¡Qué chinga…!*" He reached for her, then. At last. He took her shoulders, his strong fingers digging in—hard enough that it hurt. She didn't let herself so much as wince. She was glad—*glad* that he touched her. A little pain was nothing, not now, when there was so much at stake.

"It *is* my fault." His dark eyes burned into hers.

"No."

"*Sí. Cúlpeme.* Blame me. Because I am to blame." His voice was low and ragged. "I dragged you into this. I *worked* you, that first morning I came here to your house. I manipulated you, to get you to help me."

"Oh, please. You know me better than that by now. No one ever talked me into going somewhere unless I was already on my way. It wasn't you workin' me that got me involved. I'm in it by my own choice. It was already too late for me to back out the day that you came to town, the day I started to see that I *had* to do something, that I couldn't sit by and wait and hope that somehow, someday, someone would figure out what happened to Ralphie."

"But if I'd never showed up here, you'd have—"

"What? Done nothing? Sat by and hoped and waited. Been *safe?*"

"Yeah. You would have been safe. A hell of a lot safer than you are now."

She kept her gaze locked with his and she didn't waver. "Oh, Rio, don't you get it? I'm really glad you're here, that we're in this together. It helps. A lot. But if you're not here—if you go away, cut me out, or even if you'd never showed up in the first place—I'm on this sucker anyway. You go, I'm doing it on my own. I'm not lyin' to *anyone* that I'm out of this. Ever. So you can't cut me out and make me safe. Because I'm not safe and I won't be safe until we find out who's behind all this and make sure that person is put away."

His grip had gentled. He rubbed her arms, as if to soothe where he had hurt her. He said, so low she read his lips more than heard him, "I keep seeing my Soledad. Naked, covered in blood. I keep thinking that it could happen to you…."

She put her hands on his hard chest, felt the warmth and the strength of him. And then she lifted up to brush a light kiss on his tanned throat, lingering long enough to breathe in the scent that belonged only to him, and to kiss him again—so lightly, at that purple spot on his jaw where Dave had hit him.

His dark blue knit shirt had a collar. She smoothed it. "You have to give that crap up, you know? Just…say goodbye to it. It's nothing but macho bullshit to blame yourself for something someone else did. *You* didn't kill your fiancée. And if something happens to me, you won't be the one who hurts me. It's just really terrible logic to tell yourself I'll be safer if you're not around. Think about it. If you're not around, what I'll be is without your protection."

He pulled her closer. *Yes,* she thought. *Finally.* His warm breath stirred her hair as he whispered, "How do you do it, *Reina?* How do you make it all sound so clear and simple?"

She slid her hands around him and linked them behind his narrow, hard waist. "All right," she whispered, laying her cheek on his shoulder.

He nuzzled her hair and muttered, "All right, what?"

"You can call me *Reina* now…." Did he actually chuckle? It sure sounded like it. She lifted her face to him. "And it *is* clear and simple. You're not moving out. You're staying right here." He didn't agree, but he didn't say no, either. "Rio," she whispered. "Please…"

"You're crazy, you know that?"

"Rio. Kiss me. Please…"

He shook his head—but then, oh so tenderly, he lowered his mouth to hers.

Oh, my….

Nothing felt as good as that—as Rio's lips on hers. Whatever happened, however this all turned out, as long as she was still breathing at the end of it, she would always have this: the memory of his arms around her—of the two of them, together. Touching. Kissing. Laughing. Curled up tight in her bed in the darkest part of the night.

When she didn't have him, there'd be the memory of this kiss.

Oh, my. This kiss…

It started out slow and tender, his mouth drifting over hers, his tongue teasing, coaxing. She let her lips part enough to take his tongue inside, scraping it softly with her teeth, bringing a soft moan from him.

He gathered her closer….

And from melting tenderness, there was sudden fire.

Clothes went flying—her T-shirt, her skirt, his shirt, her bra. She put her hands on his smooth bare chest and let them trail down….

She unhooked and unzipped him, took the sides of the khaki cargoes he wore and spread them wide, catching the waist of his boxers, easing it out of the way.

She broke the kiss to look down at him, at his hard belly and the dark nest of hair and his gorgeous cock swelling, lifting out from his body in growing arousal, tenting the elastic of his boxers.

With a moan, she lifted her head again. He took her mouth, spearing his tongue inside—as she closed her fingers around him. He groaned again, and pushed his hips against her.

She steadied him, waited….

He shuddered and went still.

And then she stroked him, slow strokes, taking her time with each one, from the silky crown downward, into the nest of his boxers, all the way to the base. As she stroked him, she guided him, back to the door of her room and through it, along the side of the bed, toward the nightstand up by the headboard.

When they got there, he knew what to do. He reached behind him, groaning into her mouth, sliding the drawer open, as she continued to toy with the lovely, thick length of him—carefully, so gently, she stroked him. She didn't want him coming. Not yet.

She only wanted to drive him a little bit wild.

Yeah. Okay, it was payback, a little tender sexual torture, because he'd tried to leave her.

He couldn't leave her.

It simply was not allowed.

Not yet. Not until this was over, not until they had the answers, not until the bad guys were caught and doing time.

He had the condom out, even tore open the wrapper, but he dropped it on the bed when she sank to her knees before him on the thick bedside rug. She still had her hand around the hot length of him. With the other hand, she eased his cargoes and boxers down his hips a little, so they were out of her way.

Delicately, she stuck out her tongue to taste him, to trace the shape of him, the narrow groove at the top, the flaring rim. She felt his hand, a warm cradle at the back of her head, guiding her, and she wrapped her mouth around him. She took him in, slowly, with tender, heated care.

She took him in and she let him slide gradually out, wetting the length of him, feeling him swell, impossibly, harder, thicker, and more satiny still… A deep groan escaped him, followed by a muttered string of passionate, unknown, musical words…

And then he was taking her shoulders, pulling her

up to him. He kissed her. Deeply. And then he set her away from him—just long enough to get out of his cargoes and his boxers, his boots and his socks. He tossed his clothes in a wad to the far side of the bed, threw the boots in the corner.

One big arm came out and he took her around the waist, pulling her against his side as he reached for the condom, slipped it free of the wrapper and rolled it down over himself, all with one hand.

Once he was covered, he gathered her close again. She still had her panties.

But not for long. He eased his fingers under the bit of elastic that held them in place, then knelt and swept them down. She braced her hands on his big shoulders to keep her balance as she stepped free of them. One side caught on a flowered flip-flop, so that came off, too. He bent forward, pressed a kiss to the silly sunflower tattoo she'd gotten years ago, one weekend when she and Tiff and Rose had gone down to Dallas….

His hot tongue touched her, traced the sunflower and the so-sensitive groove of flesh where her hip met her body. She slid her fingers into the black silk of his hair, letting her head drop back on a pleasured sigh. But he only placed a quick kiss over the dark thatch that covered her sex and straightened to rise above her again.

He muttered her name and caught her to him, hands cupping her, lifting her.

The other flowered flip-flop went flying. It hit the

wall behind him as she wrapped her legs around him and he lowered her down onto his heat and hardness.

Oh, when he filled her. There was nothing else then, when Rio filled her. Her fears. The threats. The danger. The sudden, cruel rift between her and her truest friends. Everything. All of it…

Blasted away in a blinding haze of heat and glory.

When Rio filled her, nothing else mattered. Her heart to his heart, it was perfect. Right. And so very, very good.

Rio pressed so deep into her, no way to get deeper… and yet, by some miracle, going deeper still.

She locked her ankles around his waist. He turned. Two steps and he had her at the wall. He backed her carefully into it, so she could brace herself for his thrusts.

She held on tight, arms around his neck, legs locked at his waist, getting some leverage. Using the wall and her grip on him, she could move with him as he glided out—and slid back in.

All the way…

Each thrust shattered her. She couldn't take any more. And yet, somehow, every time he pulled back, she only whimpered for him to fill her again.

And he did—oh, he did. Until each nerve in her body quivered on the brink.

She was building, reaching…

And then, gripping him hard and tight, burying her head against his shoulder, whispering his name, she hit the peak.

The world exploded into pure sensation. She

pushed herself tight against him—and then held absolutely still. The deep, wonderful pulsing of her climax took her, over the edge and down into velvet darkness.

Phoebe sighed and held him tighter. Once more, on a low moan, she whispered his name.

CHAPTER TWENTY

Drive carefully, now. It's not only cars that can be recalled by their maker.

—from The Prairie Queen's Guide to Life *by Goddess Jacks*

WHEN IT WAS OVER, HE WAS SO gentle with her. He laid her on the bed and he kissed her as the sweat cooled on their bodies and the pleasure faded down to a sweet glow.

After a while, they got up and showered and dressed. She rode with him to the hotel so he could check out and get his things. On the way, they discussed the events of the night before. She told him the police had been to see Darla—and that Darla had claimed Boone had shown up at her double-wide at pretty much the same time the bad guys had broken into Ralphie's Place.

"It's interesting," he said. "Darla has a false alarm. I leave to take her to the hospital—and while I'm gone, you're attacked and your safe is robbed."

"Yeah. I noticed that, too. And I'm guessing so did the police—but that doesn't mean she's involved."

He didn't comment. He didn't have to. Even in profile, with his eyes on the road, she knew that look. He was more suspicious of Darla than ever.

She couldn't blame him—but she didn't agree. Did that make her a fool?

Maybe.

Or maybe she saw something in Darla that nobody else had—except Ralphie. Something determined, something true. Something that had Darla Jo Snider Styles fighting to make a good, honest life for herself and her baby, against all the odds.

At the hotel, Rio pulled the car into a space near a side door. She waited while he went to his room to get his stuff. Then he drove around to the porte cochere in front and headed to the main desk to check out.

She watched him disappear through the wide glass doors and thought how he wasn't like Ralphie. And he wasn't like the bad boys in leather she'd turned to in the years since Ralphie had broken her heart.

Nope. Rio wasn't like any of them. Not deep down. He was…better. Stronger, as a man, more determined. More focused. In all the ways that mattered, he was more like Hank Jacks than any man she'd ever been with.

Funny how she'd always chosen weak men: Ralphie, who couldn't stay true; the others, who were wild and bad and passionate and completely undependable. Even after she'd had such a good example of what a man could be while she was growing up, she'd somehow always managed to choose a guy she wouldn't stay with.

Maybe—at least after Ralphie—she'd wanted it that way. She ran her own life and answered to no one and that was just fine with her.

Until recently, that is, when she'd started considering the revolutionary idea of finding a good man and staying the course with him. Yeah, at first she'd decided that what she needed was a nice, easygoing, settled-down type of guy. Now, though, after knowing Rio, she wondered: Would a nice, easygoing guy be a match for her, really? What would it be like to try building a life with a slightly more…challenging man, a man who could stand toe to toe with her?

Rio emerged from the hotel and Phoebe felt a blush steal up her throat and flood over her cheeks. Getting whacked on the head must have addled her wits. She was suddenly planning their future—when she knew they didn't *have* one. Rio had made it perfectly clear to her: When this was over, he was outta here.

She reached across and shoved the door open for him. He slid in behind the wheel. "All set." He leaned closer. Did her face betray her thoughts? Worse, was she still blushing like a lovesick teenager? He must have seen something that worried him, because he frowned. "*¿Qué pasa?*"

She wanted to tell him. But she didn't. "Not a thing. Drive."

AT THE HOUSE, HE PUT HIS things away. Then he demanded to have a look at the bump on her head.

She let him look—and insisted yet again that she was fine, that it hardly hurt at all anymore.

He said, "I need to go out again—and you need someone here with you."

She promised him she was fine. He wanted to call her mother. It was the last thing she could handle right then—her mother, asking questions, giving advice, passing on messages from the spirit world. She called a neighbor whose daughter liked to babysit. The fourteen-year-old was only too happy to come over and keep an eye on Phoebe for as long as Phoebe needed watching. They agreed on an hourly rate.

And Phoebe had a sitter.

Rio left.

Phoebe didn't ask him where he was going. Probably to see her supposed friends. He would want to talk to Bernard, Boone and Darla—if he could *get* them to talk, that is—about their possible involvement in the robbery last night. And then there were Tiff and Rose and Dave; she really hoped he didn't meet up with Dave. That encounter wouldn't be friendly.

Or maybe he was headed down to police headquarters, to see if *they'd* learned anything new….

Then again, maybe he just plain wanted a break from her. He was doing things her way, yeah, but she knew he wasn't exactly thrilled about it. He still felt she'd be safer if he moved out and she told everyone she hated him.

And in the end, what did it matter where he might be and why he'd left? She'd won the round. He was staying at her place for now and they were still working openly together to get some answers. It was enough.

She tried to call Rose in the faint hope of patching things up. No answer. She left a message. "It's me. Give me a call. Please. Let's talk it out…."

By nine at night, Rose hadn't called back and Rio hadn't returned. Jeez. A girl could get to feeling downright unpopular.

She fixed herself and the sitter a light meal and then didn't have the heart to eat it. Another hour went by. Rio didn't come home and the phone failed to ring. She considered going to bed—but for what? She'd slept all day and she wasn't tired now.

Finally, at quarter after eleven, she saw the glow of headlights pulling into the driveway.

She opened the front door and pushed the storm door wide as Rio got out of the car. He came toward her up the walk. In the distance, lightning forked. The rumble of thunder followed. The air had that ozone smell—heavy. Moist.

She ushered him in and shut the door on another lightning flash. Leaning back as the latch clicked behind her, she met his waiting glance. "Storm coming."

"Looks that way."

Rio paid the neighbor's daughter and they followed the girl out to the porch to see that she got safely across the street and in her front door.

Back inside, Phoebe turned to him. "Want a beer?"

"Yeah."

She went and got him one and they sat on the sofa.

After a couple of thoughtful sips from his Corona, he told her, "I stopped in at the bar, just to have another look around. Nothing new there. I even checked the tapes to see if we'd had visitors since we left this morning. We haven't. I've also been to see Sergeant Ankerson—among other people. The police found the spot on the tape where the bad guys busted in the side door."

Her heart was suddenly beating too loud and too fast. "Did they let you see it?"

He nodded. "Two men. They wore stocking caps. And they were covered from head to toe—dark turtlenecks, dark pants, dark shoes, those surgical gloves Rose talked about. A real problem in terms of trying to identify them."

"There was nothing…identifiable about either of them?"

"One's bulkier, more muscular, average height. The other's leaner and taller. The lean one had a pack—probably containing the torch they used to bust the safe. And they didn't waste any time. Drilled the lock with a power drill, and they were in."

"Well. At least we're reasonably sure there were only two—and that they were both guys."

"They looked like guys to me. But most of the time they were in camera range, they spent right up close to the door. Not a good view, looking down on their stocking caps."

"Maybe I should see that tape. I might notice something else about them, something familiar that no one else caught…."

"Can't hurt."

"I'll call the detective tomorrow."

He tipped his beer at her. "Ankerson works nights."

So she got up and called him. He wasn't there, but she left a message. She rejoined Rio on the sofa. "You think maybe they hit me with the handle of that drill?" She reached back to finger the tender, swollen spot.

He shrugged. "Since we don't have the drill, there's no way to know."

"No way to know. That's pretty much the story here, isn't it?"

"Not really. We've got their general body types. We've got that they were too familiar with the back half of the bar to be strangers. And we've got how quick and cool they were about it. Didn't miss a beat. Didn't say a word. Didn't drop that damn drill. Took you and Rose down, in the dark, without a hitch. Got the safe open, grabbed the money and left the scene, all within five minutes or so."

"You're right. They were real pros about it."

"Which indicates they've probably done that kind of thing before. And more than once. Robbery is a high-stress occupation. For beginners especially, there's usually some kind of screwup. You don't get that quick and smooth at it without practice."

The rain started. It spattered the roof, punctuated by more thunder. Beyond the window, lightning brightened the night in flashes. And the wind was up. Phoebe could hear it gusting around the eaves outside. She picked up the remote and pointed it at the TV, hitting the mute button as soon as it popped on to a shot of Gary England, weatherman extraordinaire, a Doppler map behind him.

She looked over at Rio and found him watching her. "Hey. It's Oklahoma. This time of year, a thunderstorm can mean trouble."

"Tornadoes, you mean?"

"That's right. And by the time the siren goes off, it can be too late. I like to follow it on Doppler, get a little advance warning. Looks like the worst will pass south of here." The warnings that scrolled at the bottom of the screen didn't include Oklahoma County. At least, not yet. She glanced his way again.

He looked a little worried. "You got a storm shelter?"

"No. But they have one next door. And they share." She faced him, bringing her legs up, curling them to the side, bracing an arm on the back of the sofa. "What else did Ankerson tell you?"

"Not much. And before I went to talk to him, I dropped in on most of your friends."

"And?"

"Bernard wasn't home. Neither was Boone. I did speak with Darla. She told me what she'd already told you. I went to Tiffany and Dave's. Dave ordered me off the property, but then Tiff came to the door and wanted to know if you were all right. When I said you were, she shut the door in my face."

"Ouch." Phoebe winced, then asked hopefully, "Rose?"

"Not home—or if she was, she wasn't answering the door. I went by there twice."

"Well, you're not the only one she's not home for. I called her, to try to patch things up. She didn't answer. I left a message, but she hasn't called me back…." Outside, lightning blazed. Thunder rolled. The drumming of the rain intensified.

Rio set down his empty beer and took her hand, pulling her closer. She turned off the TV, dropped the remote on the coffee table and settled against his side, letting her head rest on his shoulder. For a minute or two, they were quiet, listening to the storm outside, safe. Together.

For right now…

Which was fine. Good. Better than good.

He smoothed her hair with his big hand. "What do you say we try and get some sleep?"

"Before the tornado siren goes off, you mean?" She felt him stiffen and laughed. "Just kidding—but you have to admit, getting hit by a tornado about now? Pretty much more of the same."

He set her gently away from him and stood, holding down a hand. She laid hers in it and he pulled her up beside him. "Come on," he said and wrapped an arm around her.

They turned for her room.

IT RAINED ON AND OFF ALL night. A real good show, lots of lightning flashing and long, hard rolls of thunder. For several minutes at a time, the rain would drill the roof as if determined to beat its way in.

But if there were tornadoes, they weren't in the metro. The sirens never called them from bed.

By morning, the rain had slowed to a drizzle. The sky was an even sheet of gunmetal-gray. Rio made breakfast.

While they were clearing off, he said he'd go with her to Ralphie's Place. "It all seems to happen at the bar. Until this is over, you're not going there alone. I'll be with you when you go—and I'll stay for as long as you stay."

She set their plates on the counter and turned to him. "Not today, you won't. Today, I'm not going in, period. We're closed and there's no bank deposit to make, since a couple of scumbags in stocking caps stole it. I've got to call my insurance company. But you know what? Even that can wait."

"I think that's smart. You can take it easy for a day. Relax a little. It'll be good for you."

She had other plans. "I was thinking I'd go with you when you try again to talk to—"

He was shaking his head. "Bad idea."

Okay, she hadn't really expected him to say yes—but did he have to say no before she even finished making the suggestion?

True, he was the professional. She'd probably just be in the way. But then again, they were *her* friends—or they used to be. Maybe she could help. Maybe he ought to give her a chance.

"Um…and it's a bad idea, because?"

"Just take my word for it."

Irritation prickled through her. "*Just take my word for it.* What kind of answer is that? You think I'll be in the way, interrupt your, er, line of questioning? Well, I won't. I won't say a word, if that's how you want it."

"Phoebe. These are friends of yours. Even if you don't try to protect them, or put answers in their mouths—"

"Hello. I said, I won't say a word."

"It's still not a good idea."

"Why not?"

"Because there could be trouble. Because there's bitterness toward you..."

"I can take trouble. That should be pretty clear to you by now. And as for bitterness, well, are you trying to tell me they're not bitter toward you?"

"Phoebe—" He reached for her.

She jerked back before he could touch her. "Answer me."

He dropped his arms to his sides. "Yeah. There's bitterness toward me. Plenty of it. They don't like me. But in the end, I'm just some nosy SOB to them. If I work them right, I might get them talking, anyway. But you...you're a friend."

She got the message. And it hurt. "A friend who betrayed them. Is that what you mean?"

"Hey..."

"Don't." She whirled away from him and fled to the window by the table. Crossing her arms over her middle, she stared out at the gray, drizzly day—and felt like an asshole. "Sorry," she said low, without turning. "I guess I'm a little on edge...."

In that silent way he had, he was suddenly behind her. His warm hands clasped her shoulders. He pulled her back against his body. She resisted—but only for a moment. Then, with a sigh, she let herself rest against him.

"I don't think you betrayed them, *Reina.*" His voice was a low rumble in her ear.

"But *they* do. Tiff even said as much. Right to my face."

"But it's not true. And you know it." He guided her around so she was looking at him. His dark eyes held hers. "You've been a good friend. A true friend. To all of them. And at least one of them has betrayed *you.*"

She nodded. "And Ralphie. Someone betrayed Ralphie in the worst way of all."

He laid a hand against the side of her face. She felt that light touch all the way to her toes. "*Es verdad.* In the worst way of all…"

She tipped up her mouth. He took it. They shared a kiss—slow and sweet and tender. When she pulled back, she put on a smile. "Okay, then. Instead of interviewing suspects, I think I'll go shopping."

He grinned. "Now, you're talkin'."

"Summer's almost here. I need more sandals. And a new bikini…"

"I wouldn't mind seeing that. You in your new bikini…"

"Better yet. If you're real nice, I'll let you get me *out* of my new bikini."

"Now, there's an offer I'll never refuse."

RIO WANTED TO DRIVE HER to the mall. He remained worried she'd have some scary after-effects from the concussion. He suggested he drop her off and pick her up later. She swore she was fine.

He said, "Call *tu madres.* She can drive you."

"Rio. Enough. I'm driving myself." She reminded him how the paramedics had said she needed watching for twenty-four hours. "It's been that long—and then some," she insisted. "Plus, I feel fine. No dizziness. No nausea. None of the symptoms they told us to watch for."

In the end, after letting loose with a series of choice words in Spanish, he gave up and let her leave on her own.

The rain started in again as Phoebe got in the car to head for Crossroads Mall. Crossroads had a couple of smaller stores she favored, stores that weren't at either of the other two major local malls.

The rain turned to hail as she eased onto I-235. She cranked the radio up and sang along to moldy oldies and refused to think that her car might get hail damaged.

Uh-uh. No dreary, grim thoughts of any kind. Not today. She wasn't worried about a thing—not a little hail, not the loss of Ralphie that still remained a complete mystery, not all the friends she no longer seemed to have.

She would shop till she dropped. Eat something loaded with fat, carbs and calories at the food court. Shop some more.

And tonight, given half a chance, she would take off her new bikini for Rio—and then jump his very fine bones.

The hail faded away, but the rain came down harder. I-235 became I-35. When she pulled off onto the service road, she had her wipers going full speed. She drove at a crawl, ducking her head closer to the streaming windshield, peering through the beating wipers, which simply couldn't keep up with the flood. Other vehicles were no more than blurred spots of color of varying sizes—blue and green up ahead, a black smudge sliding past, going the other way, a big blob of red in her rearview mirror….

She made the turn at Sixty-Sixth, no problem, since there was a light. But getting off Sixty-Sixth onto the street that circled the acres of mall parking—that one she almost missed.

Not quite, though. She spotted the turn and slammed the wheel to the right just in time. Driving at about five miles an hour, she left the mall road at the first opportunity and cut across the expanse of streaming empty parking lot, aiming the car at the flat-roofed, sprawling shape of the mall itself.

She supposed it wasn't that surprising, how deserted the place was. How else could it be on a gray gulley washer of a Monday like this one, at five minutes after the mall opened its doors?

And deserted was great, she decided. Just fine with her. No crowds. No waiting forever in long checkout lines. Yeah, she could drown on the way to the entrance, but in pursuit of cute sandals and the right bikini, sacrifices must be made.

She parked by the north entrance. Since the lot was virtually empty, she got the first space in the row across the driveway from the doors.

The rain intensified—was that possible? Seconds before, she'd thought how it couldn't come down any harder. So she sat there for a few minutes, listening to the radio, watching the windows steam up, kind of hoping the downpour might ease off a little before she made a run for it.

It didn't happen.

And hey, what was an umbrella for, anyway?

She grabbed hers from the floor of the passenger seat, hooked her bag more securely onto her shoulder and shoved open her door. Sticking the umbrella out into the downpour and sliding it open, she swung her feet out, got upright, staggered a step and shoved her door shut, turning to beep it locked with her electronic key. By then, even with the umbrella, she was soaked to the skin. Her cheetah-patterned flats would never be the same. She hesitated. Maybe she ought to just get back behind the wheel and wait some more.

But what for? She was already wet. Might as well hotfoot it for the doors. She took off, splashing through the wash of streaming shallow water, her umbrella close to her back to keep it from bouncing and maybe snagging on a stray gust of wind.

She didn't see the vehicle until it was almost on top of her. She heard an engine revving, whipped her head toward the sound.

It appeared to be her own red van, barreling toward her. She blinked. Couldn't be.

But it was. She wasted a precious fraction of a second gaping at the windshield and got a hazy view of the face behind the wheel: not a face at all. Just gleaming eyes and a black stocking cap.

Phoebe tossed the umbrella toward those eyes and launched herself at the curb.

CHAPTER TWENTY-ONE

When everything's comin' your way, hon, it's just possible you're in the wrong lane.
—*from* The Prairie Queen's Guide to Life *by Goddess Jacks*

PHOEBE HIT THE FLOODED asphalt. It was not graceful, it was not pretty. And she landed on her shoulder first. That hurt like hell—a jarring, bone-deep pain, rattling its way over to her spine and on down it.

With a sharp cry of pure terror, she rolled, sucking in dirty rainwater as it splashed off the asphalt and not caring in the least. Instinctively tucking into a ball, hands cupping and protecting the back of her head, she came up hard against the curb, throwing up more water. A wave of it spilled over her.

But the water didn't matter. What mattered was the van had whizzed by and she hadn't been hit.

She couldn't believe it.

She wasn't dead. The bastard had missed her. Scrabbling, half crawling, making mewling, whimpering noises, she surged up and onto the wide strip of sidewalk in front of the mall, certain with every stunned beat of her heart that the masked driver would try again.

But the van only kept going, skidding, wheels squealing as it made a sharp right at the edge of the building and disappeared from sight.

Phoebe squinted through the veil of driving rain, staring at the spot where the van had turned the corner and vanished, ready to spin and stagger through the mall doors if it came for her again, hardly daring to believe the danger was over.

"Not coming back…not coming back…" She heard the words and a moment later realized she was the one saying them. Oh, God.

Not coming back…

Her knees went to rubber. She sank to a sitting position, drawing her legs up, burying her head in them, suddenly freezing, shivering like some junkie desperate for a fix. The rain pelted her back and ran in miniature rivers from her hair, over her cheeks, into her mouth, down her neck.

Not coming back…

She was safe. From her own damn van. For the moment, anyway.

The spasms of shivering subsided a little. She dared to lift her head and take stock.

Her shoulder ached dully. Blood welled from angry scrapes on both knees. Her car key was digging into her palm; she hadn't let go of it. Her umbrella? The wind must have taken it; it was nowhere in sight. And her purse…?

In the driveway, smashed flat. The bastard had

missed her, but ruined her favorite bronze metallic hobo bag. Also, her skirt was a sopping-wet mess, streaked with dirt and peeled all the way back from her thighs, revealing not only the streaks of blood that ran down the outside of each thigh from the cuts on her knees, but also her drenched panties….

With a groan, she got her legs under her and pushed herself upright, tugging at her soggy skirt until it slithered down to cover her. She staggered out into the driveway again, head whipping frantically back and forth as she went, ready to leap again to safety should the van reappear.

She scooped up her flattened, soaked bag and would have kept going, back to her car, if a female voice hadn't gushed from behind her.

"Oh. My. Gosh…"

Clutching her smashed bag, Phoebe whirled toward the sound. A girl of maybe sixteen, with spiked red hair and striped knee socks stood just beyond the mall doors. Another girl, prettier, with long blond hair, came out behind her. They both held umbrellas, yet to be opened. The blonde let out a yelp of dismay. The redhead, keeping carefully beneath the overhang, protected from the rain, called to Phoebe, "Hey. You okay?"

"Not really." *Rio,* she was thinking in a numb, shattered kind of way. *I have to call Rio. Rio should know about this.* She armed water out of her eyes, opened her bag—and found what was left of her cell.

She wouldn't be calling Rio on that….

The two girls waved her forward. "Come on!" said the redhead. "You're, like, soaked…"

"Yeah," said the blonde. "Come on out of the rain..."

"Someone just tried to run me down," Phoebe said, in a voice so calm and colorless she hardly recognized it as her own. "Do you think I could borrow a cell?"

THE REDHEAD DIDN'T HAVE a cell. And the blonde had forgotten to charge hers.

"Wow. Sorry," said the blonde. "This blows."

"Oh. My. Gosh," chimed in the redhead. "Shouldn't we find a cop or something? I mean, if somebody tried to run over you, you should, like, report it, don't you think?"

The redhead was right. She should find someone in mall security, make some kind of complaint. But she was soaking wet and still shaking and just not ready to suck it up and act rationally while she talked to a mall cop.

It all seemed...much too complicated. Bizarre, even. She remembered the other night, the endless interviews, first with Officer Pulaski and then with Sergeant Ankerson. This, today, could end up the same, or even worse. If she told the mall cop everything—about Ralphie and the lipstick messages and the other night, about how it was her own van that had almost killed her, and that the person behind the wheel had worn a stocking cap just like the dirtbags who had held up her bar not thirty-six hours before...

What was mall security to do, but keep her there, soaking wet and bleeding, until someone from OCPD could be called in to ask her *more* questions?

And what had just happened sounded…kind of crazy, didn't it? And if not insane, well, it sure didn't sound real. And the van was long gone—and really, what proof did she have that it had been a van identical to her own, anyway?

She asked the redhead, "Did you happen see who almost hit me?"

The redhead frowned. "No. When we came out the doors, you were, like, out there in the pouring rain, picking up your purse." The redhead looked at the blonde for confirmation and the other girl earnestly bobbed her golden head.

So. The girls hadn't seen the van—let alone someone in a stocking cap driving it. And Phoebe should have thought faster, tried at least to get the plate number….

Two older women ran toward them across the driveway, sparing them barely a glance as they reached the protection of the overhang, collapsed their umbrellas and pushed through the mall doors.

The blonde said, "Come on. Let's—"

But Phoebe was already shaking her head, backing away, out into the rain. "No—no thanks. You've been great. Really…"

She forced a smile, thinking, *Rio.* She really needed Rio. He would know what to do. It was a ten-minute drive to her house and right now it couldn't be more than, say, twenty past ten. He'd still been there when she left. If she hurried, maybe she could catch him at home.

And even if she couldn't, there would be a phone at

home. She could call him, tell him she needed him *now*....

"Wait," said the redhead. "You don't look so good. And you really should, like, talk to—"

"Sorry. Gotta go." Phoebe turned and ran back the way she'd come, splashing across the driveway, beeping her car open, yanking back the door and sliding in behind the wheel.

ELEVEN MINUTES LATER, THE rain was back to a drizzle again and Phoebe was turning the corner onto her street.

"Oh, thank God," she whispered at the sight of Rio's big car, parked in her driveway, right where it had been when she'd left forty minutes before. He was still there!

And she was shaking and shivering again....

She swung into the driveway behind his sedan and hit the brakes just before she rammed the back of it. Then she slammed it in park, ripped the key from the ignition and literally fell out the door. She stumbled up the walk, almost tripped on the steps and finally made it to her own front door. She grabbed the handle of the storm door—locked.

Instead of trying to fumble with her keys, she pounded on it, shouted, "Rio! Let me in!"

He was there within seconds. The door swung inward and the storm door swung back. She let out a cry—of gratitude, of something hot and hurting that still managed to feel a lot like joy. "Oh, God. There you are. At last..."

He opened his arms and she fell into them.

FOR A WHILE, RIO SIMPLY held her, standing right there inside the storm door, whispering soothing words, letting her cling to him. Whatever had happened, it had freaked her out pretty bad.

He could feel fury trying to build in him—toward the *pinchi chingado* who'd done this to her. He tamped his rage down. It wasn't useful.

Finally, she pulled back enough to look at him. "Oh, God. It was awful. Rio. My own red van. Someone tried to run me down in my own red van. Someone in a stocking cap, just like the guys who broke in my place…" She grabbed him close again, buried her head against his shoulder.

He stroked her wet hair. "Easy, it's okay. You're safe now." She was shivering. He waited, holding on, until the shivering stopped.

Then, gently, he took her shoulders and held her away. "Come on." He caught her hand, pulled her toward the sofa. "Sit down and tell me everything."

She sank to the sofa. He took the wing chair to her right, and leaned toward her, bracing his elbows on his knees: close, but not touching, keeping just enough distance to watch her face as she spoke. She set her keys on the coffee table. And then she shook her head and blinked. She looked at the scrapes on the heels of her hands, at her cut-up knees that were still oozing blood. She sent him a bewildered glance. "Maybe I should, you know, clean up a little?"

He shook his head. Not till he knew what had happened. There might be evidence of some kind that needed preserving, stuff a shower would wash away.

"In a minute, okay? First, though, I need you tell me, slowly and as calmly as you can, what the hell happened to you."

"Rio. I told you. It was my own van. At the mall. It came at me while I was crossing from my car to the entrance. It was…it was all like a dream, you know? Not real. It was raining so hard and I…I…" She let out a small cry and buried her face in her hands.

He gave her a moment to get it together. When she finally lifted her head again, he said gently, "Just tell me, okay? Just start at the beginning and tell me everything you remember."

In a halting voice, she told him, about the pouring rain, the bad visibility, the van that had tried to run her down, the stocking-capped face behind the wheel, the two girls who'd tried to help her. She finished with, "I just couldn't bear to try and explain it all to a cop right then, so I came home, hoping you'd be here…." She swallowed, convulsively, and swiped away a couple of stray tears. "Oh, Rio. What should I do now?"

He picked up the phone from the coffee table. "We'll call the police."

"I know. Yes. Of course…"

"You're sure nobody else saw the van?"

"Pretty sure. If someone did, they're long gone by now."

"You're sure it was *your* van?"

"Oh, I…no. Not really. But it looked so much like it. How many badly repainted red vans of that make, model and probably that same year can there be?" She frowned and for a moment, she didn't speak.

"Phoebe. What is it?"

"Oh, I... There was something..." She waved her hand in front of her face. "But it's gone now." Her eyes went wide. She jumped to her feet. "And you know what? We need to go to the bar. Right now. We need to see if the van's still there. We need—"

He said her name, softly, and added gently, "One thing at time."

"No, I really think we—"

"Phoebe."

She pressed her lips together. "What?"

"I'm just trying to find out what you're sure about, all right?"

"Okay." She swallowed, nodded, sat back down. "I'm sure it was a red van, a red van the same make and model and around the same year as my own. I'm sure there was someone in a stocking cap behind the wheel."

"Think a minute..."

She blinked. "About?"

"Are you *sure* none of this is just your own...confusion and frustration talking?"

She scowled at him. "Do not start in about my concussion again. I am not confused because I got hit on the head. I was almost run down by a red van just now. It really happened. I swear to you it did."

"Just listen, okay? Just consider it for a moment. A red vehicle comes out of nowhere and almost hits you. You've been attacked at the bar by two characters that you know wore stocking caps. You know that the vehicle that killed Ralphie was red. So maybe, when you got that quick glimpse of the face behind the wheel—"

"No. Rio. I'm not making this up. I *know* what I saw."

"I didn't say you were making anything up."

"But you act like—"

"Just listen, okay?" He waited for her nod before continuing. "You said yourself it was pouring rain. You could hardly see to make the turn to the road that goes around the mall. You said you waited in the car for the rain to slow up. And it didn't. That means your visibility, when the vehicle came at you, had to be pretty low. And it all happened in a matter of seconds. Don't you think it's possible that it was just an accident? That the driver of a vehicle somewhat similar to your van was going too fast and didn't see you crossing to the entrance?"

She was shaking her head. "No. It was a red van like my van—more than just similar. Almost identical. There was someone in a stocking cap behind the wheel. I saw those eyes. Those eyes were looking right at me. I know the driver saw me and I know he—or she—was *trying* to hit me. It was no accident. It was on purpose…."

He knew he had to keep after her, though it grated on him to do it. The police would have all the same questions. Better if she got her story straight now, if she admitted to herself, up front, whatever doubts she might have about how it had really happened. "It was pouring so hard. I don't know how you *could* have seen whoever was behind the wheel—not clearly. I say the best you could have done under the circumstances is made out a blurred shape. Isn't it possible your mind is filling in the blanks for you?"

She didn't answer for a moment. He waited as she considered, but in the end, she only shook her head again. "Rio. I know what I saw."

They shared a long look. She *did* seem certain—yeah, she'd been under serious stress lately. But she *was* Phoebe. Not the type to go into hysterics, not the type to imagine things that weren't there.

If she was sure, he supposed that was good enough for him. He nodded. "Okay. Let's call the police and see about filing a report."

Right then, the phone in his hand started ringing. He looked at the display. Not a number he recognized.

She held out her hand as it rang a second time. "Here. I'll take it."

"You sure?"

She nodded. He passed it to her. She put it to her ear. "Hello? Yes. This is Phoebe Jacks... Oh." She listened, frowning. "But Officer, I don't see why you..." She got to her feet again. "All right...I understand... I'll be there as soon as I can." She punched the off button. And then she just stood there, the phone in her hand, staring off into the middle distance through dazed eyes.

He cleared his throat. "Phoebe?"

She shook herself and turned that blank gaze his way. "That was, um, Officer DePaul..."

Rio didn't get it. "DePaul? I don't remember any Officer DePaul..."

"Me neither. He's a patrol cop, I guess. He, um, he said they got a tip."

"What tip?"

"He wouldn't say. He just said he needed to get inside the bar and since it's all locked up, would I come over and let him in."

"He didn't say why?"

"No..."

"I don't like it," Rio said. "He could be anybody. He could be the bastard who hit you on the head the other night."

"Unreal." Phoebe blew out a hard breath. "All of this. Just totally strange and bizarre. In broad daylight, the guy who robbed the bar would call me up and *lure* me there?"

"In broad daylight, somebody almost ran you down, remember?"

SO RIO USED THE NUMBER STORED in Phoebe's phone and called the officer back. Phoebe tuned out the conversation. By then all she wanted was a bath and a long nap.

When he hung up, he said, "Okay. It's for real. Just a cop thing, that's all."

"A cop thing..."

"Cops. They don't like to let you know any more than you absolutely *need* to know. And they're suspicious. They're paid to be that way."

"Suspicious of what?"

"No way to know. Except to get over there and find out."

They took Phoebe's car. Rio drove. Phoebe was fine with that. She was still feeling shaky. She needed a hot shower and a little time to patch up her cuts and scrapes. Some Advil for her bruised shoulder would be nice, too.

Oh, and clean clothes. Yeah. Clean clothes would be heaven.

But she'd promised the officer that she'd go right over to the bar. And besides, judging by Rio's reaction to her story, she was going to need all the corroborating evidence she could get when she told Officer DePaul about what had happened to her that morning. Better to look like just what she was: a person who'd barely survived a close encounter with a too-familiar-looking red van.

Rio *had* grabbed a wet washcloth for her before they left. As they'd went, she wiped the streaks of blood off her legs and dabbed at the cuts on her knees.

They were almost to the bar before Phoebe remembered that she kept an emergency bottle of Motrin in the glove box. She got it out and dry-swallowed three of the suckers, and hoped that would cut down the throbbing in her shoulder and the pounding in her head.

OFFICER DEPAUL WAS waiting in his black-and-white around back. Rio parked the car to the side and they both got out. So did the officer.

"Ms. Jacks?" he asked.

"Call me Phoebe."

He nodded, his sharp eyes taking everything in: her matted, dirty hair, her mud-streaked torn shirt, her scraped-up knees. He asked for ID. Both she and Rio provided it. It took Phoebe a minute to dig her driver's license out of her wallet, which had been mangled pretty badly when the van had run over it.

As the cop handed back her license, he asked, "Are you all right, ma'am?"

"Well, no. I'm not. I…" She didn't know where to start.

Rio came to her rescue. Quickly and with a clarity that Phoebe found truly amazing, he brought the officer up to speed: from Ralphie's death to the lipstick messages on the mirrors, to the break-in, assault and robbery early Sunday morning.

Then Phoebe picked up the story, repeating what had happened to her outside the mall. Officer DePaul listened to the whole thing with an interested but non-committal expression.

When Phoebe finished, he said, "Let's just have a look inside now. We've had an anonymous tip on the whereabouts of the vehicle in the H and R of your ex-partner, Ralph Styles."

Phoebe's mouth went dust-bowl dry. "Someone said the car that killed Ralphie is inside that garage?"

"That's about the size of it, ma'am. So let's have a look. Once that's out of the way, I'll be happy to take your formal report on the incident at the mall."

"Uh. Sure." So Phoebe unlocked the big door and Rio shoved it up. As Phoebe stepped to the side wall to deal with the alarm, she noticed two things: there was no other vehicle, just her van. There was also water—on the floor and beaded on the body and windows of the van.

Someone had taken it out.

For a ride to the mall, maybe?

Hand shaking, she punched the code that turned off the alarm as Rio flicked on the light and he and the officer moved deeper into the garage. A moment later, she hurried to join them. By then, they were standing at the front of the van, staring at it. She hustled to Rio's side—and gasped at what she saw.

The front grill was caved in and something had hit the hood *and* the windshield; the safety glass had shattered in place in a spiderweb pattern. And there was blood—brown, old, but definitely blood—on the windshield. It looked like maybe someone's *head* had hit it. And there were streaks of blood on the hood, too—dried blood that the rain couldn't wash off. And there were bits of something she didn't want to define caught in the caved-in grill....

Red...

A *red* vehicle had run Ralphie down. An SUV, a big pickup...or a full-sized van.

Her van?

But how? "I can't...I don't understand. This van has been parked here since Ralphie died. And until today, I swear, it was fine. Undamaged."

Rio was nodding. "I'll attest to that. I've seen it. I saw it yesterday afternoon, as a matter of fact. Parked right here. The front end was fine, not a crack in the windshield or a dent in the hood or the grill."

Officer DePaul said, "Step back, please. Don't touch anything. I'm calling this in."

CHAPTER TWENTY-TWO

Don't suffer from insanity. Enjoy it!
—from The Prairie Queen's Guide to Life *by Goddess Jacks*

THEY WAITED, PHOEBE AND Rio, with a stone-faced Officer DePaul, for the original detective who'd worked Ralphie's case.

Sergeant Runson, a vehicle fatality investigator, was on what DePaul called the Signal 30 squad, whatever that meant. Runson showed up about a half an hour after Officer DePaul had put in the call.

Phoebe knew Runson, more or less. A trim middle-aged guy in gray slacks and a sport coat, he had salt-and-pepper hair and sharp blue eyes. She'd spoken with him several times in those first days after Ralphie died. He asked her how she was doing.

She told the truth. "I've been better."

He took a look at the van, scribbled some notes on a clipboard, and nodded. "Damage consistent with a head-on H and R." He told her they were impounding the vehicle. It would be processed at "the Barn," a large metal storage area, guarded and alarmed, where the guys from the lab could take their time going over it in a controlled environment.

What could she say? "Well, sure. Great. Take it away."

After that, it was Sunday all over again. Phoebe waited outside with Officer DePaul while Runson talked to Rio first. She bleakly resigned herself to answering the same endless series of questions, to reporting all the weird goings-on since she and Rio had started trying to find out for themselves who'd run Ralphie down.

But when Runson emerged—alone—from inside, he said, "You know, Phoebe, I think it would be better if you and me went on down to headquarters. We can talk there." He led her over to where Officer DePaul waited by his squad car and opened one of the rear doors.

Phoebe saw the cage between the back and the front seats. She drew herself up tall. "Sergeant Runson, am I under arrest?"

He didn't say yes and he didn't say no. "We'd just like to talk to you. Sometimes, for that, headquarters is the best place."

She held her ground. "I'd, um, like to talk to Rio first. Could you bring him out here, please?"

Runson gave her a long look and then muttered, "Just get in the car, please."

She ordered her knees to stop shaking. "Are you arresting me?"

"Phoebe. Right now, what you need to do is get in the car."

She probably didn't have to. He'd never *said* she had to. And he hadn't read her her rights. Didn't they have to do that, before they could take you away?

And what had she *done?* Nothing. She was totally innocent of any wrongdoing and as such, she had nothing to fear from a trip down to headquarters.

Right?

Well, except for the fact that she was the registered owner of the van that had very likely killed Ralphie Styles. "Sergeant Runson, I'd just like to talk to Rio first, please. Uh, briefly."

Runson looked kind of peeved, but he had DePaul go inside and bring Rio out.

Rio saw her and came right for her. And she ran to him. At that point, she didn't care if she didn't look strong, if the cops thought she needed a man to lean on. Right then, she did need a man: She needed Rio to tell her what to do next.

She flung her arms around him. "They want to talk to me at headquarters," she whispered against his shoulder.

He held her close and spoke over her head to Runson, "Is this necessary?"

Runson shrugged. "We'll check out the van. Then we may have more questions for her. It's just wiser if she comes with us now."

Rio took her by the arms and when she looked up at him, he spoke to her softly. "Go. Tell them whatever they want to know. As long as they don't arrest you, you're free to go at any time. Remember that. If it gets too bad, ask for your lawyer."

"But I don't have a—"

"You will. I'm going to get you one now. That lawyer and I will be waiting out in front at headquarters. All you have to do is ask for him."

Runson opened the rear door to the squad car again.

Rio pulled her close again. "Oh, come on. She's agreed to go with you. She'll answer all your questions. There's no damn need to increase the freak-out factor here."

Runson gave in and let her ride in the passenger seat of his unmarked sedan.

AT HEADQUARTERS, THEY LED her to an interview room. It was small and a little too cool in there, with a table and three chairs. Runson told her to have a seat—and then left.

He was gone for a long time. Phoebe sat there alone, trying to keep her head up and her expression serene, slowly scanning the room, looking for the camera that she just knew was recording her every shiver and sigh.

The longer she sat there, the colder it seemed. She wrapped her arms around herself and wished for more Motrin, for a hot cup of coffee, for a sweater, at least….

Time passed at a crawl. How long? She had no way to gauge. Why the hell hadn't she thought to put on a watch that day?

She hugged herself harder, hunched her head down into her shoulders and thought about all the strange events of the morning. The incident at the mall, the bizarre discovery of the van that looked just like hers, parked in the usual space at the bar, but suddenly with the front end all crunched up, as if…

She swallowed down the sudden urge to gag and made herself think the unbearable.

As if it was the vehicle that had killed Ralphie Styles.

But if it *was* that vehicle, then where was the undamaged van that had been sitting in its place for the past five weeks? Who, of all the people she knew and trusted, had killed Ralphie Styles with her own van, or one just like it and then…?

She sat up straighter. And in her head, she heard Rio's voice Saturday morning, reporting on her mother's dream of riding around in Darla's car with Ralphie.

Goddess. Remember. Sometimes I'd get two….

Two.

Yes!

Two…

There had been another van, hadn't there? Another van more or less identical to the one Ralphie had given her to use at the bar. He'd got them both in the same deal six years ago, hadn't he?

What had he said about it? Phoebe shut her eyes, let the words come floating back to her….

"Got me one just like it, babe. I'm keepin' it. Man never knows when he'll need to do a little haulin'…."

She had laughed, hadn't she? Yeah. She'd laughed and told him, *"Ralphie. If you need to haul something, you can use this one."*

"Yeah. But all the same, I might hold on to the other." He'd winked at her. *"For a while, anyway..."*

So had he kept it? She didn't recall hearing about it or seeing it again.

But…

Say that he had kept it.

Then it would just be…

A problem of storage.

A problem of storage, like in her mother's other dream. One van could have been used to run poor, sweet Ralphie down. And there'd still be a spare, to put in its place. Just switch the license plates and, for a while at least, till someone had a reason to check into it closely, who would guess? Who would even imagine such a thing?

Phoebe was shivering again. And not with cold. She hunched close to the table, wrapped her arms around herself tightly, and tried to think where Ralphie might have stored that other van….

She was still pondering that one when the door opened and Runson came in. He didn't look cheerful. He had a manila folder in his hand.

He threw the folder on the table. "Well, Phoebe. It's official. On two counts. The VIN numbers on the van we found at your place of business confirm that it's *your* van, Phoebe. Registered to you. And we were able to get the lab to run a couple of quick matches. Hair and fibers caught in the grill of that van are a match with samples we took from the body of Ralphie Styles."

The body of Ralphie Styles...

Tears burned her eyes. To hear the cop say it like that…to think of those strange bits of stuff she'd seen caught in the grill of the van. Bits of Ralphie, goddamn it.

Phoebe felt her stomach try to rise to her throat again. She gulped. Hard. No way was she chucking her cookies right now, in this chilly bare room, with sharp-eyed Sergeant Runson looking on.

"Well, Phoebe?" the detective said.

She sat up straight and she told him, so carefully, "I think there might be another van."

He gave her a cool, disbelieving frown and repeated loftily, "Another van." He cracked a smile, one dripping with irony. "Now, that's a good one."

She refused to rise to his easy, practiced baiting. "I'm not sure. When Ralphie gave me the van, he mentioned that he'd gotten another one at the same time. One just like it. He said something about holding on to it—he would do that, sometimes. He was always making deals, trading this for that, buying and selling things. Especially cars. Sometimes he'd…get two or three at a time."

"Where is this other van now?"

"I haven't the faintest idea. He never mentioned it again. I don't know what happened to it. But it shouldn't be that hard for you to find out if he had a van like mine at the time of his death, should it?"

"No, Phoebe." Patronizing. Doubtful. "It wouldn't be too difficult."

"Good. Because two vans would explain a lot, don't you think? One van could have killed Ralphie and then the other van could have been substituted for it, until the moment the murderer decided to put suspicion on me."

"The murderer. So. You admit it *was* a murder."

"Look. Could you just…please find out if Ralphie kept that other van?"

Runson said nothing. He looked at her, long and piercingly. And then, without saying another word, he turned and left the room.

Phoebe heaved a shaky sigh and hunched over the table again. He'd left the manila folder. Probably on purpose. Sergeant Runson didn't seem like the kind of guy who left things lying around for no good reason.

She held out maybe five minutes, telling herself she wouldn't look, that would just be playing into Runson's hands….

In the end, though, curiosity got the better of her. She slid the folder in front of her by a corner and peeled back the top cover.

Inside were photos of her van, a coroner's report and a lab report—and pictures of a body.

Ralphie's body…

Phoebe bit back an anguished cry, shut the folder and shoved it to the far side of the table. She shouldn't have looked in there. Oh, God. She squeezed her eyes shut, whispered, "Oh, Ralphie. Oh, God…"

Eventually, Runson returned. He pulled out one of the chairs across from her and sat down. "Okay, Phoebe. Let's talk this out. I understand that earlier today, you had a little run-in with someone driving a red van. Tell me about that."

Phoebe longed to start screaming, to call him a heartless bastard for showing her the pictures in that folder. But she held it together. She told it all—all over again. Everything. From the incident that morning and backward, to the lipstick messages and the break-in early Sunday morning. She told him the names of all the people who had access—and permission to use—her van. She admitted that she had no alibi for the morning when Ralphie was killed. "I was home in bed. Alone…

"But I didn't do it, Sergeant. I would never hurt Ralphie Styles. He was my friend and my partner. And you will never know how much I miss him."

"He *was* your ex-husband."

"Yes."

"Was it a bitter divorce?"

"Yes. It was also eight years ago. I'd gotten past it and Ralphie had, too."

"He wasn't much of a business partner, was he? I'd guess there were times you thought you'd do better if he wasn't around."

"Never. I never thought that. I loved him as a friend and I would never, ever have hurt him…."

It went on and on. Around and around. Runson left. Returned. Asked more questions. Left again.

Hours had passed. Phoebe asked to go to the bathroom. She was thinking that that would about do it for her. If Runson tried to keep her from taking a pee, she would do what Rio had told her to do once she couldn't take it anymore; she would demand to see her lawyer.

But Runson only went out and got a female officer

who took her to the restroom. When she returned, he offered her coffee.

It was enough to make her willing to go another round. Just barely.

And then, the next time he came back in, he told her, "All right, Phoebe. We've got word on that other van. You're right. There was one." *Almost,* Phoebe felt relief. But not quite. The look in Runson's piercing blue eyes said she could have been the one who switched the vans just as well as anyone else. "Think again, why don't you? Any idea where Ralph might have stored that other van?"

Darla. "Ralphie's widow might know."

Runson nodded. "We're already looking into that angle."

"Well. Good." What else could she say?

Runson slid into a chair again. And another cop came into the room. Runson introduced him: Major Thompson. He had soft, understanding brown eyes.

Runson leaned on her some more.

And then Thompson told him quietly to ease off.

Thompson was the one, finally, who hit her with their theory. Gently. In the kindest tones. "Phoebe. A lot of strange things have been happening to you lately. Those messages on the mirrors. The break-in and robbery. And this morning, that incident with the van at Crossroads Mall…I understand you saw someone in a ski mask driving that van."

"Yes. That's right. I did."

"Sometimes, Phoebe, when a person is feeling really guilty about something, when it's eating them up inside…well, sometimes a person in that position will punish herself." Thompson's soft eyes regarded her pityingly. "Do you know what I mean?"

Okay, she was gaping. She was gaping and she didn't care if they saw it. Her head pounded and her mind swam and the cuts on her knees burned. Her whole body was one big ache—and she couldn't believe what they were saying to her. "You think I killed Ralphie. You think I killed Ralphie and I'm so eaten up with guilt that I left myself messages in lipstick on the mirrors. I…what? Broke into the bar, knocked myself out, tied up my friend and torched my own safe? And then I *imagined* the red van this morning? That's what you think, isn't it?" She slumped in the chair and slowly shook her head. "That's what you think…."

Thompson's eyes were as kind as ever. "If you tell us the truth, Phoebe, it'll go a lot better on you. If you tell us all about it, tell us who you're working with, we'll do all we can to help you."

It was too much. Too hopeless. The final straw. They were never going to believe her. She could sit here and talk to them, answer all their questions over and over again until spring became summer and summer, fall. It wasn't going to help.

She needed out of here. *She* had questions of her own. A raft of them. She needed to get with Rio and get after getting answers. And she needed to do that ASAP.

"Major Thompson, Sergeant Runson. My lawyer should be out in front. I'd like to talk to him now."

CHAPTER TWENTY-THREE

It is impossible to lick your elbow, but that never stopped anyone from trying.
—from The Prairie Queen's Guide to Life *by Goddess Jacks*

PHOEBE'S LAWYER—A handsome woman in a great-looking, beautifully cut suit—marched into the interview room five minutes later.

She said what lawyers are always saying at such times. "Gentlemen. If you're not going to arrest my client, it's time you went ahead and cut her loose."

A few minutes later, Phoebe emerged into the waiting room at the front of the building. Rio stood from a plastic chair. She ran to him.

When his arms closed around her, she whispered, "Take me home."

Outside the glass doors, the sun was out, the air warm and moist with the memory of rain. Phoebe shook hands with her lawyer and admitted ruefully that she would probably be in touch. The lawyer went one way and Rio and Phoebe went around the building to where he'd left her car. He slid in behind the wheel. She got in on the passenger side.

Before he started up the car, he leaned across the console and tenderly cupped her chin. "*Reina.*" That was all, just his special name for her.

She gave him a trembly little smile. "I wanted out of there so bad, I didn't even think to look for a clock. What time is it?"

"About four."

She swore. "Over four hours, they kept me in there."

"Yeah. I was beginning to wonder if you would ever lawyer up." His lips brushed hers. They felt so *good.* When he moved to pull back, she caught him around the neck and kissed him again—only harder. It felt right, that kiss, it felt clean and sweet and fine. It felt…*real.* Unlike the endless hours in that bare, cold interview room.

He kissed her again. A long kiss, that time. Unbearably sweet.

And when he pulled back, she was able to let go of him. He stuck the key in the ignition.

She put her hand on his arm before he could turn it over. "Take me to Darla's."

Those dark brows drew together. "*¿Por qué?* You said you wanted to go home…."

"I changed my mind."

"You're worn out. You need to—"

She squeezed his arm. "What I need is answers. And I have a feeling that Darla's got a few of those."

"But—"

"Rio?"

"*¿Sí?*" He said the word resignedly.

"There are a couple of things you have to know…." And she told him about the other red van, which had been registered to Ralphie at the time of his death. She also shared the theory the police had about her. When she finished, she flopped back against the seat. "Yep. It's true. At the OCPD, they think I'm a real psycho-dog…."

"*Reina.* It's just a theory. You're the obvious suspect. It was your ex-husband who was run down in the street by your van. The hard truth is that most of the time, when a man is murdered, it's someone close to him that did it. As more facts come in, they'll start seeing things differently."

"I damn well hope so. But I'm not sitting still on this, not hanging back waiting for the police—or for you—to track down the truth."

"You're beat." He spoke soothingly. "If you go home, take a long, hot shower, eat something, get some rest, you'll see that—"

"More waiting. That's what you're telling me. Well, waiting's not working for me, Rio. The police need some answers. They need more information. They need another suspect, one that's not me. I intend to help them with that."

"*Reina—*"

She didn't let him get past her name. "To Darla's. Drive."

RIO HALF EXPECTED DARLA to be anywhere but at home in her cozy double-wide. He figured that by then the police would have been there, to ask her if she knew about that other red van. That would have spooked her—and should have sent her running.

But the red Sebring was sitting in the driveway and when they knocked on the door, Darla answered, wearing a lacy pajama top and a pair of battered jeans with the fly wide open, her huge stomach hanging out. Her feet were bare except for a couple of silver toe rings.

Darla ignored Rio and leaped on Phoebe. "Pheeb! I've been so scared…." She grabbed Phoebe around the neck and held on tight. Phoebe allowed that, but she didn't hug her back. When Darla finally let her go, it was only to seize Phoebe's hand and haul her through the cramped hallway to the living area, chattering away as she went. "It was just awful. I can't turn around anymore without seeing a cop. They were here again, all over me about that red van of Ralphie's…."

Phoebe dropped to the sofa and Darla sat down beside her. Rio hovered at the edge of the room. Why interfere? Phoebe was seriously on the case here. She had a look in her eye that said she would get answers, no matter what the cost.

"The red van," Phoebe repeated in a neutral tone.

"Yeah. You know. The one like the one you got at the bar. Isn't that weird, that they'd want to see that ol' thing? I swear it hasn't been out of the shed since Ralphie and I got married last December."

"The van is in the shed…."

"Well, no. See, that's what's real strange. It's not there, not anymore. I went and let the cops in there—and it was gone. *Pfffllt.* I think somebody stole it or somethin'. I just can't believe that. Someone broke in and stole that van and I didn't even notice it was gone."

"When was the last time you saw it?"

Darla's brow furrowed. "Well, I don't rightly know for sure. I never hardly go in that shed…"

"When?"

"Well, you don't have to yell at me—a couple a months, anyways."

"Darla."

Darla stiffened and craned back to peer at Phoebe anxiously. "Hey. You mad or something?"

"Darla, this morning some guy in a stocking cap driving a red van tried to run me down."

"No…"

"Yeah. I survived, as you can see. Barely. Then I got called to the bar where someone had parked the vehicle that killed Ralphie."

Darla gasped and put her hand to her mouth. "What? I don't…what are you talkin' about?"

"It turns out, that vehicle—the one that killed Ralphie—is my red van."

"But…but no. That can't be. I've seen your van since Ralphie…since Ralphie…." Darla's face started to crumple.

Phoebe grabbed her by the arms and shook her. "Don't do it, Darla. Don't you dare start blubberin' on me now. You suck it up and you answer me when I talk to you."

Darla went white, except for two spots of hot color high on her plump cheeks. But she also nodded, obediently. "Okay. Okay. I will. I promise…."

"Sure?"

Darla bounced her brown head up and down some more. "Yeah. Promise. Swear."

Slowly, those fine green eyes narrowed in fury and suspicion, Phoebe released the younger girl. "Okay. The van that killed Ralphie was *my* van. The police ran some tests and they know that much. That means—I am at least ninety-nine percent sure—that *your* van, the van that Ralphie left in that shed outside, was put at my bar on the night that he died. All this time, we've been thinking that *your* van is *my* van. Are you followin' me?"

"Yeah. Okay. Yeah..."

"Good. So I need you to tell me. Did Boone know that your van was in the shed?"

Darla rested both hands on the bulge of her belly and hung her head.

Phoebe waited for a count of three, before she demanded, "Darla. I'm in trouble here. You understand trouble?"

Still looking down, Darla did yet more head-bobbing. "Um-hm. Yeah. Um-hm..."

"The police are thinking that *I* killed Ralphie."

Darla looked up then, horrified. "Oh, Pheeb. No. Not you. Never."

"That's right. Not me. But somebody did. Somebody did it with my van, which means it was somebody we both know. By now, I've gotta bet on Boone. He's your brother and that means he's the most likely to have access to the van you kept in that shed."

Darla blinked and her eyes got even wider. "I... Oh,

Pheeb. He…well, he wouldn't. Boone wouldn't. He's…um, done a few bad things, but he'd never do murder. And not Ralphie. Oh, no. Not that…"

Phoebe picked up on the most interesting point. "What bad things?"

Darla shook her head. "Oh. Nothin'. Really. I don't know why I said that…."

"Did Boone know the red van was in the shed?"

"Well. He might have. I don't remember tellin' him, but who's to say what Boone might know—and you know what? I'm feeling a little tired right now. I can't deal with any more of you yellin' at me and stuff. It's not good for me and it's not good for my baby. So please. I'd just like you to leave now. Just go." She stood.

Phoebe tried once more. "Darla…"

But Darla only insisted, "This is my house and I want you to go."

"BOONE," PHOEBE SAID WHEN they got in the car. "Boone's place next."

Rio didn't even try to argue. He took her to Boone's.

Not that it did any good. They banged on his door and looked in his windows. Boone wasn't there—and neither was that yellow Camaro of his.

After that, finally, Phoebe allowed Rio to take her home.

The phone was ringing as they went in the door. Phoebe grabbed it off the coffee table as Rio turned off the alarm.

Rio heard her say, "Hello," and then, in a voice that

was both soft and excited, "…Yeah. Okay… All right…" He turned back to face her as she mouthed, *It's Darla.* Then she pushed the speakerphone button and set the phone gently on the coffee table with the speaker side up. She dropped to the sofa and Rio took the chair and they both hunched close to the speaker.

"Pheeb? Pheeb?"

"I'm here, Darla. Right here…"

"You sound strange. Different…"

"It's okay. I'm right here."

"Oh, Pheeb. I'm so sorry. I should have told you. Everything. I know it. But I…I guess I'm just used to lying for him. He scares me. He's hurt me before. So, well, I blew it. I ruined everything. I just…I kept hoping, you know. That he'd go away. That he'd finally just go and leave us alone. But Pheeb, after you left, I started thinking…about what you said. About those vans. About how someone killed Ralphie with yours and how my van is missin'. And I, well, I *hate* to think it, but you're right. He could have done it. He could have killed Ralphie…" She let out a cry. "Oh, my God. Ralphie…"

Phoebe said, "You mean Boone?"

On the other end of the line, Darla drew a ragged breath. And then she admitted it. "Yeah. Boone. Oh, Pheeb. Boone's not my brother, okay? He's the one I ran away from, when I came here…."

CHAPTER TWENTY-FOUR

Life's a killer. After all, at the end of it, you're dead.
—*from* The Prairie Queen's Guide to Life *by Goddess Jacks*

RIO FELT THE CRUEL KISS of cold rage. The little bitch had been playing them all—Ralphie included. It all came pouring out.

Boone had been Darla's lover. "But he would hit me. All the time. He treated me like crap. So I ran off. I didn't know I was pregnant. I found that out later. I met Ralphie. We were happy. I told him about the baby, but I lied just a little, sayin' it was only a one-night stand. Everything was fine.

"Then Boone shows up on my weddin' day. He...he thinks he *owns* me, you know? I thought he would ruin everything. But he said he had other plans. He said I could go ahead, marry Ralphie. He didn't give a damn about me getting hitched up to some old guy. He said I should tell everyone that he was my brother and I should vouch for him with you, Pheeb, so he could get himself a job at the bar. And I did. Oh, Pheeb, I did what he wanted. Partly because I was always afraid to go against him—but mostly to keep Ralphie from finding out that the baby's father wasn't who I'd said he was, that the baby's father was Boone…." Darla let out another wail.

Phoebe said, "Darla? Come on now, come on…."

And Darla pulled it together enough to go on. "Phoebe, I *loved* Ralphie. He's the only man I've ever loved. And I've been trying to get rid of Boone, I swear I have. I, well, I just know Boone's been doing things—illegal things. As long as I've known him, he always had himself a little business going fencing stolen goods—and yeah, I did wonder, if maybe Ralphie was on to him, if maybe Ralphie had followed Boone on that night last month…but I, well, I just couldn't let myself believe that. I couldn't let myself think that Boone had killed Ralphie. I couldn't… Oh, God…"

"Darla. Listen."

"Oh, what? Oh, God…"

"Are you still at home?"

"Yeah."

"Well, I'm comin' right over. You just stay there. I'll be there as fast as I can. You hear me?"

"Oh, yeah. Oh, please. I do… I need you here, Pheeb. You don't know Boone. Once he finds out what I told you…"

"What are you saying? Is he there now?"

"No."

"Is he on his way?"

"I don't know. I don't know where he is and I haven't heard from him since he called me Sunday at about five in the morning and told me to tell you that he'd been by to see me a couple of hours before."

Phoebe accused, "You provided his alibi for the break-in."

Darla sobbed again. "Oh, Pheeb. That was low, that I did that. Low-down and I know it. But you don't tell Boone Gallagher no, not unless you're in the mood to get the shit kicked out of you."

"That's a lot of lies, Darla Jo."

"I know. I do. I know…."

"But you can make it right."

"Just hurry. Okay? Boone always comes around sooner or later…."

"Well, this time he'll be too late. We're going to clear all this up, you understand? We're going to get it all straight and whoever killed Ralphie, that person will pay."

"Yes. Oh, yes. I want that. I do."

"Stay there. Stay right there at home."

"I will. I'll be waitin'."

"'Bye…" Phoebe picked up the phone and turned it off.

Rio wanted to break something. "That whining little bitch. You think you can talk her into going down to headquarters with us, telling her story to the people who matter?"

"She's going. If I have to drag her there by the hair."

"Give me a second." Rio went back to his room and got the Glock 9 mm he never carried unless he had to, though he had concealed carry permits good in thirty-one states, including Oklahoma.

He knew Phoebe saw it in his hand when he rejoined her in the living room. She didn't say a word about it. Things were that bad.

TWENTY MINUTES LATER, when they got back to Darla's place, her car was still sitting right there in the driveway.

Rio led the way up the steps. Inside the storm door, the front door was open a crack. Rio guided Phoebe back against the wall of the trailer, edging in beside her, but closer to the door. He held his Glock at the ready as he reached out his free hand, yanked the storm door open a little, enough to get his arm under there. He pushed the inner door open farther, then held the storm door ajar and signaled to Phoebe.

She called, "Darla? Darla, I'm here…."

From inside, there was nothing. Just silence.

Phoebe tried again. "Darla?"

Rio turned to her and mouthed, *Wait here.* She didn't look happy, but she did nod her agreement.

He slipped inside. On silent feet, he slid along the wall of the dim hallway.

One by one, he checked the rooms—including the shower stall in the bathroom. He went out the back door and circled around, to one side and then the other.

No sign of Darla. Or anyone else, for that matter.

Phoebe let out a yelp when he appeared behind her on the deck. "Don't *do* that. You scared me."

"Sorry."

"Well?"

"She's not there."

"Oh, God. You think maybe Boone came and got her?"

"Don't know. She's not the greatest housekeeper. That place is a mess. But at a glance, I saw no signs of a struggle."

"What should we do?"

"Look around a little. Maybe you can tell what, if anything, she took with her."

Phoebe was frowning. "You know…"

"Dígame."

"I never want to speak to the cops again—but maybe we should call them."

"We'll do better. We'll go back to headquarters, see if we can talk to Sergeant Runson, tell him everything we know—right after we have another quick look around inside."

AS FAR AS PHOEBE COULD tell, two important items were missing: Darla's denim shoulder purse, which Phoebe was pretty sure she'd seen hanging from the back of a chair in the dining area when they'd been there earlier, and the diaper bag full of baby supplies that Darla kept ready in the baby's room.

Phoebe shook her head over the rest. "It doesn't look like she packed anything. My guess is Boone was here and he left in hurry, dragging Darla with him."

"Or she got cold feet again about talking to us. So she walked out."

"On foot?"

"Stranger things have happened."

Phoebe did see his point. "Whatever. The diaper

bag thing worries me, though. Why take it unless she thought she'd be needing it? Lord. If she's in labor…"

"Since we're talking about Darla, I wouldn't even hazard a guess on any of it."

They checked the shed, which was unlocked—and empty. Then they drove to police headquarters, where they waited out in front for an hour to talk to Runson. He finally signaled them back to the squad room.

It was a little after 7:00 p.m. when they left. They'd told the sergeant everything they knew. He thanked them. He said he'd get right on it.

He still looked at Phoebe as if he had his doubts about her. By then, Phoebe didn't care what the sergeant thought of her. She only prayed that he'd do what he said.

At home again, Rio insisted she take a shower, bandage up her cuts and scrapes, and get into clean clothes. When she joined him in the kitchen, he had sandwiches ready.

They discussed what to do next as they ate.

Rio wanted to talk about her mother's prophetic dreams. "I'm thinking your mother knows way too much."

Phoebe knocked back a big slug of ice-cold, caffeine-rich Coke. "Meaning you think she's involved? Seriously? My mother?" She set down her glass. "Uh-uh. She's got nothing to do with any of this. Other than bein' psychic, I mean."

"Phoebe. It's too strange. Remember those dreams of hers, what she told me Ralphie said in them. She was right on the money, both times. *A problem of storage…*"

Phoebe gestured with her sandwich. "Meaning the shed at Darla's. I know, I know."

"And, *Sometimes I'd get—*"

"*Two.* I remember. But I'm telling you. That's just my mother. It's creepy. It's hard to believe. But she's a good woman. She drives me crazy, but she's as far from a criminal as anyone gets."

Rio said nothing for a moment. Then he tipped his bottle of beer her way and said, "I think I have to agree with you on that."

"Because you know I'm right."

"I've never been one to buy all that psychic stuff, though."

"Me neither. I tend to think of my mother's supposed 'powers' as just amazing intuition on her part—that, and an endless series of truly incredible coincidences."

"All right. Let's forget your mother, then."

"That won't be possible. She's unforgettable. But let's count her out."

"All right. So if Boone's the bad guy, who's his accomplice?"

"I'm thinking *not* Bernard. I'm guessing Dave."

"And I'm guessing you're right."

"The way Dave's been behaving, who else could it be? Plus, he and Boone are always hanging around together…."

"You think Rose and Tiff are involved?"

Phoebe's heart sank at the thought. "God. I hope not—and I know that look in your eyes, Rio. You're going over to Dave's, aren't you?"

"Soon as I finish this sandwich and drink my beer."

"And I'm going with you."

"Phoebe—"

"Don't say it. Don't even try it. There's no protecting me, no keeping me out of it. I'm in it up to my eyeballs and sinking fast. We're partners in this, Rio. We're partners all the way."

THEY WERE CLEARING OFF the dishes when the doorbell rang.

Phoebe peeked out the window before she answered: Rose. And Tiff, too. Rose looked nothing short of grim. She had a protective arm around Tiff, who had teary eyes and a red nose and a wad of Kleenex clutched in her hand.

Phoebe couldn't get the door open fast enough. She yanked it wide, pushed back the storm door. "Hey."

Rose spoke first. "Hi. It's like this. I went to Tulsa." Rose's mom lived in Tulsa now. "I shopped. I did some thinking. I was an asshole and I want to apologize."

"Me, too," said Tiff, and swiped at her nose with her wad of Kleenex. "Well, I didn't go to Tulsa. But I *have* been an asshole—worse than an asshole. I've been an idiot. A total, complete fool. Everything I accused you of—deserting the people who love you for some guy—all that is only what I was doin' myself." She spotted Rio, hanging back near the arch to the dining room and actually tried a smile. "How you doin'?"

Rio nodded. "Good enough."

Phoebe felt her spirits lift—at least a little. It had been a day straight from hell. But there was hope for her and her friends. That was something. "I'm glad you're both here. I missed you guys. A lot."

Tiff said, "Oh, God. Me, too..."

"Yeah," Rose agreed. "Oh, yeah. A lot."

"Come in. Come on..." Phoebe reached out both arms and gathered them in. The storm door bumped shut behind them.

Once the hugging was over, Rose pulled back and said, "Tiff has some scary stuff to tell you about."

Tiff sniffed. "Yeah. I do...."

Rose said, "She came to me first. She wasn't sure you would speak to her."

Phoebe looked right at Tiff. "I thought I told you Saturday. I'll always be here for you, Tiff."

Tiff nodded. "I should have known it."

Phoebe offered them Cokes. They both shook their heads as they went to sit together on the sofa. Phoebe took the wing chair. Rio moved in a little closer, but stayed on his feet. "Okay," said Phoebe, once everyone was settled. "What's up?"

"It's pretty bad," Tiff warned, and sniffled some more.

"It's been one of those days," said Phoebe.

Tiff wiped her eyes. "Today, I...well, I just got fed up, I guess. I had it out with Dave when we got home from the body shop. He'd been drinkin' all day, right there at the shop. To tell it true, he's been drunk since the night he and Rio had that fight....

"Anyway, it was ugly. I was cryin'. You may not believe this, but by the end, he was cryin', too. He told me he was in big trouble, and he told me that he and Boone had a little deal going..." Tiff had to pause to swipe at her eyes again and dab at her nose. "They, um, they would break into stores, late at night. Always outside the city. You know, Tulsa. Norman. Edmond... That way, Boone said, it would take the cops longer to see the pattern. They used two vans—one for the actual burglary and one to transfer the goods into later."

Phoebe said, "Let me guess. One of the vans they used was mine."

Tiff blinked. "How did you know?"

"Long story. Please. Tell us the rest."

"Okay. Yeah. Um, they'd use one of the vans from the body shop to carry the stuff off in. Dave would cover the body-shop logo and switch out the plates with some heap that was waiting at the shop for the insurance investigator to drop by and declare it totaled. Dave said Boone was a genius at the whole routine. He could pick out the surveillance cameras and get the tapes. He knew ways to get around the alarms. And he was fast. He told Dave what to do and Dave did it and it always went off without a hitch."

Rio asked, "How often did they do this?"

"Dave didn't say. But it started in January, about a month after Boone came to the city."

"So they broke in, took whatever money they could find and loaded up the van with goods...."

"That's right. When they had the van loaded up, they'd take it to where Boone had left Phoebe's van and transfer the stuff. Boone would give Dave his cut of any cash they'd taken and Dave would go home in the body shop van. And in a week or two, Boone would pay him off for his share of the goods."

"What did Boone do with the goods?"

"Dave never knew. Boone told him it was safer that way."

Rio must have been thinking what Phoebe was thinking. It didn't take a genius to put it together. "And the night that Ralphie died…?"

"Yeah." Tiff swiped her eyes some more. "They did a job that night. Their last job, as a matter of fact. Dave swore to me that he had nothing to do with what happened to Ralphie. He and Boone took the goods to the transfer point as usual, loaded them into Phoebe's van. Boone paid Dave. And Boone drove off in Phoebe's van. Dave came home in the white van. I remember he woke me up when he came in. I looked at the clock. It was around two."

Phoebe asked, "The messages on the mirrors?"

Tiff nodded. "Boone's idea. He thought at first he could maybe scare you enough that you'd give up asking questions."

"The break-in the other night?"

"Boone and Dave. Dave said Boone got really pissed at him, because he showed up half-drunk. But it all went off the way Boone wanted it, anyway."

"What about switching the vans?"

"Huh? What vans?"

Phoebe and Rio shared a look. Most likely Boone had handled that on his own. "Later," Phoebe said. "Where's Dave now?"

Tiff drooped against Rose. "Don't know. After he told me all that, I said we had to call the police. He looked at me, tears rollin' down his face and he said I was crazy. He'd do serious time if he turned himself in. I tried to argue with him, to convince him to do what he should. But he wasn't going for it. I was grabbin' on him, begging him not to go. He threw me down on the floor and ran out. I heard his truck peeling rubber down the street…."

"When was that?"

"Maybe an hour ago, maybe a little—" The ringing of the phone cut her off.

Phoebe picked it up from the table. "Hello?"

"Phoebe? Oh, Pheeb…"

"Darla? Darla, I can hardly hear—"

"I have to whisper. He might hear me."

"Who?"

"Boone. Pheeb. Please. You have to come and get me."

"Darla—"

"Pheeb. I swear. He made me run away with him. I hate him. He told me to my face that he killed Ralphie, ran my sweet Ralphie down in the street when Ralphie followed him and discovered his little money-making scheme. Pheeb, he *told* Ralphie, before he killed him. Told Ralphie that the baby was *his*. Ralphie died thinkin' that I wasn't true to him. But I was. I swear, I never—"

"Darla. Where are you?" She looked up. Rio stood above her, paper and pen in his hand. She took it.

"Um, I…"

"Darla. Do you know where you are?"

"Yeah. It's, um, Pilot Point, Texas. By Lake Ray Roberts." She named an address. "A yellow wood house, kind of off by itself. A wide front porch. The address is on the mailbox at the street."

"Who else is there with you?"

"Just Boone. This place was empty. He said some guy he knows owns it. Pheeb. Please. Help me. I think the baby's coming…."

Phoebe heard a soft click. "Darla…Darla?"

But the line had gone dead.

CHAPTER TWENTY-FIVE

Some people are alive only because it's illegal to kill them. Some people, even the fear of a lethal injection can't save.
—from The Prairie Queen's Guide to Life *by Goddess Jacks*

WHEN PHOEBE TOLD RIO what Darla had said, he let out a long string of bad words in Spanish. Then he added, much too softly, "No, Phoebe. I can see it in your face and the answer is no."

"He *kidnapped* her, Rio. And she thinks the baby's coming."

"She thought the baby was coming Saturday night. Remember what happened then?"

As if she could forget. "It doesn't matter. We have to—"

"She's a born liar, Phoebe. You can't tell me you believe her *this* time. If it wasn't for her and her lies, Ralphie would be alive today."

"She didn't mean for—"

"Who cares what she *meant?* She's nothing but bad news. When will you see it?"

"I do see it. I see it all. But I have to help her."

"This isn't adding up and you know it. Boone drags her off with him. She's scared to death of him—but somehow she manages to call you and tell you right where she is without him knowing?"

Rose chose that moment to speak up. "You gotta admit. It's a little too convenient."

"No. It's not convenient. The guy thinks he *owns* her. It wouldn't occur to him that she'd ever dare to go against him. He's cocky when it comes to her. He left the damn room for a minute. And she took the chance to call for help…."

Both Rio and Rose were shaking their heads. Tiff wasn't. But she did look doubtful.

Rio said, "You're not going to Texas tonight."

"Oh. Yeah. I am."

"No. You can call OCPD, see if you can reach Runson or even Ankerson. Explain everything. See if they can get in contact with the authorities down in Texas."

"Like I can't do that on a cell during the two-and-a-half-hour drive down there? Like Rose and Tiff couldn't do it. And while we're on the subject of who's doing what—what will *you* be doing while I'm on the phone trying to convince Sergeant Runson to pass the word on down to Texas?"

"I'm going down there."

"Oh. No kidding? What a surprise—alone. Right?"

"I'll get in touch with Mac Tenkiller, see if he can meet me there."

"Rio. Listen carefully. I am going. If you go

without me, I'll just get in my car and trail right along behind you."

"To save that lying little—"

"Yeah. To try and help Darla. And her innocent baby."

More angry Spanish blistered the air. "I don't get it, *Reina.* I don't understand. How a smart woman like you can be such a sucker for a piece of redneck trash like—"

She put up a hand. "You're right. You don't get it. Darla's been beaten down and abused since the day she was born. Standing up to the men who abuse her has gotten her zip—well, that is, beyond another beating. Yeah. She's weak. What else could she be, given the way she's had to live? Weak. You hear me? Weak and not evil. And I am going to Texas, Rio. Don't even dream you can stop me. You can't. That's that."

RIO CALLED THE OTHER P.I. Tenkiller didn't pick up, so Rio left a message. Then he called the OCPD. Runson was off duty. Ankerson wasn't at his desk. He left a message for Ankerson to call his cell.

When he hung up, he turned to Rose and Tiff. "Someone should go down there…."

Tiff looked absolutely terrified. "You mean…go talk to the police?"

"Yeah. Ask for Sergeant Ankerson. If you can't get him, get someone in Robbery or on the Signal 30 Squad—they're the ones who handle vehicular homicides. Tell them what Dave told you. Tell them about Darla's call, tonight. Give them the address she gave us."

"Oh, God…"

Rose wrapped her arm around Tiff again. "You can do it. I'll take you."

So Rose led Tiff to her car and they left for headquarters. Phoebe got the .38 her dad had left her and a box of shells, locked up the house and followed Rio out to his car.

He didn't speak to her all the way to Ardmore. Ninety-eight miles of angry silence, past Norman and Purcell through Paul's Valley and up through the steep-walled gorges of the Arbuckle Mountains. His nifty little GPS device on the dash told them where they were and how to get where they were going, but other than that, there was dead quiet.

Finally, she dared, "Look. We're doing this. Together. It's settled. Is there some reason you have to stay mad at me?"

He turned his head. His eyes gleamed at her in the darkness of the shadowed car. And then he looked at the road again.

"Come on, Rio. This is the only way."

More silence. Phoebe set herself to bearing it.

But then, as they passed the Ardmore exit, he spoke at last. "You got a permit to carry that .38?"

She slid him a glance. He still had his gaze on the road. But at least he'd said something. "I do. And I know how to use it, too." It had been over a decade since Hank Jacks had taught her to shoot. She hadn't exactly kept in practice since then.

But really. That was more information than Rio needed right now.

He said, "When we get there, I'm running it. You do what I say when I say to do it. Are we clear?"

"Absolutely. The way you want it, Rio. I swear."

He did look her way then. She caught him at it, tried a smile.

He didn't smile back. "The way I want it is for you to be out of it."

"Well. Other than that."

He muttered something low in Spanish. She didn't ask him to translate. She had no idea what he'd said. But she understood him perfectly.

AT ELEVEN-TWENTY, RIO'S cell rang. It was Ankerson. Rio spoke to the detective briefly.

When he disconnected the call, he told Phoebe, "Ankerson finally talked to Tiff. He's going to see what he can do about alerting the authorities in Pilot Point. He advised us to let the local police handle it."

Phoebe didn't comment. There was nothing to say.

Ten minutes later, in the rolling hills of North Texas, maybe sixty miles northeast of Dallas, they reached their destination. At that hour, in the small town of Pilot Point, all the good citizens were at home where they belonged. The streets were quiet—and empty.

Rio turned a corner and they were there. The yellow clapboard house on the north side of the street was three up from the corner and set back from the road, lots of clear space to either side, a pair of cottonwoods flanking the walk in front. On the east side of the property, a pebbled drive lead past the house and straight back to a small detached garage. Light glowed from inside the house, but the shades, at least in front and on the sides, were drawn.

Rio cruised right on by, turned the corner and parked. He had that fancy gun of his in a shoulder holster. She'd seen him load it.

She opened her box of shells and filled the cylinder of her .38.

"I hate this," he said.

She flipped the cylinder back in line, engaged the latch and lowered it carefully to rest on her lap, the business end pointed toward the door. Her daddy's gun. Loaded. Would she actually end up shooting someone with it?

"Yeah," she said. "I know. I hate it, too."

"Reina..."

She looked his way. Their eyes met. "Oh, Rio..." She set the revolver on the dash and leaned toward him.

He met her halfway, reaching out, his fingers slipping up under her hair. "You don't have to do this."

"Yeah. I do. It's not safe for you to go in alone."

She saw the faint smile as it played across his mouth. "You gonna protect me?"

"Oh, yeah."

He pulled her to him, then, across the console. His mouth touched hers. So sweet. So tender. And much too brief. When he broke the kiss, he didn't move back. His warm hand still clasped her nape and his lips hovered an inch from hers. "We can find the local police station, take Ankerson's advice, ask them to handle this...."

"And will they take us seriously? And if they do, *what* will they do?"

He released her then and sank back to his own seat. "How would I know? I've never been to Pilot Point, Texas, in my life, let alone met with law enforcement here."

"Exactly. And in the meantime, what happens to Darla and the baby—not to mention, does Boone get away?"

He didn't answer.

"Rio. That *was* the goal, remember? To catch Ralphie's killer?"

"Goals change." There were shadows in his beautiful dark eyes.

Phoebe could read those shadows. They melted her heart. He wanted her safe more than he wanted Boone Gallagher caught. A *lot* more.

She said, softly, "We're wasting time."

His eyes changed. She saw it happen, saw him accept that she wouldn't back down. He took his cell out of the holder at his belt and turned it off. When she frowned at him, he explained, "Even on silent page, it makes a buzzing sound." His voice was flat. All business. "Darla told you it was just her and Boone in that house..."

"Yeah."

"She could have been lying. And even if she wasn't, that was almost three hours ago. Things could be different now. And I didn't see that Camaro of Boone's. That would at least give us some indication they're actually there. We need a good look around. Let's see if we can get onto the property from around back...."

THE HOUSES ON THE EAST end of the street had fences, so they circled the rest of the block on foot and went in from the west. A dog started barking a block over as they crossed behind the first two darkened houses.

Rio clasped her arm. They waited. The dog let out a few more yaps and was quiet. They moved on, silently, through the overgrown grass. The waxing moon, a fat crescent overhead, provided a silvery light that turned everything ghostly, made the colors of grass and trees and houses into shadows of themselves. Phoebe carried the .38 low, the grip nestled in her hand.

The light was on in the back windows of the yellow house, the shades, as in the front, all drawn down. The small back porch—and the back door it enclosed—was screened in and dark.

Rio led her onward, to the one-car detached garage. It had a small window on the west wall. They crept to the window—and saw nothing. It was too dark in there.

But then Rio produced a tiny flashlight. He shone it in the window: a blink of brightness, and he shut it off.

It was enough to see the yellow Camaro parked inside. He signaled her to follow him around behind the garage. There, in the shadow of the building, hidden even from the ghostly light of the moon, he put his lips to her ear and, in the barest whisper, told her what they would do next.

Once he had her nod of agreement, he slipped away from her, around the west corner, the way they had come. She gripped the old revolver, told herself to take slow, even breaths—and wondered what in the hell she was doing here, what could have possessed her to force Rio into bringing her along?

Rio's knock on the screen-porch door sounded louder than any pistol shot. That was her cue to change positions. Silently, she edged along the back wall and around the corner on the east side, keeping the garage between her and the house. From there, she crept to the other end of that wall.

Now, all she had to do was peek around the corner of the building to see whatever might be happening in the silvered space of ragged lawn between the back of the house and the garage.

She didn't peek. She waited. It was what Rio had told her to do. She waited, her heart in her throat, sending frequent glances back the way she had come, alert for ambush from either side.

One minute. Two. Time stretched out into forever as the seconds ticked by.

What was that? A creaking sound. And the whisper of stealthy feet…

And a thud. A definite thud.

And after that…

Nothing. The crickets started up again, singing in the grass and the moon shone down its silvery light. And she waited some more, her mouth tasting as sour as a tarnished spoon, her heart pounding a raging tattoo in her ears.

In a shifting of shadows at the back end of the garage, a figure appeared. Her heart stopped dead as she swung her body that way, bringing the revolver up to shoot. The figure put up a hand.

Rio.

The breath fled her lungs. She knew the aftermath of terror; a sudden, knee-knocking relief.

He signaled her toward him. She went.

When she rounded the corner to the back of the garage again, she saw the still figure, crumpled in the shadow of the back wall, unconscious: Boone. Rio had not only knocked him out, he'd cuffed his arms behind his back with some clever-looking lightweight woven restraint. His ankles were tied in the same way. His mouth was taped. Phoebe saw the other pistol stuck in Rio's belt—the one he must have taken off of Boone.

Rio wrapped a hand around her arm and pulled her close. She felt his warm breath across her cheek as he whispered to her. "Stay here. Don't get any closer to him. Keep that revolver pointed at him until I come back. Clear?"

She nodded and aimed her .38 at Boone's bent head as Rio vanished around the corner again.

For maybe thirty seconds there was silence, except for the crickets and a bird trilling out a lonely string of notes some distance away. Then Boone began to stir. He groaned—a muffled sound behind the tape. He shifted, went still.

And then, slowly, he lifted his head and looked right at her. Phoebe stared back at him, keeping her .38 pointed, steady, between those mean, gleaming eyes.

He grunted some more. He strained at the cords that held him.

Phoebe said nothing. She guarded him as Rio had told her to do. She wasn't real good at this job, and she knew it. Better to be careful and silent and concentrate on following Rio's instructions to the letter.

There would be time later to think how she had believed she knew this man, how she had trusted him—with the keys to her business, with the combination to her safe, with her own safety and well-being and the safety of those she loved….

She heard the back door slam, and the screen porch door after that, and then swift feet shushing through the grass. She kept her weapon on Boone, but she was ready to raise it and shoot whoever came around the corner of the building if she had to.

It was Rio. Thank God. He dropped to his haunches, cut the restraint around Boone's ankles, grabbed him by the elbow and hauled him upright, jamming that fancy automatic pistol into the small of his back.

Rio spoke out loud to her. "Coast is clear. And Darla needs you. Lower that weapon and come on inside."

IN THE CRAMPED BACK bedroom of the house, Darla huddled in a heap on the floor, shaking, sobbing softly, holding her stomach. Her jeans were wet, a stain that spread from the crotch and downward. Fluid spattered the floor around her.

"Darla," Phoebe said. No response. She tried again, "Darla…"

With a terrified sob, Darla looked up, cringing farther into the corner at the same time.

The bastard had hit her. More than once. Her lip was bloody. One eye was purple and rapidly swelling shut.

"Darla. Honey. It's okay. It's me..."

Darla gasped, put her hand across her mouth. And then, with a hesitance that tore at Phoebe's heart, she reached out her arms.

Phoebe set her .38 on the stand by the bed and went to her. "It's okay, okay..." Kneeling, Phoebe gathered her in.

Darla whimpered against her shoulder. "My water broke. I told Boone I had to get to a hospital. He told me shut up. I didn't. I begged him to take me to a doctor. My mistake. Oh, Pheeb. My mistake..."

Rio, in the far corner, holstered his pistol and got busy securing Boone to a chair. Once he had the abusive son of a bitch securely tied, he slipped his cell from the holder on his belt. He flipped the phone open and turned it on. Waited. Swore. "Wouldn't you know? Not a single damn bar." He waited some more as Darla sobbed and Boone struggled in his restraints. Finally, he shut the phone, stuck it back in his felt and chucked Boone under the chin. "Mind if I borrow your cell?"

Boone jerked his head away and grunted behind the tape that covered his mouth.

Phoebe smoothed Darla's sweaty hair. "Rio needs to call 911. Where's the phone you used to call me, honey?"

Darla blinked and panted. "Um. Living room. And in the front bedroom, I think..."

"The house phone works?"

Darla moaned and nodded. "It's how I called you…"

"Don't move," Rio told Boone wryly. "I'll be right back." He went to make the call.

"Come on," said Phoebe. She helped Darla to stand.

It didn't last, though. One step toward the bed and Darla doubled over and sank toward the floor again, head bent over her giant belly. "Oh, God… Oh, God… it hurts…hurts…"

Phoebe knelt down with her again, making soothing noises. "It's okay. Easy. Breathe. Just breathe… We're gonna get you to the bed. Make you a little more comfortable until—"

The cold kiss of metal against the back of her head cut her off. "Don't move," whispered a male voice. "Now. Real slow. Stand up." Slowly, Phoebe rose. "Turn around. Slow, now…" She did and found herself looking down the barrel of a gun and into Dave Tolby's narrowed gray eyes.

Darla, still riding out a contraction, didn't even look up. She held her belly and moaned as Dave grabbed Phoebe's arm and shoved her to the corner where Boone sat tied to the chair. Dave backed into that corner, nice and tight, right up beside Boone, holding Phoebe in front of him, the gun pressed into her side.

She felt movement. She looked over as Dave took a pocket knife to the tie that held Boone's wrists. Boone's hands came free. He ripped the tape off his mouth. Dave gave him the knife to finish the job and shoved the gun harder into Phoebe's ribs to remind her who had the upper hand.

About then, Darla's contraction faded off. Panting and whimpering, she lifted her head as Boone rose from the chair. Her brown eyes went saucer-wide. She sucked in a breath to scream, but Dave shoved the gun harder into Phoebe's ribs as Boone put a finger to his lips.

Darla got the message. She put her hand over mouth, as if to still her own whimpers, and wildly shook her head.

They waited. Seconds that seemed to stretch into eons. There was silence, except for Darla's strangled sobs. Phoebe strained to hear Rio's voice on the phone from the front of the house.

She heard nothing. Had he made the call? Had Dave taken care of him first?

Oh, God. Was he *hurt…?*

No. If Rio was out of commission, she wouldn't be backed in a corner playing Dave's human shield, with Boone standing still and silent beside them.

Another endless span of time crawled by.

Finally, Boone got tired of waiting. His voice cut the silence. "Show yourself, Navarro. Or Dave's gonna pop your woman. Bam. Right through the heart."

Rio stepped into the room, raising his gun as he moved, drawing a smooth bead on Dave.

Boone laughed. "You know Dave'll get Phoebe when you get him."

Dave swore. Since Phoebe was in front of him, she couldn't see his face, but he didn't sound too happy about ending up dead. "Don't try it," he said. "Or I *will* shoot her." Again, to make the point, Dave shoved the pistol hard into Phoebe's side. She'd have bruises there tomorrow.

Well, if she lived that long…

On the floor in the other corner, Darla let out another animal moan and crumpled over her stomach again.

"Darla…" Phoebe dared to take a step toward her. Dave yanked her back and poked her another good one with his gun.

Darla held her belly and groaned louder.

Boone said to Rio, "Turn that pretty Glock around. Hold it by the barrel and put it on the floor." Phoebe watched in horror as Rio did what Boone had told him to do. "Good. Mine, too." Rio pulled the other pistol from his waistband and set it beside his own. "Stand up tall." Rio rose to his height as Darla cried out again. "Shut the fuck up," said Boone pleasantly, not even bothering to glance her way. Darla bent closer to the floor and swallowed her moans of pain. Boone smiled at Rio. "Gently slide 'em to me—one at a time, now." With his boot, Rio eased the weapons over, Boone's first and then his own. Boone crouched, stuck his own gun in the waistband of his jeans and rose holding the Glock. He checked the magazine. "Fully loaded. Very nice." He shoved the magazine home.

Dave said, "I don't like this, Boone."

"Glad you could make it, Dave." Boone clucked his tongue. "Real glad. And such good timing. For once. You even had sense enough to sneak in the back."

"Just give me my money and I'll—"

"Shut up, Dave." Boone kept the Glock on Rio. "In

case you didn't notice, we've got a situation here. And we don't have a hell of a lot of time to be dealing with it. My guess is the ambulance that Rio here just called will be showin' up much too soon now, and probably the men and women of law enforcement right along with it."

Dave did some more swearing. "I'm not up for this. I never done murder and I'm not startin' now."

"Sorry, Dave. But you know what? We don't have a choice. They gotta die…" He was smiling. He turned Rio's gun on Phoebe. "Bitch," he said cheerfully. "I warned you, didn't I? In writing. Complete with those cute little hearts over the *i*'s…"

Dave backed away from her, shaking his head. "Boone. Uh-uh. No. No way…"

Phoebe looked down the barrel of that Glock and knew she would die.

Until Rio said, "Boone," and took a step forward.

Boone swung the gun on him, shrugging. "All right. Have it your way. You first."

No. All wrong. Not Rio. No... She saw Boone's finger pressing the trigger and she knew she couldn't let him do it.

Phoebe whirled and stepped sideways. That was all it took to put her own body between the gun in Boone's hand and the man she loved.

Rio shouted, "No, Phoebe!"

Darla screamed.

And Boone finished pulling the trigger.

Rio grabbed her from behind, trying to shove her clear. But it was too late. Phoebe heard the shot—so loud in the small room. Something punched her, hard, in the belly, as Rio took her down.

They were on the floor and she glanced at her stomach. Red bloomed, spreading, eating up the white on the T-shirt she wore.

She looked up, blinking, not quite believing. Boone was standing over them, aiming the gun again.

A second shot exploded.

But not from Boone's gun.

Phoebe blinked some more, shook her head. But when she opened her eyes again and looked at Boone, that red hole was still there, right in the center of his forehead.

Time slowed to a crawl. Boone's eyes rolled back. His knees buckled, his lifeless body shifting sideways as he dropped to the floor.

Phoebe gaped at him, lying there. Definitely dead. Amazed, she turned her head—toward Darla, who stood by the bed, holding the .38 Phoebe had left on the nightstand in shaking outstretched hands.

"Darla?" Phoebe whispered wonderingly. "Darla?"

Rio had her in his warm, strong arms. He bent close, said her name. She moaned against the awful burning pain and focused on his beloved face above hers as the wailing of sirens split open the night.

CHAPTER TWENTY-SIX

> Any fool girl can face a calamity. It's the day-to-day livin' that does a woman in.
> —*from* The Prairie Queen's Guide to Life *by Goddess Jacks*

IT WAS TWENTY MILES to the hospital in Denton and there was only one ambulance—for Darla, far gone in labor, and Phoebe, to share. As they loaded Phoebe into the ambulance, Rio swore he'd be there waiting when she arrived.

The ride was crowded and it was noisy. The paramedics went about their business, looking after Darla, taking care of Phoebe, too: staunching the bleeding, hooking her up to an IV. There was that great, clawing, burning pain in the center of her, at first. But they must have given her something, because not long after they put the IV in her arm, the searing, breath-stealing pain faded off to a dull throb and a sense of great well-being stole through her.

She heard Darla moaning and screaming and huffing and puffing. In between the screaming, there was whining. "I can't do it. It hurts, I can't…."

Phoebe roused herself from her doped-up fog and told her, "Damn it, girl, just breathe, okay?"

"Pheeb. Oh, God, Pheeb. It hurts, it hurts…."

"It'll be fine. Breathe. And push when they tell you…." The words kind of faded off. She was just too out of it to speak.

Darla moaned and screamed and whined some more.

And then, Phoebe thought she heard the miracle: a baby's cry.

Someone said, "It's a boy."

Phoebe smiled and closed her eyes and let the darkness take her.

WHEN SHE WOKE, SHE WAS IN a hospital room. The other bed was empty. She turned her head on the pillow and saw her mother standing by the lone, narrow window, looking out. Beyond the window it was daylight.

"Mama…"

Her mother turned—and smiled that special smile, the one that made her fine-boned face seem to glow from within. "Baby. You're awake…." Goddess hustled over. She bent close, pressed a kiss on Phoebe's forehead. "You're gonna be all right, honey. It was a clean shot. The surgery went just great and the doctor says a month from now, you'll be almost good as new."

Phoebe's mouth was so parched, her lips kept sticking to her gums. "Water?"

"Not yet," said her mother. "They need to hear bowel sounds first."

Phoebe wrinkled her nose. "Bowel sounds. EEEuuu." She swallowed, straining to do it, her mouth was so dry.

"How 'bout a nice glycerin swab?"

"A what?"

Goddess took a swab from the container on the nightstand and rubbed Phoebe's lips and gums with it. It tasted of lemons. "Not as good as water," she said when her mother was done.

"But better than a swift kick with a pointed boot."

"Yeah. I guess so..." Phoebe sank back to the pillow. "Darla...?"

Goddess tossed the used swab in the wastebasket by the bed. "She had her baby."

That news did Phoebe's heart good. "I think I heard that baby cry, in the ambulance...."

"A month early, but still six pounds, one ounce. And breathing fine on his own. She named him Ralphie. They're both—Darla and that sweet baby—doing fine."

"Boone?"

"Dead. May the good Lord have mercy on his everlastin' soul."

"I knew it." She closed her eyes, remembering the confusion of those final moments: the blood. The searing pain. Rio holding her, Darla sobbing. And Dave... "I think Dave ran out...."

"He won't get far."

"Oh, Mama..." Phoebe felt the tears welling. She blinked them back.

Goddess gently smoothed her hair. "I'm here, baby. Right here."

She dared to ask, in a whisper, "Rio?"

"He's getting me some coffee. Don't you worry. He'll be back real soon."

A nurse bustled in. Goddess stepped out of the way as the nurse examined Phoebe's bandage, checked the monitors above her bed and tucked a tube in her hand with a button on the end of it.

The nurse said softly, "You just give a little push when the pain gets too bad...."

Rio came in as the nurse went out.

Goddess beamed at him. "Look who's awake."

He gave Goddess her coffee and he turned to the bed. Phoebe looked in those black eyes and felt happy tears welling again.

"We made it," she whispered.

He came close, took her hand. She twined her fingers with his. He bent close, kissed her cheek. *"Sí,"* he whispered. *"Es un milagro."*

"¿Milagro?"

"A miracle."

She nodded. "A miracle, oh yes..."

DARLA HAD A COUPLE OF long interviews with the police—first in Texas and then at headquarters in Oklahoma City. In the end, though, they decided not to charge her with anything. She'd shot Boone to save Phoebe. No one could fault her for that. As for all her lies, well, except for the false alibi she'd given Boone for the night of the robbery, not a one of those lies was to the police. She was an abused woman who'd finally fought back—and she swore, with a fervency convincing enough to sway the most hardened homicide cop, that she would never lie again.

Hers was simply not the kind of case a smart D.A. could expect to win.

Dave was caught holding up a 7-Eleven in Fort Worth, indicted and held for trial. Once they were through with him in Texas, the OCPD would get their turn.

After a few days, Dave started talking. He told everything he knew. The police took it from there. They discovered that Boone had been renting out space in an empty storefront a block down from where Ralphie was killed. When they got in there, they found stolen goods.

A week from the morning Phoebe woke up in the Denton hospital, they let her go home. She still needed weeks of convalescing to get back on her feet.

Rio took over at the bar, with the help of Tiff and Rose and Bernard—and Darla, too. The Queens reported that he did just fine. He even got with the insurance adjustor and got their money back from the night Boone and Dave robbed the place. The only thing he couldn't do was get up at closing time on busy nights and sing them all a song.

Tiff and Rose did that. Darla told Phoebe that they were "dang good." The Queens agreed that once Phoebe was back working again, they'd all get up together when closing time came around. Phoebe looked forward to that: the Prairie Queens onstage again.

At home, Rio was…careful with her.

Too careful, really. And she knew why.

As soon as she was strong enough to handle things at the bar again, he would be leaving. It broke her heart to know that. And she intended to fight.

But for a while there, she was just too weak to face the coming confrontation. She felt him, every day, retreating a little more from her.

He'd moved back to the spare room when she'd returned from the Texas hospital. Her bed was pretty much her whole world then and he wanted her to have it all to herself.

But as she got better, he never mentioned joining her in her room again. She didn't mention it, either.

She feared his answer too much.

He was so gentle and kind to her. And he ran her business for her.

A wonderful man. The man she loved…

And she was losing him.

ON WEDNESDAY, JUNE FIFTEENTH, two months to the day from Ralphie's murder, Phoebe got up in the morning and found Rio's pack waiting by the front door.

In the kitchen, he had breakfast ready, the table all set. He was dishing up the chorizo and eggs. She poured herself a cup of coffee, turned to lean against the counter. Sipped.

"Don't go," she said.

He carried the empty frying pan over and set it on the stove. "Sit. Eat."

She took the chair across from him, but she didn't pick up her fork. "Rio," she said. "I love you. I will always love you."

"I love you, too. *Siempre.* Can you deal with having Darla as a partner?"

She set down her coffee cup. "I, um. What?"

"I know I said I'd sign my half of the bar over to you. And I will, if that's how you want it. But I was thinking that Ralphie would have wanted Darla to have a share. I was thinking two-thirds of Ralphie's half to Darla, the other third to you, so you'll keep controlling interest. What do you think?"

"I think you're not hearing me. Rio. Don't go..." She felt the tears rising.

"Reina..." His chair scraped the floor as he shoved it back. In three long strides, he was around the table and reaching for her hand. With a cry of loss and misery, she rose into his arms.

For the last time? Oh, God...

"Hey. *No llore.* Don't cry..." He cupped her face, thumbs gently rubbing at the two fat tears that escaped and trailed down her cheeks.

She could see in those wonderful midnight eyes that it was hopeless. Still, she had to tell him. What she knew at last. What she'd learned.

"Oh, Rio. Why can't you see? Life is just plain messy and anything worthwhile is going to be risky. Rio, I've had it wrong. So very, very wrong..."

But he was shaking his head. "That bullet you took was meant for me. I hate that. And as long as you're with me, it could happen again."

"It could, yeah. Or maybe I'll step outside my bar onto Western one day and get hit by a truck. Because this is life. And the thing about life is that eventually it kills you."

"But it's the *way* it kills you when you're with me. The way my mother died. And Soledad…"

"So, all right. Let's talk odds. It happened twice to women you loved. Odds are, it's not gonna happen again."

He smiled. The sweetest smile. "I want you to find that nice, steady guy you've been looking for. Have babies. Be safe. You'll never be safe if you're hanging around me."

"No. Uh-uh. That's faulty thinking."

"Reina…"

"Safe? We're not safe. Never, really, in this life. We're not safe and a smart woman has sense enough to see that what she really wants—what she damn well *needs*—is a good man at her back. A good man like *you,* Rio."

"A better man than me."

"No…"

"It's the right thing."

"No. It's not. And you know what? If you insist on leaving now, fine. Okay? Fine. I'll be waitin' right here when you come to your senses."

"Shh…"

And he kissed her. The world was in that kiss. All the sweetness, all the pain. All the years they wouldn't have…

Somehow she managed not to cling to him when he lifted his head and whispered, "You'll see. I'm right. It's the best way."

It wasn't. But he was going. She'd told him what was in her heart and it hadn't made him see the light.

They sat down. They finished breakfast. And she agreed it was a good idea: a third to her. The rest to Darla.

He told her he'd already shipped the equipment he'd bought to use in the hunt for Ralphie's killer. She agreed to handle turning in his rental car.

At a little after nine, he rolled his bike out of the garage and loaded it up.

By nine-fifteen, he was gone. She stood on the porch and she waved him goodbye. Even after he turned the corner, when she could no longer see him, still, she stood there.

Listening.

Until the roar of that fine, big, powerful engine faded completely away.

PHOEBE RETURNED TO WORK. She kept busy. The days weren't so bad.

The nights, though? The worst. Those endless hours between closing time and dawn when a woman most needs the one she loves, safe and warm in bed at her side…

A week after Rio's departure, Goddess received a communication from Ralphie in the world beyond the grave. She showed up on Phoebe's doorstep at six in the morning to share what she'd learned.

"Ralphie's spirit is at peace now—except for Rio leaving. Hon, you're not to worry. Ralphie's seeing what he can do about that. It might take a while, but in the end you'll have that man back here in Oklahoma where he's always belonged."

Phoebe smiled. "Thanks, Mama," she said, not believing a word of it. In spite of the uncanny way her mother's predictions sometimes came true, Phoebe remained a both-feet-on-the-ground kind of gal.

She hugged her mother good and hard, and then led her on into the kitchen, where she put the coffee on.

The weeks went by. Another and another after that.

On the Fourth of July, Goddess, the Queens, Darla and the baby went downtown and watched the fireworks shoot high and proud over the canal. Phoebe had a great time. She was one of the lucky ones. She had a fine life and good people to love.

Her love for Rio?

Stronger than ever.

Too bad each day made her just a little bit more certain that he was never coming back.

And then, at four in the afternoon, on the second Tuesday in July, as she was setting up the usual for Dewey, Purvis and Andy, a big, shiny black pickup slid into one of the spaces out front.

A Harley-Davidson motorcycle sat in the bed in back.

Phoebe shut her eyes and offered up a little prayer.

And when she dared to look again, that big Harley was still there. And Rio was getting out of that truck.

Dewey said, "Hey, Phoebe. Earth to Phoebe. You in there, beautiful?"

"Oh, yeah. I'm here." She plunked his drink in front of him, and scooted out from behind the bar.

She was right there waiting when Rio pushed through the door.

She braced her hands on her hips as he took off his sunglasses. "Well?" she said, out good and loud.

And he said, "Okay. It's like this. I can't sleep. I keep having bad dreams. It's not working out for me, being away from you. I keep thinking about what you said, that last day. About risk. About how there's no safety in life, anyway. And I'm thinking now, *Reina,* that maybe you were right. Maybe after *mi madre* and Soledad, I stopped taking the kind of risks that matter…."

Her throat felt so tight, she had to swallow to loosen it. "So…?"

"So I'm scared out of my mind. But okay. I'm willing, if you are. I'm ready to take the biggest risk of all—that is, if you'd be my partner. And I mean in everything, *Reina. Todo. Para siempre.* You and me."

She let out a whoop and she ran to him then. He caught her, whirled her around and then crushed her close in those big, strong arms.

Back at the bar, Purvis, Dewey and Andy burst into applause.

Phoebe hardly heard them. "Yes," she whispered. "Absolutely. *Para siempre.* It's a deal."

THEY WERE MARRIED A WEEK later, outside, in Goddess's tree-shaded backyard.

Tiff's new boyfriend took the pictures: of Rio and

Phoebe saying their vows; of Goddess, dancing. Of baby Ralphie smiling in his mother's arms.

And of Phoebe, Rose, Tiff and Darla—Ralphie's wives—laughing, together, on Phoebe's wedding day.

#1 New York Times
bestselling author
NORA
ROBERTS
has cooked up two
very special romantic
concoctions to tempt even
the most discriminating palate.
Dessert chef Summer Lyndon's legendary willpower is put to the ultimate test when she develops a taste for her delectable boss in Summer Desserts. And publicist Juliet Trent's newest client, a charming ladies' man and chef extraordinaire, is determined to whet her appetite for love in Lessons Learned.
Table for Two
In stores now!
Silhouette®
Where love comes alive™
Visit Silhouette Books at
www.eHarlequin.com
PSNR542